*Wings of*

| | DATE DUE | |
|---|---|---|
| | | |
| | | |
| | | |
| | | |
| | | |
| | | |
| | | |
| | | |
| | | |

# Wings of Morning

## William Cobb

CRANE HILL
PUBLISHERS

*Also by William Cobb*

A SPRING OF SOULS

SOMEWHERE IN ALL THIS GREEN:
NEW AND SELECTED STORIES

HARRY REUNITED

A WALK THROUGH FIRE

THE HERMIT KING

COMING OF AGE AT THE Y

Copyright © 2001 by William Cobb

Cover illustration by Tres Taylor

Published by Crane Hill Publishers
Printed in the United States of America

Library of Congress Cataloging-in-Publication Data

Cobb, William, 1937-
  Wings of morning / William Cobb.
    p. cm.
  ISBN 1-57587-177-7
    1. African Americans—Fiction.  2. Civil rights movements—Fiction.
3. Southern States—Fiction.  I. Title.
  PS3553.O198 W5 2001
  813'.54—dc21                                            2001042224
                                                            CIP

10      9      8      7      6      5      4      3      2      1

For

Winston Smith

*In Memoriam*

Always a good friend,
Always ready with wit and laughter,
A poet, literary scholar, historian, and master teacher.

In our youth we loved the crumbling old houses,
the cedar encrusted cemeteries,
the Old People and the stories they told.
Together, as boys, we listened breathlessly to the tale of the ring,
The seed from which sprang this entire narrative.

I miss immensely the sharing of it with him again now.

If I take the wings of morning and dwell in the uttermost
    parts of the sea
even there thy hand shall lead me, and thy right hand
    shall hold me
If I say, "Let only darkness cover me, and the light
    about me be night,"
Even the darkness is not dark to thee;
    the night is bright as the day.

Psalm 139

Now, from the Gates of Hercules we flood

Westward, westward till the barbarous brine
Whelms us to the tired land where tasseling corn,
Fat beans, grapes sweeter than muscadine
Rot on the vine: in that land were we born.

—Allen Tate, "The Mediterranean"

# Part One

# Rachel

HIS NAME IS BILLY SINGLETON BUT EVERYBODY CALLS HIM Billy Simpleton, and he won't leave Rachel alone. He sharecrops part time on land owned by the Legrand family—land still, even in 1964, called Rose Hill Plantation. His daddy sharecropped, too, before he got too old to labor. Billy lives a little more than three miles from Rachel's house, all the way on the other side of the Legrand place, in a whitewashed house with scraggly flowers planted in old tires in the front yard. His wife, Jessie Merle, is fat and blonde and wears polyester pants suits, bright blue and pink. They have a pack of tow-headed, snotty-nosed youngsters. When the weather is good and the back roads of Rose Hill are passable, Rachel sees them drive by her house all packed into Jessie Merle's dusty old Pontiac—blue with a lime green hood—on their way into town.

In addition to sharecropping, Billy Simpleton also works at Chemco Managed Waste, the huge toxic waste dump built by the Legrands shortly after World War II on Rose Hill land over near the Bigbee River. Carter Taylor, Rachel's older brother, works there, too, driving a forklift. Carter was the first black man hired to work at Chemco other than in a janitorial position. "Of course Carter will work there," Mr. Oscar Legrand said when Carter finished high school. "Taylors have been on the place almost as long as Legrands have! Carter is like family!"

Billy Simpleton has been the cause of a lot that's happened in Rachel's life. They're the same age and grew up together on the Legrand plantation. In their teens, Billy, a pale freckled white boy with cow shit on the cuffs of his overalls, introduced Rachel to beer and then pot. He grew marijuana in the swamplands along the Bigbee and sold reefer cigarettes across the river in Hammond, in the alleys behind the poolrooms and cafes, both white and colored. Rachel loved the stuff, and the two of them used to get high together and make a kind of awkward, fumbling love in haylofts and on old quilts thrown down on pine needles in the woods.

Now Billy, minus some teeth but still swaggering, won't let her forget that. He stops his big-wheel pickup one cold January afternoon when he sees her in her yard. He gets out and leans against the fender.

"Come on, Rachel," he says, "you know you want it." And he cups his hand around his privates. She laughs to herself, remembering his pecker, long and thin, pale as a frog's belly. Rachel is tall and lean, her skin the color of cafe au lait. She wears bandannas around her head, sometimes red, sometimes blue.

"What you wear them things for, Rachel?" her mother asked when Rachel came home from New Orleans to help take care of her when she got sick.

"I wear em for all the black women who've gone before me," Rachel replied, "who cooked for and nourished children and menfolks and sewed quilts to keep em warm in winter, sewed until their eyes went bad." Her mother just looked at her from where her head lay on the pillow.

"I ain't never wore no bandanna in my life!" she laughed.

People have always told Rachel that she's beautiful, but she does not believe it. Her face is narrow with high cheekbones, and her body is hard. Her breasts jut out like the prow of a skiff. Her hips are firm and plump, her legs long. Her skin looks polished, like the finish on a fine pecan-wood tabletop.

Even as a child she'd been beautiful. She was Billy Simpleton's play-pretty.

"Come on, Rachel."

She just stands there looking at him, a pair of pruning shears in her hand from trimming back azalea bushes. "Git outta here, Billy," she says. When she lived in New Orleans she thought she'd never come back here, never come home. And he was one of the reasons.

He keeps rubbing his crotch. "Once a gal's had some a this, she's bound to need some more."

"You want to keep it, you better keep it in your britches."

He stomps his heavy work boot on the ground. He laughs and sneers. "Come on. We'll drive down to the creek."

"You want it to turn purple and drop off?" she asks.

His eyes are opaque and doubtful. He knows she's a Mam'bo, a hoodoo, that she'd come home from New Orleans one. Everybody on this side of the Bigbee knows it, as does the black side of town over in Hammond, and even some whites.

"That's just nigger-shit," he says, but she can tell he's not sure, not sure at all.

"Keep on messin with me and you'll find out," she warns.

One fateful day back when they were fourteen or fifteen, old Jim Burton, a black man her own mother's age, walked up on them in the woods. Bloodshot, mean eyes and a long razor scar down one cheek, he suddenly appeared, shotgun over his shoulder, heavy black rubber boots floppy on his legs, and they had lain there on the quilt, naked and vulnerable and frightened. Jim Burton looked down at them and said, "Git yore ass outta here, white boy." Billy struggled with his overalls and his shoes and went hopping off into the woods, whimpering and crying. Then Jim Burton let his pants drop around his ankles and said "Lemme show you what a black dick looks like."

He said he'd tell Rachel's mother she was smoking reefers and fucking a white boy. He'd turn her over to the high sheriff for the dope. He gave her whiskey, which she loved as much as marijuana and beer, and she couldn't get enough of that either. And he told her he'd beat her if she didn't do what he told her to do. "You know Abe Chadwell?" he had asked her. Later, Abe Chadwell, old with coarse gray hair and snuff in the corners of his mouth, made her get on all fours and mounted her that way. He had hurt her and laughed at her pain. After that Rachel got a job working behind the counter at Hanson's Store down in Crockers Crossroads to have money for drugs and harsh raw white lightning, clear moonshine in mason jars. She used a string of young men to try to cleanse herself of the old dirty ones. But nothing worked. Finally, the only thing she could do about it was to simply leave. To go away. And she bought a bus ticket to as far away as she could think of. New Orleans. Where she stayed fifteen years. Until her brother Carter came down there and found her and brought her home to help care for their mother, who was dying of cancer.

"I mean it," she says to Billy Simpleton, "leave me alone."

"I ain't botherin you, Rachel. You know you want it. I can see it wrote all over you."

The winter sun is warm on her head. She wears the bandanna with jeans and a long-sleeved denim shirt, worn and frayed. Billy's eyes, eyes full of questions without answers, set close together in his skull, give him a pale, owl-like appearance. She knows he still grows marijuana and now runs a still back in the swamp over near Maconoco Creek. On Legrand land. If they knew about all that, the Legrands would offer Billy no second chance. Mr. Oscar would have him thrown in jail. Or maybe Miss Amy would deal with that, now that Mr. Oscar is governor. He lives full time in Montgomery, even though Miss Amy still lives at Hawthorne, their house in Hammond. At the very least Billy Simpleton could be fired from Chemco and kicked off the land his family has lived on for generations. Rachel shakes her head.

"I can see it wrote all over you," Billy repeats.

"Ain't nothin wrote on me," she replies.

"Let me look closer and see," he says, coming into the yard. He wears khaki pants, greasy and with a hole in one knee, and a light jacket, navy blue with CHEMCO stitched over the breast pocket in red script. He gets closer and her blood runs faster. He scares her.

"Let me be, Billy," she says.

"I just want a little nookie. Don't you remember how good it was?"

"Naw," she says, "I remember how bad it was."

"Come on," he grins. Nobody can really see them now through the thick scuppernong and grape arbors, the fig and chinaberry trees that crowd Rachel's small cabin. His grin fades into a sneer. "You don't mean that. It was good and you know it."

"You can't fuck worth a shit," she says. Billy glares at her but seems more confused than angry. She knows he doesn't know what to feel. He's empty-headed and dangerous. "You fuck like white trash," she adds, goading him into a fury. She hears his breathing whistle in and out of his nostrils. She smells his sweat.

"You nigger bitch," he sneers. He wants to hit her. But she knows he's scared of her. Suddenly she realizes he may hit her anyway. She balls her fist, still holding the pruning shears in her other hand. He looks at the shears. "You would cut me with them things, wouldn't you?" he asks incredulously. "You'd cut a white man!?"

"Cut his balls off."

"Why you nigger bitch," Billy growls. He moves faster than she anticipates, knocking the pruning shears from her hand with one swift blow. With his other hand he rips the front of her shirt open and she feels the winter air like chilled water on her breasts. She backs away from him, but he keeps coming. His breath comes in snorts. His hand hurts her arm when he grabs her. "I'll show you," he spits. She's forgotten how much bigger he is than she. He's heavier now, too, fleshy, and he pulls her toward him and tries to kiss her. She turns her head away and butts him on the mouth. "Goddam," he cries, astonished as he wipes blood from his mouth. "Goddam it!"

He punches her then, and she falls to the ground, numb. She doesn't move. She wants to get up and run but doesn't move. She knows she can't get away. The side of her head throbs. She squints against the dim afternoon sun, the high gray sky. He wipes his mouth with his handkerchief. The sight of his own blood seems to infuriate him. He stands over her. "I'm gonna kill you, nigger," he rages. "But first I'm gonna fuck you good!"

She lies still as death. She only half feels his hands as they rip at her jeans, pulling them down. She feels the air on her lower body, harsh and icy. She stiffens, holds herself rigid. He struggles to get her jeans and panties over her heavy shoes. He breathes heavily, whining and crying. She feels his body on hers, feels him fumbling between her legs, smells his rancid breath, tobacco and whiskey and rotten teeth. It hurts her when he forces himself inside her, but she doesn't wince. It happens to her and it doesn't happen. He smears the blood from his lips onto her breasts. She doesn't care. It'll wash off. He grunts like an old hog and drops his body's dead weight on top of her, crushing the breath out of her. She cannot breathe at all. She feels herself getting dizzy, fading.

Then he is standing over her. The side of her face and her eye still throb, and she knows they will swell and blacken. Billy looks frightened now, like a terrified child, scared to death that he's done something that'll get him in trouble. He looks around, then back at her. "Rachel?" he says. She doesn't answer. She hates him. "Get up." She doesn't move. Her eyes focus on a brown blade of grass. She doesn't even blink. She can feel him sticky and cold between her legs. She keeps herself as immobile as she can. She doesn't even breathe. The world—Billy, everything—completely disappears. She is like death itself; an ant crawls up her cheek and into her eye and she doesn't flinch. Billy sees that and turns and runs back to his truck as fast as he can. He thinks she's dead. He thinks he's killed her. She hears him crank up, hears the truck rumble down the road.

Much later, Rachel sits up. She doesn't know how much time has passed, but the light in the chilly air is faded, muted with the declining afternoon. Her body is stiff, chilled all the way through. She is dazed, unable for a moment to remember what happened to her, and then it all comes crashing back. She can still smell Billy, still feel him on her.

She looks around. She sees her ripped shirt in the dirt. She sees Billy's handkerchief, where he dropped it, spotted with blood, dried now in the late-afternoon air. She picks it up and holds it on her palm. After a long time she smiles. It was one of the first lessons she learned at the feet of Delvane Debene, the old hoodoo woman, a high priestess and Mam'bo, who took Rachel in off the streets of New Orleans and made her a novitiate: *To do evil to someone, first take something that belongs to them, some personal possession....*

•  •  •

They all know the baby will come in the rain. It's January, the month when the black mud swims and squirms, makes the thin gravel back roads difficult, almost impassable—except by four-wheel drives, big-wheeled pickups, and, of course, mules—forcing everyone to walk the mile down to the big house and then take the chert drive out to the paved road. They know Karla, Carter's wife, will not be able to walk that far after the pains start. Earlier Carter had said, "She can go over and stay in Hammond, be close to the hospital. She can stay with Hester's daughter until her time comes."

"No," Rachel said, "ain't no need. Justina is all she'll need."

"That's right," Karla agreed. "I don't need no hospital."

"What if something goes wrong?" He looked at both women, their eyes dark and dancing.

"Ain't nothing going wrong," Karla replied, and the two women looked at each other and laughed at him because he was a man.

Carter and Karla live with Carter and Rachel's mother, just down the road from Rachel's cabin. It is the house Carter and Rachel grew up in, the only house Carter has ever known. Their mother, Rosa, lies dying in an old iron bed in one of the two bedrooms, and they are all thankful, even in their grief, that soon there will be new life in the house. At five in the afternoon—on the same gray and sullen day—the heavy clouds hanging so low they touch the treetops, Karla tells him that it's time. And Carter walks across the back pastures and through the pear orchard, past the old baseball field. It is dark when Carter passes behind the big house to the row of cabins where Justina Beasley, the midwife, lives. Justina tells him she's coming, to go on back. On the way back home in the full night, an inner radar guides him, an instinct developed by all his years on the place. He knows every cow path, every clump of Cherokee roses and patch of blackberry vines, stiff now and frozen in the winter's dark. Carter's years of labor at Rose Hill and his father's years before him—and God knew who the others were, the ones who'd come before his father—all those years seem to creep up his legs like cold from the damp ground and cling to him like a scent. But Carter knows that his child will be part of a new day. As his heavy shoes slip and slide in the thick, rich mud, black as motor oil, black as night, Carter finally sees the lights of his mother's house glimmering ahead. As long as she's alive, it is his mother's house, Rosa's house, not his.

He and Rachel had been born there. His father had died there when Carter was small. All Carter remembers of his father is the sound of him, the hollow thump of his heavy boots on the porch when he came home—and the smell of him, sweat and tobacco and raw whiskey. Carter knows his mother soon will die in the house, and his son will be born there. Carter pulls his heavy coat more closely around himself in the dank cold. He feels fear mingle with anticipation and dread. It is all strange and mysterious. He has lived so long as only himself and now there will be an extension of him, of his own flesh. He hurries. Inside the house Karla winces in pain, and it's gut-wrenching to see her, to watch the sweat pop up on her forehead. Rachel is already there, praying and shaking rattles in the corner. She lights the candles and the old oil lamp, and Carter sees the tiny flames glittering on Rachel's skin. Karla is darker than his sister, and the whites of her eyes flash as her eyes roll back in her head and she cries out, slumped and stiff at the same time. And then Justina arrives, tells her to push, to push, and Carter stands out on the porch in his shirt-sleeves, the air like a cold shower, listening to the women inside laugh and talk and even sing, and then the cries of pain come more and more frequently until there's a long wail and Carter's back inside, just as Justina pulls at the little creature while Rachel chants Hail Marys. Carter wants to tell her to shut up, to stop. But he stands hypnotized by what Justina is doing, working with the reds and the purples and the glistening wet slick surfaces and his mind races.

"It's a boy, Carter," he hears Rachel shout.

"It's a boy, Carter," Karla calls to him. "You've got a son."

And Carter sees then that his son has come into the world with small juttings of bone on his tiny, narrow back. Covered with clean, brown flesh, the bumps appear just under the shoulder blades on both sides of his back. And two stubby protuberances crown the top of his head, almost like the beginnings of horns. Rachel, her eye discolored and swollen, opens a small white bag of gris-gris powder and methodically makes overlapping geometric patterns on the floor. Justina holds the baby aloft, and Carter feels a great flood of joy and excitement, of happiness. They all look at the tiny deformities on the baby.

The three candles Rachel placed on the mantel—along with a wooden bowl of white corn meal and an egg—suddenly go out, as though snuffed by an abrupt burst of breath, and Justina says, "It's Carrie."

And everybody in the room feels her presence. They cannot see her but they feel her like a quick gust of cold air, and the flames in the gas floor heater sputter and spit like they're alive. All they know about Carrie is that she was their mother's mother, and she often walks the night to the farthest reaches of Rose Hill Plantation. People see her mostly on moonlit nights, when the air is almost as bright as daylight—silver light rather than the gold of day—and she moves quickly and gracefully three feet off the ground, a young woman barely more than a girl in a plain gray smock made of flour sacking. Buried nobody knows where. "That's why she walks," the old people say. "She ain't got no marker on her grave."

"That ain't all why she walks," Justina says, but she won't say more. "Y'all'll know the truth before I'm dead, which won't be much longer anyhow."

Justina doesn't know her own age, but she thinks she's almost as old as the white man she cares for, Mr. Williamson Dupree Legrand Jr. living alone in his late nineties in the huge old columned mansion, Rose Hill, with the four towering magnolia trees in the front yard. Justina often has to send Gilbert Washington, the other ancient house servant, out to the circular chert road leading up from the highway to chase away the people who drive up to see the house, park their cars, take pictures, or just gawk. "This is one of the finest examples of Greek Revival architecture in the entire South," a man with a yankee accent once told him. Gilbert sized up the man, whose camera hung around his neck on a leather strap, and replied, "No it ain't. It a man's house, and he ain't invited none a you."

When the old man's son Oscar Legrand became governor, a gate was put up and kept locked until Mr. Oscar decided it was bad politics, bad public relations. "People want to see where I came from," Mr. Oscar said.

"Huh," Justina said.

Justina swaddles the baby, being careful of the fleshy swellings on his back. "They're wings," she says. "He'll fly. Fly away home."

"Fly to Jordan, the promised land," Rachel says. "He Exu, come again." She pronounces it A-shoo. It will be the boy's name for the rest of his life. Eshu. Rachel makes the sign of the cross, then looks at the icon of the Virgin Mary painted on a piece of barn board on the mantel behind the candles and the wooden bowl. The candles still smoke, thinly, like gray threads suspended from the ceiling. "Carrie wanted to see her great-grandson," Rachel says. "She came to see him."

"Yes," Justina agrees.

Carter feels the presence of his grandmother like a cold, clammy hand against his skin. As a child he'd been frightened of her. He first saw her when he was seven years old, walking in the pear orchard near the big house, and again when he was fourteen. That time she sat on the roof of the old smokehouse looking upward at the ice-white sliver of moon. At sixteen, he was walking home drunk one night, stumbling in the ruts in the road, and he saw her sitting on a rock holding an old mandolin. He heard music. It was the old mandolin that had belonged to his father, the one his mother still has in the house. Dry-rotted now, it has suffered a botched repair job where somebody tacked on a metal plate to hold the strings. But it's still beautiful with its gourd-shaped sound box made of a hundred varying-colored strips of wood no more than a quarter-inch wide and the struts on its arm inlaid with mother-of-pearl, some of it long since missing. He had not known the song Carrie sang, though it sounded as familiar as his breath. Emboldened by the corn liquor, he approached her, blundering through the high weeds in the ditch, to find only an empty rock. But he could still hear the music, faint as a dream.

Now Carter stands in the room beneath the naked overhead bulb, the room where his son has just been born. He feels the cold of the winter night in his bones. He is filled with awe, astonished but not surprised at the protuberances on his son's head and back. His son. His firstborn. He looks at Karla, her head back on the pillow, exhausted from a long labor. He is proud of her. In the other bedroom, his mother, Rosa Carter, lies sick and dying. As he thinks of her the thick grief overwhelms him and floods his eyes. He looks at the walls, plastered with old newspaper. This is Rosa's house. She does it the old way, walls covered with layer after layer of newspaper. Justina's house is that way, too, and Gilbert's. They are all that's left of the old way, they and old man Dupree, confined now to that high four-poster bed upstairs in the big house, his face wizened and shriveled.

Carter thinks of the marches happening across the river in Hammond. Marching for the vote. A new push is coming, one that somebody said is the strongest one yet, one that may bring Dr. King back to Hammond.

●   ●   ●

Albert "Mose" Bell, the pastor of the Oak Grove Calvary Baptist Church in Crockers Crossroads, sits in a pew near the front door of the whitewashed frame church talking with Eldon Long. Long is the pastor of the AME Zion Church, the biggest black church in the area, located across the river in Hammond. He is also a friend of Reverend King's and the leading local organizer for the Movement. This morning, a premature spring day, the two men talk, their heads close together. Albert is much older, gray haired and heavy, Eldon thin and dark, full of restless energy. An intense man, Eldon rarely smiles.

In the meeting room at the back, Rachel Taylor teaches nine children ranging in age from two to five, teaches with her swollen and blackened eye. She told Carter and everybody that she ran into a low branch of her fig tree. Rachel knows that if Carter knew or even suspected the truth, he'd kill Billy and spend the rest of his life rotting in a white man's prison. Besides, she knows she can take care of Billy herself. The meeting room houses a preschool and daycare provided by the church for working parents. Rachel reads the children "The Three Little Pigs" but embellishes the story with her own details. The little pigs live, for example, in Crockers, and the wolf is the high sheriff of Noshobe County. The children find this very funny.

Rachel organized the little school when she first came home from New Orleans. Nobody in Noshobe County had ever heard of daycare, but she knew of it in New Orleans and started her own version of it. Mose Bell had been skeptical.

"How we gonna keep the church open during the week?" he asked. "We can't hardly pay the light bill as it is, just using it on Sundays."

"The Legrands," Rachel replied. "Maybe they'll pay it."

"Huh," Mose said. He eyed her. His eyebrows, gray and stiff like his hair, raised into little arches. "I reckon if anybody could get it out of 'em you could. You or Carter one."

So Rachel caught a ride into town to go see Miss Amy Legrand at Hawthorne. It was still summer then, still hot. She walked the last few blocks to the house. The street was familiar to her. She and Carter had practically grown up at Hawthorne. Their mother, Rosa, had been the nurse for the Legrands' son, Dooly, who was Carter's age, all grown now and long since gone. Williamson Dupree Legrand IV, called "Dooly" in the family because that's the way Carter had pronounced Dupree when they were both babies. After Dooly was older and no longer needed a nurse, Rosa worked as Miss Amy's personal maid (her "upstairs" maid, as Miss Amy called it). As boys, Dooly and Carter had been inseparable, as close as brothers. Carter worked around the house, mowing the grass and helping Miss Amy with her garden, and hunted and fished with Mr. Oscar until he finished high school and went to work for Chemco. And Dooly went off to school and got married. Now he's a priest at a big Episcopal church in Nashville, Tennessee, the same kind of church as St. Paul's in Hammond, the church Miss Amy won't let a Sunday go by without taking her place in her pew.

Rachel, the youngest of the three, always tagged along behind the boys, the butt of their jokes and tricks. They would tell her she was "it," and as she counted to a hundred they would simply go off downtown or up along the river somewhere and leave her there in the garden that sloped down toward the river bluff. She would search for them for hours until it dawned on her what they had done.

"Them boys full of devilment," Hester the cook would tell her. "Don't pay em no nevermind." Hester was the first woman Rachel had ever seen with dreadlocks. She was tall and as yellow as the yolk of a boiled egg, with dark little moles all over her face.

"But I ain't got anybody to play with," Rachel would say.

"You got her," Hester would say, pointing out the back window to the statue of the naked woman that stood in the middle of the garden. Boxwood hedges, neatly clipped, surrounded the statue, whose only adornment was a scarf around her neck that hung down in the back almost to her rounded buttocks. The statue, pink marble, was seven feet tall, and the boys would hold each other up so they could feel her titties and giggle. They would cup her buttocks and moan.

"Stop that," Rachel would say, and Carter and Dooly would laugh at her.

"Her name is Aphrodite," Dooly said. "Venus. You don't know what that means. You're too young."

One day when the boys weren't around, Hester said, "Hush! Watch now." The two of them stood in the sunlit kitchen, silently watching the statue. Through the open windows, Rachel could hear the distant faint liquid chugging of a riverboat coming down the river. She could see the tug and the barges, riding low in the water with coal or iron ore from Birmingham, bound for Mobile. "Watch now," Hester whispered, "she gonna turn her head and watch for the riverboat." Rachel trembled and Hester's hand kept her still. And they stood there and watched until the boat was around the bend, Rachel watching for the statue's head to turn slowly to follow the boat's progress down the river. It did not move.

"That ain't true," Rachel said.

"Didn't you see it, girl?" Hester asked accusingly.

"Hell no!"

"Don't talk like that, girl. She always does that when a boat comes down the river. Watches it till it's out of sight. I seen her do it often. Don't know why you can't."

"I don't believe it," Rachel spat.

"Well, I saw it," Hester spat back at her.

Years later Rachel walked through the black wrought-iron gate and up the driveway between the house and the carriage house and around to the back door. As she mounted the back steps she could see the statue in the garden, and she raised her hand in a silent greeting. Hester was in the kitchen shelling peas at the table.

"I want to see Miss Amy," Rachel told her.

"Miss Amy busy," she replied. "You can't...." and before she could finish Rachel had already passed through the swinging door into the dining room and then into the front parlor where Miss Amy sat at her tall desk she called a "secretary," writing in a leather-bound book. She looked up. A heavy, squat glass on the desk next to her hand contained pale amber liquid that Rachel knew was whiskey.

The parlor was crowded with furniture, red velvet chairs and sofas and gleaming tables, a heavy sideboard with cut-glass cocktail glasses and decanters that sparkled like jewels in the sunlight. Pictures lined the mantel and the walls, spooky paintings of old dead Legrands whose eyes would follow you all around the room. The parlor ceiling was frescoed plaster, angels and cherubs and a saint that Miss Amy once told her was Cecilia, patron saint of music. This had been the music room when the house was built way back before the Civil War by Francis Mansfield, who later became a member of the Confederate senate. Mr. Oscar Legrand bought the house when he came home from law school and opened his office in Hammond. Raised at Rose Hill, he wanted to live in a fine house. Even though Hawthorne was run down, divided into apartments occupied by poor whites, Mr. Oscar vowed to restore it, to make it as splendid as Rose Hill, and he did.

"Rachel," Amy said. "What a pleasant surprise." Her eyes flicked over Rachel, neutral eyes, registering neither approval nor disapproval. Rachel wore a skirt she had brought home from New Orleans, a skirt long and black with African symbols of the phases of the moon. She wore a frayed denim shirt and a red bandanna. The parlor was cool, a soft, comfortable cool. Miss Amy wore a plain sleeveless housedress, pale lavender. When she raised her glass to her lips and drank, her thin arms clanked with gold jewelry. In her early sixties, Miss Amy was still a handsome woman, though there were lines around her tired eyes. Her hair was coal black. "How is your mother? How is Rosa?"

"Well," Rachel replied. "As good as you could expect, I guess. She's not having much pain now."

"Tell her I'll come out to see her soon. Bring her some magazines. I've got stacks of them." Periodically, since their mother had been sick, Miss Amy would show up in her chauffeur-driven limousine with magazines and paperback books and boxes of candy. She sent cut flowers and dish gardens, which Rachel planted in her mother's yard.

"Miss Amy," Rachel said. "I need to talk with you about something."

"Of course."

And Rachel told her. Amy Legrand listened, nodding now and then. Only once she asked, "A school?"

"A pre-school," Rachel answered. She knew, of course, why Miss Amy was asking that. She knew her concern. But she waited.

"This wouldn't have anything to do with all this agitation, would it, all this business?" Miss Amy finally asked. It was as though she couldn't quite give it a name.

"Nome," Rachel replied. "It's daycare, mainly. Most of the parents work at Chemco or on the place."

Miss Amy nodded again and pursed her lips. "I see," she said. After a minute she said, "Of course. Tell Mose to send the power company bill to me every month and I'll pay it."

Rachel stood. "Thank you, Miss...." But Miss Amy stopped her.

"Wait a minute," she said. She turned to her desk, found a black-covered pad, and began to scribble. Then she handed Rachel a check for a thousand dollars. "For books and supplies," Miss Amy said.

●　●　●

"The old people are scared," Albert says to Eldon Long, the two men seated in the church. "They don't know what's gonna happen."

"I don't know what's gonna happen," Eldon admits. "Nobody does. But it's building. Like a boil. Or a volcano. We're planning a march. A big one. All the way to Montgomery on foot to present the governor with a petition for voting rights."

"On foot? All that way?"

"Yes."

Albert thinks for a moment and then he looks back at Eldon. "Governor Oscar Legrand ain't gonna like that much," Albert cautions.

"No, he's not," Eldon agrees. "You know him. You've known him since he was a boy."

"Yes. He's a stubborn man. Mean, too, if he takes a notion. Always was. His daddy is, too. Look like old man Dupree Legrand be too mean to die." He chuckles. "He's three days older than God and still countin."

"What do you think he'll do?" Eldon asks. "The governor, I mean."

"Do? When?"

"When we get to Montgomery."

Albert shakes his head. He clucks his tongue, looks at the younger man. "You ain't gonna ever get to no Montgomery, cause he ain't gonna even let you start no march like that. Mark my words."

•  •  •

This is what Rachel does about Billy: She walks through the woods carrying a cane pole over her shoulder, a lard can punched with screwdriver holes and full of crickets, and an empty pail. At Cottonmouth Bayou on the edge of Maconoco Swamp, she stops and fishes until she catches a three-foot catfish. She will filet the smaller ones she catches and cook them with black spices for dinner, but she stops fishing when she gets one exactly three feet long. She carries the fish home in the bucket full of water, careful to keep him alive. When she gets home she removes the three sharp spikes from the catfish's back. She dries them over the gas flame on her stove and then pulverizes them into a powder. She mixes the powder with cayenne and graveyard dirt. She writes Billy Singleton's name three times on a piece of paper, making sure the names cross each other. Then she folds the powder mixture up in the paper and, walking back through the woods to Cottonmouth Bayou, she puts the folded paper into the catfish's mouth and releases him, live, back into the water.

That evening Billy's wife, Jessie Merle, finds a warty old bullfrog crouching in the corner of their bedroom. She picks him up on a broom and tosses him out the window.

•  •  •

Rose Hill Plantation, comprised of a hundred square miles of Alabama's richest, blackest river-bottom land, is nestled in the crotch of two rivers—the Bigbee on the west and the Coosa on the south and east. Below this the rivers join to form the Big Cahaba, flowing south to Mobile Bay and then to the Gulf of Mexico. Well into the twentieth century the land's crop is cotton. Vast cotton fields stretch as far as you can see in all directions, the fields being planted, chopped, and finally picked by an army of slaves and then by their descendants, all presided over by a line of Legrands stretching back to old Nicholas Desnouettes Legrand. He left St. Tammany Parish in Louisiana in 1820 with his wife, three children, and six slaves to come through the gulf and then upriver from Mobile to a grant of land he received from the government in exchange for serving as an Indian agent. At the confluence of the two rivers, in the wilds of Creek and Choctaw territory, Nicholas built a log cabin on a hill in the wilderness— the cabin still standing, used for many years as a smokehouse. Gradually he and his slaves cleared the land of thick bamboo, canebrake. He then spent over seven years constructing the grand house, Rose Hill, on the same rolling knob, positioned so the landing on the Bigbee five miles away across the broad flat fields was visible from the widow's walk atop the house. Nicholas Legrand designed the house himself and knew where every peg and brick and panel of wainscoting should go. Rose Hill, with its glass windows and its furniture and rugs and chandeliers imported from France and brought painstakingly upriver on flatboats, was a showplace, a center of social activity during the dry season, with balls and barbecues. But it became almost isolated in the wet winter and spring when the thick, rich loam of the land became impassable. And later, when the little village of Hammond across the Coosa grew into a booming river town, the family moved to a house on Commissioners Street during the wet seasons. That rambling fourteen-room frame house, called "The Legrand Cottage," burned to the ground in the winter of 1921. By then, crude roads and an improved ferry across the river made Rose Hill more accessible.

The first Williamson Dupree Legrand was born to Nicholas's son Alexander in 1845. Old enough to serve in the War Between the States, which had already claimed the lives of his two older brothers, Dupree was wounded at Shiloh and then again at Gettysburg and returned to Rose Hill after the war a vanquished, bruised, and scarred young man. He married Amelia Lyon from the neighboring plantation of Gaineswood. Shortly before his early death in 1869, Amelia gave birth to Williamson Dupree Legrand Jr., the same Legrand who now in 1964 still lies upstairs in the bed at Rose Hill, an ancient man who recognizes no one, who seems locked forever in his own past, cared for by Justina Beasley and Gilbert Washington. Late in life he married Marie Louise Chaudron Legrand. Their first son, Williamson Dupree Legrand III, was killed in World War II at Pelelieu in the South Pacific; their second son, Oscar, is now governor of the State of Alabama.

Rose Hill, which has not been a working plantation in decades, is dotted with sharecroppers, both white and black. Many of the blacks—like the Taylors—are descendants of the very slaves who worked the land before the Civil War. Several small dairies now operate on the place, wedged between pastures of beef cattle and fields of soybeans, some cotton, alfalfa, and corn. And shortly after World War II, Rose Hill became home to Chemco Managed Waste, the largest hazardous waste facility east of the Mississippi River. Deep fissures have been carved into the limestone beneath Rose Hill's layers of rich alluvial soil. Those limestone beds now contain large quantities of benzene, Benzidine, cyclodine pesticides such as haptachlor, endrin, and dieldrin, which were produced in large volumes by American firms in the late forties. From 1949 on, Chemco has served as the final resting place for waste residues used in the manufacture of pesticides, plasticizers, and caustic soda, all brought in 55-gallon drums on trucks from all over the country, to be stacked in the limestone hollows below ground.

That part of the plantation is surrounded by a high chain-link fence with red signs warning DANGER! DO NOT ENTER, WARNING: POSSIBLE HAZARDOUS WASTE AREA, and NO TRESPASSING BY ORDER OF CHEMCO MANAGED WASTE, INC. Inside the fence, besides the dump itself, are swamplands along the Bigbee River and a hundred-acre lake once used for swimming and fishing. As everyone knows, it's now so polluted that no fish live in it, no thick-legged bullfrogs thrive along the banks. In fact, the lake sludge, brown scum with a silvery slime running through it, gives off a sweet, etherlike odor, a smell like creosote.

•   •   •

Billy Singleton, Jessie Merle, and their three children live on the northern edge of Rose Hill. For as long as he can remember, Billy has awakened in the pitch dark of early morning to milk, seven days a week, rain or shine, hot or cold. He knows he'll never escape it, never get ahead. His father, a bitter old man who lives just down the road, used to beat him with a stick of stove wood when he was little. He beat him when he did something wrong and beat him when he did something right. Billy has tried every scheme he can think of to go up in the world: He grows pot and cooks shine, in addition to selling milk to one of the dairies, raising his twelve scrawny beef cattle, and working at Chemco. (He doesn't like it that he has the same job—driving a forklift—as Carter Taylor, a Negro, and he mumbles and complains about it. Too many Negroes work at Chemco to suit him anyway. Billy belongs to the Klan, and he knows they'll do something soon about the Negroes and all these marches. Very soon.) He has sold Amway. His wife sells Mary Kay, taking phone orders and writing them in a ruled notebook with a yellow pencil until Billy gets home from his shift at the waste facility to help her fill out the pale pink order blanks and put them into the pale pink envelopes and send them off. Jessie Merle thinks she's going to earn a pink Cadillac one day, but Billy knows better. Billy finished high school. Jessie Merle didn't; she ran off in the eighth grade and got pregnant, then gave up the baby and came home. Billy met her when she was working the candy and popcorn counter at V. J. Elmore's over in Hammond.

Billy thinks that his high school diploma gives him a more realistic attitude than Jessie Merle, who is ignorant and also letting herself go to fat. Every six months or so, she goes to the Upper Room I Am Temple, a Holy Roller church over near Boligee, and gets the Holy Ghost in her. She goes to the church, rolls around on the floor and blabbers in tongues; then she comes home and gives him worry about his drinking and his moonshining. She doesn't know about the pot. Billy doubts she even knows what it is. The Holy Ghost usually leaves her within a couple of months and she becomes the old Jessie Merle again, smoking cigarettes and drinking beer with him, gossiping on the phone, yelling at the kids to shut the hell up and leave her alone.

They have had five children, but only three are alive. One was born with an enlarged heart and died within days, and the other one died of infantile leukemia before he was two. Jessie Merle blames Billy for their deaths, because he drinks. "God will punish sinners, Billy," she says.

"God ain't got nothing to do with it," Billy replies.

"It's the devil that lives in you. My poor little innocent babies."

"You got three more, ain't that enough?" Billy asks.

"Billy Singleton! The Lord will strike you down for that!" She is giving herself and their oldest child, Nancy, a Toni Home Permanent, and the whole house smells like goat shit. "Don't you ever say anything like that in front of my children again!"

When Billy recently started having pains in his gut, old Dr. Mason over in Hammond couldn't find anything wrong with him. "It ain't appendicitis," Dr. Mason had told him, "cause I cut that out of you when you were little. Maybe it's an ulcer. If it doesn't go away in a week or so, we'll run some tests." Jessie Merle insists she knows what it is.

"See? Ain't you sorry for what you said? And you can't take it back, neither. God won't let you take nothing back, and he hears everything!" She looks smug and self-satisfied. "God is giving you that pain!"

Billy drinks to ease the sharp pain. They sit in the living room watching "Peyton Place."

"I dreamed last night I had a fish growing inside my stomach," Billy says during the commercial.

"A fish? What was it swimmin in, rotgut whiskey?"

"I'm serious," Billy insists.

"What makes you think I ain't?" Jessie Merle retorts.

The pain goes away and then returns two nights later, when he has the same dream again. He sees the fish clearly in this dream: a slick, gray catfish.

•   •   •

Billy sees Rachel Taylor walking down the narrow, unpaved street behind the Silver Moon Cafe, a Negro cafe on Jackson Street that sells barbecue and fish sandwiches and hot dogs and shots of Billy's whiskey. He's relieved she's not dead, though he knows he would have heard about it if she were. He can see no signs of their fight on her, no traces of a black eye, no swollen lip, nothing. For a moment he wonders if it really happened. He wonders if she has told anybody. Like that smart-ass brother of hers. Billy can hear the Silver Moon jukebox thumping away, hear laughter from inside. It's crowded, before noon on a Thursday, which is unusual. Lots of Negroes are in town today, almost like a Saturday. Rachel doesn't look at him, ready to pass him in the street without acknowledging him.

"Hey, Rachel," he calls out. "You want a funny cigarette?"

"I ain't studyin you, Billy," she says.

"On the house."

"You better get on outta here before you get lynched," she laughs, her eyes sparkling in the sunlight. A red bandanna covers her hair, her thick hair, which he remembers running his hands through. He wants to do it again. He dreams about doing it. When he doesn't dream about the sleek catfish he dreams about Rachel's hair. He suddenly remembers that last night he dreamed about spiders. He shudders. He sees her watching him, a big smile on her face.

"What the hell you laughing at?" he asks.

"You," she says.

"Listen, Rachel..." he begins.

"I ain't got time for you, Billy," she interrupts.

He looks all around, sees Clutter Blue, who owns the Silver Moon, watching him from the back door. A big, heavy man, Clutter cooks the best barbecue in Noshobe County. White people all over Hammond hire him to cater their parties. One white man from Hammond, who went off to college in the East and then made millions on the stock market, gets Clutter to send him jars of his barbecue sauce all the way to New York City.

"I see your eye ain't still black," Billy comments.

"All of me is black," she replies.

"I'm sorry I...."

"I ain't got time to hear it, Billy," she says.

Billy looks around. Several other men join Clutter behind the cafe and they all watch Billy. He shuffles his feet nervously in the dust of the unpaved street lined with lime rock ditches. A row of shanties with narrow porches and steep shingled roofs faces him across the street, all of them painted a dark maroon. They are crowded together with no more room between them than a passageway that only a small child could walk through. The yards are sandy, and Billy can smell the raw odor of backyard privies and the chicken yards, and he can smell Clutter's barbecue cooking, too. Rachel is watching him, eyes as black as a starless sky.

"What's goin on?" he asks.

"What?"

"Everybody come to town. What's happening?"

"March."

"March? What kinda march?"

"March to the river," she answers. "Catfish march."

He screws his eyes up. His heart begins to pound. She frightens him. He cannot believe that her face shows no signs of his fist at all, no scars. He hit her hard. He saw the blood. He saw his own blood. Catfish march, she said. He feels a kind of clammy squirming in his belly. Sharp, prickly pains. Jessie Merle wants him to go with her to the Upper Room I Am Temple and let Kenneth Grable, the preacher there, cure him. Kenneth Grable handles snakes. Billy doesn't believe that any holiness preacher fool enough to pick up a live rattlesnake can cure anybody.

"What the hell is a 'catfish march'?" he sneers.

"When the other side of the moon comes around," she answers.

"Huh?" She confuses him. He doesn't know what she's talking about. Secret voodoo shit. He knows the men behind the Silver Moon are laughing at him. He doesn't know why, except that he's a white man. They laugh in a threatening way. Something is going on, something menacing and serious. He feels nervous again.

"Ain't the moon round?" Rachel asks him. "Like a ball. It ain't got no end and it ain't got no beginning."

"If you say so," he says, sneering again. He sneaks a look at the men behind the cafe. There are more of them now, and a couple of women, too. They all just look at him. Yes. Something is going on.

"You ever heard of a white boy gettin lynched?" Rachel asks.

"Naw," a voice says, up close behind Billy, and he jumps and turns to see Clutter Blue who has crossed the narrow backyard and is leaning on the fence made of part weathered board and part rusty wire. "If it happens to a white boy they call it murder." He and Rachel laugh. They laugh as though it's the funniest thing they've ever heard in their lives. Billy just stands there. Clutter is very black, like soot on a stovepipe. His heavy jowls shake when he laughs and he sweats even in the cool air. His dingy apron is covered with splotches of barbecue sauce, like dried blood. "You makin a whiskey run, Billy?" he asks.

"Naw, just cruisin with some reefers," Billy replies.

"Then maybe you better get on outta here, if you know what's good for you," Clutter warns, and Billy obeys.

• • •

Carter sits at a table in the Silver Moon with Karla and the baby. Karla is a happy woman who laughs a lot. When Carter married her five years ago she brought laughter into the Taylor house. Carter met her six years ago at a three-day singing and dinner on the ground at French Creek Landing up on the Coosa. It looked as though she would never conceive a child, and she didn't until Rachel came home from New Orleans.

Carter married late. A loner since his early teens, he spent his time hunting and fishing back in the swamps alone, sometimes for days at a time. Carter enjoys his job driving the forklift at Chemco, because there are long periods of time when he doesn't have to talk to another human being. Carter has always been quiet. He broods. "Still waters run deep," Rosa would say, and Carter would duck his head and smile a shy little smile, "Yes sir, still waters run deep."

After Carter and Karla had been married for five years, Rosa said, "I want a grandchild. I need a grandchild before I die." Rachel said nothing. Her mother already had a grandchild, but she didn't know it. None of them knew it but Rachel and old Delvane Debene. A little boy named Cap, in honor of Rachel's and Carter's long-dead father: Captain, called Cap. Cap Taylor. Her son was the child of a white man, an anonymous thin-chested boy in greasy jeans with a wispy, reddish mustache and whiskers, someone she'd taken up with and lived with in a dusty, partly furnished room with the mattress on the floor. He was long gone by the time the baby was born. A perfect little boy with astonishingly white skin, pale blue eyes, hair as soft and fine as an angel's. A white child. Delvane said that God was punishing her for where she'd allowed her life to go. "He the devil," Delvane said. "He come out of black white and ain't got no color. You can't see him in a mirror."

But Rachel held him up to the mirror, where she saw his perfect features there, his eyes alert, registering the world around him with an acute and perceptive calm as though patiently waiting for the power to speak what was already on his mind. Delvane wanted her to sell him. "You can get good money for him," Delvane said. "White folks don't know no better." But Rachel loved him intensely. She loved him too much to sell him. She had known a woman with thick, rimless glasses, some kind of social worker who sometimes walked the streets down around Jackson Square, talking to old men who drank wine on the grass and the young people— like her baby's father—restless and homeless young white people with long, stringy hair who were beginning to show up in droves on the streets. And the woman told her that yes she could get the boy into a white adoption agency, one that didn't require any background on the parents. Rachel trusted the woman's thick, substantial hips, her heavy, practical shoes, her authoritative white demeanor. She decided that little Cap's only chance was to trust her.

"He's white. I sent him where he'll have a chance," she told Delvane.

"He'll turn black before he's twelve," Delvane said, "I can read it."

•   •   •

People in the cafe gather around to look at the baby. "What his name?" Lucille Chapman asks. She wears a tight red dress and heavy red lipstick, hair piled high on her head. Married five times, Lucille hangs out in the cafe all the time, drinking beer.

"Eshu," Karla tells her.

"Eshu?" Lucille questions. "What kind of name is that?"

"A name name," Rachel responds.

"Uh-huh," Lucille says. She is half drunk already, but she'll march in the march to the courthouse anyway, and white people along the way will hoot at her and make fun of her, because she will stagger on her high spike heels. Lucille doesn't care.

"Who hit you, anyhow?" she asks.

Rachel's fingers go to her swollen cheek, the scab beneath her eye. The side of her face is still misshapen and bruised. "I ran into a fig tree limb," she says.

"Uh-huh," Lucille says again.

The Reverend Fred Shuttlesworth from Birmingham has come to Hammond for the march. He and Eldon Long are meeting with people down the street at the AME Zion Church. Reverend King is in Selma. In towns all over the Black Belt, people plan to march on this day to courthouses and deliver petitions for the right to register and vote, with no poll taxes, no literacy tests, no methods designed to keep them from it.

"Who we gonna vote for anyhow?" Clutter Blue asks.

"Oscar Legrand," someone says, and everybody laughs.

"He was a good man," Carter says, "once." Everybody knows how close Carter and Rachel were to the Legrand family. They all know that Carter fished with Mr. Oscar, drove trucks for him on his deer drives, took care of his bird dogs out at Rose Hill. Everybody knows Mr. Oscar and Miss Amy. They all remember Dooly. Dooly sat right in this room many a night when he was a teenager, playing poker and getting drunk with the men in the crowd. He played cards and shot craps with them and lost big money. And now he's a preacher in some fancy church in Tennessee. "Maybe Mr. Oscar is still a good man," Carter says.

"There's a new day coming," someone else says, "and he just don't know it yet."

"Amen."

"Amen."

# Carter

STRAWBERRY STREET IS AS FAMILIAR TO CARTER AS THE SOUND of his own name—the smells and the clash of colors in the crowded signs, the glare of the sunlight on the limestone gutters—as the group makes its way toward the county courthouse. This is for my father, Carter thinks, and for my mother and for all the others long dead and buried. For my grandmother. This is the new day, beginning now, less than ten years since the people over in Montgomery rose up and said, "No, I ain't going to the back of the bus. No. This is a new day." Carter feels the hope and rage simmering within him as he walks. And this is for Eshu, too.

Carter carries his son wrapped in a blanket. He won't remember, Carter thinks, but he will know he was there. For all of it. Karla walks beside him, Rachel beside her. Up front are Eldon Long and Fred Shuttlesworth. Soon they'll turn down Washington, the main business street, and walk three blocks to the city square—everyone white and black calls it simply "the Square," but its official name is "Confederate Park." It contains a tall granite monument topped with a rebel soldier. The Square's brick-and-timber pavilion once was used for slave trading. More recently it displayed the first bale of cotton of the year from John O. Rowan and Sons Gin, a practice that ended a few years after World War II when cotton ceased to be the principle crop and the ginning of its first bale no longer symbolized prosperity, a cause for celebration. Along Washington Street white people will probably empty out of the stores to watch the marchers go by. Not nearly as many turn out as they did at first, back in 1961, when the marches started—when the Freedom Riders came through. And they're no longer as hostile, though there's still some jeering, some threats. The air is still tense and heavy. Carter sees white people he knows, people he talks to at work. They stare at him. They hate him in these moments, hate and fear all the marchers.

Most of the people who watch along Strawberry are colored. Two blocks of Strawberry Street comprise Hammond's black "downtown," lined with small stores and cafes, barber shops, millinery stores, and general stores that sell everything from groceries to feed and seeds to stiff new overalls and rubber boots. The line of demarcation between the white section and the colored one is not a sharp one. The stores tend to blend together as you get closer to Washington: There's a bakery patronized by all the citizens; a hardware store; and Andy Reese's Photo Shop, its left front window full of sample photographs—graduation, wedding, portraits—that are all black, and the window to the right all white, identical poses, identical frames, the races comfortably separated by the doorway. Carter sees Andy Reese, a heavyset man with a bulging belly straining the buttons of his shirt, standing with his camera to photograph them as they march by.

Carter sees the collection of graduation photos when they pass and remembers the morning after his graduation from Noshobe County Training School. He stood in the sunshine near the back steps at Hawthorne with Mr. Oscar, who was in the state legislature then, before he became lieutenant governor. Mr. Oscar was shorter than Carter, with a paunch and swarthy skin, a prominent nose, and black hair then just barely tinged with gray. He had piercing eyes and a prominent jaw that made him look like a fierce bulldog. The early summer sun was already hot. Carter's graduation the previous night had been held in the auditorium at the training school, the black high school, in Frogbottom, Hammond's Negro quarter.

His mother and Rachel were there, dressed in white dresses and cooling themselves with cardboard fans from E. B. Harper's Funeral Home. (Rachel would leave home in a matter of days, and no one would know where she was for a long time.) There had been only two white faces in the entire packed auditorium: Marcus Knox, the Noshobe County Superintendent of Education, and Mr. Oscar.

"I was proud of you, son," Mr. Oscar told him.

"It was good of you to be there," Carter said.

"I wanted to be there, for you and for everybody. I represent all the people, Carter. I don't forget that."

"Yessir," Carter replied.

Mr. Oscar handed him a crisp new hundred dollar bill. He seemed suddenly ill at ease, self-conscious. Carter had never seen him that way except once before. And Mr. Oscar must have been thinking of the same time because he suddenly asked, "You remember the shotgun?"

"Yes sir, I do," Carter said.

"You still use it, don't you?"

"Use it well, Mr. Oscar."

It had been on a deer drive out at Rose Hill, a winter hunt, one with men from all over the state who gathered at the big house for breakfast. Old Mr. Dupree Legrand sat in his wheelchair in the parlor with a blanket over his legs by a crackling fire. He nodded, sipped a pale weak drink of bourbon and water, and smiled vaguely at all the men who stomped around in their boots and heavy canvas pants and thermal underwear shirts, the excitement of the hunt as tangible in the air of the house as the smells of bacon and coffee, of tobacco and warm biscuits and fig preserves and plum jelly.

Later in the morning Carter had gone by Mr. Oscar's stand. Though he was only thirteen years old, he drove a pickup, taking men to their stands. Mr. Oscar motioned for him to join him. Mr. Oscar sat on a stump sipping whiskey out of a silver flask and looked at Carter with slightly reddened eyes. They could both hear the dogs, distant and high, yelping. Their breath made frosty clouds in the frigid air.

"How old are you, Carter?" Mr. Oscar blurted.

"Thirteen," he answered, and Mr. Oscar peered at him in the gloom of the woods. The stark trees rose above them, tangled against the dull sky.

"Thirteen," Mr. Oscar repeated. "You're almost a man."

"I reckon."

And the dogs grew louder, less than a half mile away. "They've raised something," Mr. Oscar commented.

"Yessir."

And Mr. Oscar stood and squinted into the woods toward the sound of the dogs. He held a new Browning automatic shotgun with silver inlay on a hand-carved stock. Carter secretly coveted the gun. He had an old rabbit-ears double-barrel 12-gauge with friction tape on the handgrip that he used to meat hunt. It had belonged to his father Cap, who'd managed the dogs and conducted the drives on Rose Hill for years before he died.

They saw the buck crossing a hollow fifty yards away, heading right toward them. Mr. Oscar was ready. When they could see the buck, a six pointer, bound across a clearing with a little stream running through it, Mr. Oscar fired. He fired again. A third time. And the buck soared soundlessly through the gray woods, disappearing even as the sound of the shots echoed around them and the sharp, hot sulfur smell of the spent shells drifted by Carter's nose.

"Shit," Mr. Oscar mumbled. Then he stood there, looking at the woods where the deer had gone, the sound of the dogs now veering off toward the river and away from them.

Then Mr. Oscar just turned and handed the new Browning shotgun to Carter.

"Here," he said.

"What?"

"It's yours. Take it. It's a gift." Carter stood there holding the new gun with awe. With disbelief.

"You...you're just giving me this?" he whispered, seeing his breath frozen in the air, his nostrils still tingling from the smell of the gunpowder from Mr. Oscar's missed shots.

"Yes," Mr. Oscar said, his breath spicy and warm with the whiskey, "hell yeah. You're a better shot than I am, Carter. And you're a better man. It's yours."

•   •   •

Rachel sees Billy Simpleton standing on the corner of Strawberry and Washington streets as the marchers turn toward the Square and the court-house. She could swear that he's lost more weight even since she's seen him earlier today down in the quarter. She smiles. She knows he is looking at only her. Inspecting her, his eyes squinting.

● ● ●

Billy sits at the counter in the Country Corner. He wonders again if he dreamed their fight, but he can still feel the way his fist crunched against the flesh, and he can still see and smell the blood. Red blood, the same color as his. Maureen Puckett, the waitress, sets a plastic glass of water in front of Billy. He and Maureen went to high school together.

"Lord, Billy," she says, "you're wasting away to nothing. You been on a diet?"

"Not hardly," responds Billy. His wife says the same thing, and he looks in the mirror and can't see it. He can only feel the pain in his gut, taking away his appetite. Earlier that morning Jessie Merle had nagged, "Ain't you gonna eat them eggs?" The two fried eggs on his plate looked like bloody eyes. "And you got to do somethin about these toad frogs," she continued. "I found another one in the toilet this morning. I like to dumped on the floor."

"Whatcha havin, hon?" Maureen asks.

"Bring me a hamburger steak and fries," Billy tells her.

"You want onion gravy with that?"

"Hell yeah, I do, what you think?"

Maureen swells up and stares at him. "Well, la-de-da. Ain't no cause to get huffy with me."

When the steak arrives, smothered in brown gravy, Billy can't eat it. He can't even cut it with his knife, fearing he'll have to struggle to get the fork to his mouth. He doesn't want the other men in the cafe to see that he can't eat. He doesn't know what to do. He just sits there. After a while he notices Maureen eyeing him.

"Somethin wrong with your lunch, hon?" she asks.

"Naw," he says. She just looks at him the way Jesse Merle does, like she knows some kind of secret he wouldn't understand even if she told him. "Ain't nothin wrong with it. I just remembered I ate a half dozen eggs and a pound of bacon just fore I come to town."

Her expression doesn't change. After a minute she says, "Sheee. How could you forget that?"

"I just did, that's all. What's it to you?"

"Sheee," she says again. She clears his plate and puts a pulpy green ticket with a greasy thumb print on it down on the counter. He sneaks a look at Maureen, already busy with other customers. She doesn't care whether he eats his lunch or not. Just as Jesse Merle doesn't care whether he eats his eggs or not.

"Shit, Billy," his wife complained. "Just stop me from fixin em if you don't want em. I got better things to do."

"Yeah? Like what?" he barked. She scraped the eggs into the garbage can under the sink.

"Like flushin down toad frogs, that's what!"

The frogs come right back up when they flush them. He flushes one down and then later goes in to piss and looks down and there it is, squatting there, looking up at him. He pisses right on the frog and it doesn't even move. He thinks it's the same frog every time, but he doesn't tell Jesse Merle that. She'd think he was crazy.

"Well, the niggers are actin up again," he remarks to the man next to him at the counter. The man, eating a hamburger, shrugs. Billy thinks he works at Alabama Power Company, but he's not sure. Billy knows several of the men eating down at the end of the counter. "Y'all go out and watch the niggers today?" Billy calls out to them.

"Parade," one says.

"They need a band, like the Mardi Gras!"

Billy wonders if they noticed that he sent his meal back. "I'll tell you one thing," he says loudly enough for everyone in the cafe to hear.

"What's that, Billy?" asks Earl Aspinall, his mouth full of food. He works out at the paper mill south of town, down along the Big Cahaba.

Billy feels the squirming and the prickly pain in his belly. "I'll tell you this," he continues, "we ain't gonna let em get away with it. Just you watch us. Whatever ain't fireproof will burn. I'll tell you that."

Earl swallows. All the men look at Billy. "That's right, Billy," Earl says, "you got anything in particular in mind? To burn, I mean?"

Billy pauses. Then he shrugs. "What can I tell you?" He holds his hands out to the side with a smugly innocent and sly look on his face.

•  •  •

When they gather in front of the courthouse, Carter looks over at Rachel. She is proud and straight. He remembers her as a child, tagging along after him and Dooly. She wanted to do everything they did. "Go find a girl to play with," they would say. "I don't like girls," she'd reply.

Eldon Long introduced Reverend Shuttlesworth, who will speak on the courthouse steps. State troopers and a few city policemen are spaced out down the street. Carter sees Bubba Tate, the sheriff of the county, and some of his deputies. A sparse crowd of whites gathers to watch.

A slight smile crosses Rachel's lips as she listens to Long's introduction. Her eyes are looking inward. The winter sun gleams on her smooth skin. Carter loves her and is glad and grateful she's home now. Carter will never let his sister go away from him again. He remembers the day he found her in New Orleans, finally located her in a narrow, dark house on North Derbigny Street, living with a crazy old woman named Delvane Debene who claimed she'd taken Rachel in off the streets and nursed her back to health. She said Rachel had been suffering from malnutrition and an untreated ulcer. And the old woman had cured her, she claimed, with her magic.

Carter had received a tip at Hanson's store in Crockers Crossroads that Rachel was in New Orleans. Someone had seen her telling tourists' fortunes at a table on Chartres, reading cards near Jackson Square. He couldn't believe she'd been that close all this time. He'd already looked for her down there and in Birmingham and Memphis. It was impossible. If you were black in the Deep South you could disappear without a trace. Even with the tip it took him two weeks to find her in New Orleans, asking all along Magazine Street and in every corner drugstore and bar in the old Storyville district north of the Veaux Carre, everywhere he thought she might be, until finally someone told him a woman fitting Rachel's description lived with a Mrs. Debene, a hoodoo woman.

It had been fifteen long years since Carter had seen Rachel, and when she came into the dim room where he was waiting, a room smelling of incense and with black furry skins hanging on the walls, skins the old woman called "painter" skins, it was like the years dropped away and she was his baby sister once again. She hadn't changed at all. Except that she was a woman now. "Hello, Carter," she said, softly and simply and without any surprise at all that he'd found her.

•  •  •

She came home with him to take care of their mother. She moved into a little house just down the road. "Mama has something she wants to tell us before she dies," Rachel said one day, and he remembers that now. He thinks about his mother and her impending death all the time. It haunts him in the night.

"Governor Legrand might as well know right now that it's gonna be a long spring and summer," Reverend Shuttlesworth says, his voice ringing out from a loudspeaker and reverberating and echoing off the storefronts and the pavement. "And we will not be denied! We are on the side of justice and liberty, and we will not be denied!" The reverend's voice startles Carter from his reverie. Eshu, in his blanket, squirms. A march all the way to Montgomery, Carter thinks. If you believe, Reverend King says, then lay down all you have, your jobs, everything, and come and follow me. It would mean his job, Carter knows, and jail for a lot of them. Carter has already been in jail twice since the Movement started, the damp little redbrick jailhouse down on Cedar Street, behind City Hall. He's more than willing to go again.

"You miss any more work for that stuff, Carter," Ernest Vance, his shift supervisor, warned him after the last time, "and you're gonna be out of a job. I don't care if you are Mr. Legrand's boy."

Son-of-a-bitch, Carter thought. "Yessir," he said. His "boy." Mr. Oscar's "boy."

"Something to tell us before she dies," and she will die very soon, something Carter refuses to believe. He cannot conceive of life on earth without his mother.

Rosa is a simple woman. No formal schooling at all. All she has known in her life is nourishing: nourishing her own children and the Legrands' son and then Miss Amy, with a singular fierce and stubborn devotion that at times seemed almost simple-minded. She's a caregiver and she asks little in return. She possesses a proud streak in her that she has given to Rachel and Carter, a kind of unyielding allegiance to one's own private sense of what's right. There's something secretive and withdrawn about Rosa, too, something even her children can't touch, as though she has chosen to withhold a clandestine part of herself from the world, something that is only hers, that she refuses to make vulnerable by sharing.

As Carter has grown older, he has come to realize that his mother is tormented, haunted. She often seems plagued by a nameless sadness, a kind of depression that he thinks not even she understands.

And Carter thinks that what she wants to tell them has to do with that sadness. He's sure of it.

"We are announcing it right now, today," Shuttlesworth shouts, his voice booming. "We are going to march all the way to Montgomery, all the way from Hammond to Montgomery, and we are going to lay these voting rights petitions at the feet of Governor Legrand. We will retrace his own footsteps from this little town to the capital, and the whole world will see! The whole world will see!"

The crowd stirs. Carter hears whisperings and murmurs, and he looks over at the Square where he sees them, the Klansmen in their white robes and hoods. Twelve of them. They just stand there at the edge of the street, watching in silence. A little girl in front of Carter begins to cry. Her hair is in braids, tied with strings of white yarn.

"Mama, what is that?" she asks. Her mother shushes her.

"White trash, honey, don't you pay em no mind."

Shuttlesworth sees them but keeps speaking. Everyone sees them, white and black alike. The white spectators give them a wide berth. The sun reflects fiercely on the robes, and some of their eye holes are crudely cut, crooked, almost comical. But nobody laughs. The sight of them is menacing, threatening. They want their presence known. They move as a group down off the curb and toward the crowd. The people instinctively shrink away from them, toward the front of the courthouse, leaving a gap of pavement.

Carter hands Eshu to Karla and moves into the gap between his people and the white-robed men. "Carter," Karla hisses, "what are you doin?"

Carter stands there. "Carter!" he hears Karla say again, terror in her voice. He looks back and Karla stands holding the baby, her eyes wide. Rachel stands next to her, looking at Carter calmly, a short sly smile on her face.

Carter turns to face the white men in their robes. He is close enough to see their eyes glaring at him through the slits in their hoods. He knows he'd recognize them if he could see their faces. He crosses his arms over his chest. Shuttlesworth's voice echoes around him. Carter doesn't listen to the words but he hears the tension in his voice.

"What that man doin', Mama?" the little girl asks.

"Hush, honey," her mother says.

Carter stands facing the men for a long time, until the speaking and the singing ends. He never says a word. The men don't either. They just stare at him. Carter is sweating in the sun; he feels it on his skin, underneath his shirt. One of them laughs once. Carter can see his eyes, a pale, watery green, focused right on him, and he can hear the laughter bubbling beneath the hood.

When the demonstrators begin to break up and drift away, the white-robed men do, too, together. And they look back over their shoulders at Carter.

"Why did you do that?" Karla asks, angry. "There wasn't no cause to do that."

"That little girl was scared," Carter says.

"Huh," Karla says, "well, I was, too, and you left me and Eshu, too, just standing there."

"They wasn't gonna do anything," Carter says, looking after the men. "They just want us to know they're here. Always here."

●　●　●

The call about his mother comes near the end of a three-to-eleven shift, when Carter is maneuvering the forklift in the orange glare of high spotlights. Ernest Vance comes down and tells him he has an important phone call. Ernest takes over the forklift for him while Carter rides a bicycle up to the office building near the main gate, where the trucks come in

and are weighed and inspected and chemical tests are run on random sam-
ples from the barrels of waste.

"Carter," Rachel says, "it's time. The doctor just left."

Carter tells a lab technician to let Vance know that he has to go home,
that his mother is very sick. They all know that anyway. He finds his car,
covered with a fine silt of limestone dust, in the parking lot.

His mother lies in her old iron bed, propped on pillows, and he kneels
next to her. Her eyes are large, out of proportion in her dissipated face. He
sees fear there, a kind of controlled anguish. She knows that she's dying.
And he and Rachel know it, too. Carter puts his face in her quilt and can
smell the faint winterlike camphor scent of the cedar chest where the quilt
is folded away and stored when it's not in use. The room is overheated,
smells of coal oil and a thousand wood and coal fires and the vague sour
odor of old ashes. His mother lets her long fingers rest on his forearm, their
touch as light and brittle as dry corn shucks. Rachel stands in the corner.

Karla in the living room feeds Eshu, rocking in the big chair near the
fireplace. The house is quiet. Rosa seems to summon strength from somewhere deep inside her and says,

"Rachel...." she whispers.

"Yes mam?"

"The key...." Rosa lies still.

"Mama? What key?" Rachel steps into the light from the lamp on the
bedside table.

"In my jewelry box. On the dresser." Rosa's breathing rattles in her
chest. "I want you to get it and open my trunk." The old rounded-top trunk
in the corner of her room has been there as long as either of them can
remember, always kept locked. Both of them tried to pick the lock when
they were children, out of devilment and curiosity. They never could.
Rachel finds the key, on a loop of cotton string. She crosses the room and
opens the trunk. "The Bible. Bring me the Bible," Rosa says. The gas heater
sputters against the wall.

Rachel places the heavy old Bible, a family Bible that neither of them
has ever seen before, on the bed. Its imitation leather cover is worn. The
room is silent. "You would find it anyway, after I'm gone," Rosa says. "It's
better that you open it while we're still together, though I don't know if it's

the right thing. I'm not sure. But I... I...." Tears fill her eyes. "When you're dying, you want to set things right," she continues. "You want your children to know the truth about you. You want to know that they love you... even...."

Carter's chest feels at though it's being squeezed with a giant fist.

He picks up the Bible and lets it fall open in the center. A folded paper is inserted between the thick, stiff pages devoted to recording a family's history, its births and its deaths. Carter opens the paper, a preprinted form, a property deed, filled in with an ornate, old-fashioned script, the ink fading but still precise and clear. He reads quickly down the page. The deed transferred ownership of the house and twenty acres of land surrounding it from Williamson Dupree Legrand Jr. to Captain Taylor for "$1 and other good and valuable considerations." It was dated "1 December, 1926." "$1?" "Other good and valuable considerations?"

Carter stares at the signatures, at his father's childish scrawl, "C. Taylor," at old man Legrand's elaborate and flowery inscription. The deed was notarized by "A. Frohsin, Hammond, Alabama, December 1, 1926."

"Mr. Dupree just gave this place to Daddy," Carter says.

"He meant to give it to me, but I couldn't own it," Rosa explains. "A woman couldn't own it, much less a colored woman."

"But I don't underst...."

"Shhhh," Rachel says, her hand suddenly on Carter's shoulder. Rosa seems very tired now, barely able to move her arm, but she gestures toward the Bible, toward the family records section.

Carter is aware of Rachel's breathing as he picks up the Bible and holds it close to his face. Rachel reads over his shoulder. The penciled entries are hard to decipher in the dim light of the room. Carter squints.

Carrie Winfield, it reads. Their grandmother. dauter of Rowser & Mary Winfield, slavery, born Rosehill plantation march 4, 1891.

Carter's eyes move to the next entry, in the same careful, labored script as the first. Rosa. dauter of Carrie and W. D. Legrand. 1 December, 1905. Rose Hill Plantation.

W. D. Legrand? What? Carter tenses. He feels his breath catch. He knows what he is reading and yet is confused by it because he cannot believe it. He looks at the silvery, wavy lines again. He feels Rachel's hand grip his shoulder tightly. He doesn't breathe for a long time. The room is deathly still.

"Who wrote this?" Carter asks softly.

"She did," his mother whispers. They can barely hear her.

"She?"

"Carrie Winfield," Rachel says, "our grandmother." Carter feels another presence in the room, as if her ghost has joined them. A chill invades his body and he shivers. He looks up at Rachel, and she just stares at him, her dark eyes level. Though there's no wind, the fig tree at the corner of the house begins to scrape its branches against the windows. And Carter thinks he hears a dog howling somewhere.

"Jesus," he says. He still kneels beside the bed. His knees begin to ache. He turns back to the book. The next entries are in a different hand, a different pencil.

Rosa Winfield marid Captain Taylor july 4 1926.

Carter Taylor feb. 10 1929

Rachel Taylor 10 May 1932.

No "son of" or "daughter of," just their names and the dates. He looks up at his mother. Her weak eyes are fixed on him. When Rosa speaks, Carter can barely hear her. He has to lean close.

"I want you to forgive me," she says. "Both of you."

"For what, Mama? For what?" he pleads, and he can feel both Rachel's hands gripping his shoulders now.

"Before I die," his mother says.

And then Carter knows, like a sudden blinding epiphany. He realizes Rachel has already known it, somehow figured it out or divined it maybe even as long ago as when she left for New Orleans. He doesn't have to turn the page. But he does.

And there, in the same hand, in the same pencil, in the same position as the name W. D. Legrand in the first entry—W. D. Legrand, the name of the man they now know is their own grandfather, the ancient white man who at this very moment lies almost lifeless himself in that tall bed up in the big house—and Carter doesn't even need to read the other name, but he does:

*Oscar Legrand.*

•  •  •

"Mama was his own sister," Carter repeats. "And he is our father." He has said it a dozen times.

They sit in the corner of their mother's darkened bedroom. It's way after midnight and Eshu sleeps while Carter and Rachel and Karla drink coffee. They can hear the ticking of the old wind-up clock on the mantel, the scraping of the fig tree branches with their new buds against the window, and the distant thunder of a storm suddenly approaching. It has turned very cold. Much too cold for March. They can all feel it in their bones. Carter feels the cold in his chest, around his heart, which seems unable to heat him. He is still stunned

Their mother sleeps, and they speak in whispers. "He knew she was his sister," Carter says. "He is the devil."

"Of course he knew it," Rachel agrees.

"He knew it and he didn't care," Karla says.

"He is the white devil."

"He knew it. He knows it." Rachel looks into his eyes. "He knows it right now."

Carter thinks of the shotgun. Of the hundred dollar bill. Of his job and a million other things, other signs. His memory of sitting with Rachel at the dining table at Hawthorne with the family leaps into his mind. He remembers that Hester didn't like it, didn't approve. She'd shake her head at them in the kitchen, her dreadlocks flopping about. "Rosa shouldn't ought to let y'all eat in there with them peoples," she'd say. "It ain't right. They's white folks." And Miss Amy, bringing home armloads of books from the white-only public library, letting Carter and Rachel pick and choose and read along with Dooly. How inseparable he and Dooly were until they were twelve or thirteen, sleeping in the same bed in an upstairs bedroom at Hawthorne. Or the old double bed on the back porch at Rosa's, the mattress and springs so worn they made a valley in the middle so that when they awoke the boys would be jammed together in the center of the bed. Or one of the four-poster beds at Rose Hill, with the sheer window curtains blowing in on the breeze and Gilbert Washington mumbling and fussing at them for sleeping so late.

"Dooly is my brother," Carter says.

"He always was," Rachel responds. "What difference does it make now?" Carter doesn't answer. The storm outside gathers intensity.

"Oscar Legrand is Eshu's grandfather," Karla says. They look at Karla. All of them think of Eshu, of the strange and mysterious fleshy growths on his back and his head. Even though old Dr. Mason and his young new associate assure them the swellings do not threaten the child's health, the growths still baffle them.

●   ●   ●

Rachel brings a centerpost into her mother's room and sets up a small altar. Karla and Carter stand very still next to the bed. With ashes from the fireplace and coffee grounds, Rachel traces on the floor a long, narrow rectangle, a coffin with handles on the sides. Then she places two straw mats over the form and makes the sign of the cross on the mats with more ashes.

On the altar are three small bowls containing a mixture of corn kernels and roasted peanuts, and in the middle of each is a small candle, one white, one yellow, and one black. Next to the bowls are a bottle of red wine and a bottle of rum. She asks Karla and Carter to go into the next room one by one and remove their clothes and put them back on inside-out.

Then Rachel crosses the sheet over her mother's frail body with more ashes. She places the bowls with the burning candles at each shoulder and at her feet. "In the name of God the Father, God the Son, and God the Holy Ghost, in the name of Mary, in the name of Jesus, in the name of all the saints, all the dead...." Rachel's voice trails off. Then she leaves the room. Still and quiet, the only sound is the soft hiss of the gas heater. She returns with the old rooster from the chicken yard out back. The scraggly old rooster looks transfigured, his red and black feathers youthful and strong and gleaming in the candlelight. She places the rooster gently on the bed, and they all watch as he goes first to the bowl at Rosa's feet and pecks, then to the bowls at each of her shoulders. He feeds on the corn and peanuts. Then Rachel picks up the cock and passes him over her mother's body. Rachel's eyes are closed as she intones, "All that is evil, depart; all that is good, enter her soul and give her rest and peace. *Tout ca qui mauves ce pour sorti, tout ca qui bon ce pour entre.*" Rachel holds the rooster in one arm and crosses and recrosses her mother's arms over her body. "Release her. Give her her new life. *Ente, te, te, tete, te.* Carrie Winfield. Carrie Winfield and all the saints, release her from pain."

Rachel's body stiffens, and she stands upright holding the old rooster. The rooster seems content to let her hold him without a struggle. Her eyes open now and she stares straight ahead. She doesn't move.

Their mother is asleep. Her chest rises and falls gently with her breathing. Her pain is gone now, and she rests easily. Rachel is as still as a statue. Her face seems altered, hardened. She looks like another, much younger woman. Then suddenly she slumps and looks around, examining her brother and Karla as though she doesn't know where she is, what she's doing, or who they are. She blinks. She leaves the room, carrying the rooster.

Carter and Karla just stand there for a long time. Rachel had earlier dug a hole in the backyard, under a fig tree, and now she buries the old rooster alive in the hole, feeling her way in the dark, smelling the dampness of the thick soil, the wind raging around her.

"It's done," Rachel tells them when she comes back into the room. Her hands and arms are covered with black dirt. "That fig tree will die before spring." She looks at her mother on the bed. Rosa's face is reposed, soft and relaxed, a gentle smile on her lips, her eyes closed in sleep.

"She's ready now," Rachel says.

The wind howls. They hear thunder but they hear no rain on the tin roof. Rachel goes to the window. She sees snow filling the backyard. It comes down like thick feathers, heavy, wet flakes that drift on the wind. The peach trees, like the fig tree next to the house, already have buds, and the white, cold snow rims the branches, outlining the buds themselves. Along the fence daffodils in full bloom bow their heads in the wind, and snow gathers around them. The snow sticks to the one dying fig tree near the chicken yard, thickening over the old rooster's raw grave. The thunder booms, like July or August, and the snow continues to pelt down and cover the ground, cover everything.

"It's snowing," Rachel says.

"What next?" Karla asks.

And they all hear it then, a high singing, almost a moaning, like the wind itself. Carter thinks of his mother, and then of the man who is really his father: Oscar Legrand. He feels a dry ache inside, like a hunger, a void, where he expects his fury to be. He hears his grandmother's singing, not a dirge, not sad but joyous and full of spirit, rich and thick, creamy as new butter. A mile away the magnolia trees in front of the big house shake in the wind, their broad, waxy leaves cupping a film of snow. And the fields and the lanes and the cabin roofs disappear under the whiteness, and over it all is the singing, the high, shrill singing.

Rachel places on a small table a salep root that she dug up in the swamp. Shaped exactly like a human hand, the root is a talisman for good luck. As she stands there she crosses herself, her head slightly bowed, and they all feel a deeper chill. Nobody says anything for a long time. They all know that Rosa's soul has left her body and is soaring into the wind, into the snow. They look over at her.

"She's gone," Rachel says. "She's in the peaceful world now."

•   •   •

In the early white morning, Justina Beasley toils slowly up the back-stairs, her hand in the middle of her back, muttering to herself. She has awakened to the snow-covered world, trekked through its silvery wetness across the backyard, across the back porch—stomping the snow from her high-top shoes—and into the kitchen of the big house. She starts a fire in the stove (she still prefers to cook on a woodstove, though the kitchen is equipped with new electric appliances) and mixes biscuit batter and takes bacon out of the refrigerator to soften. Justina prepares the same breakfast she has made every morning for as long as she can remember, though only she and Gilbert eat it. She is glad the house now has central heat. In the early years, she and Gilbert had been responsible for laying the fires on cold mornings, before daylight.

When she reaches the top of the stairs she goes down the wide hallway to Mr. Dupree's bedroom. "Mornin, Mr. Dupree," she says, as she says every morning, and he doesn't answer her. He never does. He ceased to answer her greeting years before, and she thinks nothing of it. She pulls open the drapes and the room is flooded with bright new sunlight, magnified by the melting snow. "Snowed last night, Mr. Dupree," she says, "latest snow I can remember." He doesn't respond. "You wants grits this mornin?" she asks, expecting no answer. And in the silent stillness she says, "Uh huh," nodding her head, "grits it is."

Halfway through plumping his pillows, she notices that he's not breathing, that his toothless mouth is slightly open in a grimace as though caught in mid-complaint about something. With her palm she touches his forehead, which is as cold and clammy as marble. She stands there looking down at him, at his thin hair, his pink scalp, his soft, caved-in mouth. He looks like a newborn, his body curled, a strangely empty look frozen in his eyes that is as expectant and eager and hopeful as a baby's.

"Sweet Lord Jesus Above," Justina murmurs. As she crosses the room, she removes her bright flowered apron and hangs it over the large mirror on Miss Marie Louise's dressing table, the top of which has been unused and undisturbed for almost fifty years, its polished surface only slightly dulled by a thin layer of fine, powder-like dust.

• • •

Ira Foster comes out from Hammond with the hearse and takes Rosa's body into town. The house seems empty and hollow until Eshu cries in the back bedroom. It's always good to have a baby when there's death in the house. Ira told them about Mr. Dupree.

"It's a sign," Rachel says to Carter, "father and daughter dying on the same night. It was at the same hour, the same minute."

"How do you know?"

"I can feel it. I know."

"A sign of what?" Carter asks.

"We'll know. We'll know soon."

They hear a car pull up outside, the engine shuts off. It's the first of a long parade of neighbors and friends, all carrying bowls of vegetables and potato salad, plates with pones of cornbread, pot roasts, baked and fried chicken, pies and cakes. Soon every surface in the house will be laden and ready for everyone after the funeral. Rachel and Karla and Carter will be able to eat without fixing and cooking until they finally have to throw out spoiling leftovers. Then they'll wash all the bowls and platters and return them to Calvary Baptist Church, where the dishes will be returned to the appropriate kitchens in Crockers Crossroads and Hammond and the farthest reaches of Rose Hill Plantation.

• • •

So there will be two funerals, on successive days; one at the tiny white-washed Oak Grove Calvary Baptist Church in Crockers Crossroads and the other at the Gothic redbrick St. Paul's Episcopal Church across the river in Hammond. Many of the same people will attend both.

The bishop himself preaches Mr. Williamson Dupree Legrand Jr.'s funeral. The church has two Legrand stained-glass windows, one to the right of the narthex, a rendering of Jesus standing and holding a lamb in the crook of his arm, sheep curling like kittens around his feet, the dedication on its furled glass ribbon at the bottom reading, WILLIAMSON DUPREE LEGRAND, IN MEMORIUM. The other is a large round window over the high altar, an elaborate, almost Byzantine depiction of the Ascension, with its dedication readable even from the backmost pews of the sanctuary: TO THE GREATER GLORY OF GOD AND IN LOVING MEMORY OF MARIE LOUISE CHAUDRON LEGRAND.

Hardly anyone still alive has a clear memory of Marié Louise, Governor Oscar Legrand's mother, unless it's Gilbert and Justina, who once sat misty-eyed and subdued in the first row of the family section at her funeral, in this same church, almost fifty years ago. Oscar himself was nineteen years old when she died, but he could not drudge up a lucid, unclouded memory of her. He remembers only feelings: the warmth of her hand, the softness of her bosom. And smells: the fragrance of her perfume when she dressed up, the warm scent of coffee on her breath on cold mornings. He remembers her at Christmases, Thanksgivings, and summer barbecues but can't put a face with his memory, except for the thin, almost gaunt face, high cheekbones, and black hair pulled severely back that stared out from the tinted photograph in the round silver frame on a marble-topped table at Rose Hill. Mr. Dupree Legrand had always said that an oil painting of her over one of the mantels in the front parlor didn't really resemble her, didn't capture her at all. In it she looks young, hardly more than a child, stiff in a purple dress with faint suggestions of columns and waterfalls behind her. She seems as alien as the people in the other large drab portraits in the downstairs hallway, the grandparents and great-grandparents, Legrands locked away forever in that dark, distant history where Mr. Dupree Legrand has at long last gone to join them.

Bishop Morrow, the celebrant, is a stout man with a wide, flat face. Dooly Legrand is assisting at his grandfather's funeral. Dooly's alb and surplice and chasuble are as colorful and resplendent as the bishop's. The air in the church is heavy with incense. The early spring sun slants through the stained-glass windows. It's the first time that Carter has seen Dooly in ten or eleven years.

Though he admits to having known Mr. Dupree Legrand only slightly, the bishop gives the eulogy. None of Mr. Dupree's friends or business associates or hunting partners are still living, so none can speak for him, a fact the bishop notes and uses as his theme.

"He outlived everyone he knew well, except for his family," he says, "and his time on earth was long and fruitful. He was like one of the ancient patriarchs in the Old Testament, and his name has become legend. From his seed sprang a war hero and a governor of this very state. And he was proud of his sons, justly so. The last time I spoke with him, over ten years ago, at a dinner at his gracious home, Rose Hill, he conversed with vigor, even though his health was bad, was failing rapidly even then, and he spoke with pride of his sons. When a man reaches the end of his days on earth and he can look with pride on his sons, then he is truly blessed."

"What about his daughter?" Rachel whispers to Carter. They sit in the family section, next to Miss Amy and Mr. Oscar. Carter smells bourbon on Miss Amy. And on Mr. Oscar. They've all been drinking, and Mr. Oscar is unsteady on his feet. "Carter!" he had greeted him, hugging him around the shoulders. "How are you, son?" And the word "son" cut into Carter like a knife. Carter hears the bishop's words bounce off the brick walls of the church and he knows now that there's a fine, narrow line between love and hate.

The atmosphere is not really one of mourning but more of the relief that comes with finally burying someone who has been, for all practical purposes, dead for so many years that many people who have come to mark his departing—and there are many from all over the state—actually had been surprised to hear of his death because they'd already long ago assigned him to the other kingdom.

●　　●　　●

The next day the spring sky threatens another thunderstorm when the governor's entourage causes a traffic jam on River Road in front of Calvary Baptist Church in Crockers Crossroads. Four black stretch limousines carry the governor, his wife, and his bodyguards; the blue and white lights of seven state-trooper cars reflect off the trees and whitewashed church. The governor's presence brings out the curious—especially in these troubled times—people trying to drive by and look. Other mourners arrive in pickups and old cars, even a wagon or two, weaving in and out to park as near the church as possible under the threatening sky.

Miss Amy Legrand emerges from one of the limousines, a secret service agent holding an umbrella over her head even though the rain hasn't started. She takes the umbrella and lowers it, folds it, moving quickly across the dirt yard of the church toward the front door. The crowd at the door parts to let her through. Wearing a black short-sleeved dress with a square neckline and a tiny black straw hat, she is slim and dainty, walking with a grace that from a distance suggests agelessness, even youth.

Oscar Legrand himself steps out of the second limousine accompanied by several men and begins shaking hands with people who greet him in the churchyard. He is known to all of them and he calls them by name. He grew up with most of these people, has known them all his life.

All of them either work for Chemco, or live on the Legrand place, or live in Crockers Crossroads and work across the river in Hammond. The Legrand family is considered their people. They are proud Mr. Oscar has done so well, in spite of his politics, in spite of his pronouncements of "Segregation Forever." The elderly men and women tell stories of when he was a boy, hunting and fishing and sowing his wild oats with his brother Dupree. They feel a sense of ownership in him, a kind of kinship that cuts cleanly across racial and political lines. They share a past, a history. He may be the enemy, but he is homefolks.

Inside, the church is packed. Cardboard fans move back and forth, back and forth, as a quartet of old men sing a spiritual called, "I'm Goin Home on the Mornin Train," then, "Oh Mary, Don't You Weep, Don't You Moan." The windows darken, and a loud, sharp clap of thunder pierces the singing. The overhead lights dim and flicker, and the rain begins to drum on the roof. Oscar Legrand sits very straight in the pew. The Legrand family occupies the first row on the right side, in the family section, Dooly wedged between his mother and father.

The rain stops when the crowd gathers around the open, yawning grave, the flower-draped coffin, but the ground is slick and muddy. In the row of chairs next to the grave sit Carter and Rachel. Miss Amy joins them, but the others stand behind them and out of sight, and Mose Bell delivers the final words. Then they stand, and Rachel places a single red rose on the now-naked lid of the gray casket. A sudden thunderclap startles them all. Before they turn to leave, a single yellow butterfly comes out of the woods and settles briefly on the top of the coffin, then flutters away. Rachel nods and makes the sign of the cross. Then they leave Rosa to be lowered into the rich, black loam beside her husband.

Dooly waits for Rachel and Carter in front of the church. He has driven his own car and is heading back to Nashville immediately. He and Carter are the same height, an even six feet tall. He hasn't changed much at all since they were boys. His hair is thick and blond. Though he wears steel-rimmed spectacles, his eyes are still bright and eager and young. No one would ever have thought that Dooly would become a priest. At one time he had been the wildest boy in Noshobe County.

His eyes well up with tears as he hugs Carter. "Rosa," he says, "Ahhhh, Rosa. My other mother. May light perpetual shine upon her. Amen."

"Amen," says Carter.

Mr. Oscar mumbles and makes his excuses about needing to return to Montgomery right away. Carter has trouble looking him in the eye. When his black limousine pulls away, the traffic, directed by the state troopers, gradually thins. Soon several big trucks that have been held up lumber through, loaded with stacks of black metal drums, their transmissions whining, their engines groaning.

Of the Legrand family, only Miss Amy comes to Rosa's house afterward. She sits regally in the small living room, balancing a plate and a cup and saucer on her knee, the only white person in the crowded room. She embraces Carter and Rachel warmly. She calls everyone by name, asks after children and grandchildren, their sick and their elderly. She is still a handsome woman with flawless skin and a lean, willowy body. The only blemishes on her beauty are faint dark circles under her eyes. Full of energy, she laughs with Rachel, their heads together, some private joke, and her laughter rings musically over the steady, chaotic drone of conversation.

●  ●  ●

Justina Beasley can't wait to tell them about it. She is anxious. With Mr. Dupree dead, she can tell it at last. Before the old man was even cold, before the hearse returned to town with the body, she wanted Carter and Rachel to know about it. But she waited, because Rosa was dead, too, and they needed time to mourn their mother. Two days after Rosa's funeral, Justina calls them and asks them to come to her cabin. Rachel and Carter walk at dusk, the two of them, across the fields to a stand of cottonwood trees along Rabbit Branch, a broad, shallow creek that winds its way through Rose Hill to the big lake. Fishing spots and picnic places have been worn grassless and smooth along its banks. They walk by old swimming holes and crude wooden benches made from planks nailed between two trees.

They continue across the fields to the big house—looking empty now, silent, almost abandoned—and turn down the lane to Justina's cabin. The western sky is streaked with color, pale lavender and fiery yellow. The air is chilled now in the twilight. Only two of the houses are neat, kept, along the gravel lane bordered with overgrown privet. Justina's and Gilbert's. Carter and Rachel cross the porch, its tin roof covered in thick wisteria vines just now in bud. They knock on the screen door. Justina yells for them to come in. In the dim and overheated living room, she sits in a rocker. Carter and Rachel sit on an old vinyl sofa. They see Justina's face, shriveled and prunelike, the wrinkles crossing and turning back upon themselves like strands of a spider's web. Her hair, thin and iron gray, oily, clings close to her scalp. She wears a faded housedress that drapes on her body in folds, and a crisp, starched white apron. Her feet are bare, her gnarled toes appearing to clutch the rough, unpainted floor boards.

"You got to promise me you won't tell nobody," Justina begins. "I thought maybe I ought to just let all this die with me, because it won't be long for me neither and then there wouldn't be nobody to tell it. Tellin it scares me. If the high sheriff hear this, he gonna come after me. I know that. Old colored woman like me. Tellin somethin like this on Mr. Dupree, they put me under the jail." Justina leans over and spits into a wrinkled brown paper bag next to her rocker. They know that it contains an empty coffee can.

"But you need to know the truth, all the truth, and I hope the truth will set you free like the Bible says. I say this for you, Carter, cause you a man: If the truth make you raise your fist against your brother, the way Cain did Abel, or against your own blood, then you ain't no better than Cain and you don't deserve no better fate."

Carter feels oddly like a child about to hear a story of some faraway imaginary land. But his mouth is dry. Curious and fearful at the same time, he looks out the window at the flaming sky. "All right," he says.

Justina settles back and fixes them with her gaze. "Carrie Winfield, your grandmother, was the daughter of slaves, or at least people born in slavery and then freed after the war," Justina begins. "You know that from what she wrote in that Bible that Rosa showed you. She was born right here on Rose Hill, and she was not yet fifteen years old when she died. Your mama was born in 1905. That would put Carrie's death that same year, in late 1905, not more than weeks after your mama was born...."

"Wait now...." Carter interrupts.

"You wait," Justina tells him. "And you'll know." She pauses. Her voice, husky, rich, and deep, has a tremor in it. "The reason there ain't no headstone for Carrie anywhere is because she ain't buried in a cemetery."

"Where then?" Rachel asks.

Justina waves her hand in a sweeping circle. "Here. Somewhere on Rose Hill. It's somewhere near the big house." She cocks her head to the side and peers slyly at them. Carter knows then that she knows exactly where his grandmother is buried, but she won't tell them. Not now. She rocks, and the chair creaks against the floor. After a long silence, the only sounds their breathing and the creaking of the rocker, Justina continues.

"Carrie was a pretty girl. Feisty. Yeah, she was feisty. She could walk down the road and every man and every boy old enough to've found his gonads would be steppin on his tongue. And she had a smart mouth. She wouldn't take nothing off nobody. She was always laughin. Every time some older person, her parents or her aunt or uncle, anytime they would say somethin serious to her she'd laugh at em. She'd swim naked in the creek, and the men on the place would lather up the mules ridin em by there to try to get a look at her. She didn't care. She wouldn't even notice em.

"Well, Mr. Dupree Legrand noticed her. He and Miss Marie Louise hadn't been married all that long then. Mr. Dupree had done waited until he was practically an old man before he married. And even then..." She pauses. "Mr. Little Dupree was just a lap baby and Mr. Dupree rode about the place on a stallion all day. That's what all the coloreds on the place called 'em, Mr. Dupree and Mr. Little Dupree. Mr. Dupree had one of these leather riding crops and high boots. I was just a young girl myself then, but I had already been working in the kitchen at the big house for almost four years, and I would see em every day. Mr. Dupree wore a broad-brimmed hat with a peacock feather in the band and he would race that stallion up and down the roads like the devil himself was after him. And somewhere that devil caught him. Got in his veins, because he took up with Carrie. No man who had dominion over her could have resisted her. And Carrie would come to the house, in the rainy season or in the winter when Miss Marie Louise would take the baby to stay with her people over in town, and they would sleep together in that same big old four-poster bed he just now died in, the same bed he fathered Mr. Little Dupree and Mr. Oscar in, and I would hear em laughing and carryin on up there, and sometimes Carrie would slide down that curved banister in the front hall like she was bout eight years old, Mr. Dupree laughing and eggin her on all the time. I never did see Mr. Dupree happier than he was right then, but I knew it was a happiness bought with a pact with the devil. I knew no good could come of it. And I was right.

"Mr. Dupree had given Carrie a ring, a silver ring shaped like a tiny snake, with the snake's head where a stone would be and little tiny rubies for the snake's eyes. And she showed it around and bragged to some of the people on the place that she was married, that she had jumped the broom with somebody, and she would laugh and carry on and the folks on the place didn't pay much attention to her because she was always funnin, wouldn't get serious over nothing. Then she started to get big in the belly, and course there was whisperin and gossipin goin on, and her goin right on like she hadn't even noticed it.

"Well, then all of a sudden she took to sayin that she was goin off to the North, goin off up there to New York or Washington or somewhere where she could marry a white man if she wanted to, that colored and white could do that up there. Miss Marie Louise and the baby were there— it was Indian summer—and they would all sit out under the scuppernong arbor in the evenings, and Mr. Dupree would drink his toddy and they would laugh and talk and watch Mr. Little Dupree, who had just started to walk then, toddle around and try to grab the ducks and the chickens.

"And by the time Carrie's baby—your mama—was born it was winter again and the roads were muddy and gettin so you couldn't go on em by car or wagon. So Miss Marie Louise, before Thanksgiving, had taken little Dupree back into town to the cottage to spend Christmas with her people. December the first, it was, when your mama was born in one of them shanties in that row near the barn, in the dead of winter with a coal fireplace for heat. With my own mama for a midwife. And I was there. It was my first birthin, so I would remember it for that if for nothin else. But that ain't the fourth or the half of it.

"Anyhow, some days went by—cold, gray days, one of the coldest winters I can remember, damp bone-cold—and it must have been during that time that Carrie got that Bible that your mama kept all them years, bought it probably from somebody on the place who had got a batch of cheap ones somewhere to sell, and she wrote down that record of your mama's birth. It had to be in those few short days when she got it. Carrie must have wanted people who came after...she wanted y'all to know the truth." Justina stops then. She seems to be framing her next words, her next sentences, in her mind. She sighs and goes on.

"Because she showed up at the big house one night, I remember it was two nights before Christmas, I will never forget that—it had been rainin all day, a slow, frigid drizzle, and I had been thinkin all day snow, maybe it will snow for Christmas—and Mr. Dupree was to ride into town the next day, Christmas Eve, to join Miss Marie Louise and their son at the cottage, and Carrie had the baby with her, wrapped in a quilt, and she left it in the kitchen with me. I wadn't but round bout seventeen or eighteen years old myself at the time and scared near bout to death of what Carrie might be up to and what might come of it. And Carrie and Mr. Dupree quarreled upstairs. I could hear em screamin at each other clear down the stairs. I heard Carrie say somethin sounded like, 'You promised!' and I heard Mr. Dupree sayin 'You misunderstood me! You deliberately misunderstood me!' Then I heard what sounded like one of em slappin the other one, and more cryin and yellin and carryin on. All the time I was sittin crouched close to the woodstove, holdin that little baby in my lap, just shivering like I was naked to the cold. I had never been so scared in my life, before or since.

"I heard Mr. Dupree yell somethin bout how impossible it all was and how Carrie, if she wasn't just a 'stupid black bitch,' ought to know that. And she came right back at him, called him an 'ice cold blue-eyed soul killer' or somethin like that, and Lord knows I'd never heard a colored talk to a white man like that before in my life. I knew somethin was gonna happen. And I knew it was gonna be bad. I was just waitin to find out what it would be. I heard furniture scrapin then, the sound of glass breakin—I found out the next mornin that either Carrie or Mr. Dupree one had smashed both the water pitcher and the slop jar against the wall—and then all of a sudden everything went quiet. It was so deathly quiet so quick and sudden that I jumped. I listened, straining my ears. I couldn't hear anything for the longest time but I couldn't make myself move from the chair. The baby stirred and whimpered, and I was scared it'd start crying, but it didn't. I wanted to leave then but I was scared to move.

"Then I heard somebody on the stairs. It was a heavy creaking, more than just one person would make, and I went to the door and looked down the hall. There was just one lamp lit, but it was enough for me to see Mr. Dupree comin down the steps, and he was carrying something, and I knew that it was Carrie, and oh Lord I knew just as quick that she was dead, because I could see how limp she was, how her head hung back and down in a way that would wake a sleeping person up. And Mr. Dupree turned and came down the hall toward the kitchen, and I shrunk back and into a corner, holding the baby tight against me, and I watched Mr. Dupree come through the lighted kitchen then. I saw plainly that Carrie had part of her forehead bashed in and bloody, like she had been hit with a poker or a stick of firewood or something, and Mr. Dupree was crying, his eyes almost shut, tears just streamin down his cheeks. And he was makin this sound, a kind of moan deep down in his throat, a sound that I had never heard before and hope never to hear again, a kind of steady 'ummmmm, ummmmmmm, ummmmm.' He didn't even see me squattin there in the corner, but I knew he had to have known I was there because I had to stay every night to tend the fires. He just crossed the kitchen, walkin like a blind man who had memorized the lay of the room, his head thrown back and the tears bright on his face.

"He went out the screen door and across the back gallery and into the yard. I heard the dogs set up to barking and then stop. I went over there to the window and I could barely make him out crossing the yard. And then I sat there at the table, rockin the baby, hummin to it, just watchin the wick on the lamp burn low, until finally Mr. Dupree came back into the kitchen and just stood there lookin at me. His face was still wet and he was shivering himself now, out in the night cold in his shirt-sleeves. His boots and his britches and even his shirt were spotted with black mud, like he'd been digging, and I knew what he had been doin without having to be told."

Rachel and Carter and Justina are quiet for a long time. "He killed her," Carter says. "He murdered her."

"Yes," Justina says. "And me and Mr. Dupree never swapped nary a word about it. He went on back upstairs, and I banked the fires and went on home and took the baby with me and early the next morning I took the baby over to this wetnurse's house, Aunt Lucille Carter, who you were named for, Carter, and by the time I got back up to the house the next morning to build up the fires again Mr. Dupree had already gone, had already ridden into Hammond, and I didn't see him again until after the first of the year. And I never told Aunt Lucille nor nobody all that happened. I told her that Carrie was gone, had just left. I found that Bible in Carrie's cabin, and when I showed it to Gilbert—I couldn't read any more than Carrie's parents could, so I didn't have no idea what it say, but Gilbert could read—he wanted to burn it. But I wouldn't let him. I saved it."

"So Gilbert knows all about this, too?" Carter asks. "Everything?"

"I ain't sayin what Gilbert know. Y'all will just have to axe him yourself. I ain't told him much of nothing, and we ain't talked about it. No, he don't know nothin. You can just tell the high sheriff that Gilbert don't know nothin."

"All right," Rachel says. "All right, Justina."

"Everybody just thought that Carrie had made good her promise and had run off to the North, leaving that little girl to be raised by first Carrie's parents, who didn't have any idea who the daddy was, and then when they died, by old Lucille Carter again, who got her up to fifteen or sixteen when she passed, too, and your mama just became a sort of child of the plantation until she married your daddy. Until she married Captain Taylor."

Carter looks at Rachel then. Her eyes are even darker in the fading twilight of the room. Carter can hear a lone owl way back somewhere in the water oak and hickory trees behind Justina's house. It cries an eerie, haunted cry, as though it comes from the same old dim lost time that the story he has just heard came from.

"Yeah," Justina says, "I gave Rosa the Bible when she became a woman, and your mama lived all that time knowing who her father was, and when it happened again with Mr. Oscar she knew what the truth of that was, too. She knew what the sin of that was, too. And Cap must have known it, too, and must have thought that there wasn't a thing he could do about it. Not a goddam thing either one of them could do about it."

They all sit without speaking then. It is first dark but Justina doesn't put on a lamp. They can see, out the windows, the last golden-orange traces of the day. It will be full dark soon. Rachel and Carter both know by heart the trail home—part cow path and part gravel road—and tonight is a full moon. Carter thinks of his grandmother's grave, where it might be, that unmarked and uncelebrated burying place somewhere in the rich black soil of the place. He knows what Carrie looked like, because he's seen her. Feisty, Justina had called her. He's seen Carrie many times. Floating through the air or sitting on top of the old smokehouse. He envisions her laughing eyes—like Rachel's, he thinks. Yes, Rachel has her eyes—and he swallows.

"Why do you think she went up there that night?" Rachel asks Justina then, her voice hushed and tentative.

"Maybe she believed him," Justina says, "when he talked about love. And maybe he meant it. Maybe he loved her, too."

The snow is all gone now, forgotten, and it has turned spring with a startling suddenness. Outside in the grass and the privet, the cicadas and crickets and tree frogs, the katydids abruptly begin their chorus in unison, as though there's some invisible downbeat, some subtle shifting of the earth that only they can know. In the full night, before they head back home, Carter and Rachel can now sense the full moon rising over the cabin, the same moon that hovered behind leaden clouds on that December night sixty years ago.

"Yes," Rachel says softly, "maybe he did."

# Dooly

AFTER FOUR YEARS OF SEMINARY AND COUNTLESS SERMONS on the subject of love, after books and concordances and analyses of everything Jesus Christ said about it, Dupree Legrand, Dooly—Father Legrand— found out something totally new about love from Kitty Wiggins, a country singer whom he healed of a grapefruit-sized growth in her uterus. That he possessed the powers of healing he had not doubted in years, but the fact that he knew so little about love came as a surprise.

The shock began to register the first time he laid eyes on Kitty—in person. He had seen her on television and knew who she was, but one bright white winter Sunday morning she knelt at the altar rail at St. Thomas the Apostle Episcopal Church, the large gray stone downtown church in Nashville where Dooly Legrand served as Rector. At first he had seen only her outstretched and crossed hands, slim and tapered and with guitar-string calluses on her finger tips, as he made his way down the rail with the paten and the wafers. "The Body of our Lord Jesus Christ, which was given for thee, preserve thy body and soul unto everlasting life," he murmured. Mac Kilpatrick, his priest associate, followed him with the chalice. Father Legrand placed a wafer in the thin, callused fingers. "Take and eat this in remembrance that Christ died for thee, and...." He heard a sob. He looked into her face and was jolted.

He had never seen a more beautiful face in his life: high cheekbones and coal black eyes brimming with tears, black hair parted in the middle and flowing down onto her shoulders, skin as delicate as bone china. She wore a white, lacy dress. Dooly's tongue stuck to the roof of his mouth when he tried to go on. Mac Kilpatrick bumped him from behind. Dooly knew, in that one explosive moment, that no matter how much he might resist, he was lost, that here, finally, was the candle flame for which he would be the moth. He could see nothing else in the world but this creature kneeling before him, tears coursing down her pink cheeks. "And...and feed on him in thy heart by faith, with thanksgiving," he said, voice trembling, as she lifted the wafer to her pale lips, her liquid and questioning and begging eyes fixed firmly on his.

Dooly, for the past decade, had been as happy and content as he'd ever been. He had a wife he loved and two children he adored, and being a priest of God had become his central focus and the guiding principle of his life. There had always been something missing, of course, but Dooly accepted that as an underlying condition of his existence, something that had been true for him ever since he was a child: He lived with a void, a constant vague unrest that plagued him like hunger. But he knew, looking into Kitty's pained and desperate eyes, that she was somehow the mystery he'd been hungering for. All these years.

And he knew that he had found it and would fight it and would be lost to it.

•   •   •

She lies on the carpet before the altar in the deserted church, her form fluid, smooth, and soft. He has asked her to wear the same white dress from that Sunday. It is late at night, after midnight. Though he has done this healing ritual many times before, this time he's nervous because he doesn't want Mac Kilpatrick or anybody to walk in on them. He is already struggling with his guilt, fighting it every step of the way.

They have met several times in his office. Once they took a drive in her car, an old beat-up Chevrolet, up along the Cumberland River. "It's the size of a grapefruit," she told him. "That's what the doctor said. The size of a grapefruit. Isn't there something else to compare it to? How about a softball?"

"Doctors are not poets," he said. "They're scientists."

"I'll lose everything inside. I won't be a woman anymore."

"But you'll be alive. You should let him operate. I can't...guarantee anything. I...."

"Neither can he." She began to cry. "I don't believe either one of you can help me, if you want to know the truth."

"If you don't believe, then...."

"I don't believe much in medicine, either."

He looked at her. His body tingled at her closeness. No other woman had ever affected him this way. "You can let me try," he offered, questioning his motives even as he was saying it because he wanted her, badly, at the same time that he loved Paula and their children. He wanted her and felt overpowered by it. He was letting it overpower him. He knew that, too.

They sat looking out across the river. He glanced back over at her and she was staring at him. Just looking at her made his mouth go dry. She gave off a magnetic field that he seemed to sense with every nerve ending in his body. He had seen many women whose features were more flawless than hers, but rarely one whose face seemed to have been put together by some half-crazed and divine genius in such a way that its beauty was finally so tantalizingly elusive that it was almost inexplicable. She reminded him of a Modigliani portrait he once sat in front of for hours, in the unhurried quiet of the Phillips Collection in Washington, sat there trying to articulate in his mind the deeply mysterious quality of the woman in the painting, the long angular body with its luminous skin and rich soft burst of spongy pubic hair like a glorious celebration of that secret and fertile place beneath it, the face with its slanted green eyes like some otherworldly icon.

"You can't do it," she said. "You can't heal me."

"I can," he stated, "with God's help."

She was quiet for a long time. He could hear his own heart beating. "All right," she said, "with God's help."

• • •

The church is still and quiet. The Tabernacle Lamp glows red above them, and one soft white spot lights the altar with its wooden cross. "Let us pray," he begins. "Almighty God, who didst inspire thy servant Luke the physician to set forth in the Gospel the love and healing power of thy Son, graciously continue in me, thy humble servant, the like love and power to heal." Dooly licks his dry lips. He signs over her body. "Lord have mercy, Christ have mercy, Lord have mercy." His voice echoes in the vastness of the deserted old church. He closes his eyes and focuses on the image of the cross in his mind. He feels in the shadows around them something moving, something swelling. He feels the power of God.

He puts his hands flat upon the softness of her stomach. Her breasts rise and fall with her rapid breathing. Dooly's own breathing quickens, his body tingles. He feels himself aroused. He expected that. Her eyes are closed, her head tilted toward him. "Almighty God," he says, "who art the giver of all health, and the aid of them that seek to Thee for succor, we call upon Thee for Thy help and goodness mercifully to be showed upon this Thy servant, that she being healed of her infirmities may give thanks unto Thee in Thy holy church, through Jesus Christ our Lord. Amen."

Dooly leans forward, his face close to her body. He feels her heat in his hands, feels her body growing hotter. He can smell her. His heart pounds. Waves of pleasure begin to surge through his body. He whispers, "In the name of God most high, mayest thou be given release from pain, and may thy soul be restored into harmony with His immortal laws. In the name of Jesus, the Prince of Life, may new life come into thy body." His lips almost touch the white cloth of her dress. He feels her heat against his face. He licks her, slowly. He feels power pressing him from above. "The Lord lift up His countenance upon thee, and give thee peace, both now and forevermore. Amen."

He moves his hands over her belly. The silky cloth moves with his hands. Her stomach, swollen, begins to flatten. He knows now that it is happening. Thank God. Thank God. He feels a tremor in the great stone floor of the church, feels it tighten in his loins and run through him with a violent shaking. The silence around them is so heavy that it presses against his ears like the palms of large hands, and he feels the pressure inside his head. Her white dress glows as though it is lit from within. His hands move of their own accord now and the power moves down his arms and into her body. His face is close to her, close to her bare skin, and when his lips touch her skin they touch flame. He collapses on top of her and is still.

• • •

"The doctor is right. I didn't heal you. God did," Dooly says to Kitty. The afternoon sunlight slants through the old frosted windows of his office, lined with books. His desk is cluttered with the yellow legal pads he writes his sermons on. The downtown traffic sounds are distant and muted.

"But he said it was not possible," she tells him. Kitty has been back to her doctor, who was astonished that the tumor had gone away.

"It must have been benign, something," the doctor said, dumbfounded. "A lipoma, fatty tissue. Sometimes these things heal themselves. It's a great mystery."

"Yes," Kitty agreed. She still cannot really believe that Father Legrand has done it. She thinks the doctor is probably right; she's been raised to think that they always are. Then she remembered Father Legrand's eyes. She remembered that she felt the tumor go away, that night in the church, knew precisely when it had left her body. "I was healed," she had told the doctor, "by a faith healer."

"Come now, Miss Wiggins," he laughed self-consciously. "Your body has healed itself. Sometimes...Well, there are still some things that we in the medical profession don't understand, believe it or not."

"I was healed. In a healing service. I felt it go away." Had she? She thought so, but now she wasn't sure.

"And who is this witch doctor, if I may ask? Who is this person practicing medicine without a license?" Dr. Putnam was always rough with her, was always hurting her during examinations. Kitty thought that men went into OB-GYN because they hated women in the first place. She didn't answer. "No, that is not possible," the doctor said, shaking his head, "but I have some colleagues out at Vanderbilt Hospital, and if you wouldn't mind. I mean, it's most unusual. If you wouldn't mind my sharing the X-rays with them, perhaps we could do a, well, a study, publish the results, look into this more...."

"No," she said, thinking of Dooly Legrand's light blue eyes, the way he looked at her. "I know what happened. Forget it."

• • •

"It's stupid and presumptuous of the doctor to think he knows what is or is not possible," Dooly says to her. "Only God knows that."

"Why don't you, you know, go out and heal the world?" she asks. "Go on television or something?" He sits there looking at her. She smirks, not even trying to hide her doubts.

He has the saddest eyes she's ever seen, very pale blue, behind little steel-rimmed glasses. She knows he's an unhappy person, but maybe he doesn't even know it. He is dissatisfied, restless, not quite complete. His clerical collar and black shirt make him look handsome and authoritative. His sandy hair is cut short. She has seen the pictures of his family on his desk, a little boy and girl, a slim dark-haired woman in tweeds, a confident and polished smile. The kind of woman she has always envied. His wife probably went to some fancy finishing school and rode horses as a girl instead of a mule.

"Like Oral Roberts?" he asks. He smiles and shakes his head.

She found out about Dooly from her friend Sylvia Matthews, a songwriter who was once Miss Pascagoula, Mississippi. Sylvia and her boyfriend, Amos Collins, a cowboy truck driver, were regulars at Little Willie's, the club where Kitty sings.

Kitty, too, is from Mississippi, born in the tiny town of Quitman, north of Laurel. "A railroad track and a sawmill, and that was about it," she told Sylvia and Amos. "In those rolling clay hills that wouldn't grow anything but pine trees and corn." Her father, who had worked in the sawmill, died when she was still a young girl, died from "hard work and too much booze," she said. Her father had been a moonshiner. "We were poor as dirt, clay-eaters. He cooked shine at night, back in those hills. He made some of the best white lightning you ever tasted. It was famous." She wrote a song about her father. It's called "Cornstalk Wine."

"We lived in a house with a dirt floor," she told her friends. "It's that rough life that I want to sing about. That I want to write songs about. Mama went to Meridian, Mississippi, to live after I left home. She married a chiropractor. He drinks and they fight. Will the circle be unbroken?"

• • •

"There's no such thing as faith healing," Kitty said when Sylvia first suggested she visit Dooly. "It's bullshit."

"No, I've seen it happen," Sylvia insisted. "No shit. At a tent revival once in Pascagoula, I saw a little blind girl get her sight back."

"And a little lame boy got up and walked," Kitty smirked.

"No, really."

Kitty downed the rest of her beer. "That big gray church?" Kitty asked her then. "Really?" She'd seen the church many times, sitting on a downtown corner, the traffic on Broadway bunching noisily around it. Kitty had been crying for three days. Her surgery was already scheduled, a complete hysterectomy. "Are you kidding me? A faith healer? Come on."

"No," Sylvia said, "I wouldn't kid about something like that. The priest there, Father Legrand. He's the son of the governor of Alabama, if you can believe that. The word on the street is that he can heal. He has healed people."

"Of cancer?"

Sylvia patted her hand. "I don't know, baby. But it's worth a try."

• • •

Father Legrand continues to shake his head. "No. I would never go on television or anything like that. Why do you think Christ performed his miracles? Did he do them to impress? No. Did he do them to prove something? No, he didn't. He did them because of his love of God and of mankind." Kitty has never known anyone like him before. It had never occurred to her that Christ didn't perform his miracles to prove to the ages that he was the Son of God. Why else? Maybe he performed them for the same reason she writes songs and sings them. She knows instinctively that Father Legrand understands this.

It seems stupid to her to call someone Dooly's age "Father." The first Sunday service she'd attended had been strange to her, with the incense and the bells and the kneeling, a far cry from the little white frame church in the red clay hills of southeastern Mississippi, a Methodist church, just outside Quitman.

She knows he's terribly attracted to her. And she him. She can feel it in the air between them, like summer heat lightning. She can read everything in his melancholy eyes. He already knows what's going to happen. Her eyes keep returning to the color photograph of his family in its silver frame. She is grateful to him. Maybe he has saved her life. Maybe someday she'll be convinced of that. She knows what Dr. Putnam would have found when he cut into her.

She looks at him. He will do anything for her. Even leave the church. What she has been through has frightened her more than anything in her life. And she doesn't trust the church. It scares her even more.

• • •

Little Willie's, in Printer's Alley, is like hundreds of clubs all over Nashville; but it's one of the best, because you can't sing there unless you've sung at the Grand Ole Opry. Kitty has done two shows at the Opry, on the crowded stage at Ryman Auditorium, and the audiences loved her. She plays her guitar and sings with a single spot, wearing a man's white oxford-cloth shirt and tight, faded jeans and dark leather boots. When she sings at Little Willie's, the crowd falls silent, the waitresses stop weaving between tables, and the bartender puts down his shaker. Everybody listens.

Two of her songs have been recorded by Joan Baez. Kitty sings them every set, and the audience applauds when they recognize them: "Upriver" and "Little Ones." She also sings the new song she's still working on: "Take the Wings of Morning." It is slow and steady, a soulful song about searching and not finding, about searching for grace. Arlo Guthrie sings her song, "The Midnight Train to Mobile," during his concerts. She recorded a single of that for Half-Moon Records, backed up by "Little Ones." Now she has a contract for a new album, just as soon as she has ten songs she's satisfied with.

"You're famous," her friend Laurie tells her, as they drink a beer at one of the tiny round tables between Kitty's sets. Laurie is a female impersonator at Papa John's, a club next door. Laurie's real name is Lawrence

Dimaggio, and she's from Memphis. She takes female hormones and is very proud of her plump breasts and hairless body. She plans to have the operation in eight months. ("Then it's she all the way, baby," Laurie proclaims, "no more tuck and tight!")

"No, I'm not famous," Kitty replies. "What's famous, anyway?"

"You've been on TV, on the Opry," Laurie says and shrugs. "That makes you famous." Laurie smokes long, thin cigarettes called Eve, her lipstick smudged at the corner of her mouth. Kitty first saw Laurie one night when she dropped into Papa John's to catch the show and Laurie was grinding to the music in only a black G-string. When Kitty left, Laurie was sitting on a stool taking cover charges at the door. "Great show!" Kitty called to her, and Laurie smiled gratefully. Laurie was only nineteen years old.

Tonight Little Willie's is dark and noisy and smoky. The alley outside is shoulder to shoulder with people waiting to get in for Kitty's next set. Right now, the Steel City Shine, a string group from Birmingham, plays for dancing.

"Who is he?" Laurie asks. "Come on. Tell me."

"He's a priest," Kitty says.

"A priest?"

"An Episcopal priest. Not a Catholic priest. He...he's special."

Laurie stares at her. She wears a black, low-cut dress and her hair is piled up on top of her head. "They marry," she asks, "right? Is he married?"

"Yes."

"I mean, is he...."

"I don't want to talk about it. It doesn't matter. This is destined to be. That's all I know."

"Destined to be?" Laurie smiles. She winks. "What does he say about that?"

"It doesn't matter what he says," Kitty says, eyes narrowed.

Laurie shrugs. "Anyway," she says, tapping her ash into the saucer on the table. "Anyway, you're famous to me. And I can't wait till we get busted. They'll put your picture in the paper."

"We probably won't get busted," Kitty says. But she hopes they will.

Some street folks and students from Fisk and Vanderbilt, a group of blacks and whites, plan to stage a sit-in at a nearby Krystal restaurant. Kitty has recruited Laurie to join them. "If they throw you in jail, it'll get into the papers," Laurie cautions.

"Yes," Kitty says, smiling. Laurie smiles back at her in the dimness. "I've never been in jail before," Laurie laughs. "I guess it's time."

• • •

And they do get arrested and put in jail, and it does get into the papers, a picture of Kitty emerging from a paddy wagon at city hall in the morning *Tennessean*, with the small headline "Singer Arrested In Sit-In." Laurie is standing next to her. The caption under the picture reads "Singer Kitty Wiggins and an unidentified female were arrested yesterday afternoon along with twenty-four others for violating trespass laws. When ordered to leave the restaurant, they refused to do so and were placed under arrest."

On that clear, crisp afternoon, the crowd of demonstrators gathered near the campus to march up the street to the Krystal. Six of them planned to go in, three whites and three blacks. The street people, wearing ragged denim jackets over tie-dyed T-shirts, smelled of pot. Kitty could tell from their eyes that they were high. "If these people are holding, they're in deep shit," Laurie said to her.

"Don't worry. They got better sense," Kitty said.

None turned out to be in possession, but the cops had a field day right there in front of them. The nervous young manager of the Krystal, as though reading from a script, kept repeating, "We reserve the right to refuse service to anyone." Frightened, he just kept saying what his supervisors had instructed him to say. He looked like a college student. "I have to ask you to leave."

"Hamburgers, six apiece, all down the line," Kitty said.

"Sorry mam," the boy answered. "We reserve the right to refuse...."

"Yeah, yeah, you said that," Kitty said.

The street people and students clogged the sidewalk and blocked the door, waiting for the cops. When the police got there they wasted no time. "Jesus," Laurie said. As the cops flailed away with night sticks, the scene outside the tiny diner descended into chaos. Some of the students and street people began to fight back and resist, taunting the cops: "OINK,

OINK!" "PIGS, PIGS!" People were dragged to the waiting paddy wagons while those inside sat quietly and waited as the motion raged around them.

The police made their way through the human barriers to the diner and through the door. "All right," one of them yelled, "you're under arrest, all of you."

"For what?" Laurie asked, standing up, her hand on her hip. Her lipstick was like a slash of fire across her face. In her high spike heels, she towered six feet tall.

"For impersonating a human person," one of the cops responded sarcastically, "Jesus H. Christ!"

• • •

When Dooly sees the picture in the paper, his attention is riveted. There she is, stepping down from the police wagon, an officer holding her arm, her face tilted down, hair cascading down onto her shoulders like a sheet of black water. He sits at the kitchen table. The room is sunny and smells of coffee and bacon. The breakfast table, the entire room where he has eaten his breakfast every morning for the past five years, the room at the back of the two-story house on the leafy street in Belle Meade on the city's west side, suddenly seems unfamiliar to him, strange and foreign.

He can't take his eyes from the grainy image in the paper. He remembers the touch of her, the smell of her.

She told him that she participates in demonstrations. Yes, he thinks, yes. That's where she's taking him. That's what's conspiring here. He thinks of Carter and Rachel. There is a strong link here, and Dooly feels it like a spasm in his chest.

Holding the newspaper, staring at the photograph, he is far away and in another time. A sunny summer day when they were children…and then he remembers a recent telephone conversation with his mother: "Yes, Dooly, Carter and Rachel are in the middle of it, marching in the streets and all that. I see them. It's all madness. The whole world is being turned upside-down."

"Somebody we know?" Paula asks, shattering his reverie. His wife stands behind him with the pot of coffee, ready to pour him another cup. "Yes," he replies, "one of my parishioners."

She pauses for a moment, a moment too long. "Uh-huh," she says, not looking at him as she refills his cup.

He has not touched Kitty Wiggins except to heal her. Yet Paula knows everything. She already knows.

•  •  •

Dooly first discovered he had the gift of healing when he was a senior in seminary at Sewanee. He was thirty-one years old, already married with a child. A man named Raybob Sneed had suffered an accident, falling in the woods while hunting with his two young sons and breaking his leg. The two boys somehow managed to get the old man back to a traveled road, where somebody picked them up and brought them into town. It was late on a Saturday afternoon, and Dooly was at the chapel by himself, setting up the altar for mass the next morning (a duty called the "Lady of the Altar Guild") when the three of them appeared outside the door.

"You need a doctor. You need a hospital," Dooly insisted, walking out to meet them. The old man, who smelled of stale chewing tobacco and harsh whiskey, just stared at him. He was unshaven, in overalls with one leg ripped up to his hip and a heavy wool shirt under a frayed hunting coat stained with animal blood. His leg just below the knee twisted almost sideways, the break clearly visible beneath the skin.

"For this people's heart is waxed gross," the old man said, "and their ears are dull of hearing, and their eyes they have closed." The old man was quoting scripture, but Dooly didn't recognize it, couldn't place it. It seemed a strange choice for the circumstances. "Lest at any time they should see with their eyes, and hear with their ears, and should understand with their heart, and should be converted, and I should heal them!" He shouted the last words at Dooly. "That's from Matthew, and Jesus said that," Sneed said.

"Your leg is broken, you...."

"And you have the power, because you...."

"Wait now, wait," Dooly said.

The old man continued quoting. "For to one is given by the Spirit the word of wisdom; to another the word of knowledge by the same Spirit; to another faith by the same Spirit; to another the gifts of healing by the same spirit!"

"But I...."

"Truly the signs of an apostle were wrought among you in all patience," the old man continued, "in signs, and wonders, and mighty deeds!"

His piercing eyes, like pale green agate marbles, were insane eyes fired by madness. He quoted as though he knew the entire New Testament by heart. He probably did. The mountains around Monteagle were filled with religious fanatics, self-proclaimed prophets. Some handled snakes and followed signs and spoke in tongues. They were objects of ridicule among Dooly's fellow seminarians.

The sharpness of the old man's penetrating glare unnerved Dooly. The two boys sat quietly on the steps of the chapel. The old man propped his back against the wall of the brick building. There was no sign of a car or truck. Whomever had brought them had simply dumped them there.

Dooly had no idea what to do with them. He thought of the phone in the sacristy.

"Look...." Dooly began.

"HEAL ME, GODDAMIT, YOU SNIVELIN LITTLE SON-OF-BITCH!" the old man shouted.

Dooly's mouth dropped open. The old man's eyes attacked him like hurled darts. Dooly wanted to ask him why he didn't heal himself since he knew so much, but his tongue seemed swollen and thick. He couldn't speak at all. He just looked into the old man's fierce eyes. It was a late autumn afternoon. The lawn of the chapel was awash with leaves, bright red and yellow and brown, and the late sunlight slanted through the trees and slashed in golden streaks against the bricks of the chapel. Dooly couldn't move. It was still and quiet.

"Heal me," the old man said more softly, pleadingly, "I'm in pain." It was a prayer; and Dooly realized in that one blinding moment that the old man was a messenger of some kind, and Dooly thought, "And heal the sick that are therein, and say unto them, The Kingdom of God is come nigh unto you." The message opened like a slice of sunlight in his brain.

Before he could think, Dooly placed his hands on the old man's leg. He could feel the bone sliding under the skin and felt a wave of nausea; at the same time he felt as though someone had taken a hammer and hit him in the back of the head. He was dizzy, and his eyes went out of focus. He could smell the old man's unclean body. His hands and fingers tingled. Looking into Sneed's eyes, he saw the pain, and the fear, and something else, something so mysterious that he couldn't begin to comprehend it, and he knew it then, said it to himself: I am looking into the eyes of God.

This old man... This old man....

The eyes of God. Dooly was prostrate on the grass before him. His hands moved on the old man's leg, and he felt the bones move again and snap back into place and the first thing that came into his head was that the old man's leg had been somehow out of joint and he had accidentally massaged it back into place, but he knew that was not so. He felt the break, the jagged bone about to penetrate the skin. He felt the old man's leg heal beneath his hands. The breath rushed out of him, and his head pounded. He slumped on the grass.

He watched old Mr. Sneed and the two boys walk away down the sidewalk, the old man's flayed overalls flapping around his leg. Dooly was exhausted, completely drained. He couldn't move for a long time.

●　　●　　●

"Maybe you can raise the dead, too," Paula says sarcastically, sitting in the den, working some needlepoint. She doesn't like his healing. She's seen it with her own eyes and doesn't like it. "It's dangerous, Dooly," she warns, "it's tampering with something you don't understand." She's angry with him all the time now, and it freezes his heart.

"It's simple," Dooly says, "what could be more simple?"

"It's not. It's complicated. It's...it's spooky."

The bishop has warned him, too. Austin Philps, the bishop of the Diocese of Middle Tennessee, is a tall, baldheaded man with a slight lisp, a brilliant biblical scholar with a degree from Harvard Divinity School. "I have heard about things, Dooly, that you have been doing in the name of the church, and they disturb me. You may be going considerably beyond your duties as a parish priest here."

"Yessir."

"Frankly, this stuff smacks of medieval superstition, a return to the Dark Ages."

Dooly thinks of old man Sneed and quotes from the Acts of the Apostles to the bishop: " 'So when this was done, others also which had diseases came and were healed.' "

"Don't you dare quote the scriptures to me, son," the bishop bristles. "Let's just leave that sort of stuff to the fringe element, all right? The fundamentalists and all this 'new day' we keep reading about in the papers."

"The 'new day,' " Dooly says, "is the new age of Christ, begun in a manger."

"Yes, well," the bishop responds impatiently, tossing his head and glaring at Dooly. Dooly has made him very angry. The bishop does not like to be instructed about anything. Especially by one of his priests.

Even if he is the son of Oscar Legrand, the governor of Alabama.

●   ●   ●

When Dooly was a teenager, he sat with four men at an old card table, one of its legs fastened on with baling wire, in the back room of the Silver Moon Café. They played poker with a deck of greasy, limp cards, the air thick with acrid cigarette smoke. It was like a hundred other games, but this time tension filled the air, a sense of pent-up danger. Dooly, half drunk on beer and swigs of Thunderbird, was the only white person present, and the room, a little larger than a closet, was lit with a single naked 40-watt bulb that hung from the ceiling. It was Clutter Blue's game, and you bought in for twenty dollars from which Clutter cut out one dollar for himself, leaving ninety-five dollars in the game unless a player went to his pocket, which Dooly had already done twice because he was losing heavily. Nobody took any money off the table. Clutter had a strict rule against rat-holing, and men were reluctant to break any of Clutter's rules. He enforced them with a sawed-off pool cue he kept behind the counter up front.

They played six-card stud, a game Dooly heard them call "Pitty-Pat," one card down, four up, and then the last one down. It was cold outside, but the room, which smelled of cornmeal and hot grease from the kitchen, felt close. All of them were sweating. Henry Barnes was dealing. The jukebox up front was playing Nellie Lutcher's "Come On A My House." They all helped themselves to an open pack of Chesterfields on the corner of the table.

Dooly had an ace in the hole and a ten up. His ten up was high, so he bet fifty cents. Carl Trotman, sitting to his left, raised him a quarter. Carl was a mechanic at Wigginton Pontiac. Carl's right eye was permanently bloodshot from a welding accident. He had to squint at the cards, holding them up close to his face. He had a nine up.

Jack Dubose, with a five up, called. Henry, a six, called. Buddy Ed Morgan, the janitor at the Dauphin, the movie theater downtown, called. He showed a trey.

"Deal the goddam things, Henry," Jack said impatiently. He was losing, too, losing big, a steady drain of his coins and wrinkled bills. And he was mad about it. A sharecropper on Dooly's grandfather's place across the river, Jack was a large and heavy man. He wore overalls without a shirt, his black skin with its sheen of sweat gleaming in the weak light from the hanging bulb. Henry dealt. Dooly got an eight. Carl Trotman got another nine, a pair showing. Jack said, "Shit!" He watched the four of clubs fall on top of his five of diamonds. Buddy Ed got another trey, another pair showing, and Henry dealt himself a deuce.

The cards continued to fall, and Dooly knew that even though there were no aces showing he wouldn't get another ace to go with his first one. It was one of those nights. He took the pint of Thunderbird Jack offered him and slugged it down. It was sweet and syrupy, and Dooly realized he was drunk. Carl Trotman's pair of nines held up and were still high after the last card was dealt. He bet a dollar, the limit on the last card. Jack raised him a dollar. Everybody looked at Jack's cards. He didn't have doot showing. The four and five, an eight and a jack. He's paired the jack, Dooly thought. Carl stared at the cards for a long time. Everyone else had folded. Then he raised Jack back. Jack called.

Jack turned over his cards. He had a pair of eights down, three eights. He glared at Carl, as though he knew what Carl was going to turn up. And he did. A third nine, that Carl had had from the start. "Goddam mutherfuckin son-of-a-bitch," Jack shouted, the anger and frustration exploding from him, his eyes bulging. He stood up and backed away.

Before anybody even saw him go to his pocket Jack had a switchblade knife in his hand. The room grew so quiet they could hear the click as the blade opened, long and sharp, the dim overhead bulb glinting on the razor-honed edge. All the other men stood up. Dooly could see Jack's eyes, strained open and staring. He'd known Jack all his life. Once, over at Rose Hill, when Dooly was four or five, Dooly had begged his grandfather for a pig from a new litter. His grandfather told him he could have one if he could catch him, knowing full well that he couldn't. But Jack, who'd been squatting on the back porch, having come up to the house to run some errands for Justina, caught the pig for him and showed Dooly how to hold it. His grandfather then let Dooly take the pig home to Hawthorne, where he tried to raise it as a pet. But it liked to root out of its pen and run all over town. Once Miss Amy had been walking to town to shop and met the pig coming home, and the pig had sniffed her and turned around and followed her all over downtown. After that the pig was sent back over to Rose Hill.

"Don't, Jack," Dooly pleaded.

"You stay out of this, Mist' Dooly," Jack said.

But Dooly moved around the table, toward him. "Please, put the knife down," he said. "You don't want to do this, Jack."

"You don't understand, little white boy," Jack spat, his eyes large and unblinking, determined. "Git out the way, now, 'cause I want some a Carl. I…"

"He ain't done a thing," Dooly said.

"This ain't none a your business, boy," Jack said, turning his eyes on Dooly for the first time, and Dooly saw intense hatred there, a concentrated rage that shocked and frightened him, and Dooly took a step toward him. "Listen to me, boy," Jack said, and nobody else in the room moved. Dooly froze.

He could hear movement behind him, and Jack seemed to crouch and then spring, knocking Dooly backward into the table as the table and cards and money and beer cans and empty wine bottles went flying. Dooly was on the floor and someone stepped on him, on his arm and then his hand, and he could hear bodies being hurled against the wall and grunts and shouts and crying and scraping of furniture and then someone fell heavily on top of him. Dooly felt the warm blood splatter against his cheek. The man's breathing was rattling and bubbly, an agonized wheezing that grew weaker, and Dooly shut his eyes and began to cry.

•   •   •

He was sixteen years old. His father had bought him a green Porsche that Dooly drag-raced on Spring Hill Road south of town. He and another boy, Sonny Blankenship, had been caught dragging, beer cans rattling around on the floorboards of their cars, and Dooly's father had to come down and get him out of jail.

At that time his father was in the state legislature. "How the hell do you think this looks, Dooly?" Oscar asked, his face red. "If you don't give a shit about me, at least think of your mother!"

Dooly's mother had been sitting in the darkened parlor drinking when they got home. She cried. "Leave him alone, Oscar," she said. "He's just like you and the rest of them. He's Legrand through and through!"

His mother had been an Estes, from Mobile. She and his father had met at the university in Tuscaloosa. Dooly's maternal grandparents were transplanted northerners who moved to Mobile during the Depression from Rochester, a little town in Vermont. "Your grandfather was a Marxist, Dooly," his mother told him one afternoon as she sat on the back porch staring out across the river, holding a glass of gin and tonic. "And your grandmother was cultured, a ballet dancer when she was young. They were not from this magnolia-drenched and history-ridden place. They never belonged here, were never at home here." What she didn't say, but what Dooly even then knew she meant, was that she didn't belong here either.

He and his mother were close. She doted on him, she made no bones about it. His mother was a painter. One of the upper floor bedrooms overlooking the river was her studio, and as a small child Dooly would emerge from the studio covered in oil paint where she had let him play in it all he liked. His father was an unenthusiastic churchgoer, but Amy made sure that Dooly was raised in the church, drilling him on his catechism and taking him each week to Sunday school and to church at St. Paul's, where Dooly would stare at the stained-glass windows dedicated to his great-grandfather and his grandmother Legrand. His mother gave Dooly his first prayer book when he was confirmed. "To be a priest, Dooly," she said to him, "would be the greatest way to cope with this ignorant and heartless world." He didn't want to be a priest. But he didn't want to disappoint his mother.

And then there was Carter Taylor. Later in life Dooly would look back and marvel at the irony of the fact that his confirmation into Christ's church seemed to mark the end of his relationship with Carter, his best friend, the one person after his mother to whom Dooly had been closest. But he knew that his confirmation simply coincided with that late adolescent period in which, in that part of the world at least, racial barriers were raised that had not existed before.

Dooly's memories of his childhood, an innocent time, a time flooded with summer sunlight, were inextricably bound up with Carter. Carter and his little sister, Rachel, were always at Hawthorne, along with their mother, Rosa. Often Dooly would go home with them, across the river, to spend the night at their house, rising in the crisp morning to roam the plantation or to hunt or fish, sitting at the table eating Rosa's heavy cat-head biscuits laden with butter and molasses or coming back later in the day to eat thick, sticky oatmeal cookies, large and round as saucers, fresh and warm from the oven and spread with peanut butter. He and Carter were together constantly. And suddenly they were not. When they became young men, they were no longer together.

•  •  •

The night of the fight at the Silver Moon, Dooly's father left him in jail all night, and Dooly heard the talking, the moaning and the cursing from the other cells in the dank little jail with sweating redbrick walls. Shivering on the thin naked mattress of an iron cot next to a seatless toilet full of dark, stinking water, Dooly heard the talk that Carl Trotman somehow took Jack's knife from him and that Jack Dubose was dead, his throat cut from ear to ear, and Dooly could still feel Jack's body on top of his, Jack's blood still sticky on Dooly's cheek and neck even though he had washed a thousand times in the stained sink attached to the wall. The four men who survived the poker game were in jail. Carl Trotman, in the next cell, cried and prayed all night.

"Sweet Jesus," he moaned, "sweet Jesus above."

And Dooly did not sleep but had waking dreams all night, of how quickly it had happened, the sudden brute force of it, the fury and defeat that generated its own powerful energy, and all night he could smell the thick male bodies heavy with work sweat and liquor and tobacco. He could still see Jack's eyes and he knew he would see them for the rest of his life. He had seen there such hopelessness and rage. As he lay awake in the agonizing long hours he came to believe that Jack had planned it that way, that Jack had wanted to die. Dooly couldn't understand why any man would want to die, and he cried for him.

The next morning Oscar Legrand made Dooly stand at attention on the back porch in the cold in his shirt-sleeves while he paced back and forth. Carter was waiting in the garden. He had come with the pickup to take Oscar across the river to go duck hunting up along the Bigbee.

"Why, Dooly? Why?" his father asked him. "I can understand a boy sowing his wild oats, son, but in a nigger beer joint? It could have been your throat cut instead of Jack Dubose's. You ever think of that?"

"Yes sir," Dooly said.

His father peered at him then, his eyes narrowed, his jaw working. His father's face was broad and flat, his hair thick and curly. His body was chunky and solid. "Are you just shiftless, son? Sorry?" His father wore a new hunting coat with suede elbow patches and a suede collar. "You need to start thinking about what you're gonna do with your life. I know you're still in high school, boy, but the time is coming faster than you know. You need to change your ways."

"Yes sir."

"Law school, maybe. Just what the hell do you want to do, son?"

"I think I want to be a priest," Dooly said.

There was a long silence. His father just looked at him. The winter sunlight glinted on the gray highlights in his hair. "Well, I'll be god-dammed," his father said. Dooly said nothing. "A priest? This is something your mother has cooked up and filled your head with, right? Well, you're going in about the opposite direction from becoming a priest, I'll tell you that."

"I know. That's the point."

His father stared uncomprehendingly at him, confused. He had no idea what Dooly was talking about. But Dooly knew even then how hard he was running from what he knew he was and always would be.

# Rachel

"BILLY?!" JESSIE MERLE SHOUTS. "BILLY?!" SHE STARES AT HIM from the bathroom doorway, gaping at him as though he's some kind of monster.

Billy vomits into the toilet bowl and gags. He just tried to eat. He backs away, his eyes wide and panicked, mouth rimmed in bloodless white.

"Flush it, goddammit, flush it," he stammers, his whole body trembling with a sudden gripping and painful chill, his eyes fixed on what look like swarming minnows on the surface of the water, a writhing and wriggling mass of silver gray.

"Flush it, I said," Billy pleads.

And Jessie Merle leans over and pushes the handle. The toilet gurgles and she steps back and stares with horror at her husband, now grown as skinny as a scarecrow.

•   •   •

On that same day, an achingly beautiful sky-blue April day, Mose Bell and his grandson take a shortcut from Mose's house in Crockers Crossroads to the river where they often go to fish. The old man has worn his own path up the hill behind his house to a place where Chemco's high chain-link fence has sagged and rusted. Entering there, they cross the high earthen dam of the hundred-acre lake that had once been the glimmering center-piece of Rose Hill Plantation. The path then winds through the woods and swamplands to an unlocked gate near the Bigbee River.

Mose and his grandson Hardy Siddons—Mose's daughter's boy—pause on the dam, look down at the sweeping view, at the houses in the village, the two rows of whitewashed frame cottages, Mose's church with its steeple that leans slightly to the north, the concrete block and frame Hanson's Store at the end of the street, and next to it the ruins of the old store and tavern once run by a white man named Crocker back in the middle of the last century, a man now long forgotten except for the name he passed on to the crossroads community. The lake is dammed between hills that are the highest points on the place. South of the village, they can see the rivers, their junction, and beyond that the haze surrounding Hammond. In the opposite direction they see the big house atop its own rise in the river basin: Rose Hill, gleaming white in the spring sunlight. The sun glitters on the smooth black asphalt of the highway, and as they watch, a large 18-wheel truck loaded with 55-gallon metal barrels rumbles by on the way to the hazardous waste dump three miles away.

"Papa, let's fish in here," the boy says. He suggests it every time they pass the lake. Not yet five years old, Hardy looks out across the broad, still surface of the lake. Both of them carry long bamboo poles.

"Ain't no fish in there, Hardy," the old man chuckles. He squints against the sun's reflection on the water. His whiskers are a startling white against his black skin. His overalls are too large on him. Hardy, barefoot, wears identical overalls.

"Why not?" the boy asks. It's like a ritual with them.

The old man chuckles again. "All the fish dead. I remembers when there was more fish in there than you could shake a stick at. Bluegills big as my hand and bass that'ud snap your line like sewin thread."

"Where they at now?" The little boy's nose, is running, and Mose takes out a wrinkled handkerchief, wipes his nose, and makes him blow.

"All dead, son," he says, putting the handkerchief in his back pocket. He removes his red baseball cap and scratches his head with one finger. All the trees and undergrowth on the edge of the lake are dull brown, some of the trees nothing more than empty black skeletons against the sky, and the old man knows that in the shriveled undergrowth are carcasses of animals that had come to drink, mostly wild but some domestic ones as well that got away from their owners and found holes under the fence. Mose has seen the sun-bleached bones of hogs and dogs, as well as deer and turkeys and alligators, possums and raccoons.

"That ain't even water out there," the old man says. "Looks like it but it ain't. Ain't nothin but sludge. Look here." The old man takes a stick and stirs it into the lake and pulls it out. Green slime clings to the stick. Where he disturbed the surface they see brown scum with a kind of silvery oil running through it. "Used to be a lake, but ain't no lake no more. Don't nobody ever come round here no more." He pauses, his head cocked to the side. "Listen. You don't hear nothin, not even any birds singin. Ain't been no birds in here since I don't know when. Ain't nothin here."

"How come, Papa?"

"All that waste over there at Chemco, I reckon. Don't nobody ever come here. They don't even know about this shortcut, nobody but me and you. I reckon they think that gate locked over yonder. Come on."

In the middle of the dam they come to a large ditch and they can see the stained and discolored ground where the contents of the lake have leaked through. They cross the ditch carefully. "Don't get your bare foots in that mess," the old man cautions, "or your mama kill me." He laughs. "This ditch gettin deeper and deeper. Ever time I come over here, after it been rainin, more and more of that stuff leakin through. I reckon them people from the state keepin up with it. They needs to fix this dam fore it give way. But I reckon that's Mr. Oscar Legrand's business, now ain't it? And he the governor of the whole state." Mose laughs again. "Yessir. Maybe he too busy to worry with it."

The old man looks around him, at the glimmering, diamondlike surface of the lake and at the sky. He seems lost in thought, a vague, far-off look in his eyes. "Yessir, somethin real wrong here. When I was a boy your age I was already choppin and pickin cotton. The whole Legrand land was cotton fields, stretchin away far as you could see, like the ocean. All of us chopped and picked, and we hunted and fished and lived off the land. That was part of our sharecroppin agreement with the Legrands. All you could catch and kill you could eat. You couldn't do that now."

The sun hurts his eyes and makes him squint, and his grandson looks up at him expectantly. The old man grows pensive, and the boy knows his grandfather is getting ready to preach a sermon. "Like the Good Book say in Deuteronomy, 'The Lord your God is bringin you into a good land, a land with flowin streams, with springs and underground waters wellin up in valleys and hills, a land where you will lack nothin.'" He stands very still. The boy watches him, his gaze steady and intense. "That was what it was like in the old days. It ain't the way it is no more, boy. You got to walk these two miles all the way to the river just to wet a hook. And you can't hunt nothin no more. Ain't no squirrels at all, and the ducks just fly right over. We used to get our turkeys for Thanksgivin and Christmas right out here. Now you got to go to the Piggly Wiggly."

"Yessir," the little boy says.

They walk on, their poles slung over their shoulders, the boy a miniature reflection of the old man, the soft, faded denim legs of their overalls flapping as they walk. The old man moves stiffly, and the boy skips on every third step or so, watching his bare feet in the dust. They are unhurried, leisurely. The man carries a pail of earthworms nestled in moist soil, and the boy dangles an old syrup can full of crickets, its top punctured by a screwdriver for air holes. The old man knows of a perfect place on a slough of the river, where they can settle in the shade of tall trees and watch their corks float on the water all afternoon.

Behind them, warming in the late-morning sunlight, the ditch marks the place where the dam is most acutely and severely cracked, where deep-seated fissures have formed from the yearly spring rains that raise the lake's water level. Directly down from that point is the village, and beyond that the flat plain between the rivers. At the bottom of the ditch, where the old man had stepped with his heavy brogan, his shoe print fills slowly with a thick, oily liquid, glistening globules of what appear to be a mercury-like substance that oozes from the earth. No one is there to see and observe it, to note it, and as the old man's and the boy's voices fade away there's only a noiseless and ponderous silence.

●  ●  ●

"I'll lose my job," Carter says, "we'll all lose our jobs. But I'm ready."

"There'll just be a few of us," Eldon Long explains. "We'll walk all the way. We'll camp alongside the highway."

"Mr. Oscar ain't gonna be studyin you when you get to Montgomery," Mose Bell says. "If you get to Montgomery."

Eldon ignores the older man. "What I plan is this," he continues. "We'll start on a Sunday. That way everybody can be there, old and young, everybody, and we'll all walk across Rooster Bridge together, carryin our petition, and then once we get on out on the highway all the other people can come on back. And the rest of us will go on. I figure it'll take almost a week. Friday. Friday morning, bright and early, we walk through town and up Dexter Avenue to the capitol. People can drive over for that, join us. Folks in Montgomery, people all along the way, can join in."

"They can do that anyhow," Mose points out. "Ain't no sense in walkin all the way from here to there."

"It would be just another march that way," Long argues. "Like Reverend Shuttlesworth said, this way the whole world will be watching."

"Huh," Mose says. "The Klan be watchin. White trash will come outta the woodwork then. Who gonna watch out for you when you 'campin'?"

"Guards. We'll have guards. Armed guards."

"You think Sheriff Tate or the state troopers gonna allow that? You bitin off more than you can chew here, Eldon."

Rachel listens to the men talking. They sit around a table in her classroom in the back of the church. She knows Mose is right to feel apprehensive. She feels it, too, knows it in her bones. The men sit in children's chairs, and their knees stick up almost to their shoulders. They look at a large Alabama highway map that Rachel has tacked up on the wall. "Mobile Bay," Rachel says, and the children all point. "Sand Mountain," and they point again. "Now show me where Crockers is," she challenges, and they all yell and scramble to be the one to touch it. "Right here," "Here tis," "Dare, rat dare!"

Rachel observes Eldon Long. His eyes blaze when he speaks. She was in New Orleans when his daughter was killed, and though she rarely read the papers, someone had told her about it. She remembered his little girl from when she was a baby. Rachel knows Eldon's wife, Cora. Everybody knows that Cora Long loved a white man who moved off to Birmingham. Rachel thinks, then, of Mr. Oscar. She feels a frigid void in the middle of her chest when she thinks of him. It's as though her heart is replaced with a chunk of ice. But she thinks she has somehow known it all along, since she was a child. She recalls once snapping at Hester when Hester corrected her about something, "You can't make me, you're not my mama!" And Hester had said, "You hush your mouth, girl. You don't know who you are," and then looked at her with a look that chilled her all the way through.

What they have discovered haunts Carter worse, she knows. He would be lost in a brown study, sitting at the table letting his coffee grow cold, and he'd suddenly say something like "Daddy knew. He had to have known it all. Maybe that's why he...." His voice would trail off.

"A man don't need an excuse to drink himself to death, Carter," Rachel responded.

•  •  •

Carter wants to talk about it all the time. He walks down to Rachel's cabin after supper, and they sit on the narrow porch in the chilly dusk.

"It don't matter, Carter," Rachel says. "It don't change who we are. Go look in the mirror. You're still the same person you've always been. That's all that matters."

"You know better than that, Rachel," he says. "We're the products of white man's sin." He is brooding. She knows he has been drinking.

"Mama didn't sin," she adds.

"Shit. Everybody thinks their mama can't sin." Even in the fading light she can see the tracks of his tears on his cheeks. He's hurting all the way to his core. They sit quietly for a long time. Then he looks at her. "Why don't you put a hex on him?" he asks.

"Because," she says. "Because he carries his own hex. He'll carry it with him to the grave."

"He's the governor! He's a big shot!"

"He's eaten up. Inside. He's a miserable, unhappy man."

"Shit," Carter mutters.

"He's full of hate. He always was."

"But he...I..." Carter stares at the scuppernong arbor.

After a few moments she finishes his sentence for him: "You loved him. All right. He loved you, too, still does, probly. If he loves anybody. But he's white folks. Love for him is always on his own terms. White folks' terms. He lives on the other side of the moon."

One lone cricket starts up.

"I just want him to know I know," Carter says.

• • •

Little Hardy Siddons has been absent for a week, and Rachel is worried about him. He has had a bad cold off and on all winter and has missed school, but never as much as a whole week. She asks Mose about him when he comes by the church.

"They carried him over to the doctor in Hammond last Monday. He bad sick," he tells her. "The doctor say they shoulda brought him a long time ago, but they didn't know." He stares at her, almost curiously, his eyes tired and bloodshot, as though he hasn't slept.

"Bad sick?" she asks.

"The Lord have mercy." Tears flood the old man's eyes.

So when her day is over and the other children have all gone home, Rachel walks into the village to see about Hardy. In the late afternoon sunlight she passes Hanson's Store with its shed over the gas pumps, its benches in the shade, the storefront splashed with multicolored signs: RC Cola, Best By Taste Test, Garrett's Snuff, Martha White Flour. She then turns down the narrow dirt lane to the Siddons's house.

The lane is lined with open limestone ditches, green-stained with moss, several inches of clear water flowing through them. The houses are small three- and four-room shanties with diminutive porches on the front, little more than stoops, some still with privies out back. Most of the places have running water now, but not all. Some of the backyards are high fenced, and Rachel can smell hog slop and chicken droppings mixed with the smells of supper cooking: greens and pork and warm, sweet cornbread.

A few people sit on the porches in the lingering warmth of the day, older people who don't work anymore, and they nod and speak to Rachel when she passes.

"Hardy Siddons must be sick," Rachel says, and they grunt or moan in reply.

"Old winter cold got him and won't let go," one old lady comments.

"Sure the truth," another, across the street from the Siddons house, adds. "That boy must be sick, to stop him from running. He run everywhere he go!"

Almost at the end of the lane, the second house from the end, underneath where the earth slopes sharply up to the hills of the old lake, Rachel walks through the gate in the sagging fence. Rigged to swing closed with a chain and an old cast-iron tractor wheel, the gate thumps behind her as she goes up the sandy walkway lined with dusty verbena with tiny new buds. She raps on the screen door with her knuckles and peers through the single window in the door. The front room is empty, and she opens the screen and knocks more loudly on the door. She sees May, Hardy's mother, a young woman, lean and yellow, cross the room and pull open the door. She just stands there looking at Rachel.

May wears men's khaki pants and a white, unpressed blouse. Rachel can see that she's been crying. Her eyes are sunk back into her head. Her hair is matted and tangled.

"What...?" Rachel starts to ask.

May cuts her off. "We just got back from Dr. Mason," she tells her, "over in Hammond. He say the tests come back. He say Hardy got leukemia. He say Hardy dying."

"But...but..." Rachel stammers. May does not move back to let her in. She stands squarely, as though blocking the door.

"Something been wrong with Hardy all year, since he started down there at the church," May says. "He's had this cold since way last fall. He can't get shut of it. He ain't got no energy now, can't hardly even get up out the bed. Last Monday he couldn't even hold his head up."

"Can I..." Rachel begins.

"No," May interrupts. "No you can't."

And then Rachel knows what she means, knows what the sullen, fearsome look in her eyes really is.

"You don't believe...you don't believe...."

"Dr. Mason say there was two others with this same thing. Childhood leukemia, he call it. Both dead. One of them was white, Billy Simpleton's little girl, you remember? They both died round bout the time you come back here."

"I didn't have anything to do with that, May," Rachel says. She is afraid her knees will give way and she'll sink to the porch floor. She cannot believe it. Just days ago Hardy had been prancing about the little classroom wearing a coloring book on his head, giggling with the other children, listening intently to the stories Rachel read, his brown eyes dark and full of wonder. And now May thinks she has caused this, and maybe even Mose thinks it, too, the way he looked at her earlier in the day. "I love Hardy, May, I wouldn't...."

"You're a hoodoo. Everybody knows that. It ain't modern. It's old magic stuff. It's evil. I should have known better than to ever let Hardy...."

"May! You know better than that!"

"Then how come all these children dying when you come back to Crockers? I don't want you in my house. I'm scared of you!"

"You ain't scared of me, May. You know me."

"Don't nobody know you, Rachel."

Tears stand in May's eyes. Rock solid in the doorway, she is not going to move. Rachel thinks then of her own son Cap. She feels that same hollow aching in her gut that she felt when she watched the social worker walk away with him. Taking him away from her forever as though he had died to her. She feels as alone as she felt then.

"Don't come round here, Rachel," May warns. "We don't want no hoodoo round here."

And she steps back and closes the door in Rachel's face.

The old woman on the porch across the way looks at Rachel as she comes back through the gate, the tractor wheel and the chain clanging as it slams shut behind her. Sitting in a rusty metal glider with a frayed, patchwork quilt thrown over it, the old woman leans forward and spits a brown stream of snuff juice into the yard.

"May upset," she says, "she ain't herself."

"Hardy is sick," Rachel says, "he's bad sick." She walks almost in a trance. Her legs are heavy, and her skin tingles. The setting sun turns the sky overhead a bruised purple. She feels the first chill of the approaching night.

"Sho is," the old woman says, "he bad sick." Her name is Ruby. She had come to Rachel once to ask if there was some way she could cause her son and daughter-in-law, who was a whore, to break up. Rachel told Ruby to find a mockingbird's egg and, next time she was at their house, to break it in the corner and that would break whatever peace was left in the house and the couple would separate. The old woman later told Rachel that it worked. Her son is now married to a woman who goes to church and doesn't drink.

"May is young," Ruby says. "She don't know what to think."

"Yes." Rachel stands very still in the road. She can barely see the old woman through the shadows of the smilax vines hanging over her porch but she can see the whites of Ruby's eyes.

"When you live as long as I is," Ruby continues, "then you know old man death come on everybody like a thief in the night, sooner or later. And sometimes them that lives the longest got the biggest burden to carry."

"Amen, Ruby." With great effort, Rachel starts the long walk to her house.

● ● ●

In addition to her kitchen and eating area, Rachel's cabin has two rooms—her bedroom and her Altar Room. The windows in the Altar Room are draped with black cloth and the room is lit with coal oil lamps and candles. Rachel built the altar, a waist-high wooden table, from rough planks. On it and around it are artifacts and icons she has collected and that she adds to from time to time: a three-foot plaster of Paris statue of the Virgin Mary she brought from New Orleans, a full-color print of St. Patrick with snakes curling around his feet that she found in a magazine, a bottle of rum, an opened Holy Bible (her grandmother's Bible has now replaced the one she had originally placed there), a crude wooden cross and a nine-pointed iron cross, a collection of candles of various hues and lengths and thicknesses, a wooden bowl of Holy Water, and a jar of honey. Dried flowers, plastic figurines of animals and birds, a goblet of clear corn whiskey, and a bowl of white cornmeal with an egg propped upright in it. In back of the altar, the centerpole is decorated with bits of bone and feathers and streaks of glitter-filled paint.

The rest of the room is bare, lighted now only by the candles, which flicker as air moves through the tiny cracks between the wallboards. She writes Hardy's name nine times on a piece of paper and places it on the altar. She begins to chant in the language that old Delvane Debene taught her:

"*Caroline saisie; ce loa moin.*
*Dambalah Wedo*
*m'a p'ba ou Bon Die.*
*M' ce Creole Congo,*
*m' pas sotto oh!*
*Dambalah Wedo,*
*cote ou ye?*
*Soleil-a leve lan pays Congo!*"

The language is Delvane's version of a kind of Creole French. Sometimes in New Orleans, Rachel would walk down Rampart Street chanting in the language, and people would stare. Every now and then someone would stop and stand stock-still and then point to her. "Delvane Debene," they'd say, and cross themselves over their hearts.

Rachel holds prayer beads between her fingers and chants the words over and over again. She doesn't move from the spot for a long time.

● ● ●

The moon rises over the cabin, a fractured disk as white as snow. Owls in the swamps begin to answer back and forth, and hound dogs howl at the midnight brightness almost as light as noon. Most people sleep, except for the men on the graveyard shift at Chemco Managed Waste. Unaware of the moon because of the spotlights, they can't hear the owls over the grinding of the trucks' gears and the rumbling of the forklift engines. Nor can they hear the faint music coming from the direction of the old smokehouse, where Carrie Winfield sits with her mandolin. "Swing low, sweet chariot," she sings softly, "coming for to carry me home."

•   •   •

Long after midnight Rachel leaves the house. She wears a loose-fitting garment, a gray smock that comes down to the tops of her bare feet. She wears a red bandanna, tied in three knots, and gold hoop earrings. Rachel takes the well-worn path down along Rabbit Branch, but instead of turning toward the big house, she crosses the creek on a fallen log. There is plenty of light to see, and she finds a shadowed and silver path through the woods lined with ferns and tangles of briers. The ground grows damp and swampy. Thick streamers of Spanish moss hang from the trees overhead.

A half mile from the clearing she has made along Maconoco Creek— made for these rituals—she begins to hear the drums. They're ready for her, the drums beating their slow, inviting rhythm. Her people wait. There are not many of them anymore, not nearly as many as used to gather along Lake Pontchartrain when Rachel was in New Orleans. Though there never were many in this part of the world, there are always a few. Rachel remembers an old woman named Rosalie who lived in Frogbottom over in town, and people used to say that when she was young she had held voodoo dances and ceremonies up along the Bigbee. As a shriveled old woman with cottony gray hair, Rosalie dispensed potions and gris-gris from her little house on Spocari Street. Rachel remembers seeing her on the street and being frightened. She also remembers an old man named Greensboro who used to walk up and down the streets of Hammond beating on a worn old bass drum. The children were scared of him, too, because people would point to Greensboro and say, "That old man a bluegum."

"What's a blue-gum?" Rachel asked Hester.

"You don't need to be knowin," Hester warned. "Don't mess with him. He a hoodoo."

Rachel sees the bonfire through the trees. Golden sparks rise in spurts into the sky and twist toward the moon. When she comes into the clearing the drums stop. The four young men playing the drums are naked except for black loincloths, the flickering fire glowing on their bodies. Five young girls with gray smocks like Rachel's sit on a log across the clearing from them. Before the fire a white sheet is spread out on the ground, lighted candles all around it. In the middle of the sheet are five empty bowls. Behind the fire is a centerpole, nine feet tall and painted with streaks of red paint.

Old man Joe Bynymo sits in a cane-bottomed chair near the fire. He wears a long black overcoat, even though the night is warm, and a black bullwhip is slung over his shoulder. Next to him on the ground, a rusty wire cage contains a rooster with slick red and black feathers. Bynymo, a hermit, lives in a little shack way back in Maconoco Swamp. One of his eyes is grotesquely cocked and stares off into space. A long razor scar runs down his forehead and through the cocked eye and down his cheek to the corner of his mouth, where his lip curls up and his snuff-stained teeth show through. Bynymo sometimes comes out of the swamp and walks the streets of Hammond, trailing his bullwhip in the dust like a snake. In the cold of winter, he wears only his shirt-sleeves, and when the weather is warm he dons the overcoat. In town little children, black and white, hide in the bushes when they see him coming and then jump out and dance around him chanting, "Bynymo, Bynymo, Hit him in the Belly with a Fawty-fo!" He unleashes the bullwhip and whirls it over his head. As they scatter in every direction, he pops it after them, the loud cracks echoing like pistol shots. They run screaming in mock terror.

The young men remove a crate from an old deserted corn crib near the edge of the woods. Rachel opens the crate and takes out a crown of thorns she made from dried rose vines. She places it on old Joe's head. Joe sits with his palms on his knees. He doesn't move. Rachel nods her head, and the drums begin again.

The five girls move out toward Rachel and begin to sway to the beat of the drums. One by one they approach Rachel and curtsy. She takes each girl by the hand and helps her make three graceful turns. They are young girls, in their teens. Their bodies move with the rhythm, and Rachel moves with them. All of them feel the cadence in their bones. They are as graceful as swans.

Rachel chants, "The Angel of the Lord said to Mary that she would conceive of the Holy Ghost. Come, My God, Come. Grace, Mary, Grace.

Holy Mary, Mother of God, pray for the Saints....

Dambalah Wedo, assuage your children

Dambalah Wedo, we are all angels...."

The moon hangs low over the clearing. Rachel chants his name: "Hardy Siddons, Hardy Siddons, Hardy Siddons." All their movements are smooth and easy, without jerks. Rachel goes back to the crate as the girls continue to dance. She puts on a necklace made of blue and white beads interspersed with snake vertebrae. She takes out a butcher knife honed to razor sharpness and bottles of Florida Water, barley water, strawberry soda, and then eggs and herbs and roots and a mason jar of graveyard dirt. She pulls out and puts pictures of St. Patrick and the Virgin Mary on the spread-out sheet.

The drums grow more furious, and the girls move faster. One by one they pull the loose smocks over their heads and begin to dance naked. Their bodies, lean and oiled in the firelight, move sensuously. They rub themselves between the legs. Their breasts jiggle and yank in tune with the drums. They begin to moan and shout. Rachel begins to feel it completely, begins to know that Dambalah will be present. Dambalah will take possession of her.

She feels her arteries and veins begin to burn with Dambalah's blood. She removes her own smock, tossing it into the darkness, and feels the spring night on her naked skin. She throws off the bandanna and looses her thick black hair. She wears nothing now but the necklace and the gold hoops, and they tug at her ear lobes as she sways and jerks. "O *Legba! Commande!*" she chants. "O *Dambalah! Commande! Commande-yo!*"

She feels free of her body now. She closes her eyes and feels herself soar over the clearing like a bird. She sees old Joe sitting on the ground and the boys with the drums and the girls writhing and twisting in the flickering firelight. Now she's with them. The drums beat like her own pulse, the fire burns like her own body heat. She opens the jar and scatters the dry graveyard dirt over the dancers' bodies. She flings the empty jar into the dark woods. A powerful force pushes her to the wire cage where she removes the rooster and holds him over her head. The drums speed up even more. The rooster flaps his wings, and she hears the shouts from the girls who surround her now, and she can smell the acrid smoke of the burning hardwood and the girls' sweating bodies. She holds the rooster by his feet and lets the bird flail the air with his wings.

Her movements are swift and smooth and sure. "Saint Andrew and Holy Angels," she shouts, "behold us at your knees at the feet of Mary!" The girls whimper; they move frantically with their eyes closed.

*"Dambalah! Dambalah! Take this death as your own.*

*Take this death instead of Hardy!*

*Bwenga, manman moin! Si ou alle, pas tounin.*

*Pousse alle, Zo, oui!"*

She takes the butcher knife and smoothly slits the rooster's throat, and the rooster continues to flap his wings and yank his feet even as its hot blood begins to spurt in jerks, and Rachel catches some of the blood in the bowls and lets it run down her arm and across her breasts and down her belly. The blood splatters on the writhing, snakelike bodies of the girls. The drums reach a crescendo, ear-splitting and deafening, and Rachel drinks the rooster's salty warm blood directly from his neck while he still moves, and the girls all scramble for the bowls and drink, holding the bowls before their mouths as their bodies jerk and thrash about in unison with the movements of the dying rooster.

The drums echo through the trees and out into the swamp in almost one continuous sound now, and Rachel and the girls move spasmodically, their heads thrown back and their eyes closed. Their breasts bounce and sway. The flames of the bonfire roar and spout toward the black sky beyond the treetops. The wavering light from the fire glows on their bodies, on the sweat and blood, on the particles of dirt that cling to them.

•　　•　　•

Justina Beasley hears the drums, a distant, dreamlike murmur, as she lies in her bed in the dark, unable to sleep because of her arthritis. Jessie Merle Singleton hears them, too, sitting on the toilet to relieve the full bladder that awakened her. Jessie Merle thinks they must be the sounds of earth-moving equipment at Chemco.

And in a dim, close bedroom in Crockers Crossroads—too far away to hear the sound of the drums—Hardy Siddons, who earlier in the night had sunk into a feverish coma, sits up in bed and looks around, his eyes bright, and cries, "Muh-dear, where am I?"

And his mother, May, slumped in the corner keeping what she believed was a hopeless vigil, stands and clasps her hands in front of her and shouts, "Praise Jesus!"

# Part Two

# Dooly

PRINTER'S ALLEY TEEMS WITH PEOPLE. CHET ATKINS PLAYS
at the Carousel; the Limelighters, in town to cut a record for RCA, jam
every night at Chez Lulu's. Loretta Lynn headlines at Mother Spacks.
Katrina Starr, with fifty-four-inch breasts, strips at The Tulip Is Black.
A crippled man on the corner tries to sell mangy baby chicks left over
from Easter.

Lights and music spill into the alley, mostly the twang of guitars and
the wail of country voices. But there's jazz, too, from the Kit Kat Klub, and
saxophones squawking from the strip joints, and rock-and-roll blaring from
Papa John's. Here Laurie bumps and grinds, shaking her breasts to a recording of Little Richard's "Long Tall Sally." Dooly Legrand and Kitty Wiggins
sit at a table in the corner and watch.

"That may get you thrown out of here," Kitty says, pointing to Dooly's
clerical collar.

"So be it. It's me." It makes him feel reckless to wear the collar down
here, even though no one seems to notice it.

Kitty laughs. She's given to sudden bursts of spontaneous laughter,
which wash over Dooly and warm him. He can't stop smiling.

Kitty wears a baseball cap she got in a souvenir shop near Ryman
Auditorium. Red with a blue patch in the front, it reads: "If You Don't Like
Country Music, You Can Kiss My Ass." She wears it high on her head,
the bill low over her eyes. "I wanted one that said 'Keep America
Beautiful: Shoot a Redneck,' but I didn't have enough money for two."
Her eyes dance with laughter. She drinks a beer from out of a long-
necked bottle.

Dooly's spirits soar just looking at her. She's happy. And free. She reminds him of the first girl he ever loved, of his own youth.

"I'll buy the other cap for you," he offers.

She looks over at him. She smiles. Her eyes glitter. "All right."

He knows she's kidding about not having the money. With royalties from her record and fees for performing at Little Willie's, she has plenty of money. But she doesn't seem to care about it, doesn't spend much. She lives in a run-down apartment building out near Vanderbilt. Dooly knows the building. He knows some students at Vanderbilt Divinity School who live there and call it "The Catacombs." She drives an old beat-up black Chevrolet. "My starter car," she calls it, "only sometimes it doesn't start!"

Kitty rarely eats anything but fruit. With the beer now, she eats an apple, slicing and sprinkling salt on it. As Dooly watches her eat it, he asks, "Are you a vegetarian?" She shrugs. She grins at him, chewing. One of her front teeth is slightly crooked. Peering up at him from beneath the bill of the cap, she says, "Maybe." Her eyes glow. The frantic music swirls around them. It seems to grow louder, and they can both feel it thumping in their ears.

She grows moody all of a sudden, staring at Laurie on the stage. Her moods change as abruptly as switching on and off a light. "Look at her." She points to Laurie, who grinds against the curtain, her back to the audience. Her buttocks are smooth and plump, divided by the black thong. Only the broadness of her shoulders gives her away. When she turns to face them, her breasts are startling, bouncing and swaying with her movements. "God made her, too," Kitty says.

"Yes," Dooly says, but not like that, he thinks, not like that. And Kitty stares at him, knows what he's thinking, he can tell. Her gaze fixes on him, her eyes the color of dark, rich chocolate. They're active, aggressive, grab him like hands. There's something completely physical in the way Kitty looks at the world, at him.

"Maybe Laurie is the lowly of the earth," Kitty says, "that Jesus talked about. That Jesus walked among."

The music stops and the sudden silence is deafening. Laurie disappears from the stage to scattered applause, mostly devoid of energy or enthusiasm. Some tables barely look up. They focus on their drinks, their conversations. Dooly sips his beer. He glances back at Kitty, her eyes still locked steadily on him. He coughs, feels uncomfortable.

"Yes," he says, "I think you're right." And at that moment he knows she's right, and he's bothered.

Like a shrewd animal that senses fear and vulnerability, she says quickly and sharply, "It's bullshit, you know. That doctor was right. My body healed itself."

"All right."

"I mean it, Dooly." She looks around. She takes a napkin from the dispenser and begins to shred it between her fingers. "That's the truth of it. It's too frightening otherwise. You know?"

"All right," he repeats.

"Stop saying 'all right,' goddammit!"

Dooly says nothing.

"I mean," she says, "how can you do that church service, over and over? It's so sterile, so stiff. It's...it's removed from life. It's not life. Don't you know?"

"Yes," he says.

She nods toward the empty stage. "Jesus would adore her. Jesus was like her. They...." She pauses. "They have a lot in common. Jesus was...two things, too."

Yes, he's thinking, yes. The cigarette smoke reaches up to the ceiling of the dark club. Surrounded by harsh laughter, Dooly says, "I am trying to work within the church. The church is my life."

"The church is nobody's life. The church is somebody's death. That cross...."

"That cross is eternal life."

"Shit. You healed me because you wanted to fuck me!"

• • •

Kitty walks around the apartment wearing nothing but the baseball cap and a pair of sheer blue bikini panties. Dooly can hardly look at her. He thinks if he keeps on looking at her he will be struck blind. Her body and legs are long and slim. She's so exquisite that she must be reserved for the divine.

Now she sits cross-legged in the middle of her bed—a mattress on the floor—with her guitar across her lap. She sings him some of the song she's writing. "The Morning Star...The Child Star...Holds you in its hand. You soar above the earth, you take the wings of morning...."

"Well?" Her eyes plead for his approval.

"It's lovely," he says.

She just looks at him, her head cocked to the side. Her hair spills straight down over her naked shoulder. She shakes her head back, tossing her hair, a habit that intrigues him. Her eyes drift away from him, as though she's thinking of something else, something far away. Then they focus on him again. He stares hungrily at her breasts. He cannot help it.

"I've got some good weed," she tells him. "Would you like some?"

He doesn't hesitate. "Yes."

•   •   •

In the dimly lit room, the smoke hangs heavy like a spicy incense from the joint they pass back and forth. Kitty's stereo, turned up loud, plays the Joan Baez album with Kitty's two songs on it. Joan Baez sings "Birmingham Sunday," the beat insistent, persistent. Kitty stands in the middle of the room, smiling at him. Completely naked now, she poses for him. Her breasts are small and plump, the nipples dark and no bigger than dimes, her pubic hair soft and fluffed. She's the most beautiful woman he's ever seen.

She laughs and begins to dance in an imitation of Laurie, giggling all the while. She licks her fingers and reaches down and gently begins to massage herself, her fingers softly probing the folds at the top of her vagina. When she looks at him her face is flushed. Her breathing is quick and her laughter bubbles in fragmented jerks. He cannot bear it any longer but he cannot move. She takes his hand—her fingers still wet and warm from her own body—and pulls him up and toward her. He surrenders.

•   •   •

Mac Kilpatrick looks at Dooly for a long time. Mac wears wrinkled Bermuda shorts and a sweat-stained T-shirt. He's been mowing the grass in the courtyard. Finally, he asks, "What's going on? Have you lost weight?"

"No," Dooly responds, "not that I know of."

"Something...."

"It doesn't concern you, Mac," Dooly interrupts.

"Well, excuse me." Mac feigns being offended. He mocks everything. He's older than Dooly, too old to still be a priest associate. Dooly knows that he drinks heavily. He's not married and seems to have no one in his life. Dooly has wondered if Mac is gay.

•   •   •

The vestry meets in the Parish Hall. The senior warden, Alois Richfield, teaches psychology at Peabody. An imposing woman, she's the only female senior warden in the Diocese of Middle Tennessee. The first woman to earn a Ph.D. from the University of Chicago, Alois doesn't call herself the "only" anything. She calls herself the "first." "I think we should invite colored to the church," she announces to the group. Dooly cringes at her use of the word colored. He grew up with the words "colored" and "darkies" and "niggers," words that were once comfortable words on his own tongue.

"You're right, Dr. Richfield," Dooly says. (He had once made the mistake of calling her Miss Richfield. "Don't call me 'Miss,'" she snapped, "because I haven't missed a damn thing!") "The church must become involved in this push for civil rights, for justice."

"Hold on," Judd Pasinetti says. "The Bible doesn't say anything about 'civil rights.'" Judd is a businessman.

"The Bible doesn't say anything about a lot of things, Judd," Dooly responds.

"No, it doesn't," says Wooster Gamble. He is an attorney. Dooly has never seen him without a suit on. Tonight he wears a gray one.

"I think the church ought to be concerned with what the Bible says, the salvation of souls, and not all this social agenda and everything," Judd says, sounding a lot like Bishop Philps. "And I think I represent the thinking of most of the members of St. Thomas."

"We can invite them into our church," Alois Richfield argues, "without marrying them."

"Amen to that," Clara Dingle says. "Where will it all stop?" Clara Dingle and her husband, an executive with Life and Casualty Insurance Company, live in Belle Meade, on Graymont, the next street over from Dooly and Paula.

Dooly sits with his mouth clamped shut, his lips a thin, narrow line across his face.

• • •

"Tell me why you did that. What made you do it?" Dooly asks Kitty. He's obsessed with her arrest at the sit-in trying to integrate the Krystal Restaurant. He knows that he's envious. Four years ago he read about Eldon Long's daughter being killed and wanted to go down to Hammond. Especially for the burial, when Martin Luther King was there. It was all so new then. He hadn't gone. Paula didn't want him to. "Your father would faint," she had said.

"I did it because I had to," Kitty responds matter-of-factly.

"You're from Mississippi," he argues. "You were raised just like I was. You had all that race stuff pounded into you from before you were even old enough to understand it."

"I did it because it was the right thing to do. Sing the praises of the right thing to do, right?"

"All right. Yes. Three hundred years of wrong. The church must...It must...."

"The church is impotent," she injects.

"All right. But you were healed in the church, whether you want to admit it or not. Your life was saved." He looks at her across the table. She eats a salad while he works on a hamburger. They are at a Shoney's Big Boy way out on Granny White Pike.

"Like I say," she shrugs.

"Well? Weren't you healed in the church? Yes."

She looks at him, chewing. She swallows. "Maybe. If I was, it was you, not the church." She stares levelly at him and finally asks, "Do you believe in angels, Dooly?"

After a minute he replies, "Yes. Of course. Yes, I believe in angels."

She reaches across the table, touches his hand.

"Then you need to know that Laurie is an angel."

Dooly puts his hamburger on his plate and looks at her. "Of course. Yes. Of course I know that Laurie is an angel."

"Do you?"

"Yes."

She toys with her salad, moving a slice of tomato around on her plate. "Angels bring messages, Dooly. That's what happens in that Bible of yours, right?" He doesn't answer. "Laurie has two missions in her life. First, to find out who she really is. And then to learn to live with who she is. Right?"

"Yes," he says. "I understand now that Laurie is more whole than the rest of us." He can't keep the slight sarcasm out of his tone.

"Then you've been paying attention."

Only days ago he would have thought she was joking. Now he knows how serious she is. She shakes her hair away from her face with that toss of her head.

"You have no idea, Kitty," he says, "how immersed in life I am. You mustn't sell me short."

She smiles. "You're still a stockbroker, Dooly, only now you're speculating in souls."

"And I take what I do very seriously."

"I know, I know." She reaches out again and lets her hand rest on top of his. "Come with me, Dooly, when the time comes."

"Where?"

"I don't know. Wild flowers don't care where they grow." It's a song she sings. "Somewhere right, we'll know when the time comes. There'll be signs."

He swallows, and his saliva wants to stick in his throat.

"All right," he says.

• • •

Long after the children have gone to school, Dooly walks downstairs. "Where were you, Dooly?" Paula asks. Her face is drawn, her eyes tired.

"I was with John Berry," Dooly lies. John Berry, a recovering alcoholic nine years sober, does Twelve Step work with AA. Dooly sometimes accompanies him on his missions of mercy.

Paula sits across the table from him, a fresh cup of coffee before her. Since the children were born, Paula has grown lean and hard. She exercises regularly and ferociously. She jogs. She now wears her hair in a pixie.

"Well? What's happening to us, Dooly?" she asks without looking at him. She knows he's lying about John Berry. He doesn't know how much she has figured out. They're too close for her not to know the truth.

They met when they were undergraduates at Vanderbilt. Paula was a basketball cheerleader, an honors student. Dooly, on the other hand, was barely getting by. A business major (to please his father), he had joined his father's fraternity, Kappa Alpha. Paula, the daughter of a barber in Columbia, Tennessee, was impressed with his family, their prominence, their money. When they graduated, Dooly went to work for Boggs & Simone, a brokerage firm in Atlanta, and they bought a house in Buckhead. They were happy, had lots of friends.

Then one morning Paula found Dooly in their bedroom crying. At first he couldn't tell her what was wrong. Finally he explained that he was unable to move because he could not decide which suit to wear. Diagnosed with severe clinical depression, Dooly saw a psychiatrist for two years. Then he came home one evening to tell Paula that he'd quit his job and was going to seminary to become a priest.

"You what?" she responded incredulously. "You what?" She couldn't believe he was serious. Then she resented him, naturally, because she was unable to understand. But she stuck by him. She had borne him two children. The years passed and they loved each other. She was a good woman.

She sighs, still is not looking at him. "Are you sure you weren't seeing her?" she asks softly.

"Who?" he asks, feeling stupid, guilty, a child caught at mischief.

"I don't know. But you of course do. Unless of course you've been see-ing prostitutes or something. I don't know. I don't know anymore."

"No, I was with John Berry," he insists. He hates lying. His voice is dry and hollow. He sips some orange juice that tastes lukewarm and bitter. They sit there for a long time, neither speaking. Finally he says, "It happens."

"Yes," she responds, "shit happens."

"No, not shit. Something good. Something pure. Something...."

"Stop it, Dooly! Spare me, okay?" He looks up to see tears tracking down her cheeks. "You can fool yourself into thinking that, but don't try to pull that on me, okay?"

"I couldn't help it, Paula."

"Oh, you could've helped it all right. Of course you could have helped it." She stands up then, walks across the kitchen floor, stands in front of the windows. Morning sunlight streams in. She turns to face him. "What's the matter, Dooly? Am I not good enough for you anymore?" She isn't crying now. She smirks at him. Her eyes look almost amused. "Huh? What is she, younger than me? Of course she is. A tootsie. A trophy. I would have thought you would be better than that, Dooly. But I should have known better. Yes. You are no better than your father." She spits it at him.

"No, I...."

"Yes! No better than that mean, evil old man! You are your father made over, Dooly!"

"You don't understand. I'm talking about love."

"Hah!" She laughs, a cackle, a stage laugh, edged and tart. Then she begins really laughing, throws her head back and bellows. When she looks back at him, still chuckling, trying to get her breath, he sees that the tears in her eyes are now tears of mirth. "Hah!" the laughter still bubbling up. "Love? Please, Dooly!"

"All right," he says, turning away.

"Love?" She grows suddenly serious again. "Love is those two little children who go to bed almost every night asking me where their daddy is."

"Don't."

"Love is staying with a person for almost eighteen years, in spite of reversals and abrupt switches in directions and downright crazy and destructive and abusive behavior, because you love him! When it's true and really love, you're not in love, you love! And that's...."

"Abusive?" Dooly asks. He stands, too. "Abusive? What the hell are you talking about?"

"Silences that go on for hours, days! Moods! Cutting me and everyone else off. You don't like anybody, Dooly! Maybe you should try like instead of love! Maybe you should want the people who love you to like you, instead of you always trying to please some remote father who doesn't give a doodly shit about you...."

"Please him? My God, I've been running from him. I've been rebelling my whole life against him and what he is. How can...."

"It's the same goddam thing, Dooly! Can't you see that?" Dooly stands very still and stares at her. "You are as far away from your own children as he is from you, and you don't even know it! And you are about to seal that distance for the rest of your life!"

Tears fill Dooly's own eyes now. He blinks them back. He can see a drawing of a dinosaur, remarkably detailed, attached to the refrigerator door with magnets, a drawing Oscar did in school. And he remembers the feel of Marie Louise's lean little body as she sits in his lap for reading, lithe, almost weightless. Curious and eager, she turns the pages in the book. She smells like vanilla and has his sky blue eyes.

Dooly cries openly now. Paula circles him, calm and predatory. "I'm not good enough for you, huh?" She hits him in the chest with her fist and he doesn't move. She stands very straight, gathering her strength, and hits him again in the same place. He shudders. She backs away from him. Slowly she unbuttons her blouse and then tosses it aside, standing in the middle of the room in the beams of sunlight, wearing only her blue shorts. "Not good enough," she says. Her breasts swell, dark tipped, pulled downward with their own rounded weight. They are as familiar to Dooly, their texture and their weight, as if they were a part of his own body.

She unbuttons her shorts and lets them slip down her legs. Her body, tanned, hard, an athlete's body at forty, is one of his regular rituals, for eighteen years of his life, as dear to him and as satisfying as any other. He cannot imagine living without her. It will be like learning to live without a vital organ or a limb. The prospect terrifies him, fills him with dread. He can't imagine being in the world and not seeing his children every day.

But there's no turning back. He knows that his old self has been destroyed and he's been created anew. Paula stands naked before him. "Make love to me, Dooly," she says, her eyes heavy-lidded, narrowed, "make love to me one last time."

Trance-like, he unbuttons his shirt. His fingertips tingle where they touch the buttons, like tiny electric shocks. He wears an old pair of gray sweat shorts, thick and soft from countless washings. He loosens the drawstring. He realizes that he's terribly aroused, but his member seems apart from him, detached, governed by another mind and another sensuality separate from his own. He thinks of Kitty, thinks for a moment that it's she and not Paula who stands there.

And then like an explosion behind his eyes he sees Rachel, Rachel thirteen years old and naked, in one of the empty cabins on the lane behind his grandfather's house. He can't recall where Carter was that day, nor why they were in the vacant cabin, only that they'd taken off their clothes and looked at each other's bodies, the sunlight streaming through the curtainless windows, the old cabin smelling musty and unused. He can see her now, every detail, like a vivid photograph, the way the light played over her smooth skin so much darker than his and yet lighter than he had expected. He could tell that she knew what the sight of her naked body was doing to him. He was sure he could have her, simply because she was a Negro. But when he moved toward her, she moved away, giggling.

"No son," she said. "Look at that thing," pointing to his erection. "It look like it gonna bust!" She laughed, dancing away from him.

"Rachel," he said, following her.

"No!" She turned back toward him, the ease and the laughter gone, her eyes hard and cold, lifeless. "No! I ain't one of your white whores!"

The memory of that moment pains him now—simply because she was a Negro—and the image of Rachel's young naked body moves inside his head now even as Paula moves slowly around him. "Make love to me. How could you do this to me, Dooly? To us?" And he knows he's so full of sin that it's strangling him. He lets the shorts drop and steps out of them. He remembers that when her mother died, the first thing Paula wanted to do when she found out was make love. And she cried and wept all the way through and screamed out in agony when she had an orgasm.

She pulls him down on top of her, hot and uncontrolled, right on the kitchen floor in the morning sunlight, and Dooly can smell the old shuck smell of that deserted cabin over twenty-five years ago. It's as though in some wild surreal way, something interrupted is now becoming complete. He knows that he's insane.

The two bodies writhe on the floor, their breathing coming in harsh pants and grunts. They try to hurt each other, to conquer. They roll and squeeze, cry out and moan. "How could you?! How could you?! How could you?!" she chants, her fists pounding his sweating, arching back, and he thrusts as fast as he can and with all the strength he can muster.

•   •   •

Dooly stands behind the antique carved wooden pulpit and looks out over his congregation, a lake of upturned faces, some expectant, some already bored, some eager, some indifferent. He sees Paula and Oscar and Marie Louise and he imagines that he sees Carter and Rachel at the ages of his own children sitting beside them. But there are no black faces here at St. Thomas the Apostle Episcopal Church. None at all. He wishes Kitty were here. He looks at Paula, and she stares back at him with a level, steady gaze.

He looks down at his notes. "As Jesus says in today's gospel," he begins, "'have you believed because you have seen me? Blessed are those who have not seen and yet have come to believe.'" His voice echoes in the old stone church. He looks out at them again but his eyes do not focus on them. Instead he sees the round stained-glass window with the angel at the back of the church, and he remembers that when Oscar was a baby, barely able to talk, he'd been fascinated by the window, had called it a "nangel." When he was a little older he told Dooly that the angel was peeking in the window at them.

"Jesus has just appeared to the disciples again after his resurrection," he goes on, "for the second time, and Thomas is now present, doubting Thomas, and he has placed his hands on Jesus's wounds and has exclaimed

'My Lord and my God!'" Dooly pauses. He looks back at his family and is astonished to see Carter and Rachel still sitting there, as big as life, both dressed in well-scrubbed and faded cut-off overalls, their summer uniform. And Dooly thinks he should be there, too, a boy their age, not dressed in overalls because his mother would no more have let him wear overalls than she would have let him walk naked down Washington Street at high noon on Saturday. Carter and Rachel sit calmly, and no one notices them. Not his family nor Alois Richfield nor Judd Pasinetti nor any of the rest of them, not Mac Kilpatrick who sits dozing against the wall beside the high altar, nor Bobby Gamble, this morning's thirteen-year-old pimply-faced acolyte. And when Dooly looks at Bobby he sees himself, dressed in identical vestments, kneeling in the cool dimness of St. Paul's in Hammond, looking up in awe at the huge window depicting the Ascension, the window dedicated to the grandmother that Dooly never knew. Everything he looks at plunges him into the past. His past. He blinks his eyes, looks out at the faces all washing together like dogwood petals on a Hammond sidewalk after a spring rain. And he can smell the rain, cool and sweet. His mind reels. He feels and hears the words coming from his lips and he doesn't know what they'll be until he says them.

Then he says, "What will you all think and feel when you get to heaven and find out that God is a Negro woman?"

He can sense how stunned they are. The incense from a thousand processionals and recessionals hangs in the thick air. After a long silence there's a stirring. Judd Pasinetti grins. He thinks Dooly is making a joke. Most of the faces of those who've heard him are turned down in frowns. Others stare blankly and then look around wondering what they've missed. "What will it take for you to believe that?" he asks. His voice rises, booms. "God is also a crazy old man who lives way back in the hills over near Monteagle, who lives off roots and nuts and berries, and who rages all the time about Jesus and nobody ever hears him because they don't want to know about it. How many people do you think actually heard John the Baptist cry out in the wilderness? Huh? How many? How many were gathered alongside that stream that day, when crazy John baptized the Christ? Three? Four? Would you have been there?!! Or would you have wanted proof before you bothered yourself?" Some heads nod in a kind of puzzled agreement. Paula's eyes have not left his face, her expression tentative and waiting, like a cocked pistol.

"God is a Negro woman," Dooly repeats, "and if you don't believe in that possibility, then I submit that YOU DON'T BELIEVE IN GOD!" His voice rolls out over them. They stir uncomfortably. In the corner of his vision, Dooly sees someone at the back of the church get up and leave. Others stand. Judd Pasinetti frowns now, his face red and swollen with anger. Dooly realizes he's on the verge of losing his own mind completely, that he's indeed insane. Everything is changing by the moment. Carter and Rachel still sit there looking at him, their eyes dark and round, sitting in the bloom of childhood. He'd not seen them for years before those two recent funerals in Hammond. It was as though time had robbed all three of them—not just of his grandfather and their mother—but of part of their substance, their core. Their identities had changed, and seeing them jolted him with that same knowledge about himself.

His voice, deep and strong, reverberates in the church. "You people don't know the pain, the horror that lurks just under the surface of your own hearts. You are too comfortable, too complacent. It's enough to make Jesus puke!" There is murmuring in the pews. "How can you hold yourselves above another human being? Do you seriously believe that Jesus would walk that walk with you? Whose side do you think Jesus would be on in this conflict raging about us right now? I'll tell you! He'd be walking in the streets with our black brothers and sisters, that's where he'd be! 'For what ye have done to the least of these my brethren, ye have done it also unto me!' Open your ears! Open your hearts, people! If you would be God's people, open your hearts!" He can feel the hostility radiating back toward him like heat. Many turn their backs on him and leave.

Dooly looks down at Carter and Rachel. Both smile at him. They know him better than anyone else ever will:

He's lithe and lean, twelve years old again, whirling and shooting the basketball at the goal tacked up on the side of the barn. When it goes through cleanly, Carter says, "That was pretty good, for a white boy." And Rachel's laughter gushes like an artesian spring.

The winter sun bakes them, packs the black mud of the barnyard as dry and smooth as asphalt. They smell the dry scent of hay and the rich odor of manure mixed with the acrid smoke of the coal fires up at the big house and in the cabins. The smoke streaks the high pale sky. "Let me play," Rachel begs, and Carter says, "No, you're a split-tail." "A split-tail," Dooly echoes. They have just learned the word. The boys laugh. "Shut up," Rachel says, "you don't know nothin, neither one of you."

And when he turns around one day and looks at Rachel, she has turned into a woman—the girl-woman in the deserted cabin—a lovely woman who has suddenly and unaccountably gone so far beyond the boys that their ages seem irrelevant. She knows more already than they ever will. Dooly knows now that it was the Eve in her, the Eve and the Mary, too, but he didn't know it then. "Don't forget I ain't one of your white whores." Her words reverberate through his mind. Her eyes flash like a spark on flint.

And Carter, bigger and stronger than Dooly, seems always to be Oscar Legrand's favorite, more like a son to him than Dooly. It's clear that he prefers Carter's company. That hurts Dooly more than even his adult self can admit. It is why he has grown apart from his father, opened the chasm as wide as an ocean.

"If you cannot open your hearts to your brothers and sisters, whether they be black or white or purple, then who can you open them to?" he asks the congregation. More people leave out the back of the church now. Parents usher young children toward the doors. "You turn your backs to me, you scorn me for what I say. When you say the Confession every Sunday it is hollow! Empty! Do you think God hears such a rote petition as that? Do you? Is it your words or your actions that God wants? Huh? LISTEN TO ME, YOU PEOPLE!"

He sees Paula stand and her lips shape the word "no." She says it several times. His children look at him inquisitively, as though he's a stranger. Only Carter and Rachel nod and smile encouragingly at him. They are pleased that he is creating a ruckus, as though the three of them are children together again in some mischief.

He raises his arms above his head. His chasuble flares out behind him like a cape. He imagines his eyes as beams of light, burning them all. Almost everyone stands now, gathers their wraps. The scene suddenly strikes Dooly as comical. His laughter floods out over their indignant comments, their shaking heads, their glares. "AND THE GUILTY SHALL

FLEE!" Dooly shouts and laughs louder. "GET OUT!" he shouts, "GET ON OUT OF THE TEMPLE! HURRY!"

• • •

The early Tennessee spring is still cold as Dooly and Kitty walk in the woods on the banks of the Harpeth River, the dogwood trees around them erupting with brilliant white. The air is clean, the sky clear.

It just happens, Dooly thinks, it just happens. It is sometimes only just beyond our understanding. But...but.... At night he dreams of Kitty. And he dreams of himself stretched out on the cross, hands nailed to the wood, and he awakens startled and sweating. So real was the dream he can taste the blood in his mouth. It takes him a while to reorient himself to their bedroom, to the glowing nightlight against the wall. Paula stirs, rumples the covers. Out of habit he puts his arm around her and presses close to her familiar warmth. She wakes slightly, enough to be aware of him, and inches herself to the other side of the bed, as far away from him as she can get.

Now in the woods he holds Kitty's hand. The skin of her hand is rough, perhaps her only physical flaw, he thinks, that and the slightly crooked tooth. The insides of her fingers feel like sandpaper. Wearing jeans and a plain gray sweatshirt that she has bought at Sears, she smells like soap and like rain-soaked trees. Dooly wears an old blue sweater and wrinkled khakis. Low briers grab at his cuffs as they walk along a path bordered by wild strawberries, pine needles, and stands of stunted ferns. Dooly thinks it's much too early for all the yellow butterflies they see dancing about, fluttering from bud to bud.

"Look," Kitty says, and they watch three butterflies weave in an intricate pattern just above the ground, as though they're playing some prescribed game. Kitty points at them, a smile on her lips. The butterflies, darting, pass through a shaft of sunlight and disappear.

"I...." he begins, "I...." Tongue-tied and clumsy, he can't go on. He had never intended to make such a choice, such a binding choice. "No," he says, "no, I can't do this." He thinks of his children, of Paula. Of his church.

"You've already done it," she points out.

He knows he can't erase his outburst in the church. Or all that Paula is going through. Now waiting calmly for him to leave, she's become withdrawn, miles away from him already. "But I can undo it. Something. I don't know what has gotten into me. This...this frightens me."

"Of course," she agrees. "I'm scared, too."

He thinks of Paula, just that morning, looking at him with large sunken eyes full of hurt. "Why, Dooly?" she asked him for the thousandth time. "Why?"

"There comes a time," he said, "when you have to lay it all down and follow."

"Lay us down, too, huh?"

"Yes."

Her eyes flashed with rage. "You should have thought of that before you married me. Before we had children. You son-of-a-bitch."

He looks at Kitty, at the sunlight in her hair. He knows there's no use resisting. He knows his fate was sealed that first day he saw her at the altar rail, when he looked into her eyes and felt his vicarial powers melting away. It was like coming back abruptly from self-hypnosis, from an hallucinatory state, a sudden wrenching return to the temporal that reminded him forcefully that he was first of all a man. But Jesus was, too, he thinks, Jesus was a man, too, maybe not first of all but a man nonetheless. He was human. And without sin, we are not human.

Kitty watches him, sees how the sunlight brings out the gray highlights in his blond hair. His eyes are a calm, sad blue, a brooding blue. She doesn't think she's ever known such depth in a man before. Not her father, certainly not her father. He would never have had the courage to do what Dooly is doing. All the other men in her life have been momentary, thin images, like shadow forms flashed on a wall and then gone. She had grown to like it that way, had grown comfortable with it, but Dooly grips her, solidifies something in her, excites her. He's dangerous because he's both momentary and forever.

She reaches out and touches his arm. He looks at her, his eyes yearning, eager, sad.

"Don't worry, Dooly," she reassures him. "This is right."

"All right."

"Lighten up, son." She punches him on the arm. She runs ahead of him. Laughing, he catches up. Their laughter echoes in the woods, among the saplings and the new growth. Crocus is in full bloom and daffodils, and redbud, blood-crimson, and dogwood blossoms like a mad painter's random and manic splashes of white.

She grabs him and holds on tight. And Dooly thinks *And is it in this time that we are reborn?*

●  ●  ●

On Sunday night, Kitty and Laurie have a party. A keg sits in a corrugated wash tub in Kitty's living room. The apartment is crowded. Laurie meets Dooly at the door wearing a low-cut sequined green evening dress. She kisses him on the forehead. They're almost the same height. Dooly knows that her kiss will leave lipstick on his forehead.

On the stereo a Julie London album plays. Cigarette and pot smoke hang in the air. Laurie's roommate, another female impersonator at Papa John's, arrives in male clothes but is heavily made up. His name is Cecil and he dances as Cecile. He's gay and has no intention of taking female hormones like Laurie. He thinks Laurie is crazy to do that. He tells Dooly, "I would never cut off my cock. I love cocks."

"You've introduced me to a whole new world," Dooly tells Kitty, and Kitty punches him in the ribs.

"Stick with me, son, and you'll really go places."

Kitty wears skin-tight jeans and a loose-fitting dark gray blouse. She gives Dooly a toke in the bedroom and kisses him on the cheek. People sit around on the floor and on the mattress. A man with a beard strums a guitar, competing with Julie London in the other room. He sings "Michael Row the Boat Ashore," and several others sing along with him. Then they give Kitty the guitar, force it on her, and she sings "Upriver" and then "The Midnight Train to Mobile."

A girl in a leather mini-skirt sits on Dooly's lap. She kisses him on the ear, puts her wet sticky tongue in his ear. The party spills out into the hallway and down the hall. A boy and girl argue in murmuring tones in the corner. Shrill laughter rattles the close air of the party. Hoop cheese and soda crackers and mounds of pretzels in plastic bowls fill table tops. Canned smoked oysters and boiled peanuts. Everyone throws the shells on the floor.

They want Kitty to sing again. They always want her to sing. People jostle for positions on the floor before her or stand around the edge of the room three deep. She decides to try out "Take the Wings of Morning" on them:

"If you want to fly
Away from heat and rain,
Away from tears and pain, then
Take the wings of morning..."

Tears glisten in her eyes as she sings. The song has a gospel flavor, high and tinny. It comes out of those clapboard churches that dot the scrubby red clay hills where she's from. Her voice is clear and pure as mountain stream water. At the same time it's rough and coarse—strong and powerful and as vulnerable and brittle as new crystal, full of confidence and fear, of bravado and coyness. As she sings, the room is silent as falling snow.

"You are far from harm
You are home again...
You fly to outstretched arms...
On the wings of morning."

When she finishes the song her voice hangs in the air like an echo.

•   •   •

One of Laurie's friends from Fisk University calls and tells them to watch the late news on Kitty's small portable black and white. A local newscaster reports: "In what surely will go down in history as 'Bloody Sunday,' hundreds of Negro demonstrators were dispersed by force and ridden down by Alabama state troopers on horseback in a confrontation at the historic Rooster Bridge, just outside the small town of Hammond." They see grainy film then of the troopers, the horses and their hooves; then the troopers on foot swinging their night sticks, wading into groups of people, some of them women and elderly. Dooly goes warm and cold with the beer and the wine he's drunk and the pot he's smoked. His brain floats. The voice-over of the announcer continues. "Hammond is the hometown of

Alabama Governor Oscar Legrand, who, early reports say, ordered the troopers to stop a planned march to the state capitol to deliver voting rights petitions." The pictures go on and on: a woman, old with gray hair, falls to the ground while a mounted policeman flails at her with his stick; panicked groups of demonstrators run into the deep ditches alongside the highway. "The governor's office issued no statement today, but Putnam Lawley, the head of the Alabama state troopers, said that the dispersal order was issued to preserve the peace and security of the state highways. The Negroes, he said, were guilty of illegal assembly."

Dooly stands transfixed, transported, pulled back again to his beginnings. The images of Rooster Bridge are familiar. "In an exclusive interview with NBC News," the announcer says, "the leader of the Negro demonstrators, the Reverend Eldon Long, said the demonstrations would continue." And Dooly sees Eldon Long, a man that he's known most of his life. Standing next to him is Carter. Dooly's heart stops. Carter holds a bundle. It looks like a baby, wrapped in a blanket.

"We will march all the way to Montgomery," Eldon Long states. His right eye is bandaged. "We shall not be deterred and we invite everyone all over the country to come and join us. We shall overcome!" "Yes, Yes," cry those around him. Carter Taylor peers into the lens of the camera as though he's looking directly into Dooly's eyes.

Carter holds the baby in the crook of his arm. Dooly sees Kitty looking at Carter and the baby, too, her eyes shining, and he feels such a surge of love for her and for Carter that it almost knocks him off his feet. He can't move. He thinks he must be very high because he hears old man Raybob Sneed's voice then, quoting scripture: "My name is Legion, for we are many."

The blanket-wrapped child seems to pulse white in Carter's arms, to glow, and Dooly sees that Kitty recognizes the glowing, too. He reads the message clearly in her eyes; he knows they'll go down there, together. Dooly knows that the bundle Carter holds, the child, Carter's child, is the sign that Kitty had predicted that day they sat across from each other in Shoney's Big Boy. Dooly had known the sign would come, the sign for him to come back home.

# Carter

AS GRAND DRAGON OF THE LOCAL HAMMOND KLAN, Lucious Willie knows he holds a desirable and powerful position. He can't think of a better platform from which to promote his main agenda: the protection of America from the Africans and the Asians and the other dark hordes of the earth.

He'd been kidded about his name all his life. Even his father, who did little but sit around in his undershirt and drink beer all day, teased him. Lucious awoke one morning years ago and said to himself, "All right. All right. If my daddy and mama gave me a nigger name, then I'll get back at them by killing me some niggers." Lucious had grown to intensely hate all people of color, convinced that their very presence mocked him. So he began his campaign against them by helping to plant the bomb at Eldon Long's church that had killed Long's daughter. He was also there in '61 when the wop-yankee-white-nigger-outside-agitator was tortured to death. He's never been caught for these crimes. Except Lucious doesn't see them as crimes. He considers them patriotic acts.

On the Saturday morning before the confrontation at Rooster Bridge, Lucious sees Billy Singleton checking out at Waite's Store. Billy's buying a pound of baloney and a sack of cornmeal. He's lost so much weight that Lucious barely recognizes him, then he thinks to himself that Billy looks like what they mean when they say the wrath of God. Lucious and Billy are friends. They're in the same Klavern. They drink together sometimes at the Good Lady's, a beer joint that sits up on stilts at the edge of the swamp near the Coosa River Bridge. You can sit out on the screen porch and listen to the tree frogs and katydids and bullfrogs.

"Billy, my man, you been on you a diet, I see."

"No goddammit I ain't been on no diet," Billy says, visibly angry.

"Well, I mean, you done trimmed down some."

"What's on your mind, Lucious." As a boy, Billy had teased Lucious mercilessly about his name.

Lucious shrugs. They walk out the door together and stand on the sidewalk next to Billy's pickup. The spring sun is hot, bright.

"Big doins with the niggers," Lucious tells him. The word is that tomorrow they'll meet at all the churches, march through town, and gather out at Rooster Bridge. "The National Guard's on standby." Lucious squints in the sunlight. His face is pale and freckled, his hair a reddish orange. The sidewalk is Saturday-crowded, and he lowers his voice as a group of Negroes walks by. A family from out in the country somewhere. "There'll be almost two hundred state troopers tomorrow. That's the word."

"Uh-huh," Billy nods, and Lucious peers at him. Billy seems distracted, uninterested in what Lucious is saying.

Annoyed, Lucious says, "I thought you, as a good Klansman, would be interested in all this."

"My mind is just on a lot of other things, Lucious."

"Well, you better get your mind back where it belongs!"

Billy doesn't look at him. "I don't know, Lucious. I... I got some, you know, personal problems."

"Wait a minute, now. Is this here the Billy Singleton I know? Now you listen here to me, boy...."

"Just let me alone!" Lucious thinks he looks like he's going to cry. Personal problems. That must mean that wife of his is spreading it around on him. Lucious is surprised because he thought he would have heard about that.

"You can't let personal problems get in the way of your patriotic duty," Lucious lectures sternly. Billy tries to move away, and Lucious grabs him by the arm. "You owe it to all your buddies, Billy. We depend on each other. You better straighten up and fly right, son."

Billy hangs his head, then looks up at Lucious. His face is skeletal, his eyes sunk back into his head. "All right," he replies.

"Whatever personal problems we all got ain't nearly as important as our mission. Don't be forgettin that."

"I won't," Billy says, "I promise."

"All right. Well. There's gonna be a countermarch or something. We'll think of something. Sometime next week. We can't let them niggers get away with it."

"With what?"

"With everything!" Lucious continues to inspect him curiously. "Goddammit, Billy, you sure as hell got to get your mind on it."

Billy puts his hand on his truck door handle. "I got to go, Lucious."

"Well, go then, goddammit. But I'll look for you next week. Don't think I won't."

"All right." Billy hoists himself up into his truck with its deerskin-upholstered bench seat. The knob of the gear-shift lever is decorated with a color picture of a naked woman. Billy's high school graduation tassel dangles from the rearview mirror. A gun rack in the back window contains only Billy's casting rod. "I'll see you, hear?" Billy calls.

"Yeah." Lucious watches Billy back out and turn down the street. Now there's a man who wants to back down, Lucious thinks. There's a man who needs to be encouraged. Lucious smiles. The tailgate of Billy's truck has a faded LEGRAND FOR GOVERNOR bumper sticker.

●　　●　　●

As soon as they see the troopers on horseback massed on the other side of the bridge, the marchers know there will be trouble. ("Ain't nothin gonna happen," Carter had insisted to Karla, "they ain't gonna do nothin!" "No, you can't take him," she had wailed, "my little baby!" "He's goin. He's gonna see this. He's gonna know it all firsthand!" "He's just a baby, Carter!" He had left her crying at the house.) The troopers appear to be poised and alert, like a cavalry unit. Rachel and Carter walk near the front of the column of marchers, Carter holding Eshu. The sight of the troopers thrills Carter. He wants something to happen, longs for action and change. He's made up his mind that he'll walk all the way to Montgomery. Ernest Vance warned him about losing his job, but he doesn't care. He imagines facing Oscar Legrand at the end of the line, walking up to him, holding out Eshu and saying, "Here. Meet your grandson." In his imagination he puts Eshu down, then slices Mr. Oscar's pale throat with a straight razor. He can see the bright red blood gush. Tears spring to his eyes. He winces at the image.

A soft breeze ruffles Eldon Long's necktie and Mose Bell's, too. They march in the front line, along with an old woman named Estelle Benson and a young boy named Kenneth Collins. Almost a thousand people, dressed in their Sunday finery, form lines four abreast that reach down Jefferson Road and on back into town. They stop traffic where Jefferson Road intersects Highway 80 and turn east on 80 toward the bridge and Montgomery fifty miles away. Because all the law officers wait on the other side of the bridge, the marchers halt the traffic themselves. Horns blow at them, and one man in an eighteen-wheeler shakes his fist, his face red.

●   ●   ●

It happens so fast that nobody realizes what's going on. They expect the troopers to try to stop them. Governor Legrand's office issued a statement that the march to the capitol cannot take place because it's "an endangerment to public safety." This phrase is tossed about and draws much laughter. It's a beautiful day and everybody is in good spirits. There is loud talk, laughter, some singing. They expect Eldon Long to be faced down by whomever is in charge of the troopers, maybe even Putnam Lawley himself. The word among the marchers is that Eldon will refuse to stop. If the troopers physically block them, they plan to disperse and try again tomorrow. And then the day after that. Some newspaper reporters and television cameramen hover near the bridge, as though they expect something big to happen, as though they've been forewarned. One cameraman has climbed up near the draw of the old bridge itself.

After the first twenty-five or thirty rows of marchers cross the bridge, the troopers on horseback make their move. They begin to trot toward the marchers. The marchers stop as the troopers trot toward them. It quickly becomes apparent that the troopers on horseback don't intend to stop. They plow into the marchers, riot sticks flailing, to the shocked screams and yells of the crowd. Carter protects Eshu with his arm and tries to shield Rachel as well, but he's sideswiped by a horse and pushed into the ditch. Carter goes down on his knees and only then realizes that his forehead is bleeding. "Rachel!" he yells, "Rachel!" Hunched over in the ditch, he cradles the baby, grits his teeth, feels his muscles tense so tightly that they pain him. He hears grunts and moans, the dull, metallic clanking of the shod hooves on the pavement, the yells of the troopers. Amidst the chaos, Carter sees two young men clinging to the stirrups of a horse. He watches the uniformed man and the horse go tumbling into the ditch, the horse rolling. Trooper's bullwhips lash the air. Tear gas canisters pop like firecrackers, and the acrid gas drifts along in streams in the breeze. The air is dense with the gas and dust and cries of pain and fear. Carter's eyes fill with tears. He hugs Eshu to his chest and covers the baby's face with the blanket. He braces for whatever will come.

● ● ●

Sam Michaels's eyes sting and water from the gas. Twenty-six years old, he is two months out of the police academy. He feels his powerful horse move between his legs, the thick muscles rippling. He can smell the horse, like dried straw. He can smell the people, too, as they struggle and break and run, sweat and lilac perfume and the clean, bleachlike odor of Sunday clothes. His senses are as acute as they have ever been in his life. He thinks of his horse—named Limerick—as swimming in a human flood. Excited and frightened half to death, Sam feels his heart race in his chest.

Sam doesn't want to hit anybody. But he doesn't want the others to see that he doesn't swing his riot stick. He sees his buddy Jimmy Houghton jab somebody with a cattle prod and hears the scream even above the roar. He thinks that maybe this is only a bad dream, that he'll wake up any second. But he knows better. It's a nightmare, but it's real. He hears the screams, the cries, and the grunts. Limerick stumbles, then surges forward. Sam sees someone, an old man, go down beneath his horse's hooves.

His horse turns sideways and rears, and Sam waves his riot stick over his head like a cowboy twirling a rope. Feeling stupid, he wonders why he is here, why they're doing this. Like a good soldier, he's following orders.

He has never thought about colored people much; they've always just been there. Almost choked on the tear gas, he realizes that up on the horses, the troopers are getting more of the gas than the people on the ground. Most struggle to put on their gas masks. Sam makes no move toward his. The gray gas drifts by his face as though he's flying through a cloud. He knows it's stupid not to put on the mask.

The trooper next to him, a man he doesn't know, his face red with effort, hits a white-haired old woman with his stick. Sam hears the dull thunk the stick makes on her skull and he watches her go down in a clump of crabgrass beside the pavement. She reminds him of the old woman who used to cook for his grandmother. Hess. He thinks for a moment that it is Hess, then he remembers that Hess is dead; besides, his grandmother lives a hundred miles away, clean on the other side of the state. Troopers all around him drop their riot sticks and bullwhips and cattle prods to struggle with their masks. The horses' shoes make sparks fly from the pavement. That strikes Sam as funny, and he begins to laugh. He laughs and laughs.

• • •

Carter deflects the blow with his one free arm, locks arms with the trooper, and pulls him from the saddle. The trooper's heavy boots hit the asphalt, and his gas mask comes off. A white man with a paunch, he seems stunned to be off his horse, standing on the ground, face to face with Carter. He breathes in short, quick gasps. Carter knows the panic he's feeling; the stinging hot gas is closing his own throat, burning it like liquid fire. The two men just look at each other. Then the white man pleads, "Don't cut me. Please don't cut me." He wears no side arm. No shots have been fired. They are armed only with the hard, dense riot sticks, like shortened pool cues.

Carter would cut him if he had his razor. He wishes he'd brought it, tucked it into his shoe or looped it around his neck on a cord like some of his friends do, like the razor in the waking dream about his father. Carter used to carry a razor back before he got married. Now his straight razor, honed so sharp it can draw a drop of blood with a mere touch, is hidden away in some drawer. Someone bumps Carter from behind. At the same time a horse whirls behind the trooper and its flank crashes into him. Carter sees the startled, scared look on the trooper's face as his legs fly out from under him and he hurtles into the ditch. Carter backs away, looking all around him, holding his baby boy close against his chest.

• • •

Eldon Long won't run. He eases Mose away from the troopers into the weeds of the ditch, holding onto his arms and settling the older man into the bushes like putting him to bed. Then he turns and faces the troopers and holds his arms over his head. Straight up, as though he's reaching to heaven. "Jesus is Lord!" he shouts just as a blow comes from nowhere and bounces off his forehead, causing him to drop to his knees with bright squiggly stars flickering through his head. He knows his knees are skinned raw on the rough pavement, the britches of his new suit ripped. But he thinks first of his wife, Cora, and then thinks *they are not trying to really hurt us they are trying to humiliate us like a pack of dogs and we mean no more to them than dogs, than...*

• • •

Carter looks around. He doesn't know what to do. The men seem to avoid him now, probably because they see he carries the child. The gas chokes him. Despite his urge to fight back, he can't with Eshu in his arms. He keeps the blanket tight over the baby's nose and mouth. Then he spies Rachel, standing in the road. He thinks she stands in the exact same place she did when it all started. The melee seems to part and flow around her, as though she's a sturdy tree in a violent flood. Nothing touches her or harms her at all. She stands very straight, the bandanna on her head, a smile on her face. A strange, resigned smile.

• • •

It's over as quickly and abruptly as it started. It just stops. A sudden silence is gradually broken by whimpers and choking sounds and coughing from people on the ground, by the horses' hooves growing distant and muf-fled. The chemical burning smell of tear gas hangs in the air. The remote, faraway clock on the courthouse tower downtown chimes two times. Two o'clock. The same sound the clock makes every workday and every sleepy Sunday early afternoon, ringing out over Hammond and settling into all the crannies of peaceful post-church, post-Sunday-dinner quiet.

● ● ●

They sit at the kitchen table in their mother's house. Carter still thinks of it as his mother's house. He has a slight cut on his forehead and a small lump; it had been a glancing blow. Karla brags that she knew all along what was going to happen to them. "Mose said it would," she says. "He predict-ed this a long time ago."

"That they would stop us, yes," Carter responds. "Not what they did."

"You shouldn't oughtta took Eshu. Didn't I tell you, now?"

"He's fine. I can take care of my son."

"You didn't have no business goin either, Rachel," Karla adds. "That's man's work."

"Shit," Rachel utters.

Carter senses bad blood growing between his sister and wife. They'd once been close. His mother served as a calming, steadying influence. And her death has set them all adrift.

Karla resents Rachel's attitude toward Eshu. "It's like he's hers," Karla complained bitterly to Carter a few days ago. "Hers and yours! Like y'all had him together and not me and you!"

"Shut up that talk," Carter responded, angry. They lay in bed in the darkness, before sleep, not touching.

"Well, she don't need to stay up here so much. She got her own house."

"All right!" Carter turned over, turned away.

Karla resents that Carter and Rachel went to the march together, have experienced it together, though she could have gone with them. They practically begged her to go. A heavy, thick silence encircles the table. Everyone is nervous, on edge. Word is out that Reverend King is on his way. Eldon Long thinks the federal government will force Governor

Legrand to let them march. They will regroup and try again later in the week. Eldon Long appeared on television, inviting everyone to come to Hammond and join them.

"You can't take Eshu on that march," Karla says.

Carter doesn't answer.

"You'll lose your job," Karla warns.

"So be it," Carter says, and Karla cuts her eyes away and pouts.

"You've got a son now," she reminds him.

"Yes I know I have a son. You don't have to tell me that."

The only sound in the room is the ticking of the clock. Rachel fingers her earrings, big gold hoops. After a few moments she says, "When I was in New Orleans I heard of policemen grabbing women's earrings and just yankin em off, right through the flesh. They would round up women off the street and rip their ears. I don't know why. Because they could, I guess. I thought maybe they might try to do that with me today." She sits very still. "But they didn't." Carter and Karla both look at her. "They couldn't," she says.

Carter still cannot get everything straight in his mind, the events of the afternoon. Nobody was killed, but Estelle Benson has been hospitalized with a concussion and a broken shoulder. Others with broken bones have been treated and released. Old Dr. Mason showed up with his bag and fixed up scrapes, bruises, and some cuts. His new assistant, Dr. Hughes, fresh in town, helped him. A tall, thin young man, Dr. Hughes kept saying over and over, "This is a travesty! A travesty!"

Mose Bell came away with a split lip and brier scratches all over his legs, and Eldon Long a purple knot on his head. After the troopers pulled back, everyone retreated back across the bridge, straggled in groups toward town. Instinctively they returned to the churches: Rising Star AME, New Hope Baptist, Mount Zoah Holiness. Whichever church they'd come from they went back to without instruction, without orders. Carrying Eshu, Carter and Rachel cut down Jackson Street toward Shiloh Baptist Church, where they'd left the car. People milled around everywhere.

Carter was brought up short by the sight of a white woman in the throng, and then he saw immediately that it was Miss Amy Legrand. Wearing a dark blue polka-dot dress and a blue straw hat with a veil, she spotted him in the crowd and started toward him. People moved aside to let her pass. All of them knew her. "Afternoon, Miss Amy," they greeted, as though it were an ordinary Sunday afternoon. And she nodded to them, called them by name, all the time her eyes fixed on Carter.

"Carter. Rachel," she called. "You are all right."

"Yes," Carter said.

She stood looking up at him, her eyes like bits of flint. The sun shone directly in her face, but she didn't squint. She'd just come from church and held a small red leather-bound prayer book. She looked around at the milling people and then back at him.

"This is madness," she said.

"Yes mam."

"I don't think Oscar...that Oscar knew...." She didn't finish. She shook her head, then looked at Rachel. "Rachel, are you all right?"

"Yes, Miss Amy, I am."

The older woman's eyes darted back and forth from one to the other several times. Then she looked at the baby. "This is Eshu," not a question but a statement. She reached out and touched the blanket, pulled it back to reveal his face. Eshu's eyes were wide and alert. "He was there," she said, "he was in this crazy thing."

"Yes mam," Carter replied.

"When you were babies, when you both were children...." she began, but again she didn't finish. She just looked at them, an ache in her eyes so deep that it seemed part of the color. Carter knew in that moment that Miss Amy knew everything, too, had known it all along. Her eyes were moist. "Thank God you are all right," she said.

●   ●   ●

The dim, low-wattage lights in the Upper Room I Am Temple burn into the night. "Devil worshippers!" Brother Kenneth Grable shouts. "They are all around us, they are everywhere!" He wears a white shirt open at the collar, cuffs rolled halfway up his forearms. Sweat drips from his face, his yellow hair matted and damp. Twenty people sit on crude benches and cool themselves with cardboard fans. Leland Williams, a skinny man with soot-black hair, sits on the small altar-stage with his electric guitar across his lap. Jack Simmons, his hair cut in a flattop over his broad, flat face, sits behind a set of drums. "Je-heee-sus saves us," Brother Grable shouts, "by his blood and his mercy! Amidst them out there," and he waves toward the black windows, "who are agents of the very devil who would drag you down, drag you away from the Lord and Savior Jesus Christ! Amen! Amen!"

Leland starts to play and Jack follows. They pick up each other's beats in a jazzy version of "Leaning on the Everlasting Arms." There are no hymnals, but they all know the song. "What a fellowship! What a joy divine! Leaning on the everlasting arms!" Brother Grable paces back and forth, waving his arms, conducting like a maestro. "Leannning… Leannnnniiiing.…Safe and secure from all alarms…!"

Billy and Jesse Merle sit in the front row. Jesse Merle sings, her shrill voice rising like a siren in a storm. "Leeeeeeaning…leeeeeeaning.…" The drums and cymbals beat and clash, the guitar screams with a voice of its own. Billy is doubled over with a pain that sears his belly like a hot poker. It's hot in the cramped little white-framed church, as hot as an oven, though the spring night outside feels cool.

The hymn grows more frenzied, more insistent. Brother Grable opens a wooden box at his feet and pulls out the snake, a brown timber rattler, thick, about five feet long. His arms bulge with the effort of lifting it. The snake's head weaves back and forth as though in time to the music, its dry rattling merging and melding with the drums' whisper. Brother Grable holds the snake before his face, then lifts it over his head and prances around. The people, still singing, press forward, raising their arms and reaching, but Brother Grable yells, "No. No. This snake is Billy's. Billy's!"

Billy, almost drunk, stands up, and the room swims and rages. In preparation for this, he consumed a half pint of Cabin Hollow Bourbon and smoked two reefers. The pain in his stomach feels like a dull knife. His head and his ears hurt with the noise of the music. He sees the snake weaving in the air. He thinks for a moment that he's going to puke. The snake is looking at him. Billy has killed thousands just like it in the swamps, has shot them with his shotgun. He'd held them down with a forked stick and ground their heads into the stones with the heel of his boot. He'd caught them in his net when seining for minnows and held them underwater until they drowned.

He wonders if the snake knows what he's done to its brethren. Maybe it does. It is the old accursed one, the one that God made to crawl on its belly on the earth. "Leaning...Leaning...." They sing the song for the third or fourth time. The presence of the snake makes everyone delirious. Billy thinks it makes everyone crazy, including him. Brother Grable's eyes shine like a madman's. He holds the snake out to Billy, and Billy reaches. Brother Grable pulls it back like a child playing a trick.

Billy stands, his hands held out. He'll take the snake. He'll try anything that might relieve his pain. Brother Grable walks coyly about, ignoring Billy. He pretends that Billy's not there. Billy wants the snake; he wants it now. He wants to feel it, to hold it. The music pounds in his ears. He wonders whether he should be singing, too. He doesn't know the words to the song. He doesn't know anything but that he wants the snake.

Now Brother Grable stands in front of Billy. Sweat glistens on his face, and his hair sticks out wildly from his head. "Take it, Billy," he commands, "this one's yours." Billy reaches out, grasps the snake. Cold to the touch, it's much heavier than Billy had expected. Billy lifts it in front of him and can feel the snake's muscles rippling beneath its skin as it slowly revolves. The snake smells like rotting cucumbers.

The frantic music and the babbling and the shouts soften as though some hand has reached in and lowered the volume. Everything around him moves in a kind of dreamlike slow motion. The only things in the world then are Billy and the snake, bound up together as though they're one. He holds the snake up level with his face and looks into its eyes. The moment seems to last forever.

Then the serpent—so quickly and deftly that Billy doesn't really see it, only feels it— the serpent strikes him on the cheek, a swift thumping that jars him like a small child's fist. Billy's eyes widen in disbelief and horror as he begins to feel the sting, and he watches helplessly as the snake strikes him on the arm. He sees the two tiny red spots that rapidly become one larger spot, one pool of blood that begins to spread like a stain, and Billy flings the snake against the wall. He hears Jesse Merle scream. He hears everyone scream. What had been a vacuum in his head fills again with noise, and he whirls as though to flee.

"No! No! Don't let him run!" he hears someone yell. He thinks it's Brother Grable. He slumps toward the floor as hands grab him from every direction. Colors whirl around him. Then everything goes dark and silent.

• • •

Billy awakens the next morning in his bed, when the sun is already high. His head aches from the bourbon, and his tongue feels dry. He sits up. Jesse Merle's not there. The house is quiet. He looks at the clock and sees that it's already after ten. He realizes with a start that the pain is gone completely from his gut. He cannot believe it. His arm is dotted with two tiny clotted fang wounds, but there's no swelling, no pain. He struggles out of the damp and tangled sheets and into the bathroom and throws on the light. He looks into the mirror.

He sees the two punctures like tiny pinpricks on his cheek, just above his morning whiskers, which look like tiny black iron fillings on the skin. "Why by God," he says aloud, "that wasn't even no poisonous snake!" He stands there, looking into his own hollow, sunken eyes. But the pain is gone, he thinks, the pain is really gone. His stomach feels sweet and empty. He is hungry. He grins. He starts to whoop with joy but then stops. But if that wasn't no poisonous snake, he asks himself, then why, then, is the pain gone? It was poisonous, and the poison has not hurt him. It has cured him. Stunned with the magnitude of this revelation, Billy cannot speak for a long time. "Sweet Jesus," he finally utters softly.

• • •

They come from everywhere. News footage of the confrontation at Rooster Bridge, televised all over the country, all over the world, also featured an interview with Eldon Long inviting everyone to join the march. It played over and over. President Lyndon B. Johnson issued an order that the march must be allowed to proceed, and he threatens to send in federal troops to protect the marchers. Governor Legrand's statement stipulates that if the marchers are protected, then he will allow it. He will protect them himself with the Alabama National Guard. "My only concern," he states, "as it has been all along, is the safety of the citizens of Alabama."

They arrive by the hundreds. Young white people dressed in ragged denim with long, messy hair. Nuns in their old-fashioned habits. Celebrities: Harry Bellafonte; Joan Baez; Peter, Paul and Mary; Sammy Davis Jr.; Pete Seeger; and Stokely Carmichael. Martin Luther King Jr. is already here, along with Ralph Abernathy, and they've set up headquarters at Shiloh Baptist Church, located on the edge of town in a field that's rapidly becoming a huge campground, with tents and tarpaulins. Marchers continue to come from everywhere: Michigan and California, the Northeast and the Midwest. Black people from all over the South migrate to Hammond. They stay in every spare room, on every porch, sleeping in hammocks and on pallets on the floor.

Hammond resembles a giant military encampment. Smoke from cook fires arises every noon and evening, hanging like a low, thin cloud amidst laughter and music, singing, and nightly services in Shiloh Baptist Church. King, Abernathy, Andrew Young, and Eldon Long preach fiery emotional sermons greeted with cries of AMEN and YES, YES, UH-HUH! "We shall not be moved," they shout. "We shall overcome," they all sing.

The people of Hammond have never seen anything like it. The closest thing was the so-called "Freedom Summer" a few years back, when the Freedom Riders passed on through on Highway 80, crossing Rooster Bridge on their way to Meridian and Jackson beyond. "Outside agitators" had also been here before, like in the Spring of '61 when SNCC sent in several young white people to organize voter registration in Noshobe County. One of the workers had been murdered. That was followed by the explosion that destroyed part of Eldon Long's church and killed his daughter. People had gathered for her funeral march back then. Even Martin Luther King was present, but it had been nothing like this.

"Bunch of goddam beatniks," Wallace Walker, the butcher at Waite's Store, calls them. He is talking to his co-worker Gloria McMillan. Wallace has just waited on two young boys with hair down to their asses who told them they were from New Hampshire. He ground them two pounds of hamburger. They had called it "hamburg." "They don't even know how to talk American," he says disgustedly to Gloria.

"Sheeeeeeeit," Gloria adds, "you can't tell the girls from the boys."

"Probly ain't much difference," Wallace shrugs. They've done a booming business since the beatniks started arriving. They've sold case after case of soft drinks. Mr. Waites just told them they're completely out of beer and will have to wait for the truck from Tuscaloosa to deliver more. "Niggers and nigger lovers will put away the beer now," old Waites commented, as though revealing some great truth to them.

"Some of my friends went over there to watch em last night," Gloria tells Wallace. Thin and blonde, she wears a white apron streaked with brown, dried blood. "They seen Harry Belafonte walkin around. Now, he's good-lookin for a colored man."

"He's mostly white," Wallace points out. Wallace's belly pushes out in front. His thinning hair is dark, and he wears long, thick sideburns. "He's near about all white is how come he's so good-lookin."

"They seen two boys kissin one another on the mouth, right out in the open. French kissin," Gloria reports.

"Now that's some scum there," Wallace says. "I wouldn't give you two cents for no goddam queer."

•　•　•

The two boys, Philip Music and David Miles, are from Esto, New Hampshire. Nineteen years old, they have been lovers since they were twelve. David Miles is short and heavy and has no neck to speak of. Philip is of medium height with sandy hair and lanky arms. His face is angular and tanned. One of his front teeth is chipped. They call each other Sal and Dean, after the characters in *On the Road*, and they even tell other people that those are their names. Most people don't even respond. Occasionally someone will look long at them and shrug and say, "Shit."

They cut through alleys on their way back to the campgrounds. They cannot believe the kind of poverty black people live in down here. Neither of them ever knew a black person until they left home. The first one they met had been a young pool hustler in Scranton who'd taken every last dime they had. He told them he was from Harlem, but the man who ran the poolroom told them he was from Brewster, New York, and was a scholarship student at Bennington. They learned that you couldn't trust anybody, a lesson they learned over and over again. "You can't believe what anybody tells you," Philip Music would say. They'd been sold magic mushrooms that made them deathly sick instead of high. They smoked rabbit tobacco laced with oregano. They snorted talcum powder. They'd been beaten up in boxcars and arrested for loitering and thrown in jail in Naperville, Illinois.

They came to Hammond with a girl they had met in Florida, a woman, really. About forty, her name is Chestnut Paw Paw. "What the hell kind of name is that?" they asked. "It's the name of the new heart," she told them. She wore dresses made of strings of beads. The three of them had lived together for a while in a wooden shack on a sandy back street in Destin. She told them she was a poet. "Everybody is going there," she said, "let's hit the road." "Where the hell is it?" Philip asked. "Alabama." "Alabama? Jesus!" "Stay here, then," she said, "but it's where it's happening."

Among the hundreds of people descending upon Hammond, they lost contact with Chestnut Paw Paw shortly after they arrived. Someone told them she had left with a trucker, going north. They were disappointed and saddened, because they'd been with her for more than three months. She'd become a kind of surrogate mother to them, cooking and keeping them both warm at night. They have not been in contact with their own parents in more than two years now.

Besides, there'd still be three feet of snow on the ground in Esto. Down here it's already hot. They're used to it, or at least aren't surprised by it anymore. When they traveled through Houston last August, they wondered how people could actually live in that sauna. New Orleans was worse, smelling like everyone on the street had farted at the same time. They wintered in the little town of Destin, Florida, working sporadically in a seafood processing plant, cutting the heads off jumbo shrimp. Their clothes and their skin still smell like shrimp, but they don't notice it any more. "Here come the fishhead boys," people yell, "wheweeee!" A black kid from Hammond they'd met, whose nickname seemed to be "Honeychild," said in front of them one night, "Shit can't smell itself, cause it don't know it's shit." And everybody sitting around the fire passing a joint laughed. They called them "reefer cigarettes" down here.

Philip Music carries the brown paper bag with the ground meat and cans of beans. Both boys wear boots and greasy jeans and denim jackets. Their jackets have patches they bought at a head shop in New Orleans. David's says: Get Your Shit Together. Philip's says: Fuck for Peace. "That one was made for you," David commented. "I haven't heard you complaining any," Philip replied.

"These black people down here act happy," David says.

"Happy?"

"Yeah. All this singing and Jesus stuff."

They are both uneasy with all the religion.

"I don't think that's exactly happy."

"It's weird, man," says David.

"Jesus and all that," Philip says, "is not happy. I mean, you got to die, right?"

"Die?"

"Before you can go to heaven and all that. Right?"

"I guess so," David answers.

"So while you're here, you ain't shit, right?"

"Right."

They see the man approaching down the alley but they're almost upon him before they really notice him and are brought up short. He's very old and seems to be staring at them from his one good eye, which is overlarge and bloodshot. His other eye is cocked to the side and looks off into the distance. A long, furious scar marks his cheek. He is black as coal dust, and his graying beard looks as though it has been cut with a hatchet. He wears an old felt hat crammed on his head and a heavy overcoat, black wool and dusty, even though the day is turning quite warm. They both instinctively move to the side to let him pass, but he moves in front of them. They stop. They edge closer to each other. The man just glares at them with his one eye.

"Hey there," Philip Music says. The man seems hostile. Even angry.

"What's happenin, man?" David asks. He doesn't know if he has ever seen quite so menacing a figure before. Dangling down the front of the man's overcoat, buttoned from top to bottom, is the smoothly worn wooden handle of a long bullwhip. Slung over his shoulder, the whip trails after him in the dust of the narrow road. The eye fixes on them and freezes them. Save for the distant noise from the activity at the church and in the field, the alley is quiet. High wooden fences line the ditches on both sides of it. The boys are isolated with the old man.

Philip sticks out his hand. "Philip Music," he says. The old man doesn't move, doesn't respond at all. For all they know, he might not have even heard him. He just stands there, his flared nostrils swelling slightly as he breathes.

"Joe Bynymo," the old man says suddenly. They jump at the sound of his voice. "Hit im ina belly widafawtyfo," he mumbles.

The two boys look at each other. They feel like they're in a different country. The way people speak, especially black people, sounds like a foreign language. "What's that?" Philip Music asks.

"Bynymo, Bynymo," the old man says more slowly, "hit him in the belly with a fawty-fo."

"A fawty-fo," Philip repeats. "A forty-four. A gun." He elbows David. He grins. "You got you a pistol, old timer?"

The man doesn't answer. The alley smells of hog slop and backyard chicken houses and privies. Everything down here is skewed, off-center. They decided early on that the sun had baked people's brains. It's like a family that is rotten underneath: Everyone is polite to each other, but underneath there simmers rage and hatred barely held in check.

"You're welcome to anything in that sack," David offers, his voice squeaky and nervous. "Nothing but beans and ground beef."

"You look like you could eat this hamburg raw, right out of the package," Philip comments.

David says quickly, "Shut up, man!"

"I'm just bein friendly, man."

"Don't make him mad." David wants to run for it. The old man's eye reminds him of a picture of a Cyclops in a book he had as a child. He'd look at the full-color picture and shudder. For a while it gave him nightmares, made him afraid of the dark. He thought that the eye was trying to communicate something to him. He didn't know what but felt it was important, something spooky from the world of grown-ups that he didn't understand. Something he was not meant to understand. "Let's get outta here," he says.

"Are you goin on the march, old timer?" Philip asks.

"Bynymo, Bynymo," the old man says.

"Yeah, you said that."

"Shut up, goddammit, Philip." David backs up a few steps, as though he intuits that the old man is about to explode. Philip, holding the wrinkled sack, continues to stand there as cocky as a bantam rooster. Maybe the old man wants what's in the sack. Maybe he can smell the meat like an animal. "Give him the sack."

"What?" Philip looks back at him. "He doesn't want the sack. Do you, fellow?"

"I don't want nothin," the old man responds.

"There. You see?" Philip grins at David. He motions with his head for David to come back closer to them. Then David sees the old man unfurl the whip and begin to limber his arm.

"Philip, you better...." he begins, but the old man whirls the bullwhip over his head and cracks it. The sound is so unexpectedly loud, almost ear-splitting, that David cannot move but stands with his mouth hanging open, empty of words. He thinks he sees sparks fly from the end of the whip, and he sees fibers from the grass rope tip burst in a silver cloud in the sunlight and drift through the air, the whip whistling like a windstorm as the old man whirls it again. "Run, goddammit!" David yells.

And he hears the crack like a shot right behind him. At the same time he feels the pain across his buttocks as searing as a red-hot sword. He leaps forward and lets out a loud whimper of astonishment as much as of pain, and his legs suddenly fail him. His boots are as heavy as anvils. He hears the high, whistling sound of the whip again, a more distant pop, and Philip cries out. The crack comes again at his butt, and he thinks it rips clean through his tight jeans and cuts into his flesh. He's sure he's bleeding.

The white boys flee frantically to opposite ends of the alley as Bynymo rocks back and forth, expertly wielding the whip, popping the boys precisely on the right back pocket of their britches. His low, guttural laughter rumbles as he watches them jerk and leap and scramble to get out of his range. The bottom of the sack the tall boy carries rips open. Cans of pork and beans spill into the two cinder-filled ruts and roll into the ditch. When the boys disappear around the corner, Bynymo cracks the whip two more times for good measure and then strings it out and replaces it over his shoulder. He smiles. "Bynymo, Bynymo, hit him in the belly with a fawty-fo," he mutters under his breath, walking down the alley toward town and toward the Silver Moon Café, where Clutter Blue's wife, Martha, will fix him a fish sandwich in the back room.

●   ●   ●

"Here he is," Frank Fite announces when Lucious Willie walks into the room, "the man with two first names!"

"Red on the head," Billy Singleton adds, "like a dog's dick!" Everybody laughs.

They are meeting at the old Maylene School, a rambling wood-frame building out in the Flatwoods that's no longer used for anything official. Its windows are boarded over with plywood, and whitewash peels from the walls. Students who used to attend Maylene, grades one through four, are now bussed into Hammond. But the place still smells like a school—chalk dust and moldy books and old crayons. A bulb connected to a long extension cord run from Frank Fite's nearby filling station lights the room. The old first- and second-grade room is now furnished with cast-off sofas and chairs.

About thirty men and two women gather tonight. Billy sits in the first row. One of the women is Mesta Follett, a harsh-faced blonde from Birmingham, pretty in a tired, worn way. The other woman, Sister Myrna Ruple, a revivalist preacher, large and heavy, almost six feet tall, pretends she didn't hear the remark about the dog's dick. She leads them in prayer. Then Lucious conducts the meeting. They plan what they'll do if the protesters carry out their threat to march all the way to Montgomery. The Klan decides to stage a countermarch across Rooster Bridge in robes and hoods—carrying their flags. Johnny Lee Bobo, the Imperial Wizard of East Mississippi, is coming over from Meridian with more than a hundred Klansmen. Mesta Follett reports that Birmingham will send down at least a hundred, maybe more. She announces that she herself is joining the throng of protesters that will march to Montgomery.

"I'm originally from Ohio," she explains, "I can talk like one of them. I'm gonna infiltrate the ranks."

"Naw!" Frank Fite says, "you kiddin us, or what?"

"The nigger preacher said everybody come, so here I am," she continues. "I already been hanging out up there. We got some strange humanity in our midst, brothers. That little pygmy Sammy Davis. And them nuns take the cake." Sister Ruple snorts in agreement. "You wouldn't believe some of the stuff I've seen with my own eyes."

"Yes we would, too," Lucious replies.

"I say we take our guns and slaughter ever goddam one of em," says Billy, who boasts a new energy, a new purpose. He hasn't experienced the pain in several days. His appetite has been good, and he even thinks he's gaining some weight back. "I told you, didn't I?" Jessie Merle said smugly, "Jesus bit you through that snake!" "Uh-huh," Billy agreed, "uh-huh." He didn't know what had happened. Whatever it was was good.

"There'll be plenty of time for that," Lucious says.

"You're chickenshit is what's the truth," Billy challenges.

"You can't talk to me like that," Lucious responds, his voice rising.

"I can't?!" Billy says. "Well, listen to me, then. What am I doin?" He stands up.

"Jesus Christ, Billy! What's done got into you? A few days ago you was about to quit, hang dog like some goddam coward...."

"I ain't no coward, Lucious! Say that again and I'll...."

"Boys! Boys!" Sister Ruple intervenes. Mesta laughs. Half the men laugh and half are mad. Billy doesn't care. He'd just as soon get the guns and go after them now as later. Billy sits back down on a stool made from a barrel sawed in half and watches the other men get all worked up. Half of them want to start shooting, and the other half don't. He watches Lucious's face grow redder and redder. Before he realizes what's happening, he feels a sharp ache in his gut and can't believe it. He's caught by surprise. Since the incident with the snake, he has felt sure that he'd been cured. He tells himself that it can't be coming back. He hopes it's just a bad gas pain. If he could just go outside and fart he'd be all right. But he knows better and he feels the prickly slivering in his gut. He knows that the fish pain is back. He wants to cry. His face breaks out in a cold sweat. His skin feels clammy. His tongue tastes like old pennies.

An overwhelming sense of disappointment settles over Billy, and he begins to whimper. The men sitting close by look at him. Billy needs to burst into tears but he can't do that in front of them. The relentless throbbing settles in his lower intestines. He thinks for a minute that he'll mess his pants. He tightens himself. He stands up, and a searing cramp grabs his testicles like an angry hand. He doubles over. Jesus! "Scuse me," he mumbles. His legs are stiff as he makes his way across the room, out the door, and down the dark hallway to the dingy old bathroom. He knows all their eyes follow him as he goes.

The narrow, high-ceilinged room, lit by a Coleman lantern hanging against the wall, has just one toilet with no seat. Stained yellow and brown, the toilet has no water in it. In his rush to get his pants down, Billy wonders what the women do. The cold porcelain is like damp ice against his flanks. As he tries to force downward, he knows his asshole is ripping, but he cannot stop. It's too late. It feels like shitting broken glass. He can't believe it, thinks he'll pass out any minute. The stench is suffocating. And then, as quickly as the pain had come, it's gone. The whole middle of his body feels suddenly cool and hollow. He's finished. By damn, he is finished! He can think, for the moment, only of that.

He uses his wrinkled handkerchief to wipe and he sees bloodstains on the handkerchief. His rectum stings like a wasp's bite. He stands and pulls up his pants. He moves gingerly, as bowlegged as a wrangler.

After a few steps he crumples to the floor and lies there in a daze. When the meeting breaks up they find him leaning against the bathroom wall. They assume he's drunk and help him to his pickup. Lucious drives him home.

Later, someone remarks about the catfish he saw, that some kid, some vandal, tried to flush down the old toilet that hasn't flushed in years and won't flush ever again.

# Rachel

AMY ESTES LEGRAND GETS HER DRIVER, LEROY BRYANT, TO take her out to Rose Hill Plantation. She hasn't been out there since the old man died. She supervised Justina and Gilbert by phone in closing up the house, covering the furniture, pulling the drapes to shut out the daylight. She knows they've done exactly as she instructed.

The only things Amy covets in the house are a few pieces of furniture. She wants to inspect and get measurements on a couple of exquisite sideboards, massive pieces that she's not sure will fit in the smaller rooms at Hawthorne. Wearing a black dress, pearl earrings, and a pearl necklace, she looks as though she's on her way to a formal occasion. "Elegant," Hester said when Amy passed through the kitchen, "you looks elegant this afternoon, Miz Amy." She sits lightly on the rich leather seat of the limo, almost too slim, almost weightless. After crossing the Coosa River Bridge, she notices the lush green fields of soybeans and some cotton stretch away on both sides of the highway. Legrand land now, as far as she can see, in all directions. And no Legrand lives on it now, she thinks, except.... And she stops herself from thinking of Carter and Rachel. No, no Legrands now that that old he-devil Dupree Legrand has died and gone to join his spiritual father in almighty hell. He never liked Amy, nor she him, really. He resented her from the start, from the first time Oscar brought her home from the university to meet him.

She'd given up formal training in art—over her parents' strenuous objections—to marry Oscar. She went home with him to the huge old house where Mr. Dupree Legrand would sit in that wheelchair, his long, thin, gray hair flaring out around his head like a horse's mane. He'd glare at her out of his diseased old pale eyes. Glare, she knew, simply because she was a woman and there hadn't been any other woman except Justina in that house for almost fifteen years then. And those same eyes popped up in Dooly, eyes that every time she looked into them, even when Dooly was a baby, she thought, Yes, God, I'm sure this is your amusing way of reminding me that my offspring is forever a Legrand, will be a Legrand throughout eternity, Dooly—my pride—my 'special charge.' Dooly, always there to remind her. In spite of his tender heart, Dooly possessed those steel—even cold—blue eyes that announced to Amy that the blood that ran in her child's veins was not Estes blood but Legrand blood.

As a small boy, Dooly had come crying to her one day and told her that Carter had killed a bird, a sparrow, with an air rifle. Dooly clung to her and cried his eyes out. Carter said "Awww, Miss Amy, we're hunters." She wondered if Dooly was the only Legrand in history who detested hunting, who could not bear to kill.

When he was a teenager, Dooly wanted to do everything he could to antagonize his father, to embarrass him. He'd been wild as a buck, drinking even more than his father, and chasing after every little piece of female white trash that wagged her tail at him. But underneath it all, Amy knew, he possessed a goodness and a purity that were incorruptible. She wasn't surprised when he turned to the priesthood. She'd known all along he would. She'd shaped him that way, created him the way she created her paintings.

Leroy steers the limo up the circular driveway and stops in front of the house. The long lawn slopes up to the veranda, and the four old magnolia trees stand rooted and constant beside the crumbling brick walkway. The six columns across the front rise to the second-story roof. The house seems lifeless. With their drawn drapes, the windows on both sides of the heavy, ornate door—and above it on the second floor—look like closed eyes. The air is still; no breeze disturbs the thick, waxy leaves of the magnolias. The lawn, spotted with clumps of crabgrass, already needs mowing, and even at this distance Amy can see that the glass in the windows is streaked with dust.

Amy pauses on the worn bricks of the front veranda. It's a cool day, the low clouds hanging overhead like a gray flannel sheet. She detects the faint ammonia smell of the Chemco landfill. Then Amy sits in a wooden rocker on the porch. She knows that it's dusty but she doesn't care. Beyond the black limo in the driveway, she sees the fields rolling toward the Bigbee River in the distance. She remembers the view, especially the one from the widow's walk around the cupola at the top of the house. From there you get a clear view of the hills around Crockers Crossroads as well as the river landing. And an unobstructed view of Chemco as well, with its enormous crater, its vast white limestone quarry. She thinks again of old Dupree Legrand and the many times his eyes must have looked at exactly what she looks at now.

Amy stands. She rummages in her purse, finds the key, and opens the door. It creaks on its hinges. Gilbert hasn't oiled it in a while. She thinks of Gilbert and Justina in their cottages on the lane behind the house. She reminds herself to stop and see them. The inside of the house is dark. She switches on a light. The furniture, covered with white muslin cloth, looks like mounds of cotton or snow. The eyes in the portraits on the walls stare down at her. The only sound is the slight cacophonous ticking of several clocks. The house smells faintly of tobacco, even of whiskey. Man smells.

She finds the first sideboard and pulls off the cloth. She doesn't even have to measure. The piece is much too large for any room at Hawthorne. It's dark-stained mahogany, reaching almost to the ten-foot ceilings, its mirrored-back top crammed with silver goblets and soup tureens and ladles, even a huge punch bowl etched with hunting scenes. All the silver gleams, kept polished all these years by Gilbert and Justina. Amy crosses the hall-way and goes into the parlor. She measures this sideboard for the upstairs hallway and is pleased to see that it will fit. Made of pecan, lighter and more delicate but still bulky and overlarge, the piece holds heavy crystal glasses with matching decanters. She opens one and sniffs. Scotch. She pours a couple of inches into a glass and sips it.

"Hello, Amy." A deep voice startles her. She looks quickly around but sees no one. She thinks maybe Leroy followed her to the house, but he'd never call her Amy. She stands there for a moment, gripping the glass, listening to the ticking of the grandfather clock against the front wall between the windows. No one is there.

"Help yourself to a whiskey drink, Amy," the voice continues, and Amy knows that she's being woofed, that someone has sneaked in to play a trick on her.

"All right," she responds. "Come on out, whoever you are." She smiles and takes another small sip of Scotch, smooth and easy, sweet in her throat. "Justina?" Amy calls. "Gilbert?" No one emerges. She looks out into the hallway. Nothing. She smells tobacco again, stronger now. The emptiness and silence of the house make her nervous. She feels a presence as real as a sudden change in temperature. She shudders. She knows her imagination is playing tricks on her. Then she sees him standing before the fireplace and she jerks back and spills some of the whiskey onto the rug.

"Who...what...." she mumbles. A man. A handsome man in a black, broad-brimmed hat with a peacock feather tucked into the band. He wears dark wool trousers, a homespun shirt without a collar, and thigh-length brown leather boots. She notices that the boots are muddy. She's never seen him before; she feels terrified. Someone who has broken in. But he called her by name.

Standing very straight, she aims her chin directly at him. "Who are you, sir?" she asks. "My bodyguard is just outside, I...."

"You don't know who I am, Amy?"

"...can call him in in a second, and he is armed. So...."

"You really don't know who I am?"

"Why should I know who you are?" she snaps. "How did you get in here?"

He laughs. His teeth are gleaming white in the dim room. She squints at his face and turns on another light to get a better view of him. She can see his face clearly now, a striking face, angular and even beautiful, and his eyes.... His eyes. She thinks of Dooly. His eyes. "My God," she mutters.

"Yes. Hello, Amy."

She stands flat-footed, not knowing what to say or do. She knows her eyes are tricking her, that she's hallucinating. "What do you want with me?" she demands.

"This is my house," he says, "you are the stranger here. Maybe I could ask you the same question."

The air she breathes now is musty like old cloth and tingles her nostrils. She sees motes of dust drift in narrow shafts of gray light that sneaks between the drapes. Her mouth is dry, and she takes a drink of the whiskey and coughs. Young Dupree Legrand grins at her. It's impossible for her to think of this young man as Dupree Legrand, the hateful old man in a wheelchair, a stick figure wasting away on yellowed linens on a bed in an upstairs room. She notices his long black hair flowing beneath the hat, curling on his neck. Hair that had already grown stiff and gray when she first met him.

"No," she says, "it cannot be."

"It can, Amy, and it is."

"What do you want?" she asks. "Leave me alone."

"I don't want anything. I am long past the time of wanting anything."

"You hate me," she says. "You always did."

"No, I don't hate you. I never hated you. I rather liked you."

"You had a funny way of showing it, then."

"You just were never as perceptive as you thought you were. There haven't been many women who've understood us very well. Us Legrands. You, for example. What do you really know of love, Amy?"

"Hah! You're one to talk of love! Hateful. That's what you were, hateful." She shakes her head and drinks the rest of the whiskey, feeling it warm her.

"No," he says, "you have no way of understanding me, because I was haunted. All those long years I was haunted. You wouldn't understand, you couldn't. You would have some damn fool 'woman' way of looking at it."

"Of looking at what?"

"You already know in your bones. You were born knowing, just like Eve." He smiles. His teeth are even and strong. He seems solid and substantial, not like a specter at all.

"Eve?! Good god, old man, don't talk to me about Eve!"

"Why not? I'm well acquainted with her. I had to carry her stain all my life."

"Hah," she says, "her stain? I think you've been identifying with the wrong person in the story."

"No, I am Adam."

"I was thinking of the snake," she says, "the serpent." He laughs. His eyes glow with a youthfulness long departed when she'd first met him.

He seems for a moment to grow vaporous; she blinks. He changes density with her blinking and she knows she's imagining him. But she also knows that if she reached out she'd touch him. His legs are muscular and powerful in the tight wool pants. The white shirt open halfway down his front reveals tufts of black hair, the swells of his chest. She sees tiny beads of perspiration, a slick moistness on his skin. She can smell him, like horses and sweat.

She hears a long, slow rumbling and she thinks at first that someone is moving furniture upstairs. Then she realizes it's thunder.

"It's going to rain," the ghost tells her, continuing to smile. He is young, younger even than Dooly, in his early thirties. They stare at each other for a long time. She hears the thunder again, distant and muffled.

"Well, Amy," he says.

"Well what?" She's uneasy, even though she doesn't for a moment think he'd harm her, that he can harm her. He is a figment, a shade of her own imaginings, but she's frightened of him nonetheless.

"You are still a beautiful woman, Amy." He bows slightly toward her.

She suddenly realizes she feels a strong physical attraction to him, to her husband's father, and it disgusts her. She feels a surprising—and alarming—stirring in her loins. She speaks quickly to mask this. "All right, all right. Fine. I'm still a…You people were never lacking in charm, you…."

"What people do you mean?" The smirk on his lips tells her that he knows full well what she just felt.

"People like you. It's all a show. Not for your family, not for those who are supposed to love you. You win people over with your graciousness, your good manners. A disguise. A cover for your real selves." She hears her mother in her voice, her mother going on about southerners. "Magnolia-ridden" had been her favorite term for them. "Sin-stained" another.

"Legrands, you mean?" he asks, and he reaches out toward her, a slow, seductive gesture, his face cocked to the side, and she pulls back.

"Don't you dare touch me," she says. "You always wanted to, didn't you? I could see it. Even in that wheelchair, when you could hardly walk, you wanted to. When you could hardly hold your head up you leered at me." Her breath quickens. Her skin feels dry and hot.

"Oh, come now, Amy."

"No. I know. At the bottom of everything with you people is sex. That's what it comes down to. That's...."

"No, Amy," he interrupts, "you just don't understand. It's not sex. It's power. You women think it's sex. All of you. But women are stupid about the real ways of the world, Amy, because those ways are men's ways."

She's so angry now that tears spring to her eyes and blind her. But she's confused. She wants to put her hands on his legs to see if they're real, to see if they're warm. She wants to run her fingers through his hair. She wants to tighten her fingers around his throat and choke out whatever life he has somehow managed to wrest back from the dusty air of the old house. Her legs go weak, and she reaches out and steadies herself with her hand on the hutch.

In that instant she, too, is transported back in time. She stands on the party porch of Oscar's fraternity in Tuscaloosa and sees him for the first time, his stocky body, his startling eyes like those of a man too old for his body, his face. She hears her long-dead mother's voice as clearly as if she were in the room as well, as clearly as if there were three of them—ghosts all—in the room: "Amy...Amy...they're not your people."

Amy closes her eyes and feels him close to her. The floor begins to tremble under her feet. The whole house shakes. She hears laughter. When she opens her eyes she expects to see Oscar, a boy in a tweed jacket and with a bottle of beer in his hands. But she sees an old man, laughing, his eyes now liquid and watering, his mouth toothless, and she feels his arms feathery and light as they go around her. She feels his body pressing against her, smothering, stifling her. She can't breathe. The laughter, dry and sharp, rings loud in her ears. The body moves against her, inside her, in the quick throbbing of her blood. There's nothing she can do.

"Goddamn you," she screams. "Goddamn you to hell." She stands for a long time with her eyes clenched shut, until the laughter is gone and everything is still.

She hears something behind her in the hallway and she jumps, startled again. A voice says, "Miss Amy?" She sees that it's Gilbert. Her heart races, and she works to catch her breath. She turns back to the fireplace and old Dupree is gone. The space he had occupied now an intense vacuum.

"Miss Amy, I seen the car," Gilbert quickly explains. His hair and his mustache silver against his black skin, Gilbert wears a gray vest and pressed blue trousers that she knows he put on for her. "I didn't go to startle you so."

She cannot gather her voice to speak. She stands there, drained, exhausted. She looks at the hearth, the mantel, the two crystal candlesticks. The dull black andirons, cast right there on the place years before even Gilbert had been born. Nothing moves. The yellow lamplight glows on the marble of the fireplace, on its pink veined surface. Amy knows that there's a brick in the back of the fireplace with LEGRAND stamped on it. When he was little, Dooly would kneel close to the fireplace and strain to see it behind the flicker of the flames.

For a long time she stares at the place where Dupree Legrand had stood just moments before. Then she looks at Gilbert and sees that he too stares at the same spot before the fireplace. She knows that he has seen old Dupree also. She doesn't know what else he saw. She still cannot speak. She'd thought she was finished with the old man forever, that she'd escaped his clutches, his lust. She thought that his death had ended it all. Gilbert looks at her.

"Yes mam," he nods.

•   •   •

The town is like a stage set before the last act, the final curtain. Dooly walks down Washington Street in the sunshine. The redbrick storefronts haven't changed since he was a child. There's a constancy here, but also a sense of something old and fading, about to disappear. The past, ancient and stubborn, doesn't want to give way. The town square, dappled under the towering and gnarled old oak and elm trees, is crisscrossed with sidewalks scrawled with hopscotch squares. The sagging merry-go-round, green-painted, still operates; and a round concrete fish pond still draws people to watch fat goldfish swim lazily just under the water's sparkling surface.

Dooly finds his mother in the garden behind the house. She doesn't say anything when she sees him, just stands looking at him. He can tell she knows everything, has heard all about it from Paula. Her eyes look him up and down.

"You don't have to dress like a field hand, Dooly," she finally says.

"Yes mam, I do."

He embraces her. Stiff at first, she returns the embrace and steps back, her mouth pursed.

"At least you're still wearing your collar," she sighs.

"Of course. Why wouldn't I?"

"From what I hear, the bishop wanted to rip it from your neck," she responds. In spite of herself, she smiles. But he can see the tiny glint of tears in her eyes. She shakes her head. "Oh, Dooly, Dooly, what in heaven's name am I going to do with you?"

"How is Carter?" he asks. "And Rachel?"

She stands looking at him, behind her the fresh new green of the April gardens. Her eyes are blue, not the pale blue of a Legrand but darker, richer. She wears a plain gray sleeveless housedress. Her body is as lithe and shapely as a teenager's. Her dark hair is fixed, perfect. For as long as Dooly can remember she has had it done every Friday without fail. She has always seemed to Dooly to be one of those people who is almost totally complete within herself.

"Why are you doing this, Dooly?" she asks. "Have you lost your mind?"

"No, but I may find it."

She snorts. "I want you to stop this nonsense. I want you to come home to Hawthorne. Stay with me. For awhile. Until all this blows over."

"'All this,' Mother, is not going to blow over."

"I forbid it. Who is this woman? This hillbilly singer? You're making a complete and total fool of yourself. And I forbid it."

"I'm not a child, Mother." He smiles.

"Well, you act like one. I am serious, Dooly."

"I know you are, and I'm sorry. I didn't mean…."

"This is serious business, Dooly. Deadly serious. It's not a game."

"I know that. Believe me, I know that."

"And it's madness. I told Carter and Rachel. I told Carter that it's madness."

"Yes," he says. "How is Carter?"

"You belong in your church, Dooly, with your people." Amy ignores his question. "Everything here is doomed, rotten and corrupt...." She stops herself, turns away, gazes toward the river. "My mother warned me. She said we were cursed here, that we...."

"Don't, Mother."

"Your father is a madman, Dooly," she continues. "But you know what? You know what the truth is?" She looks back at him. Pools of tears stand in her eyes now. She trembles, her thin shoulders shaking. "He hasn't changed. He was always like that. He...." She looks as though she wants to say more. The tears spill down her cheeks. She begins to sob. Dooly holds her, pulls her light body against his. He rubs her stiff hair. He brushes his lips against her cheek. He holds her for a long time, until her sobs slowly subside.

She pulls herself free, steps away, dabs at her eyes with a Kleenex she takes from a pocket. She sniffs, straightens her back. She seems embarrassed that she cried, even in front of him, her only son.

Finally she looks back at him. "Carter. His son, his little boy," she starts, then looks off at the river again as though searching for something far away. Dooly says nothing. "He's a special child."

"I know," Dooly acknowledges.

"The child is deformed. Was born deformed. I want you to heal him."

"I can't."

"Why not?" she asks. Her lips form a thin line across her face. "Why not?"

"Because," he explains, "my powers to heal come and go. I...." He pauses. He's sweating, takes off his jacket and slings it over his arm. He can see the statue of Aphrodite, the spring-green azaleas and darker boxwoods, and beyond all that the river, lying cola-colored and glinting under the afternoon sun. "What's the child's name?"

"Eshu," Amy replies. "What new nonsense is this, that you can't...."

"Eshu," he says. Eshu. He dreamed of Eshu last night and he awakened, startled, not knowing where he was, knowing only that he was not in his comfortable bed at home with Paula. "I don't know why," he says. "But I can feel the powers leaving me the way I can feel pain. I just know it when it happens. It's there and then it's not. For a while."

"No," she insists, "God is not like that."

"It's not God. It's me."

She stares at him. A sweet, rain-promising breeze drifts in from the river. "Because you're living in sin," she says.

"No. Not that. We all live in sin. Forever."

From Aphrodite's perspective, they would look like bookends, matching and yet different, a man and a woman, two generations. They appear to be so much alike they seem like two halves of the same person.

"Sin is not the issue," Dooly says.

"The only issue here is the child, his health."

"Yes," Dooly agrees.

"Yes."

* * *

The sunlit streets teem with people. It's a zoo. Rachel wonders where these white people have come from all of a sudden. She wonders where they've been all this time. Carter is excited about it, has attended all the preachings. Karla won't go with him. She doesn't want him to go on the march. But Rachel knows he will, and she knows she will as well.

People avoid and shun Rachel now. The word had gone around that she's the cause of little Hardy Siddons's illness. Carter tells her to ignore them. "To hell with em."

"I know better than to blame you, Rachel," Mose Bell told her earlier, in the back room of the church. "I pray to the Lord to give me strength. But still...."

"It's not me causin it, Mose," she insisted.

"I know it, I know it," as though he wanted to convince himself. "But thank the good Lord Hardy's better."

Rachel knows what's causing it. One of Billy Singleton's little girls died of the same thing, childhood leukemia, right after Rachel had come home from New Orleans. And a little boy in a family she didn't know, a family that sharecropped over near the lake. Just the other day Rachel had been gathering roots in the woods near there and saw the skeletons again, the bleached bones of animals that had come into the low swampy places to drink. And she stood for a long time on a high, flat place that Carter, Dooly, and she used to call Cherokee Bluffs—pretending to be Indians shooting arrows at settlers on the water below. Looking out over the shimmering, metallic surface of the lake, she knew what was causing the sickness. She stood there breathing in the rancid smell and said aloud, "Yes."

Today the whole town throbs with an invisible intensity and anxiety. There's the promise of violence—in the flowers, in the moist heat, in the sunshine, as well as in the crowds of people. Rachel feels the tension as she walks. She can hear it in the air, in the shrill laughter, in the chatter.

Rachel turns down Jackson Street, toward the riverfront, toward where the old city dump had been located when they were children. She and Carter shot plump rats there—so fat they moved slowly and languidly—with one of Mr. Oscar's twenty-twos, but Dooly wouldn't do it. He wouldn't kill even a rat. "White boys is sissies," Carter taunted.

"And niggers are Africans," Dooly responded. Rachel watched them with large eyes. They were so much bigger than she.

"Sho I'm an African, and proud of it, too," Carter said, and hit Dooly on his upper arm with his balled-up fist. Dooly hit him back, and they started to laugh and wrestle in the dirt. Rachel sat on a battered and sagging old sofa they'd found in a pile of trash and watched them, holding the rifle. She was a good shot, a better shot than Carter. Carter was best at everything else. He could already hit a baseball farther than even the grown men over on the place. The boys were thirteen then. She was ten. Carter had taught her to shoot pool at Shorty McCrae's poolroom on Strawberry Street, and she'd gotten to be so good that all the sharks in town wanted to challenge her. She beat a lot of them, too. By the time she was fifteen, she even beat Shorty, who was famous all over the Black Belt.

Some of the same children who badger Joe Bynymo when he comes to town now lie in wait for Rachel. When she turns onto Grist Street, away from the crowds, there they are. One of them throws a piece of chert at her. It misses, but she hears it ping against a mailbox at her elbow. "Blue gum!"

a boy yells. "Blue gum! Go on back over to the swamp where you come from!" They giggle and keep their distance. There are seven of them, four boys and three girls. Their eyes and their teeth look harsh white against their dark skins. Rachel points at them. She makes some sort of sign with her fingers, and they shrink back. She only makes up the sign, but they don't know that. Three of them take off running.

"Git on outta here, chillen," Rachel calls to the others. They watch her from across the street. "Go on!"

"Mama say you brought a hex," yells one of the little girls, her hair up in braids and tied with white yarn.

"Papa say you a blue gum," one of the boys screams.

"And I eat chillen, too," Rachel growls, baring her teeth at them. They break and run. Rachel stands looking after them. She feels tired, her limbs heavy and sluggish. The children remind her of Hardy. She looks up and down the street, shading her eyes with her flattened hand. Not as many people walk here, but the ones who do pass on the other side of the street and stare at Rachel. Jackson Street is paved with crushed limestone and ashes. Rachel can smell the coal fires that have taken the chill off the early morning. Small shotgun houses, some with rusty screen porches, line the street. Rachel walks by a house with budding pink azaleas growing in the swept dirt yard.

She hears someone behind her and turns to see a young girl, fourteen or fifteen, thin, a wrinkled gray sundress hanging on her frame. Her skin is smooth. Her eyes, big in her gaunt face, dart about like those of a frightened animal.

"You got to help me," she begs.

"How?" Rachel asks. She has no idea who the girl is.

"You got to give me a potion, somethin."

"What is it?" Rachel can see that the skin around the girl's eye is swollen and puffy, with a break underneath, a fine line like a cut. "Who hit you?"

The girl's eyes snap away and around, as though she has little control over them. She walks a few steps down the street and then stops and looks back at Rachel. Rachel follows her. They walk along in silence for almost a block, then stop by a burned-out house overgrown with kudzu and honeysuckle and Cherokee rose. An old rusty stove sits on the caved-in porch of the house. The girl stops and looks at Rachel, her eyes like saucers.

"It's my daddy. He won't stay offa me."

"You mean…."

"Yeah."

"And he hit you, too, he…."

"I got to have a potion. I got to have somethin to git him offa me."

"All right," Rachel says. The girl starts to cry. She looks even younger than at first. "You've started gettin your period already, haven't you?"

"Yes mam. But he been doin it…he been doin it since I was little. He…."

"How old are you?"

"Thirteen."

Rachel feels the sun on her head through the bandanna. She looks at the girl and sees herself when she was young. When Rachel inspects her closely, the girl's eyes look older. She seems bent under the weight of all she's carrying. "What's your name?" Rachel asks softly.

"Martheta," the girl answers. "For my auntee." Then Rachel knows who she is. Rachel knows her aunt Martheta Williams. And she knows Martheta's brother James, the father of young Martheta. She has seen him drunk, loud, and ugly at the Silver Moon. Fired from the Veneer Mill for fighting. James Williams. She saw him just a few Saturdays ago sitting on a bench in front of McCrae's poolroom on Strawberry Street. When she walked by, he called out, "Hey, Rachel, wallow for a dollar!" "Keep your dollar, boy, wallow on it yourself and don't mess with me," Rachel said.

"Come over here," Rachel says to the girl. They walk into the overgrown yard. Rachel squats behind a hedge and opens her bag.

"I ain't got no money." The girl stands looking down at Rachel. The girl is scared to death. Of her, Rachel knows. And of what's in her bag. She's heard all the talk, too.

"That's all right," Rachel responds. "You ain't got to pay me." She pulls out a small bottle stoppered with a cork. "This is Adam and Eve oil," Rachel explains. The girl takes it hesitantly, holds it in front of her. Then Rachel holds out a small gnarled stick. It rests in the pink palm of her hand, and the girl kneels down and looks closely at it. "This is a piece of High

John the Conqueror Root. The only place you can find it is in Maconoco Swamp, buried way down. And down around Houma, Louisiana. Only two places in the world. It's rare. But it works." The girl takes both the bottle and the root. "What you got to do is grind the root up. Take a hammer and pulverize it on a brick. All right? Then you got to mix it with the oil. Now, listen to me. This is the most important part. You got to wait till he's asleep. Then you got to clip some of his hair, off his head and off his privates. Put that in with the root and the oil and then stopper it back. Shake it and mix it up real good. Then you got to get some of his urine. Without him knowin it. Just a little. When he drunk he probly pisses on the floor, and you can get it then. You got to mix it with your own menstrual blood, just a little of it, and then you got to slip that mixture in his food. Or in his coffee. Don't matter, so long as he consumes it. You listenin?"

"Yes mam."

"After he has consumed it, and when he goes to sleep, put the bottle of mixture under his mattress."

The girl sits on the ground now. She sits like a child listening to a story, hugging her knees to her chest. She stares at Rachel, her eyes still frightened. "What'll happen then?" she whispers.

Rachel pauses. "He won't never bother you again. He won't never bother another woman again, for as long as he lives."

Martheta looks long and hard at Rachel. The two sit in the shadows of the hedge and the kudzu climbing on the charred timbers of the old house. "Will he die?" Martheta asks finally.

"No," Rachel replies, "but he'll wish to Jesus for the rest of his life that he'd never done what he did to you. He'll wish he was dead."

The young girl rises with the oil and the root. She dusts off the seat of her dress with the flat of her hand. "Thank you, mam," she says. Then she's gone, her bare feet soundless on the sandy dirt. Rachel squats on her haunches. It's cool in the shadows, quiet. She hears horns blowing, traffic sounds in the distance. She stays there awhile, hidden away. When she resumes walking down the street, there's a new spring in her gait. She's smiling.

•  •  •

They spot each other at the same time. Rachel, Dooly thinks when he sees the familiar figure, the loping walk, and the bandanna. There is Dooly, Rachel thinks, come to be with his mother in all this.

Dooly crosses the Square toward her, passing by the seesaws. Rachel never sees the seesaws without recalling what it felt like as a child to stand on the sidewalk and watch the white children playing on them and be warned by her mother that she was not to set one bare toe on the grass or the playground itself.

One hot afternoon Dooly suggested that they play on the swings. Carter told him, "You know we can't go in there." Dooly looked puzzled for a moment; then after a long silence they had gone on to gather fool's gold along the chalky limestone bluffs, filling sections of an old bicycle inner tube they had closed with wire on the ends. They added it to their stockpile in one of the outbuildings at Hawthorne. They had what they figured was a million dollars worth. Sometimes they traded it with two white boys, Earl and William Wembley, who lived with their parents in a leaning tarpaper shack down near the dump.

"Rachel!" Dooly greets her. He stops, stands apart from her, hesitates, and then embraces her. "How are you, Rachel?" he asks, stepping back, and she shades her eyes and squints at him. He is taller than she, but not by much. He and Carter are almost the same height. She tries to see their same blood behind his eyes but she can't. He's too white. She thinks of little Cap, her own son, as white as a freshly washed sheet in the sunshine, and her heart lurches.

"What's wrong?" he asks.

"Nothin," she answers, "nothin's wrong. I'm fine. How are you, Dooly?"

"Okay. How's Carter?"

"Carter is all right." The sun reflects off the whiteness of his collar. It seems too big for his neck, as though he's lost weight even since she last saw him at the funerals. The two funerals. "He misses Mama," she tells him. "We ain't over it yet."

"You don't ever get over it. You just learn to live with it."

"That's right."

"Well..." he smiles. "It's good to see you. So good to see you."

"You, too," she responds. He peers at her, his eyes narrowed as though he's trying to get her into better focus. As though he's inspecting her for something. They're still the same people who gathered fool's gold along the river. But they're not the same people at all. Rachel's eyes are as deep as the sea. They remind Dooly for a quick moment of old Raybob Sneed's. They glint like sunlight on dense leaves in a forest. Too many shades to even see.

He reaches out toward her. His eyes looked pained. "Tell me about Eshu," he says.

"What about him?"

"Mother said...." He stops, shakes his head, and looks away. People pass them on the sidewalk and stare. All the locals know who they are. If Dooly weren't standing talking to her, with his arm still outstretched, his fingers almost touching her arm, they'd be greeting him. "Mother said he was born deformed, that he...."

"No," she says and begins to walk. He falls in step beside her. "No, she's mistaken."

"But she said...."

"She sees what she sees," Rachel says. "He was born special."

They walk fast, and Dooly keeps pace with her. "All right," he says. They turn at the corner, and Dooly knows they'll walk around and around the Square. They'll retrace old footsteps, a charted path. All right, he thinks, he was born special. Mother said that, too. All right.

"It's the poison that comes from the dirt," Rachel tells him, "it comes out of the ground itself, it's the poison. Mama's cancer, too, I figured it out. It's..."

"Wait," Dooly interrupts. "The poison? What...."

"Yes. The old lake is full of it. It's not even a lake any more. It's a sump. Everything there is dead. It's all dead."

"Dead?"

"Yes. It's in the black ground. It shakes in the trees and makes the snakes crawl. It's evil come there."

They walk even faster now. "I don't follow you, Rachel," Dooly says. "I don't know...."

"There's a lot you don't know," she responds. They walk along in silence and turn another corner. People part to give them room. "Little children get sick. They die. Black and white both, don't make any difference. When the evil come outta the ground it take white and colored alike. You know that. You're a preacher man."

"Yes."

"Things ain't right. The dead won't stay buried. They roam the sacred groves. They roam the igbodu. Zombie. Man named Carl Narcisse, lived over there at Coatopa, died twenty years ago, and the other day his family come upon him sitting beside the road eating sardines out of a can. He didn't hardly know em, but they knew him all right. He was alive, and they had every one of em stood there and watched him buried all those years ago. He told em he'd been working in a sugar cane field down near New Iberia all that time. Said he'd been a slave, like in the old days. First Zombie round here in many years."

"Rachel, the poison you're speaking of, it...."

"Yes. It comes down out of the sky like rain. It bubbles up outta the ground like a spring. You can smell it. Get close to the lake and it smells like a flooded privy. It smells like the alley behind the filling station. It smells kind of like when you pass the beauty parlor on a hot day."

On the other side of the Square now, near the swings, they stop. Rachel stands looking at him. There are tiny beads of perspiration on her forehead.

After a long moment she says, "You don't believe me about the Zombie, do you?"

"Of course I believe you."

She stares at him for a long time. His glasses gleam in the sun. He carries a blue jacket over his arm. "You are my brother, but you are still a white man," she says. He has no idea how literally she means it. No idea. But he will. Soon. And even then she knows that there are things he'll never be able to know, never be able to understand.

"We are what we are," he replies.

"Yes."

He takes her hand and guides her off the sidewalk into the park. The swings hang limp and unused, the seats worn smooth. They pick out swings side by side and push themselves back and forth with their feet.

"We gonna get arrested," she says, laughing.

"Not any more. Not ever again."

She cocks her head to the side and stares at him. "It's a long time comin," she says.

"A long time comin," he repeats. He laughs, too.

The sound of the cars on Washington Street are distant, a whisper. His jacket and her bag rest on the grass. They swing back and forth, higher and higher. Rachel begins to laugh again, her laughter like warm syrup. Her eyes glitter. She kicks her feet out to force herself higher, and Dooly notices that she wears worn high-top work shoes. She throws her head back, and the sound of her laughter rolls out over the playground. He remembers her laughter from years ago, when she was small, when she would delight in the smallest of things. He remembers it as clearly as if it were today.

# Dooly

MARCUS HANSON LOOKS UP FROM BEHIND THE CASH REGISTER when Dooly walks into his store in Crockers Crossroads. Rubber boots and harness hang from the rafters. Cigarettes and candy bars and cellophane-wrapped cakes line the glass counters; farther back are canned goods and flour, cornmeal and salt and sugar, bolts of calico cloth, and racks of stiff new blue denim overalls and pants and jackets. The cool air of the store smells of cinnamon and lye, of tobacco and the faint sour scent of last winter's ashes in the potbellied stove in the back. An old-fashioned drink box is stocked with bottled drinks sitting in ice cold water. Dooly fishes one out, a Nehi grape. He sees hoop cheese on the counter and a hand-lettered sign, reading, "Cigarets, 3 cents apiece." He can remember many the day when Marcus sold him and Carter and Rachel loose cigarettes, which they'd smoke along the creek bank, lying back in the sun and feeling grown up.

Marcus, tall, thin, and bright yellow with a severely receding hairline, slouches over as though to make himself less tall. He squints. His eyes have been bad for years, and he doesn't recognize Dooly in the dim light of the store.

"Good afternoon, Marcus," Dooly says.

"Evenin," Marcus nods. He takes Dooly's dollar bill and gives him ninety cents change. He does not ring it up; the old upright, rounded cash register has been rusted and locked into an open position for years. Marcus simply uses the protruding partitioned drawer for his cash.

He looks at Dooly out of the corners of his eyes, wondering who this white man is who knows his name. Dooly isn't wearing his collar today. He wears an old plaid shirt Kitty bought him at a thrift store. Dooly sticks out his hand.

"This is Dooly," he says, and Marcus breaks into a grin.

"Lord Jesus, it's Mistuh Dooly," he exclaims. "I ain't seen you, son, since you was knee-high to a hoppergrass!" It's a lie. Dooly saw him at Rosa's funeral. But Marcus thinks such pronouncements are expected of him. "Where you goin, up to the house?"

"No." Dooly doesn't think he wants to go up there.

"Ain't nobody up there now but Gilbert and Justina. You ought to go see them."

Dooly takes a long drink of his cold soda. "I will while I'm in town," he says. "Where is everybody?" Usually several people sit in the shade of the front shed, behind the two gas pumps, having cold drinks and talking.

"Everybody gone to the preachin over cross the river. Big doins over there. Say they gonna march all the way to Montgomery."

"I know," Dooly says. "I'm goin on the march, too."

"You is?" Marcus asks. He cocks his face to the side and looks curiously at Dooly. He shakes his head. "They say they's lots of white folks over there. I ain't been over there myself. Mose say they college students. Must be like them boys that was here back three, four years ago. One of em got his-self killed."

"I remember that." Dooly turns the grape drink up. It's ice cold and soothing. Sweet and thick.

Marcus still watches Dooly suspiciously. "What your daddy gonna think about you goin on that march?"

"What do you think?"

"I say he gonna shit a brick."

Dooly laughs. Marcus chuckles. "Lord, Lord," he shakes his head again, slowly back and forth.

"I came over here to see the old lake," Dooly tells him.

"What you want to go up there for?" Marcus asks. "It's dirty."

"Dirty?"

"Yeah. Ain't fit for nothing."

"What's the quickest way to get up there from down here?"

Marcus leans his elbows on the counter. "Well," he says, almost in a whisper. "Now I don't want to get Mose in trouble or nothing."

"Mose?"

"Yeah." He leans forward, and Dooly leans closer to him. "You got to promise you won't tell nobody over at Chemco. And Lord, don't tell your daddy."

"Cross my heart," Dooly promises.

"All right. Mose got him a path up through there, to get to the river to fish. He told me they's a break in the fence up the hill from his house. They got all them signs and all, and Mose say he knows he trespassin, but he go through there all the same. Go on down the street to the end, where Mose's house is, and go round back and you'll find the path. Mose carries his grandson up there to fish."

"In the lake?"

"Lord, no. Ain't no fish in there. Ain't been no fish in there in a long time. Like I say, he cut through to the river. It stinks up there, too. Ain't much at all up there no more, clean to the river. You know I was raised over there, on some land inside where the fence is now. I used to seine for crawdads all in that swamp. Big old mothers. Them restaurants in New Orleans and Biloxi and Mobile used to beg for crawdads from around here. Swamp lobsters, they used to call em. Juicy things, big as your thumb. Ain't been none there for fifteen or more years now."

"Thank you, Marcus," Dooly says. "My lip is zipped." He hands Marcus a fifty-cent piece. Marcus smiles and puts it in the drawer.

In Kitty's old car, Dooly drives down the narrow, unpaved street between the two rows of houses that are little more than shanties. He parks at the end where the ground begins to slope upward. He finds a well-worn path that goes up the side of the hill through waist-high Johnson grass, bright green and sharp-edged in the spring sun. Dooly wishes he had heavy boots as he makes his way up the path, passing through bushes of briers and around thickets of blackberry vines and clumps of beggar lice. Near the top the path levels out and broadens, and he sees the ten-foot chain-link fence with its red signs.

He goes through the gap in the fence and comes out at the lake. It's much worse than he had imagined. He passes through a stand of dead pines and hardwoods to get to the dam. There he sees the surface of the lake shimmering in the high sun, its veneer almost like a metallic skin. The chemical smells engulf him, make his eyes sting. He feels sick. Carefully he makes his way down a gap in the dam, its raw red dirt gaping nakedly, and he goes up the other side. The surface of the lake is up to the very top of the dam. He can see lots of seepage, a black brackish liquid tar that fills the bottom of the breach and leaks down the hillside into the dead trees toward the village.

On the other side of the dam Dooly descends a muddy, moss-coated path into a thicket of dead magnolias and water oaks, hickory trees, and thick hotweed. Even though it's spring now, there's not a single mosquito or squirrel or bird in the branches overhead. A murky stream leads into the swamp. Dooly picks up a branch and plunges it into the stream's bed. He scoops up a blackened clump of noxious sediment with a poisonous metallic scent. In the hole left in the streambed flows a silvery oil.

"Shit," Dooly says aloud. He cannot believe it. In his childhood, the place had been like an Eden, green and fertile.

Dooly breaks several branches from one of the dead oaks that line the stream and holds them close to his face. A black liquid runs down the middle of the fragile sticks. He walks down along the shallow creek. The trees are thick, brown, and discolored; the dry vines tangled; and the ground on both sides of the path is covered now with turbid water. He has entered the floodplain downriver from the landfill. The swampland gives off a sweet, etherlike odor that's beginning to make his head ache. He sees an occasional 55-gallon drum in the bayou water, apparently swept downstream from Chemco during a heavy rain. Dooly watches perch floating belly up. Near one barrel is the shell of a dead loggerhead turtle with a skull about sixteen inches in circumference. The harsh chemical odors mix with the unmistakable smell of decaying and death.

All around him is a heavy silence, as still as a lifeless exhibit in a museum. Dooly swallows, but there's no saliva at the back of his throat, and he can taste the harsh chemicals that surround him in the air. His eyes burn. He remounts the dam and can see a row of trees across the lake, trees now spindly and black against the high spring sky. On one tree, a tall water oak, an old tire swing hangs motionless in the still afternoon. Long disused and forgotten, the swing triggers Dooly's memory of the day he and Carter had strung it. Suddenly, he doesn't know whether tears or irritation from the chemicals fill his eyes.

He stands still but hears no birdcalls or humming of insects. He sees no butterflies, hears no distant owl call or squirrel chatter. Just an empty, deep and abiding vacuum, the stillness of something almost prehistoric, of something becoming fossil, of something long ago departed and extinct.

●　　●　　●

As he drives back from the lake, Dooly thinks of his father. Oscar has been absent from Dooly's life for as long as he can remember. Absent physically as well as spiritually. Like the Old Testament Jehovah, Oscar was the distant father, godlike and above. When Dooly was a small child, his father stayed in Montgomery for long periods of time. During his brief visits home, he always had Dooly stand at attention for inspection, like a little soldier, to measure his height against the doorjamb in the dining room and get a ritual hug. Even when he was home, Oscar spent most of his time at Rose Hill hunting and fishing. Your father's coming home, Hester or his mother would whisper reverently. Dooly remembers the mix of excitement and terror that he would experience. And his jealousy of Carter. Even as a child, Carter seemed to have more in common with his father than Dooly did.

Dooly notices the police car behind him and checks his speed. He is driving well under the limit and surprised when the blue lights and siren come on. At a point where the highway widens, Dooly pulls over, the police car behind him.

Dooly gets out of the car. A county deputy approaches him.

"I'm..." Dooly begins.

"I don't give a shit who you are," the deputy shouts. A short man, swarthy, his belly pushing against his thick leather belt, he wears a khaki shirt, blue pants, and a Smokey-the-Bear hat. The cop looks vaguely familiar. Though the man doesn't seem to recognize him, Dooly is sure that he's someone he knows, someone he went to school or shot pool with.

Dooly reaches for his pocket, his billfold with his license. Reacting to Dooly's sudden motion, the policeman hits Dooly across the mouth with his fist. Dooly's head snaps back, and he tastes warm blood on the inside of his lips. They sting and tingle, numb and dull, already swelling, and he falls back against his car. Incredulously, he instinctively covers his face, protecting his glasses.

"You seen him, Leon, didn't you?" he hears deputy ask. "You seen him reachin for his weapon?"

"Yeah. Son-of-a-bitch."

"Looks like we got us one of these here outside agitators," the first one says. They turn Dooly roughly to face his car, yanking his arms behind him. One of them grips the back of his head and grinds his face into the top of the car. The car's metal is hot from the sun. The metal frames of his glasses bend and cut into his skin. The dust on the top of the car mixes with Dooly's sweat and his blood. Sharp pains shoot through his upper arms and shoulders.

"Wait..." Dooly attempts.

"Shut the fuck up. Just don't say nothin. This here car has been seen over at the march site. Tennessee license plate number forty-three-dash-nine-nine-nine. Davidson County. You think we ain't got tabs on all you sons-a-bitches? Huh?" He twists Dooly's arms. The pain is almost unbearable. His eyes are shut tight, and he thinks he might pass out.

"We don't need your kind around here. Fuckin queer," the second deputy says. Dooly doesn't even know what this man looks like. He thinks for a moment that he's going to be executed by someone he's never seen.

Dooly smells the oiled asphalt of the highway, the sour, murky mud of the bar pits. He smells his own blood, salty and rich. His arms are yanked upward again, and Dooly grunts. Then he feels a paralyzing blow against the backs of his legs, and his knees buckle. He starts to go down, scraping his face against the car, his knees skinned instantly by the gravel, burning like fire. Again his head is pulled sharply back by his hair. The short deputy slaps him across the face, and his glasses go flying. Dooly kneels there, feeling the gravel cutting into the flesh of his knees. He gets a blurry look at the other one now. Older, taller, the second deputy wears his

Smokey-the-Bear hat at a rakish angle. He wears horn-rimmed glasses, and a little salt-and-pepper mustache covers his upper lip.

"Beg," he yells, "beg, you asshole, and we'll let you go."

Dooly says nothing. He kneels there, his arms locked behind him, his whole body numb from the pain, rigid. He's prepared. Father, be with me. Give me strength.

"Beg."

"No," Dooly says.

"Beg, asshole."

"No, I will not beg."

After a long silence, a car goes by very fast, in a great whoosh of hot wind. Dooly wonders what the people inside must think. As the sound of the car dies away the first cop says, "Well, Don, we got us a hero."

"Yeah, we ought to shoot him and wrap him in chains and throw him in the river."

The older one, Don, takes out his pistol. It's chrome-plated, shiny as silver. He holds it close to Dooly's face. So close Dooly can smell the cleaning oil, the powder. He presses the barrel against Dooly's forehead. He holds it there. Dooly's breath catches in his throat, comes in pained gasps. He clenches his eyes shut, sees only blackness. Yea, though I walk through the valley....

"Beg."

"No."

Dooly braces himself, sure now that it is coming. Bless me at the hour of my death, Father. A peace settles over him, a calm. He wants it to be over. He thinks of old Raybob Sneed, and he remembers Kitty. He thinks of his children. The image of the old tire swing against the pale blue sky lodges itself at the front of his mind. It's like the image of the cross.

He feels the pressure of the cold gun barrel ease. He senses their hesitation and realizes they're not going to kill him. He knows that they just want to hurt him, to scare him. Relief washes through him.

"If you know what's good for you, asshole," the tall cop sneers, "you'll turn this car north and get your ass back to Tennessee. And consider yourself lucky."

Dooly doesn't look up as the men walk away from him. He hears their boots crunch in the gravel. A big eighteen-wheeler goes by, building up speed for the long haul up the Coosa River Bridge to the south. Dooly hears the police cruiser start and then head toward town in the wake of the truck. He kneels there. The stones cut into his knees. The ground is still cool from the morning, but the high sun touches his head like warm fingers.

He stays there in that posture for a long time. His figure is small next to Kitty's dusty car, beside the dark gray highway that cuts as straight as the edge of a board through the low, flat land between the rivers, north of the gracefully curving concrete bridge that crosses the Coosa into Hammond.

• • •

In the Silver Moon, Carter sits at a table near the back, buys a half-pint of Early Times Bourbon, and pours it over ice in a Dixie Cup. The place is crowded, tense. The air smells of close bodies and cooking—the hot grease of the deep fryer in the kitchen, the pungent scent of collard greens cooking slow with pork fat, ribs cooking over coals. The cigarette smoke is so heavy that Carter hardly needs to light his own Chesterfield. The noise is deafening, the laughter and talk and music: Lightnin Hopkins's "Back Door Friend" plays on the jukebox.

Some men at the next table goad Carter. They want him to arm-wrestle their friend, a large, dark man named Abraham something-or-other from Uniontown. They're restless, looking for a release, something to absorb their burning energy. Carter had once been good, taking on all comers for bets that sometimes got as high as fifty or a hundred dollars. Some of his matches were notorious, with the side betting getting up into the hundreds of dollars as well. Wiry, with a hard and narrow upper body that was deceiving, Carter could beat much larger and stronger men with ease. He knew how to make them wrestle defensively from the start and he'd often have them beaten before they realized the match had begun. But recently he's done little more than drive the forklift and he's not in as good a shape as he once was.

"Naw, man, I ain't studyin you," Carter tells him.

"You're chicken," Abraham replies.

"Naw." Carter lights his cigarette and blows the smoke toward the ceiling. He looks around the darkened room. Whenever someone opens the door, shafts of blinding sunlight penetrate the gloom. With lots of people, white people, in the street, only two white faces sit inside the Silver Moon, a man and a woman. They hover near the front door, lean up against the counter. They must feel the hostility toward them in the crowded place. They order beer but don't know what kind of food to order. They ask Clutter in a clipped, blunt accent if he makes hamburgers. He tells them yes he does. Lucille Chapman, sitting at the counter, asks them don't they want some chitlins. They smile, nod, don't know how to answer. Lucille asks them, don't they want to buy her a drink, and they do.

"You're chickenshit, Taylor," Abraham yells, and the other men laugh. Abraham's arms bulge in his shirt, and his coal black skin glistens with a sheen of sweat. Completely bald, Abraham works in a sawmill, lifting logs onto a conveyor all day.

"I got twenty on Abraham," a man named Cletus announces. "Who'll take it?"

"I said I ain't wrestlin," Carter insists. He drinks his bourbon and smokes his cigarette. They know he'll wrestle. They know he can't resist the challenge.

"I will, I'll take that bet," Carter hears a voice say, a white voice, and he looks up and squints in the dimness and the smoke. He sees that it's Dooly, grinning at him. His lip is swollen, and tiny scabbed cuts line his eyes. He looks like someone hauled off and punched the shit out of him. Rachel had told him that Dooly's in town. Carter smiles. "I'll cover that twenty," Dooly offers.

"Hello there, brother," Carter greets him. He stands and they shake and pound each other on the back. The other men all know Dooly. They look at him curiously. Someone brings him a cup of ice and Carter pours him a drink.

"You're home," Carter says when Dooly settles across the table.

"Yeah."

"What happened to your face?"

Dooly shrugs. "I ran into a door."

Carter nods. All right. He knows from Rachel that Dooly is here for the march. Carter is surprised. He doesn't know what to think of it. Except for brief visits at Christmas, when they both seemed to be playing roles, he hasn't known Dooly as an adult. It hasn't been the same since they were boys.

Carter sees old man Dupree Legrand's coloring in Dooly, sees the old man in the tilt of Dooly's head, hears him in the timbre of Dooly's voice. Carter can remember Mr. Dupree as he looked when they were small boys, before he was confined to a wheelchair. Striding about in his shined boots or sitting on a horse so high that he was up there majestic and close to the sun, he seemed older than God even then. Though his hair was gray and thinning, he was vigorous, his body trim and rigid, with an aura of power and control about him. He commanded complete respect, even awe, from everyone on the plantation. His presence loomed large over the boys' long summer days, the hot, still, dusty afternoons filled with idle playing or fishing. If it were Saturday or Sunday, they often played baseball near the pear orchard in the east pasture, which Mr. Dupree had ordered the grounds to be kept mowed for that purpose. Every year he sent off for enough equipment to furnish two teams with gloves and bats and balls and he'd sit in the shade of a chinaberry tree in a wicker rocker that someone had lugged out from the big house and watch the games, jubilantly waving his walking stick in the air at a home run or a good defensive play. Carter and Dooly were allowed to play with the men and older boys, mostly blacks with some whites—sharecroppers and their sons—woven together in the combat of the sport. When they were little boys, Carter and Dooly were permitted to play right field together as though they were one player. Carter remembers roaming the dense, neatly clipped grass, freshly mowed, smelling the new cowhide of the glove, feeling the leisure sun on his head—it was different from the workday sun, the weekday sun. He and Dooly both occupied the one spot in the lineup, sharing the time in the batter's box with three strikes apiece.

Dooly's eyes fix tightly on Carter's, as though he's transfixed. Finally he says, "You have a child."

"A son," Carter replies. "His name is Eshu."

"Ahhhhh. Eshu," he repeats. Dooly seems thinner than when Carter last saw him. He wears a wrinkled blue cotton shirt that's too large for him.

"He's the most important thing in my life," Carter adds, "I love him more than anything. More than life."

"Of course."

"You have children, you know…." and Carter stops. Dooly thinks of his children in Nashville. He knows now that what he's done is irrevocable.

When he returned to their tent earlier, his face covered with blood, Kitty looked at him with wide, astonished eyes. "Dooly, my God! My God, Dooly!" She didn't come to him. Instead, just for a moment, she backed away as though she couldn't bear to touch him in that state. Then she helped him, washing his face and removing his blood-stained shirt, finding him another shirt and his spare glasses. "What happened?" she stammered.

"Some of Hammond's finest," he told her. "The police."

"Why? What were you doing?"

"They don't need a reason, Kitty. We're here, that's enough."

"Okay, okay, if this is what…." Her eyes jumped around nervously. Her face was flushed, she wore no makeup at all. In a shapeless old red sundress, faded almost pink, she smelled like wood smoke from the camp fire. "The bastards," she uttered.

"You have two children," Carter continues, "Oscar and…."

"Marie Louise," Dooly adds.

"And how is Paula?"

"Paula is fine."

The two men stare at each other for a long silent moment. It's as though they communicate completely with their eyes. Dooly knows Carter will surmise everything he needs to know about him and Paula without being told.

The smells of the cafe are so familiar to Dooly that he feels like he's never been away. Many the night he sat right here, at this very table with its wooden top worn mostly smooth but etched with liquid stains and scratched initials. Carter raises his cup and tilts it toward Dooly. They nod and smile. He drinks the bourbon. The men at the next table watch them solemnly, suspiciously.

"You ready?" John Hardin calls. "Have yourself another drink and get ready."

"All right," Carter responds without looking over there. He pours more bourbon and drinks it down and then crunches ice between his teeth. "All right. I'm ready." He pulls out some wrinkled bills and slaps a ten on the table. Abraham puts his own ten on top of it and pulls his chair over to their table. He adjusts it and sits, a Camel dangling from his lips. He puts his elbow on the table and moves his large hand slowly back and forth. He clenches and unclenches his fist, his fingers thick and callused.

Dooly puts his twenty on the table. Other bets are made. People crowd around, pushing and shoving. The white couple at the counter doesn't know what's going on. "Just two brothers back there measuring each other's dick," Lucille tells them. They look amazed and confused and laugh self-consciously. Their hamburgers, topped with something like slaw, are greasy and very good.

Carter finishes his cigarette and moves to crush it out in the overflowing ashtray. "Wait," Abraham says, "let's make it interesting." He holds his smoked-down Camel between two fingers. The end is damp and shreds of tobacco protrude. He measures carefully with his eyes and puts his cigarette butt, still glowing, on the scarred table top precisely where the back of Carter's hand will come down if Carter loses. He nods toward the table.

"Naw." Carter shakes his head.

"Come on."

An expectant, tense silence falls around them. Carter sits there for a moment and then places his own glowing coal exactly opposite Abraham's hand. An appreciative murmur ripples through the onlookers. The two men lock eyes and then carefully place their elbows on the table. "You count," Carter instructs Dooly.

"All right." Dooly stands over them. Their fists clasp together, palm to palm, their bodies poised, ready. Dooly can feel their trembling power and their strength, still tentative, waiting. Two thin gray lines of smoke, like strings, rise straight up from the smoldering cigarettes. Dooly can smell them scorching and burning the old veneer of the table. "One…" he counts, "two…." The force of the two men, barely held in check, gathers in their eyes, still locked together. Dooly feels them vibrating like a stretched rope. "Three."

In a moment of suspension, almost of weightlessness, their strength comes together. Both men grunt. Then Dooly sees it in their eyes. Each man knows, instantly. Abraham's fixed look grows desperate and Carter's victorious. To groans and whistles and laughter, Abraham's hand starts steadily toward the glowing coal. It slams into the table, on top of the lighted cigarette. Dooly can see the intense pain in Abraham's eyes now, but the huge man doesn't cry out. Beads of sweat break out onto his face until finally Carter releases his hand and picks up the two tens, flexing his fingers, then picks up Abraham's spent Camel and snubs it out in the ashtray.

"Well, shit," Abraham mutters, cradling the back of his hand in his other palm. "Well just shit."

Dooly picks up the wrinkled bills. He smiles at the men.

"What the hell you lookin at?" Cletus asks Dooly.

"Cletus...." Carter begins.

"No, wait, I asked the gentleman a question. What the hell you lookin at?" Cletus stands up, as does John Hardin. Abraham watches them. The crowd around them falls silent again. "You ain't wanted in here," Cletus shouts. He's about Dooly's height, medium build. Cletus and John Hardin both have their hands in their pockets. They take a step toward Dooly.

"Goddammit...." Carter begins again, standing now too.

"Keep out of this, Carter," John Hardin warns. "This ain't none of you."

"None of me?!" Carter asks.

Cletus reaches out and pushes Dooly in the chest. Dooly staggers, looks around. A thick wall of people surrounds him. The two men stand close to him, their eyes inflamed. Dooly smells the whiskey they breathe out. The huge Abraham stands up behind them. No one speaks; the jukebox shrieks and thumps in the corner. The stale air feels close and hot.

Dooly is sweating. His hands tremble. Then Carter steps in front of him, between him and the other men.

"All right, all right, goddammit," Carter says, "you want to get to this white boy, you gonna have to come through me!"

"Git out of the way, Carter," Cletus yells.

"Come on," Carter goads. "Come on, pull them knives outta your pockets! Come on."

"This ain't your fight!"

"I'm makin it my fight!"

A long, tense silence follows, as though everyone in the room is holding his breath.

"We don't want none of you, Carter," John Hardin says.

"I don't reckon you do," Carter replies.

For what seems like minutes, they all stand in a fixed tableau. Finally the men sit back down at the table, grumbling, picking up their glasses and beer bottles. They don't look at Carter and Dooly.

"Let's get the hell out of here," Carter says.

•  •  •

"They were right," Carter says, "you didn't have no business in there."

"I came to see you," Dooly responds.

Carter is driving. He passes a quart of white lightning, wrapped in a brown paper sack, back and forth to Dooly. He drives toward the river bluff, away from where the crowds gather around the church. Near the bluff the town is building a marina where the old dump used to be. Carter and Dooly find a grassy place near the construction site, under a mimosa tree with its delicate, pink, spiderlike blossoms. They had come here many times as boys, sneaking away with a bottle they'd either stolen or bought with coins carefully saved from chores. Carter still seems angry. Dooly is still shaken from the encounter in the Silver Moon. They look out over the river toward the low, flat swamps on the other side.

"There's gonna be bad trouble soon," Carter reflects. "You saw it. People are feeling mean. That was a just taste of it. Things are bound to get rougher."

"I'm prepared."

"Shit! We ain't never prepared!" Carter replies. They drink the smooth, clear shine directly from the jar. Its fumes tingle Dooly's nose. The shine dissolves his fear and calms him. "Was you prepared for whoever mashed your face in?" Carter asks. Dooly laughs. He's getting high, and it all suddenly strikes him as funny.

"What's so goddam funny?" Carter asks.

"I don't know," Dooly chuckles. "Everything." Then he gazes off across the river.

"Well, you owe me one," Carter states. "I ain't layin my ass on the line for you again."

"Okay, thanks."

Carter doesn't acknowledge him. They sip the whiskey.

"What are you doing here, Dooly?" Carter asks after the long silence.

"I don't know," Dooly shrugs. "I had to come. When I saw you and your son on television, I had no choice. I knew it then. Right then." They lie there in silence on their backs, propped on their elbows. A buzzard, little more than a speck against the sky, circles over the swamps on the other side of the river. "I knew that if I was ever to be whole again, then I had to begin here. Where it all started."

Carter doesn't answer. Dooly has no idea what Carter is thinking. He still seems angry and distracted. Troubled.

"What is it, Carter?" Dooly asks.

"It ain't nothin, Dooly," Carter says. "So just shut up."

Carter drinks the clear, fiery liquid that looks like water from the jar. He wipes his mouth with the back of his hand, then stands, unsteady on his feet. He fumbles for his cigarettes and lights one, flipping the match over the bluff toward the water far below. He wears his work uniform: khaki pants and khaki shirt with CHEMCO embroidered in red script over the pocket. He worked the eleven-to-seven shift then drove into town after only a couple of hours of sleep. He drags on the cigarette, looking off into the distance.

"The old lake," Dooly says, "have you seen it?"

"Yeah."

"It must be caused by the Chemco landfill. How long has it been like that?"

"Years. Rachel thinks it's the cause of some children's sicknesses. She thinks it caused Mama's cancer. I don't know."

"Who's supposed to be looking after that? Isn't it monitored?"

Carter seems impatient. "I reckon. People from the state come to the landfill from time to time. They check the scales. They check the logs in the lab, all that. I don't think they look at the lake, though." Carter looks at Dooly. His eyes are red-rimmed and tired. "The fact is the governor of the state owns the business, don't he? So who cares?" His tone is bitter.

"It's terrible. It should be reported," Dooly says.

"To who?" Carter stares at him for a moment, then looks away. He walks closer to the edge of the bluff. The muddy water crawls below. The river is high from the spring rains and deep against the tall chalk bluffs. Though the current is barely visible on the surface, it's strong at this bend. When Carter exhales, the breeze whips his cigarette smoke and pulls it away, over the river.

"When this is over, we'll have to report it to somebody," Dooly replies. "That dam looks like it's about to give way. It's dangerous. We'll have to...."

"When this is over? This ain't gonna ever be over, Dooly." He takes a swig then hands Dooly the jar. The harsh chemical smell of the liquor reminds Dooly of the way the lake smelled. He takes a long drink, the shine like mild fire in his throat, burning his tongue and gums. He feels its heat in his belly.

"Whew, we ought to have some water to chase this," he mutters, handing the jar back to Carter.

"What's the matter? You still a sissy?"

"Something like that." Dooly wants to laugh, but Carter's tone isn't a joking one. Dooly knows that something deeply troubles his old friend, something Dooly doesn't understand. Carter stands too close to the sun now, forcing Dooly to shield his eyes and squint. Even then Carter is mostly silhouette.

"I know it, Carter," he agrees, "I know it's not gonna ever be over."

"And maybe it's too late for you to even come here and pretend it will be."

Dooly hears the naked anger in Carter's voice, intense, directed at him, only at him. Dooly swallows. He still tastes the shine. "Just because we can't see it being over doesn't mean we can't do what we can, what we have to do. All of us."

"All right."

"It's not just your fight, Carter."

"Hah." Carter glares at Dooly. "Not just us niggers' fight, huh? Well, it is." He takes another drink from the jar. "It ain't white folks' fight. White folks can't do nothing for us. They ain't got nothing we would want."

"Come on, Carter."

Carter sits back down, leaning against the mimosa tree. He fixes Dooly with his weary eyes, then smiles, more a mirthless grin, and shakes his head. "What you don't know, Dooly, would fill a book."

"I know that, of course."

"No, you ain't got any idea."

"Then tell me. Tell me some of what I don't know." Dooly is beginning to slur his words.

Carter looks up at the high, clear sky, at the thunderheads gathering on the western horizon. The mason jar is two-thirds empty. Both men are just this side of being drunk. Carter laughs to himself, then out loud. His eyes are level on Dooly now but they're soft and unfocused. "Lemme ask you a question," Carter says, nodding.

"All right."

"Just how far do you think your precious daddy's political career would go if word got out that he's got a nigger son and a nigger daughter?"

"What?!"

"Me and Rachel, asshole," Carter slurs.

"No." Dooly's reaction is instinctive, quick.

"Yes." Carter's eyes steady on Dooly's.

Dooly hears the words but can't grasp their meaning. The liquor clouds his mind as though his head is suspended in a vacuum. Something registers in his brain but he's not sure what. The glare of the sun hurts his eyes. He swallows. He wants to ask Carter to repeat what he said, but Dooly has heard it with such clarity that its import cannot be mistaken. Preposterous and farfetched and unlikely. Yet it's something so factual, so common that he's known it all his life, known it in his soul even before he was born. Rosa! Of course he'd known.

"So...." Dooly sighs. He feels suddenly drained, as though all the vitality has escaped from his muscles. *So this is what I was called back here to find out, to know....* He can hardly take it in. It's too much. Yet he cannot think of anyone he'd rather have as a brother than Carter. Or a sister than Rachel. But it knocks him off balance. It feels as though his life up to now has not been real, as though he must now go back to the beginning and revise it, relive it. He realizes that surely this is what has been missing all along, that this is the source of his unrest, his discord. He has known it without ever being able to articulate it, even to himself.

Carter continues, "Yes, your father...."

"Our father...."

"No! My father died a long time ago. My father died when I was little."

"Wait, slow down." Dooly massages his temples, closes his eyes tight. "Wait. Father and Rosa?"

"Yes, for years. And Miss Amy knew it, she...."

"You talked to her about this, and she told you she knew it? That she...."

"No. She didn't tell me. But I know she knows the truth. Or part of it, anyway."

"Part of it? Jesus, Carter. There's more?"

"No," Carter answers. "Nothin you need to trouble yourself about. Not now, anyway. I didn't even know if I'd tell you that much. I didn't want to give you the satisfaction of knowing. I don't want to ever even discuss this with your father. All I want is for him to know that I know. That's all."

"But...."

"You can't change the past, Dooly. You can't change what's been."

"Sure you can! Absolutely! I believe that, Carter. What you do today and tomorrow alters it, changes it...."

"No, buddy. No way. It don't make a speck of difference. Me and you, our relationship was fixed solid a long time ago." Carter takes out another cigarette. Dooly watches him. "Remember this one?" Carter asks. He chants. "'Fight, fight, nigger and a white, who's the nigger and who's the white?'"

"Goddammit, Carter! We're brothers. Real brothers."

"No, we're not," Carter replies.

"You called me 'brother' back there. At the Silver Moon. You said...."

"And I'll call you brother again. But we ain't brothers. We ain't never been brothers and we never will be. My name ain't Legrand. It's Taylor."

The way Carter says it, the name echoes in the air all around them. Taylor. It pulses and vibrates, hangs there, as palpable as a banner. Taylor. The two men look at each other. They both stand now.

"Fight, fight, nigger and a white, who's the nigger and who's the white?" Carter chants. He thinks of Mr. Oscar, then of old Dupree Legrand, then of his mother, his mother the way she must have been as a young woman. Suddenly he swings. His fist catches Dooly on the side of his head, and Dooly goes down on one knee, still raw from this morning. He cries out in pain and shock and surprise at the sucker punch that came out of nowhere.

"Goddammit, Carter." His anger and frustration surge as he struggles back to his feet. His head swims. He feels hot nausea burn his throat. Carter bounces on the balls of his feet, trying to be nimble, his fists bobbing in front of him. He's drunk. With his mouth turned down in a grotesque sneer, he looks like a child acting the role of a man obsessed. Dooly swings his fist, putting every ounce of strength into it, and his knuckles crash into Carter's mouth. Dooly sees blood spurt and Carter's eyes go vague and opaque as he falls back flat into the grass, sitting, his face full of astonished disbelief.

Dooly stands looking down at him, his head throbbing. Carter licks at the bright fresh blood on his lips. "What?" Dooly questions. "Did you think I would turn the other cheek?"

"Arrrrph!" Carter grunts, rolling forward and tackling Dooly around the legs. Dooly falls on top of him. They are both down in the grass, they pant, struggle blindly to get a hold on each other. They're dangerously close to the edge of the bluff, so close that their fighting shakes loose some small chunks of limestone and sends them plummeting into the water a hundred feet below. They roll in the dandelions and clover, getting green stains all over their clothes. Sweating and snorting, they gasp for breath.

Their sweat mingles together, and the blood from Carter's burst lip smears all over Dooly as they struggle. Dooly's thoughts come in quick fragments, flickering images: like a stuck pig—and already again another shirt bloodied, two in one day. He sees them as boys rolling in the dirt and almost always fighting to a dead draw. Rachel watches them—Rachel with her black, flashing eyes. Then he sees her sitting in the swing in the park, the blue bandanna wrapped tightly around her head. Dooly's arms feel as heavy as iron bars.

As boys they wrestled for what seemed like hours, but now they're slowing after only minutes. Heavily drunk, both move in slow motion as though they're underwater. They gasp for breath, then become suddenly still. They look into each other's eyes. Dooly sees in Carter an unfathomable darkness that reaches out and draws him in. Carter sees clearly the pale blue eyes of his kinsman. They are sealed together, bound up forever as brothers.

# Carter

WHEN CARTER ARRIVES HOME IN THE LATE AFTERNOON, Karla tells him that Ernest Vance called from Chemco to tell Carter he's fired and to come pick up his last paycheck. Karla is sobbing.

"You see?" she cries. "You see what's come of it? How we gonna eat, Carter? How we gonna pay the doctor bills for Eshu? Huh?" She seems to look at him for the first time. "What happened to your lip?" she asks. "You're drunk, Carter! What happened to your clothes?"

Carter doesn't answer. He shakes his head to try and clear it. What had been a vague threat that he would deal with when the time came has suddenly become real. He feels oddly liberated. He knows in the back of his heart that Amy Legrand will see to it that the doctor bills get paid if it comes to that. But he doesn't tell Karla. He doesn't want to ask the Legrands for anything. Going to them with his hand out would be worse than starving to death. He figures there will be some other way.

"We'll make out," he reassures her.

"You're a mule, a stubborn mule."

"Be careful now, Karla."

She shrinks back, looks at him as though he's a monster. "You hit me, just you hit me once, my brothers be over here on you like white on rice," she warns.

"I ain't gonna hit you. Have I ever hit you? You know better."

"You say be careful, like you gonna hit me. I know. I...."

"Shut up, Karla." He turns away. She hasn't even started supper. All the laughter is gone out of Karla now. Everything seems to be falling apart at once. He's anxious for the march to begin. He'll take Eshu and sleep under the open sky. He thinks of Dooly, of all that he'd seen in his eyes. He runs his tongue over the inside of his lip where it's still swollen.

"You've got grass stains all over your uniform. They cost money, Carter." Brave again, she knows he won't hit her. "What slut you been wallowing around with?"

"I had a fight," Carter replies.

"Huh," Karla snorts. She stands looking at him, her eyes projecting a mixture of hatred and fear. He doesn't know how to deal with her anymore. She's changed almost overnight. It has to do with Eshu. And the march. Everything that's happening around them.

"Fix me some supper," he orders, "I got to go over to the landfill. Tend to my business."

"You look like business." She stares at him for a moment, then goes back to the kitchen. He hears her slamming pots around. The noise wakes Eshu who begins to cry. Carter feels as if his head is about to split open.

●　　●　　●

"Good riddance is what I say," Billy Singleton sneers. Carter folds the pink envelope with his last paycheck in it and puts it in his pocket. Other men, white men, stand behind Billy, looking at Carter. They all grin. Carter is a joke to them, has been since he came to work there. They poured molasses in his locker, tied his extra work shirts in knots, stole his lunch and replaced it with dog turds. Some of them laugh and joke with him at break, seem to even want to get close to him, but they always back up. They look at him curiously, as though trying to figure out why he's different from them, other than his skin. He knows he confuses them. But no matter how much they want him to be afraid of them, he's not.

"Why ain't you off over there with them outside agitators?" Bobby Musgrove asks. Carter has known Musgrove, who lives over in Hammond, all his life. Thin as a rail, he has a purple birthmark over his eye and a patch of white in his close-cropped, dun-colored hair. The white patch is a birthmark, too, he once told Carter.

"Yeah. I hear y'all're marchin to Jordan," Goodlowe Lewis snorts with laughter. An older man, fat and snaggle-toothed, Lewis weighs over three hundred pounds. No one else laughs at his joke.

"We are," Carter replies. "Marchin to Jordan."

They grin. Billy looks as though he doesn't know whether to laugh or get angry. Billy, skinny now, looks as pale as a bleached sheet. His eyes look like hollows in his lean face. He smells like soured milk. "Y'all think you gonna take over the world, don't you?" he sneers. When he talks his Adam's apple floats up and down.

"Just what's rightfully ours," Carter replies.

"Go back to Africa, is what I think," Lewis says.

"You crazy man," Musgrove laughs, "Carter couldn't find Africa on a map!" Everyone laughs. Carter laughs, too. But the laughter doesn't break the tension. It hangs in the night air as tangible as the dampness. The white men are dangerous because they're afraid of him, as scared of him as if he were a ghost.

"That's right," Carter says, "I ain't studyin no Africa."

He sees eyes narrow. His tone taunts them. They want him to be humble, to show fear. They need desperately for him to fear them. However, he holds himself erect and lets his eyes go heavy-lidded. Outnumbered six to one, he looks back at them with calm amusement in his eyes. He feels their fury rise like heat. His paycheck, his last paycheck, folded in his pocket, seems cold against his skin.

He turns then and walks away from them, walks slowly to his car. He can feel their eyes penetrating his back, hear the hushed buzz of their voices.

"The black son-of-a-bitch," Goodlowe Lewis spits.

"Yeah," Musgrove agrees, "we ought to scare the shit out of him."

"Maybe worse than that," Lewis says, "maybe we ought to string him up!"

"Yeah," some of the other men mutter.

"Yeah," Billy Singleton chimes in.

• • •

The back roads on the place have turned into a muddy quagmire from a heavy late-afternoon thunderstorm. Carter parks his car near the big house, sitting dark and silent and closed behind the magnolias. He starts his walk home under the stars. Thin gray clouds sail across the sky, the almost-full moon sparkling silver behind them. Carter sniffs the air. It will rain again tomorrow. The Big Cahaba is still rising from all the rain upriver. In two weeks it will reach its spring flood stage from the rains and the thaws way up the Bigbee and the Coosa.

Carter hasn't walked more than a half-mile when he sees her sitting in a Japanese plum tree, heavy with blossom. She holds the mandolin, the same mandolin that sits on the mantel back at his mother's house, except that this mandolin has no rot, no metal plate tacked on. Its polished wood glows rich in the moonlight. Carter sees the shimmer of the mandolin's intricately worked mother-of-pearl that he has often admired. The plum tree sits near the crumbling stone wall of the old cemetery, Rose Hill's slave cemetery, filled with simple, small markers, gray lichen-spotted marble flats with only first names, "Ella" or "Blount" or "Punchy," with death dates but no birth dates. The graves date from the early nineteenth century.

His grandmother sits in the topmost branches of the tree, twenty feet off the ground. He has never seen her this plainly before. He can see the snake-head ring on her finger, glittering, the ring Justina told them about. She sings a song he's never heard, a song about home. He knows she's aware of him but she doesn't look at him. He can never get a clear look at her eyes. The song floats through the air like an aroma of something burning. It surrounds him, consumes him like a flame.

Shafts of headlights pierce the darkness and Carter is startled by the grinding of an engine, the clashing of gears, tires spinning and slipping in the mud. He hears laughter. He sees it then, heading toward him, a pickup with oversized tires weaving fishlike in the muck. He recognizes the truck: Goodlowe Lewis's. He turns back to the plum tree and she's gone, vanished, the pink-white blossoms glistening and rustling slightly where she'd been. There are shouts now, whoops and clamorous laughter.

They see him, and the truck slides by him in the mud, turned sideways. He gets a look at Lewis, wrestling with the wheel, and three other white faces behind the mud-splattered windshield, in the middle the spectral drawn face of Billy Singleton. The men in the back hold on, giggle, a half-full beer can whistles by Carter's head, sprinkling him with a fine mist. The men hoot at him.

Earlier, they found a crate of rotting tomatoes in the alley behind the A & P over in Hammond and plan to ride through Frogbottom, pelting the so-called freedom people or anyone who happens to be on the streets. As Goodlowe makes another pass, the truck wallows and spews up black mud behind it like a rooster's tail. They fling the mushy fruit at Carter. The hurled tomatoes go wild, sailing through the air all around him. "We got maters, Carter!" they sing out. "We got maters!"

Carter stands still. He smells the tomatoes, sour and acid. He watches the truck make another hard U-turn and stop, the motor gunning, the laughter ringing. The truck sits there, threatening, gathering strength. They are drunk now. He knows they are going to try to run him down. Carter remembers Rachel, the way she looked the day at the bridge when the troopers on horseback descended on them. He sees her again in his mind's eye as she stood there with everything parting around her as though she possessed some invisible shield. He remembers the look on her face, the calm serenity. He walks into the road and stands there, looking at the truck. He cannot see any of the men's faces from this distance.

The only sound is the gunning motor, as though the truck itself—a mechanical monster— sits contemplating, planning. It reminds Carter of a massive bull about to charge. Then it roars forward. Carter, in the middle of the muddy road, doesn't move. He watches the oncoming truck. He sees the blobs of white faces behind the windshield, like petals blown against the glass. The truck picks up speed and comes directly toward him. He knows for sure they're going to run him down. He doesn't move.

In the moonlight, almost as bright as day, Carter sees Goodlowe Lewis's grim face, his eyes, and Billy Singleton shouts something. The truck picks up even more speed as it hurtles toward him. There is no way it can miss him. And yet deep down he knows it will, trusts it will. Suddenly it's behind him. He feels the hot wind from it. Turning, he sees the wide eyes of the men in back, holding on, swaying and jerking with the erratic move-ments of the truck, their mouths gaping at him in disbelief.

Billy sits tense with his hands against the dash, waiting for the wet and sickening thud, like hitting a dog or a watermelon. But it doesn't come. "What the fuck?" Goodlowe yelps.

"We missed him, we missed the son-of-a-bitch," Musgrove yells.

"Ain't no way." Goodlowe taps the brakes, yanks at the steering wheel. The mud-smeared windshield makes it hard to see. But Carter was right there, in the headlights. The big truck spins. All the weight in the back causes the large tires to bite deep. The truck rocks to a stop. Its headbeams illuminate the road. The moon lights the trees and bushes alongside the ditches. There is nothing in the road. It is as though Carter has been sucked into the air.

"Shit on a stick," Goodlowe Lewis yells.

Billy smells stale beer and sweat from the close hard bodies in the cab. He smells the rancid tomatoes and the mud, the faint, tart exhaust that leaks in. His body goes cold with a sudden chill.

"Son-of-a-bitch jumped in the ditch," Musgrove explains. "He's a quick bastid, ain't he?"

Billy knows better.

"He was right there," Lewis whines.

Billy knows better. He feels the sharp pain in his gut, so much a part of him now that he's learned to live with it. It comes on him without warn-ing and causes the skin on his face to grow taut. Billy knows that Carter has evaporated before their eyes, like a puff of fog or steam. Carter is Rachel Taylor's brother. Billy knows where the pain inside him came from but he doesn't know what to do about it. He thinks if he kills Rachel Taylor then he will surely die, too. She tortures him, but he recognizes that she is some-how his only link with life, the only one who can get the pain out of him.

"It's sin eatin you up, Billy," old Brother Grable would explain. "Replace it with Je-hee-sus!" His eyes would go all dreamy and vague, and Billy would realize again that Grable was crazy as a loon. Billy knows what's wrong with him.

Billy remembers how he and Rachel used to do it in the woods, in the green woods. In his memory it was always spring, always simple and uncomplicated. When you were a child you just wanted something, and all that mattered was whether you got it or not. He had wanted her warmth, her softness. Her heat. She had given, openly and eagerly. Billy thinks that Rachel was the only person in his life who ever gave to him.

He has to do something soon but doesn't know what. Something big, some grand gesture. He's waiting for a sign, something to tell him what to do, and then he'll do it. It will make sense when the time comes.

Goodlowe stops the truck where Carter had been standing. All the men get out and stand around in the mud. They pass around a bottle of Old Crow and chase it with Pabst Blue Ribbon. Bullfrogs croak in the ditches alongside the road, and crickets chirp in the brush. The men can all smell the old lake in the distance, like a creosote mill.

"You had him in your sights," one of the men says.

"He jumped clean," Goodlowe surmises.

"Naw. He was still standin there when we went by. You just missed the fucker."

"Maybe I hit him." There are hoots and laughter.

"You couldn't hit the insides of a barn if you was locked inside," one of them says.

"Fuck it, then."

Billy stands off to the side. He drinks off the last of a half pint of Cabin Hollow. The men wrestle over the fifth of Old Crow, giggling like schoolboys. They're oblivious to what Billy feels. He knows they're not alone. Someone is watching them. Maybe it's the sign that Billy has been looking for, but he can't see whoever it is. It must be Carter.

Then the light in the night air changes, grows brighter. They all notice it now and get quieter, except for Musgrove who laughs loudly like a child at table who's unaware that the blessing of the food has started. Like parents, they all shush him and start looking around. The crumbling old stone wall stands quietly. The plum tree's blossoms glisten as bright as day, as though they're illuminated by an inner light. And the cottonwood trees behind it begin to sway slightly in the breeze. From the new-leafed branches of the trees comes a huge swarm of butterflies, darting about and flickering above their heads. Yellow butterflies, glowing almost neon in the quickening light, and for a few moments it's as bright as noon.

The leaves of the underbrush on both sides of the road take on an incandescence so that each leaf is distinguishable, vivid. None of the men can move. Their faces are open and astonished as they look around at the butterflies, which now swirl like snowflakes in a windstorm.

They think they hear snatches of music and drums, a rapid, steady drumming that seems to echo from the trees and the swamp. The drums grow louder.

"Jesus," one of the men whispers.

"We better get outta here." Goodlowe Lewis leaps for his truck, and the other men follow, shoving at each other and grabbing arms to be the first to pile in. Only Billy stays put.

"Wait! Wait a minute. Don't...."

But they don't listen, and he doesn't want to be left by himself, so he catches up and jumps in over the tailgate, sprawling face-first into what is left of the rotting tomatoes. He had wanted to stay for a moment, to figure out what was happening, to see the sign. The truck roars and grinds up the road. Everyone is silent.

•   •   •

Joe Bynymo stands in the middle of the old cemetery. He watches the red taillights disappear down the road. He hears the drums, muffled and restrained, a muted beckoning. He sees the butterflies drift in the breeze in the now-empty roadway. Bynymo smells fire, and his flat nostrils flare. His eyes glow like embers. He raises both arms to the white men in a gesture of farewell, or perhaps of greeting. His overcoat bunches at his shoulder blades and spreads behind him like a bat's wings.

"Dambalah Wedo," he calls. "Behold your children!"

•   •   •

"Whose house is that?" one of the men asks.

"Rachel's," Billy responds, before he even thinks. He panics that they'll do something to her. The little cabin is dark. It sits back from the road behind fruit trees in bloom, a quince tree, fig and chinaberry trees. There is a scuppernong arbor and honeysuckle thick on the side fence.

"The blue gum," Goodlowe says.

"The hoodoo," Musgrove adds.

"Hey, what you stoppin here for?" one of the men in the back yells.

"She ain't at home," Billy says.

"How the fuck you know that? She might be asleep." Lewis narrows his eyes and stares through the windshield at the little house. He licks his lips.

One of the men in back throws half a tomato and they hear it splat against the tin roof. Lewis hands Billy the fifth of Old Crow. It's almost gone, and Billy turns it up and takes a drink. It burns his tongue. Billy is drunk but he doesn't want them doing anything to Rachel. They might kill her. "Let's go," he calls.

"Where?" Musgrove asks.

"I got to get home," Billy says.

"Jesus, Billy, you're pussy-whipped," Lewis laughs. He reaches behind him, pulling his shotgun, a 20-gauge pump, from the gun rack. He opens the door and the light comes on in the cab. Lewis steps out, grabbing two open boxes of shells, birdshot, and buckshot. He jams some birdshot into the chamber. His laughter sounds like grunts, a kind of hunh, hunh, hunh. Billy feels sick.

Lewis fires at the house, and glass breaks. Billy's stomach turns over, and he scrambles out and jumps down off the high running board onto the muddy road. Lewis fires again, and Billy vomits into the ditch. He feels as though he's turning inside out. BOOM, the gun sounds again. As Lewis pumps another shell into the chamber, the spent shell flips right by Billy's face and into the ditch.

He fires again and again, across the front of the house. The shot breaks all the glass and ricochets off the tin roof. The birdshot shatters the windows and rips through the black curtains. In the Altar Room the shotgun blasts smash the plaster of Paris Virgin into thousands of pieces and shred the picture of St. Patrick. The altar table tips over, spilling the old Carter family Bible onto the floor along with the Holy Water and the honey and the rum. The candles scatter, and the dried flowers and plastic figurines blow about like leaves in a whirlwind.

The lone lamp in Rachel's Spartan living room is hurled against the wall and breaks. The walls of the rooms are embedded with birdshot. The entire front of the house looks as though some berserk animal chewed it up. Still Lewis fires. He shoots up a half box of shells before he stops. All the other men, including Billy, watch him with their mouths hanging open, as though hypnotized by his actions. When he stops firing, the percussion still echoes in their ears, and the sharp sulfur odor of the gun smoke clogs their nostrils.

Billy's ears ring. "Jesus," he hears one of the men say.

•  •  •

Coming up the path through the woods, Rachel steps up to the backdoor when she hears the truck stop in front of her house. She listens. She thinks she hears Billy Simpleton's voice and the vague masculine murmuring of others. She knows, this time of night, they're drunk. And dangerous. She's certain they'll do something to her house, maybe torch it. They're capable of anything. She hears something that sounds wet and soft hit the tin roof, followed by laughter.

She tenses. Though she expects something else to happen, she still jumps at the sound of the first shotgun blast. She hears glass breaking. Another shot, then another, so loud she thinks they're directly over her head. Things shatter in her house. The spraying bird pellets splatter against the interior walls. She makes herself into a tight ball, her arms shielding her head, the exploding shells so loud in her ears that she can hear nothing else, not even her own breathing that comes in gasps or the rapid beating of her heart.

After a long time, after what seems a decade, the shots stop. Rachel doesn't move. She feels the sharp edge of the stoop wedging into her back. She hears the truck doors slam, hears the engine catch and the driver rev it. The truck rumbles down the muddy road.

Rachel doesn't move at all until the sound of the truck dies. She knows it has stopped at Carter's house. Her head comes up, and her eyes are bright and sharp in the darkness. She doesn't know if Carter is home. But she's certain that Karla and Eshu are there. *Eshu.*

• • •

Karla is in the kitchen feeding Eshu when she hears the gunshots, like a dove shoot or a war, down the road toward Rachel's place. Carter isn't home yet. She figures the gunshots have something to do with him. She recognizes them as white men's gunshots. They come from the direction of Rachel's house. Her body tenses. Eshu stops sucking, sensing her fear. He knows.

When the gunshots stop, Karla soon hears the sound of a truck. She gets up, holding the baby tightly against her, and shuts off the light. The front of the house is dark. She hears the truck stop and the sound of men's voices. They chant in a singsong way, as though they are saying something like "Come on out Carter, we got a mater for you...." She stands very still in the dark, her entire body rigid and shaking. She squeezes Eshu against her. She looks up the hall and sees the reflection of the truck's headlights through the curtains at the front window. The men are milling around. She hears their laughter.

The suddenness of the blast causes her to jerk back and cry out, muffling her cry at the same time because she is terrified they'll hear her. She hears the glass in the windowpanes break and shatter on the floor and shots slash into the wall near where she stands. Whimpering, shaking with terror, she squats low on the linoleum as another burst of fire splinters the front door. Looking desperately around, she crawls across the floor and squeezes herself between the wall and the stove, still warm from the cornbread she baked earlier for Carter.

She crouches there, crying, holding Eshu. She can see his eyes in the darkness, like black pearls. The men hoot in the road. More shots tear through the front of the house and shred the furniture and walls. Some of the stray shot pings against the sink and the stove next to her head. A pitcher of milk on the table falls and shatters across the floor. Karla moans in horror. Locked stiff, unable to move, she now knows that she is going to die and that Eshu will, too, if she doesn't do something to save him. She shivers, her breath coming in quick inhalations. Then a high, long moan escapes from her, a shrill sound like some strange singing she's never heard before. She rocks back and forth on her haunches. Her eyes shut tight, she holds Eshu against her chest, one breast still free and jutting, the nipple long and engorged where his feeding was interrupted. Then she reaches up with her free arm and pulls open the oven door, smelling the lingering scent of cornbread, feeling the gentle warmth of the air inside. She pushes Eshu into the oven.

Almost immediately a blast rocks the house, followed by another, buckshot now that Lewis has spent the box of birdshot and reloaded again. Some of the heavy, hot lead balls rip into Karla's side and cause her body to jerk upright, her eyes to fly open wide. And she hears another shot, a further jolt to her body, that hurls her against the stove and wedges her there.

Then the shots stop. Surrounded by a heavy silence, Karla tries to move but can't. She hears the men's voices, distant and faint, and the sound of the truck starting, the clashing of gears. Then the truck is gone, and she's alone in the thick, cloying quiet. She tries to cry out, but no sound comes. She feels life seep out of her as her blood flows onto the floor. Eshu is safe in the warm stove, safe and guarded. She cannot close her eyes or move her hands. Then the searing pain suddenly leaves her body, the awful thirst is gone from her mouth. In the moonlight shining through the kitchen windows, she sees the spilled milk mingle with her blood on the linoleum floor. She ebbs away into darkness and silence.

• • •

Rachel makes her way down the road toward Carter's house, keeping to the ditch and the moon shadows. Then she leaves the road and cuts through a pasture to come up from the back. The new blackberry vines, wild strawberries, and briers grab at her long skirt. She's barefoot. She hadn't expected to walk anywhere tonight but on a worn path. And she didn't want to enter her house after the white men destroyed it. She couldn't bear the thought of seeing what they'd done.

Carter's house is dark, still, and quiet. Nothing moves at all. Rachel is careful not to step on the shattered glass from the windowpanes in the backdoor.

"Karla?" she whispers, then louder, "Karla?"

No answer. She pushes open the door. The darkness feels as deep as the middle earth, the quiet broken only by the ticking sound of her mother's old windup clock. Then the electric pump starts up. It hums for a few seconds and then shuts off. Rachel is almost sure the men are gone. She'll take that chance. Switching on the light, a low-wattage, naked bulb that dangles from the ceiling, she immediately sees the blood and milk swirled together on the uneven linoleum floor, the unnaturally bright red and the otherworldly white twined together like a pattern in marble. Rachel stands transfixed, unable to turn her eyes away. Even as she stares, she traces the steady flow of blood to a point behind the stove. Her bare feet slip on the mixture, feeling its heat, its coldness, as she moves to the stove. Then she sees Karla's lifeless eyes, already filming over, wide with a kind of mute astonishment, staring back at her.

"Eshu!" Rachel cries aloud. She looks around and notices that the oven door is open, the edge of blue blanket hanging from it. She knows instantly what Karla has done to save her baby. She reaches in and pulls the bundle from the oven.

She folds back the blanket. Eshu's eyes, steady and shining, frame her in the weak light of the kitchen. Flooded with relief, Rachel stands for a moment holding the child, then switches the light back off. Silver moonlight spills across the cluttered kitchen floor. Rachel puts Eshu on the table and inspects him carefully in the dimness. She can see only his face, which looks almost white in the filtered moonlight. For a moment she thinks that he's not Eshu but Cap, her baby of long ago. She cries out, "Sweet Jesus! Thank God!" Rooted to that spot, her feet sticky in the mixture of blood and milk, she squints at him. As white as plaster, as colorless as snow, he seems to shimmer and glow, almost to vibrate.

She knows the men will come back. She senses someone coming and picks up the baby. He's hot to the touch. She hurries toward the backdoor. She knows where she must take Eshu. She can see clearly as air where she must take him, where he will be safe.

• • •

Carter awakens to the sound of distant gunfire that sounds like fire-crackers popping. He sits up, alert, in the little cemetery, next to a slab that reads "JIM, 1856." He doesn't remember how he got there or why he fell asleep. He recalls only the truck as it hurtled by him or over him, he doesn't know which. He recalls only the startled faces of the men inside. Listening for a moment to the gunfire, he scrambles to his feet, suddenly remembering where he is and why.

He cuts across an open pasture toward the sound. It comes first from Rachel's house and then his own. He tries to run, but the thick black soil clutches at his shoes and drags against him. He thinks of Eshu. He knows that Karla and Eshu are there in the house. The oily black clay seems to want to pull him under, like the recurring nightmare he had as a child, running against some powerful force that slowed him to an agonizing crawl, toward some obscure destination he knew was momentous. Now he understands that dream, its purpose. It is his son.

Armed with only his straight razor, he feels it folded cold and smooth against his skin under his shirt. It will not be much of a weapon against a 20-gauge shotgun. Carter chants in his mind twenty, twenty, twenty in time with his strained breathing and laborious strides, a mantra that distracts his imagination away from the horrible images it wants to conjure up.

Before Carter manages to cross the field and hoist himself over the barbed-wire fence and into the road in front of his house, the shooting stops and the truck pulls away. Carter hears its engine start up and sees the headlights; he hears the high, shrill laughter, the shouting. As he gets closer to his house he sees the chewed-up wood siding, the shattered windows, the shards glimmering like cheap jewels on the ground. He sprints across the hard-packed dirt of the front yard, kicking the sticky mud from his feet. The screen door hangs on its hinges. The wooden door is in splinters. Carter pushes into the front room.

"Karla?" he shouts. "KARLA!" There is only silence. He switches on the light. The living room is a wreck. The lamps and figurines, ashtrays and framed pictures are scattered about on the floor, and the newspaper on the walls hangs in tatters as though peeled off in strips by a mischievous child. Carter runs down the short hallway, looking into the bedrooms. He slips when he gets to the kitchen. Its floor is littered with broken glass, milk, and blood. "KARLA!"

As soon as he sees her body jammed into the space between the wall and the stove, he knows she's dead. Grasping her body by the legs, he pulls, struggling with the weight of her. When he moves her to the middle of the room he sees that she's been shot through the middle, her body torn and bloody. He breathes rapidly, panting, and allows a whimper of mourning to escape his lips. Tears sting his eyes. "Eshu!" he screams. "Eshu!"

He searches the house, ripping the bedclothes from the crib, looking everywhere yet sensing that his son is not there. They've taken him. Exhausted, out of breath, he's terrified at what they might do to Eshu. Blind rage surges through him, a fury so hot that it sears his brain.

He rummages through the closet and finds the Browning automatic shotgun, propped barrel-up in the corner. With the silver inlay on the hand-carved stock, it's the gun Mr. Oscar gave him years ago. Filling his pockets with buckshot shells, he stands in the dead silence of his house, holds the gun in the crook of his arm, his eyes fixed firmly on the door and the muddy road beyond.

Etched permanently in his imaginings, he can hear the sound of the truck driving away, the laughter.

●   ●   ●

The wet ground is cold against Rachel's bare feet. Vines grab at her ankles, and brambles sting her legs. She hardly notices as she strides, a steady, pistonlike jog, her eyes focused straight ahead. She cuts across the field behind the big house, clutching Eshu to her breasts. Her skirt hem is already ragged and torn by the briers.

Though the moon has started its descent, Rachel finds a path. She knows this place so well the darkness doesn't slow her. She hears bullfrogs plop into the water, scurrying in the undergrowth, as she approaches. She is startled by a lean cow the sound of her footsteps scares out of its wallow. The cow rolls over and then crashes clumsily and noisily into the bushes.

She passes along the creek behind Justina's and Gilbert's dark cabins, beyond them the huge old white house glowing in the dying moonlight. She crosses through the pear orchard and turns onto the chert drive down to the main road.

Wary of walking on the road, afraid the men will come back, she walks at the edge of the woods and the fields, near the fence row, brushing plum bushes and saplings aside, shielding Eshu with her arm. All her concentration is fixed on her destination. She worries about the river bridge, doesn't want to cross the bridge on foot, because it offers no place to hide. She tries to think of another way to cross the river but can't concentrate. She keeps walking. She hears a car or truck coming and crouches in thick willow bushes until it passes, speeding down the road toward the highway. It doesn't even occur to her to see if it's Carter. She knows she can't take that chance. It's up to her, now. In her deepest heart she knows that it's always been that way, and like the depths of the sky and the slow turning of the earth it will never change.

● ● ●

Squinting through the windshield, Carter hears the chert pebbles rattle inside the fenders. His headlights pick up thin shreds of mist forming in the dark gray air, presages of an early-morning fog. He knows where Lewis lives and where Musgrove lives. He knows the truck. He'll find it.

Gripping the steering wheel tightly enough to turn his knuckles white, he chews his lower lip. The gun leans against the seat next to him. The razor nestles on his upper belly, cool there.

In the mist he imagines Karla's lifeless eyes, unfocused and vague, an image that causes his head to pound and his hands to sweat. He knows he can't focus too clearly on Karla, her maimed body, her stillness, or he'll collapse.

He turns onto the empty highway, south toward town. The center lines zip toward him like arrows, as though his car is eating them. Carter presses the accelerator to the floor. Ahead, he sees the tall white bridge curve gracefully in the waning moonlight.

●   ●   ●

Later, with the moon low in the sky, Rachel stands on the north bank of the wide Coosa and looks across at Hammond, the few lights of the sleeping town twinkling in the darkness. She's out of breath, her bones and muscles ache. The tall bridge arches above her. The river is high, near flood stage, and muddy; its current is swift, though she knows it's slower here than downriver.

At the end of a rutted road she has followed through the swampy woods is a boat landing with several skiffs, fishing boats, the boats' mooring chains and ropes tight as the current pulls and tugs at them. Equipped with oars, old coolers, and rusted tin baling cans, the boats are padlocked. But Rachel finds one with an old lock. Holding Eshu, she picks up a sharp rock the shape of a small loaf of bread. She manages to pound it on the lock over and over again. It's noisy work. An old fishing shack up on pilings about fifty yards away looks deserted. Her whole arm hurts, a pain like a hundred wasps' stings. But she keeps on lifting and dropping the rock.

Finally the rusted lock breaks. Rachel pulls at the chain, at the same time scampering into the boat, nesting Eshu in the prow where it's dry. She arranges the oars and bales out the bottom. She hopes it's nothing but rainwater, not a leak. Fixed on the house across the river, she doesn't even allow for the possibility that they won't make it. In reality she is already there. She pulls at the oars, grunting, her shoulders stiff and aching, her entire body sore. It seems a long way across the river. Looking over her shoulder at Eshu in the prow, the bundle of blanket, she cannot see his face, his eyes. She smells the murky water, the mud of the bank. She hears the current, a steady, deep pull that seems to come from the center of the earth. She knows the waters contain trunks of uprooted trees, branches, parts of outbuildings washed away and swept along. She knows this current is the most powerful force she's ever struggled against.

But she was raised on the river. It doesn't intimidate her. And she instinctively turns the boat upriver, against the current, and begins to pull harder, calculating her angles, anticipating that she'll move faster downriver than across, will be drawn by the current through the junction and on around toward the landing where a new marina is under construction. That's where she must make ground. Below that the steep chalk bluffs rise straight up to the sky.

She works automatically, methodically. Sweat plasters her blouse and skirt to her body. She battles the current that wants to take her past the town, downriver all the way to the gulf. But she has to let it propel her— give in to its power and control it at the same time. Her eyes burn and her chest aches. She thinks her heart and lungs might burst. Still she pulls at the oars. She doesn't know where her strength comes from. She even falls asleep briefly, then jerks awake, newly aware of where she is, her eyes darting to landmarks on the other side to gauge her progress.

When they pass through the junction where the Coosa and the Bigbee join, she can feel her speed increase. She hears the boiling and eddies, the deep, steady roar of the current. Scanning the shore, she sighs in relief. She sees that she's far enough on the other side of the river that she can guide the boat to shore at the landing. Even though the boat eases out of the river's gripping fingers and into stiller waters, she keeps up her rhythm, looking over her shoulder, eyeing the landing coming, the street leading down to it. These sights bring her a dull satisfaction. She just nods, and then nods again, and pulls on the oars.

The boat's prow grinds into the gravel. Stepping into the water, the sharp pebbles on the muddy bottom cutting her feet, she is so stiff that she falls to one knee, and the cold water seems to revive her. She shakes uncontrollably from the cold and her exhaustion. She looks quickly around. The landing is deserted, very dark, the moon faded in the predawn chill. She hears nothing but the steady, dull roar of the river, the sound that clings to her like a smell.

She pulls Eshu from the boat. He's so heavy she can barely lift him. Her arms and legs are weak and rubbery, her hands blistered and raw from the oars. Blood runs down one leg where she cut her knee when she fell. Her skirt is filthy, soiled with mud and perspiration and blood.

Rachel pulls the blanket back and looks at Eshu. His black eyes stare back at her, soft and luminous. He knows too much, she thinks. It's as though he can see into her soul, as though he's somehow known her since before she was born. She has thought it many times before.

"You know all the secrets," Rachel says aloud, looking long at him. She shudders again.

She turns up the road, but something makes her stop. She can barely make out the snake on the ground, a dark gray water moccasin, thick, heavy, five feet long, its head raised as though staring at her. Frozen stiff, afraid to move, she doesn't know how long she stands there. Then the snake slithers off across the crushed limerock and into the underbrush. Rachel realizes that she's not been breathing, that her heart hasn't been beating, that she's been suspended in a state not even fully alive.

All those miles through the swamps and in the thick weeds—when she had feared every second that she'd step on a snake—and then here on a street, on the town side of the river, she sees one, fat and sluggish, undulating away from her in a kind of haughty slow motion to disappear into the ditch without a sound. She thinks for a moment she dreamed it. She puts her foot down tentatively, looks all around her.

Bent with the effort like an old woman, she continues up the steep incline of the road. The baby feels as heavy as a sack of bricks. When she reaches the top, where the street levels out, she does not think she can go a step farther. She sits down for a moment on a bench in the cool darkness. She's so tired that she knows she can't rest long, that she might well go to sleep from exhaustion.

She hears a car in the distance, watches it go through an empty intersection three blocks away, coming down from the flats atop the bluffs. A soft cry snags in her throat. She's almost sure it's Carter's car. Then she's afraid that she's dreaming that, too, like the snake, and she shakes her head, grits her teeth, and with great effort stands up. Only four or five more blocks to go, to get to the big white house on the bluffs.

She turns down dark alleys and side streets, approaching the house from the river side, from the back. She walks on cinders and doesn't even feel the pain. She climbs a couple of fences, and dogs wake up and bark at her. But she pays them no attention, moving as steadily as the river current. They bark and snarl, then stop, whimper, circle her, and sniff at her legs. Finally Rachel kicks at them, says, "Gitouttahere, dawgs!" They scatter.

She approaches the dark house through the gardens. She passes by the statue of the naked woman, breasts as bare as if she were nursing a baby.

Rachel, almost giddy now with relief and fatigue, thinks, Yes, maybe she can nurse him now that Karla's gone, maybe she has milk in them stone titties, or they can just give him sweet milk or some of that new formula or whatever, because anything will be alright with him. Maybe Hester can feed him from whatever thin pale good would come from them old skinny tits of hers! Maybe he won't even need to be fed! Maybe he can just take his nourishment from the air, like Spanish moss or a ghost.

She crosses the back gallery and pounds on the kitchen door with her fist. It takes a long time before the kitchen light comes on and the door is unlocked and cracked open. And she sees Hester's face, her dreadlocks hanging down, Hester frowning at her. Hester pulls the door open wider and stands there, clutching a red chenille bathrobe to her throat. Her eyes are wide. She looks Rachel up and down, stares at Eshu in her arms.

"Yes," Hester nods. "All right. You have brought him home."

●   ●   ●

Carter finds the truck almost by accident.

He'd driven around the town with a kind of stoic patience. Goodlowe Lewis's house out in Shortleaf was dark, the driveway empty. The downtown was deserted, nothing open but the white poolroom—Red's—on Washington Street, where yellow light spilled out across the sidewalk. The square looked still and barren, the towering old elm trees casting shadows almost like midday.

Now he drives down Commissioners Street, past Hawthorne, sitting silent and unlit behind its black wrought-iron fence. Then on impulse he turns up the narrow street leading to the plateau atop the bluffs, the grassy area where yesterday he and Dooly had drunk the shine and then fought. He sees the reflection of taillights and instinctively douses his lights and shuts off his motor. This is the truck he's been looking for.

Quickly he gets out of his car, pulls the shotgun after him. The pockets of his pants sag with the weight of extra shells. Craning his ears, he listens but he hears nothing, nothing but the distant, steady whisper of the river. Moving carefully up the road, he smells the gun oil, faint, like wisps of perfume on the damp air. The truck sits facing the river, the door on the passenger's side standing open. He pauses, listens again, cups his hand behind his ear.

The interior of the cab is dimly lit, and he thinks he sees something move, someone's head, but he can't be sure. Then he picks up the scent of the rancid tomatoes, their barbed acid. The smell assaults his nose like a fist. Maters, Carter.... We got maters.... He can hear the voices, their insulting condescension. Close enough now to see the mud caked in the treads of the oversize tires, he hears something in the truck, something rustling like a squirrel in a nest. His eyes fix on the open door, the soft golden interior light barely strong enough to make out forms, bodies, men. Squinting his eyes, Carter moves closer, setting the soles of his shoes down flat on the crushed limerock.

He hears them: a grunt, a guttural command he can't make out. He pauses long enough to pull the loop of cord with the razor over his head. He flicks his wrist and lets the razor fall open. It's honed so sharp that merely touching it with the meat of his thumb raises a pearly bead of his own blood.

He moves closer to the truck, holding the razor in one hand, his shotgun in the other. He sees them now. Reared back against the seat, Goodlowe Lewis moans, his bulk crowding the cab, his head thrown back and moving from side to side. Crouching in front of him, Musgrove kneels on the running board, his head in Lewis's lap. Carter can see the white splotch of Musgrove's birthmark as his head moves up and down rapidly. Lewis cries, "All right! All right! Uhhhh. Uhhhhh."

Without even thinking, Carter moves so quickly that later he won't remember all the details. But for now everything has the clarity of crystal. He shoves the shotgun barrel in Lewis's face. At the same time encircles Musgrove's neck with his right arm, the razor against his throat. Carter knows that it's already drawing blood even as Musgrove's head bobs up. Lewis's eyes pop open wide, his thick lips blubbering, "What the...what the shit...hey...."

"Where is he?" Carter demands. Musgrove tries to pull back against him and Carter tightens his grip. "Don't move, or I slice your windpipe," he threatens, and Musgrove whimpers and grows still and tight, trembling.

"Who?!" Goodlowe Lewis asks in a desperate scream. "Who...who you mean?"

"My boy."

"I don't know nothin bout your boy," Lewis sputters. Beads of sweat cover his face. Shaking, he looks cross-eyed at the gun barrel. "Wait a minute now. Wait...."

"No," Carter shouts. "You shot up my house. You killed my wife. Where's my son?"

"I don't know, man. Honest. We didn't even...we...."

"We didn't go in the house," Musgrove pleads. "I didn't even get out of the truck. You're cuttin me. Please."

"Shut up," Carter spits, shoving the gun into Lewis's cheek. The fat man grimaces, and his lips move but no sound comes out.

"You got to believe us," Musgrove cries.

"Why? You killed my wife," Carter shouts at him.

He looks into the man's desperate eyes and has a sudden clear image of Karla's lifeless face, the splintered front door, the sound of white men's laughter. He tightens the pressure of the razor on Musgrove's throat and pulls it across, feels it slice deep. Musgrove's back bucks against him as his head falls forward. He makes a sound halfway between a shocked cry and a gurgle. Then his head turns to the side, his eyes already rolling back into his head. His hot red blood spurts out all over Lewis's pale, hairy legs. Lewis yells, his face frozen in terror. "Oh goddam, oh Jesus! Help me, god-dammit!"

Carter sees Lewis's dick then, thick, still almost hard and covered with Musgrove's shiny blood. Lewis sees him look and screams, "No! Wait a...."

With one deft motion of the razor Carter slices it clean off, and it tumbles like a fat sausage to the floor beside Musgrove's body. Lewis's blood spouts from the severed stump, his face mirroring pain and utter disbelief. He stares, shocked, at where his dick had been only a second before, engorged and sensitive, his dick of thirty-nine years. His blood splatters the dashboard and the inside of the windshield.

Lewis's eyes begin to glaze over. He leans forward. His lips quiver as though he's trying to say something. Carter swings the barrel away and brings it crashing into Lewis's face, across his nose, and his head jerks back against the seat. Carter hits him again in the head. Lewis's bloated body crumbles. Carter hits him one more time. Lewis falls forward against the steering wheel, his eyes still open but out cold. Or maybe he's already dead, Carter doesn't know.

Carter steps back. The inside of the truck is a bloody mess. Pushing Musgrove's legs into the truck, Carter rolls the window half-way down and pushes the door shut. He throws the shotgun and the razor on the grass and runs around to the driver's door. Opening it, he rolls down that window, too. He reaches in under Lewis's body and, depressing the clutch with one hand, yanks the truck into neutral. Carter throws the razor and the shotgun into the back of the truck.

Bracing himself behind the big truck, Carter begins to push with his legs. He grits his teeth, closes his eyes, pushes as hard as he can. Gradually the truck moves, only inches at first then faster. Carter turns and pushes with his hands flat against the tailgate. The big tires gather their own momentum, and the truck rolls toward the bluff, picking up speed as it goes, and Carter has to trot, still pushing as the bluff declines toward the edge and toward the wide black darkness beyond. Carter stops himself at the bluff's edge and watches the big truck glide off and turn slowly in a prolonged somersault, hurtling toward the river below. It twists gracefully as it falls but hits the water with such force that water splashes fifty feet into the air. An explosive sound shatters the predawn quiet a few seconds later. It causes two policemen on night duty, drinking coffee at the courthouse, to look up. One of them asks, "What was that?" The other shrugs, "We better go check it out."

"In a minute," the other says. Then they forget about it.

In houses along the bluff people roll over in their sleep and turn their pillows cool-side-up. And dogs look up, ears cocked. But the sound is gone as quickly as it came, its reverberations muffled and muted by the bluffs and the water and the thick swamps across the river. From high above, Carter watches the surface of the river, glittering in what is left of the moonlight, as the truck moves downriver, half submerged and then almost gone completely, only the top of the cab showing. Then nothing. In the murky water, the truck turns slowly, like a pinwheel, toward the muddy bottom eighty-four feet below. The lifeless bodies float face up in the cab, blood drifting and fanning out featherlike, growing diluted, then invisible as it's absorbed into the water that crawls steadily and forcefully back to the sea.

# Billy

IN A MOMENT OF DRUNKENNESS, BILLY SINGLETON GETS THE sign. His children swarm around the red Formica table where Jessie Merle fixes them banana sandwiches. Billy barely remembers their names anymore. The youngest, Billy John, in diapers and a smudged yellow Mickey Mouse T-shirt, eats cornflakes from the box. Standing barefoot on the linoleum floor, he stares at his father, his hand at his mouth.

"What the hell you lookin at?" Billy growls.

"Billy! For God's sakes!" Jessie Merle says over the din.

Billy drinks some of his own shine, right from the jar. He looks at Jessie Merle, the way her ass has started to spread. Her waist is disappearing. She's taken to tying her hair up in a topknot like Sister Ruple's, but it falls loose and dangles in limp wisps around her head.

Holding a table knife caked with mayonnaise, she looks at him. Two loaves of sliced sandwich bread sit open on the table. The children snatch at each other's sandwiches, and she swats at their hands with the flat of the knife. Billy takes a long drink from the jar. It burns his mouth. Its fumes make his nostrils twitch like he's about to sneeze.

"Dr. Hughes says I have a ulcer," he says. "He's full of shit."

"He's a doctor."

"And he's full of shit."

"You ought to listen to him. That stuff is poison. It's devil's brew."

"You sayin I'm the devil? Cause I brewed it."

"Stop it, Billy," she says.

"No, is that what you're sayin?" Slurring his words, he swells up, trying to look resentful and proud, things that he doesn't really feel. He knows that's not what she meant, but it's a way to pick a fight.

Jessie Merle ignores him. She holds a piece of bread on the flat of her hand and slaps mayonnaise on it with the knife.

"I don't want no banana," little Nancy whines, "I just want a mayonnaise sanwich."

"You can't eat just a mayonnaise sanwich," says Henry, dressed in short pants without a shirt. "There ain't no sucha thing as just a mayonnaise sanwich," Henry says, then pulls Nancy's hair and she screams.

"Jesus," Billy yells. "I can't come in my own house without gettin a headache."

"We need a bigger house, Billy," Jessie Merle complains, pushing Henry and Nancy apart with her elbow. "They're growing and we need a bigger house."

A big house, Billy thinks. A big house. He remembers passing by the old Legrand place, shuttered and dark in the moonlight. Rose Hill, they call it, like a bunch of priss-asses from England or something. Naming a house, for God's sake. The old man is dead. "He's the meanest son-of-a-bitch that ever lived," his father once told him, "a rich bastard that don't care about nothin but hisself." "The Big House," the Negroes still call it. Closed up, with enough room and furniture for ten families. Sitting empty, owned by the family that owns all the land for miles in any direction, the family that sits back on their fat asses and takes thirty-five percent of every acre of soybeans you raise, every gallon of milk you sell. Every goddam dozen eggs you hoard beyond what you need to feed your own family. And if you're damn fool enough to still plant and chop and pick cotton they help themselves to thirty-five of every hundred pounds of that, too! Unfair, like everything else in life.

"The Big House." Maybe that's the sign he's been looking for. It belongs to the governor of the whole state now. When they passed it last night, the house seemed to glow in the moonlight, it was so white. "If we ain't careful," Luscious Willie always warned, "southern white men are gonna be the new niggers." Billy has a vision of himself and all his buddies from the landfill, all his friends in the Klan, all dressed in overalls with bandannas on their heads, bent over picking cotton in the sun while Carter Taylor stands on the wagon with a bullwhip and a shotgun and laughs at them.

"Fuck that," he mutters aloud.

"Billy! Watch your tongue!"

His family crowds the little kitchen. They swim before his eyes. His son Henry grins at him. "Fuck that, Paw, fuck that!" he repeats.

"Shut up, boy," Billy says.

"Fuckfuckfuckfuck," says Henry.

•  •  •

Billy puts a couple of five-gallon cans full of gasoline in his truck, plus a pile of old rags thick and stiff with paint stains and turpentine. He loads up a bundle of yellowed old newspapers, too. He plans to break into the house through a front window and set as many fires on the first floor as he can. The old house ought to go up like a tinderbox, ought to make a fire that will be seen for twenty miles in any direction. From Hammond across the river and from the Upper Room I Am Temple, from everywhere.

He pulls up to the house and starts to unload, noticing the faded LEGRAND FOR GOVERNOR sticker on the tailgate of his truck. He remembers once going to see Oscar Legrand at his office at the bank, years ago, even before he had gone to work for Chemco. In his faded, patched, and shapeless overalls and heavy, clunky shoes, he went to ask for a loan for some new milking machines and to ask for a new roof on the house he was renting from the Legrands for thirty dollars a month. Oscar Legrand kept him waiting for an hour. Then he treated Billy with impatience and quickly sent him downstairs to talk with a snooty man in a suit and horn-rimmed glasses. That man turned him down flat for the loan and the roof, too. Billy left there feeling humiliated and furious.

As a boy, he often rode by Rose Hill with his father and saw the old man and whoever happened to be visiting. They'd be sitting on the veranda taking in the afternoon sun, drinking good red whiskey, the kind you can only buy in the state liquor store: Wild Turkey, Jack Daniels, Haig and Haig in those pinch bottles with wire net on them—whiskey that cost almost as much as most men made in a week.

Billy has harbored a glum resentment for old man Legrand and his family for all these years. It feels heavy inside him like nausea. He works like a dog for every little scrap he has, but people like the Legrands have everything without working at all. Billy seethes with the unfairness of it all. It has smoldered inside him for as long as he can remember. He unloads that stinking acidic waste at their landfill for hours on end so that the Legrands can sit and drink their smooth red whiskey.

He'll show them. He'll show everybody. Including that damn fool Brother Grable and that idiot Dr. Hughes. And Rachel Taylor. When she sees what he's capable of, maybe she'll take the hex off him. He'll put the fear of God in her, by damn.

He unloads the newspapers and the rags and the gasoline. Billy carries the cans up onto the porch of the old house, which is still and quiet. The towering thick magnolia trees crowd the sky and blot out the moonlight. Nervous and jumpy, Billy jerks back when he sees a man standing there. He realizes it's only a shadow, a construction of leaves and light from the sky. Nothing moves. Billy hears no sounds, no traffic, no constant drone from the television that fills his home from dawn to midnight. After moments of silence, he hears an owl, miles away, distant and deep in the swamps, a lone owl's single, entreating cry.

The ancient house feels heavy with its past, its history. Billy thinks he should be able to hear all the voices it has absorbed in more than a century. The laughter and music. But the house sits mute, ungiving, everything empty and hollow.

Billy looks around. He tries a window. It's locked, so he pulls a ball-peen hammer from his back pocket and wraps its head in his handkerchief. He knocks out a pane. The glass breaks on the hardwood floor inside, and Billy crouches and listens intently. After a minute he reaches in and unlocks the window. He raises it and lifts the gas cans, newspapers, and rags through. Then he climbs inside.

He stands blinking. It takes a few moments for his eyes to become accustomed to the dark. Moonlight slants through the closed drapes on some of the windows. Billy switches on his flashlight and shines it on furniture covered with white sheets. Dust motes float lazily in the beam. Billy has the sudden sense of being underwater, of being at the bottom of the sea. Then something moves. He's sure he sees something move in the corner by the fireplace and he shines his flashlight there. There is nothing but rose wallpaper, faded pink.

He realizes he's sweating. He feels frightened, feels another presence in the house. Perhaps he's in the company of all the Legrands who've passed through it. He keeps looking over his shoulder, sure that someone is standing there. But the old house ticks and settles in its own emptiness. Shadows bloom and swell around the high ceilings as he shines his light around at the portraits on the walls, the people looking at him with solemn recognition. He knows they know who he is. And he knows they think he's trash.

"What the hell you think you lookin at?" he demands, his voice echoing in the rooms. He hears his voice even before he realizes that he's spoken. He thinks that surely someone else asked the question. He places his light on a table, begins to pile up the rags and newspapers in the corners of several rooms. He opens the gas cans and douses the piles, the carpets, and the mounds of furniture. He slings gas onto the drapes.

"What you doin?" a voice asks. At first Billy doesn't even pause, doesn't even acknowledge it because he knows it's in his head, that he's imagining it. Then it comes again, almost in a scream, "What...what you doin?!" Billy freezes, then whirls around to see a man standing there in the hallway holding a lantern. Billy's heart leaps into his throat. The lantern light glints on the long barrel of a rifle the man holds in his other hand. Billy grabs the ball-pin hammer and raises it like a hatchet, moves with the quickness of a woods cat. He hears the sickening thunk of the hammer hitting flesh and bone. The lantern clatters in one direction, the rifle in the other. The lantern breaks and flames lick across the floor. The drapes and a pile of rags ignite with a deafening whoosh. Billy flings the hammer across the room and gropes back toward the broken window.

• • •

Gilbert Washington had been sitting in a folding chair in the cool night air under his chinaberry tree when first saw the headlights. He thought, All right, yes. It's Carter come home late from over cross the river, because they must be getting nigh to startin their walk to Montgomery by now. And then he saw the reflection of light coming from inside the house, just a flicker, like lightning behind a heavy cloud.

Gilbert often sat out here, sometimes almost all night, because he couldn't sleep very well anymore. His bones ached when he'd lie down. So he'd place his chair where he could follow the moon's arching journey down the night sky. His old hound dog, Abner Doubleday, would doze beside the chair. Though he had never seen a professional game in person, Gilbert was a baseball fan. He followed Jackie Robinson's career and pasted pictures of him torn from newspapers and magazines to his cabin walls. He also taped up pictures of Larry Doby and Luke Easter and Willy Mays. He'd listened to games on the radio for years and recently had been able to watch games on his snowy little television when the Meridian station broadcast them on Saturday afternoons. The games came from St. Louis and New York and Chicago and as far away as Boston.

Unlike Justina next door, Gilbert had schooling, could read and write. He even spent a year at Tuskegee Institute. For decades Gilbert made all the grocery lists and did all the shopping for Rose Hill while Justina kept the kitchen and the beds. They both cleaned. Mr. Dupree always bragged that Gilbert could make the best mint julep in the state of Alabama. And Gilbert drove for Mr. Dupree until he himself became too old to get behind the wheel.

Gilbert knew that someone was in the big house, burgling it. Gilbert never considered that there might be too many for him to handle or that he was too old and weak to deal with it. He went inside his cabin and loaded his old twenty-two. He had no telephone. He planned to hold the rifle on the intruders, then call the high sheriff from the house. He would call Sheriff Tate and have him send someone out to pick them up. He lit a kerosene lantern he kept on the porch and walked across the backyard, past

the old smokehouse to the big house. Thin and stooped, he wore sus-
penders that crossed his white shirt in the middle of his narrow back to
hold up his loose-fitting pants.

Gilbert unlocked the back door and slipped inside. The kitchen
smelled faintly of spices, garlic, and nutmeg. Everything was put away and
shining clean. He stood there listening to what sounded vaguely, in his old
ears, like someone rummaging about in the front of the house. Moonlight
spilled through the windows, brightening the kitchen. He thought he
heard a thump. Then he smelled raw gasoline so sharp and quick and unex-
pected inside the house that he jerked his head back.

As he went down the hall, the smell grew stronger, suffocating. Gilbert
stopped in the doorway and saw him then, in the lantern light and in the
beam of the intruder's flashlight: Billy Simpleton. Sorry white trash, his rat-
colored hair close-cropped on his skull, he was busy dousing the curtains
with the gasoline from a rusty can. Billy Simpleton.

Though Gilbert knew immediately what Billy was doing, "What you
doin?" he demanded.

Billy continued to work for a moment and then turned to face him, his
face ashen, his mouth hanging open in surprise, his snaggled teeth gaping.

"What...what you doin?" Gilbert asked again, more loudly.

●    ●    ●

By the time Billy scrambles back across the porch and into his truck,
flames shoot from the windows and lick the sides of the house. His breathing is harsh and strained. He stops his truck on a slight rise and looks back.
The entire sky glows orange from the fire. He's trembling. "Jesus," he
whimpers, "Jesus." A spontaneous sob escapes him. The old man was in the
house, in the flames. He hadn't counted on anything like that. Billy thinks
that maybe he killed the old man with his own hands. He shudders. And if
he hadn't killed him he'd left him in the fire.

When the old man's lantern broke, the inside of the house practically
exploded. Billy could feel the sudden vacuum and the heat, and when he
rolled out the window onto the porch his clothes were smoking, his eyes
were burning, there were black smudges on his hands. He didn't know if

he'd been burned or not. He was too numb to sense any pain. He hardly touched the ground as he sprinted toward his pickup. *What have I done?* he questioned. *What have I done?*

Now in his truck he watches the fire with a rapt fascination. The flames reach over the pear orchard toward the black sky. The work of his own hand. A conflagration. He thinks of all the Legrand ghosts burning up inside the house. Then he thinks of the old man with the lantern and Billy's eyes sting with tears. His clothes smell like gasoline. He's scared. The immensity of what he's done—the old man and the house—causes him to shake uncontrollably. And the flames and the sky and the stars wash together in his tear-filled eyes and make one bright smear. His smudged hands grip the steering wheel with a fierce terror he's never before known.

•    •    •

The one old fire truck on the Rose Hill side of the river, an ancient 1924 Ford ladder truck with real wooden spoke wheels, belongs to the Crockers Crossroads Volunteer Fire Department. A gift from the Hammond Fire Department some years back when they purchased new equipment, it sits in a tin shed behind Hanson's Store. When Marcus Hanson sees the glow in the sky, he knows immediately what's on fire. He calls Raymond Gant, the chief. Raymond's wife tells Marcus that he's over at the preaching at Shiloh Baptist Church. Everybody else is, too, except Joe Simmons down the road. Marcus's call wakes him up. "Good God!" Joe yells into the phone, and Marcus knows he's looking out the window.

"You want me and you to take the truck on out there?" Marcus asks.

There's a pause. "Ain't no water out here," Joe realizes. "What good would it do? Call Hammond. Call Boligee."

"All right," Marcus says.

The fire is visible from everywhere Billy thought it would be. Amy Legrand, in her studio at Hawthorne, working late into the night on a painting of herself as a little girl, looks out the window and sees it. Although she's nine miles as the crow flies from Rose Hill, she knows that the old house is the only thing out there that would make such a fire. She sips at her drink, thinks of the hutch she has not gotten around to retrieving. She thinks of the ghost of old Dupree Legrand. She thinks, then, of Karla's brutal death, of the baby downstairs with Hester, of the look in Carter's eyes when he found him there this morning.

"I'll take him now," Carter said.

"No," Amy insisted. "Leave him. He needs women."

"I'll take my son."

"Just for a while," she relented. "Until he...." She stopped. Carter's eyes, full and deep, seemed older, hardened by Karla's death. "We can take care of him," she finally said. "He's still nursing."

"He's my son," Carter argued.

"Of course he is your son." A smile plays about her lips now. It would all make a poem, she thinks. The fires of hell coming up to consume the old man who started it all.

● ● ●

Brother Kenneth Grable prays in his two-room house a half-mile from the Upper Room I Am Temple. He kneels at bedside, facing the window. Sometimes he prays for four or five hours a night, on his knees on the cold wooden floor. At first he thinks, They're burning at the landfill. Enter my soul, Lord. Enter my soul and set me on fire! The fire grows before his eyes, the entire southern sky taking on a red glow that throbs and pulses. It is the coming of the Lord, Brother Grable prays. *He is returning on the day of the Apocalypse, on the day of the final judgment! Enter my soul, oh Jesus, and make me clean!*

● ● ●

By the time the two trucks from the Hammond Fire Department get there, the house burns furiously, clumps of sparks shooting into the sky like holiday fireworks. Even the tank truck they bring isn't enough. The Boligee Volunteer Fire Department arrives, and then the one from Forkland, but the men can do little but watch it burn. They hose down the smoldering magnolia trees. They hose down the outbuildings, the old smokehouse, the roofs of Justina and Gilbert's cabins, just to be on the safe side, even though the cabins sit almost a hundred yards from the house.

Wearing a faded blue bathrobe over her flannel nightgown, Justina stands beside Marcus and Joe Simmons in the road in front of her house. They watch the house burn, can feel its intense dry heat even at this distance.

"Chief Davis say somebody set it," Marcus says. "Say he could smell gasoline even after they got here, after it done been burnin for a while."

"Where Gilbert?" Joe asks.

Justina doesn't answer him for a moment. Then she almost whispers. "I seen him out the window. Goin up to the house." She looks at Marcus. "Right fore the fire started."

"Gilbert?" Marcus scratches his head. "You ain't sayin...."

"Naw," Joe says.

"He had his rifle," Justina says, "and a old kerosene lantern."

"Naw," Joe says. "Where he at now?"

Justina nods toward the fire. "I reckon he in there. Where *you* reckon he is?"

•　•　•

Billy drives to the clearing alongside Rattlesnake Branch, near where all the butterflies exploded on them last night. He's trying to get away from the fire, but its light follows him like a shadow. He knows it will follow him for the rest of his life. Using a spade he carries in the back of his pickup, he digs a deep hole in the moist dirt along the creek. He takes off all his clothes, everything, even his shoes, and buries them deep. The air feels cool on his naked skin. He packs the dirt down with the shovel. Behind him the red glow hangs in the sky like a bloody mist.

Billy wades into the creek and bathes himself, his teeth clattering in the icy water, the cold sucking the breath right out of his lungs. He splashes, scrubs with handfuls of sand from the bottom, rubbing until his skin is pink and raw. He can still smell the gasoline, as though it seared itself into the linings of his nostrils.

With nothing to dry himself with, he climbs dripping wet into the truck. The deerskin seat feels like ice on his balls. He shivers. Water streams into his eyes and blinds him. He wipes it away with his already-wet fingers. He cranks up and eases the truck back into the road. He feels foolish sitting in the truck as naked as a jaybird. He feels tiny, like a child pretending to drive. He can't imagine what Jessie Merle will say when he arrives home like this, what he'll tell her. He hopes he doesn't have a flat or an accident.

The dirt road is slick from all the recent rain. He remembers Goodlowe's truck wallowing in the mud, recalls the look on Carter Taylor's face when they bore down on him, a look of fear at first and then defiance and refusal. Then he remembers the old man. Gilbert, he now remembers his name—and he chokes and bites his lower lip, leaning forward and squinting through the windshield. He hadn't meant to do that. He hadn't meant to do that at all.

He pulls into his front yard. Miles away from the fire now, he can still see it. A light is on beside the door. Billy hopes the children are not still up. Sometimes Jessie Merle doesn't discipline them at all. Sometimes she lets Henry ride his tricycle through the house at all hours of the night. It'll be Jessie Merle's fault if he walks into his house buck naked, dick dangling, and there sit his three children watching "The Jack Parr Show."

He pushes open the door. The television is on, bathing the room in its pale gray light. Sitting on the couch, Jessie Merle looks up at Billy. Nothing registers on her broad, flat face. After a minute she blinks. She says nothing.

"Well?" he asks gruffly.

She blinks again. "What happened to your eyebrows?" she asks.

He touches above his eyes and feels only smooth skin. They're gone. She continues to regard him with her level, benign gaze. "You don't seem to have a eyebrow left to your name."

# Part Three

# Dooly

"I'M TAKING HIM ON THE MARCH WITH ME," CARTER SAYS.

"No," Amy argues. "He's a baby. He doesn't belong in this...."

"Yes, he belongs."

"There are doctors, Carter," Amy says. "I'll spare no expense...."

"There's nothing wrong with him," Carter interrupts.

"Now wait a...."

"No, you wait," Carter yells. Amy just looks at him. Thick silence fills the room.

"Carter!" Hester says sharply. "You oughtta be ashamed of yourself, talking to Miss Amy thattaway!" Everyone in the big kitchen—Dooly, Rachel, Carter, Miss Amy—watches Hester.

"But...."

Hester continues. "All she done was take this poor child in, this...."

"This what?" Carter asks. "This half-white half-Legrand child? Or is it not that much white? Or more than that? Yes. More than that because..." He stops in mid-sentence and looks at Dooly. "More than that because Mr. Oscar wasn't the first Legrand to have a nigger in the woodpile? And not only that, he killed her, he murdered her...."

"What?" Dooly questions. "What?"

"What in heaven's name are you talking about, Carter?" Amy demands. "This is..."

"No!" Rachel interrupts. "Stop! All of you. Just stop."

The room still reverberates with Carter's outburst. Miss Amy stands stiff, one hand gripping the back of a chair. Her crisp blue housedress reflects the color of her eyes. Her lips form a thin line across her face She speaks softly, her voice taut.

"You must remember, Carter, that you are not the only one who was wronged here. It takes two people to create an adultery. I...."

"No," Rachel insists. "My mother was helpless. She was black. And she was a woman."

"You don't know," Miss Amy replies, "tell them, Hester."

Standing next to the stove, Hester says nothing. Dreadlocks framing her drawn face, she shakes her head, looks away.

"Nothing either of you could say would ever convince me otherwise," Rachel challenges. "I know what I know."

"All right," she sighs. "It's history, buried in the past. Let the dead bury the dead. Let the living...."

"Wait," Dooly interrupts. "What, Carter? What murder?"

Carter stares at Dooly. Dooly sees something new in his eyes, a depth of rage that seethes with killing, with death. It's plainly written on Carter's face.

"Tell me," Dooly urges.

"It didn't start with Mr. Oscar," Carter begins. The room fills with tension, tension and anticipation. Hester and Amy and Dooly have no idea what Carter is about to say and yet they know. Carter's words bring their knowledge to the surface, form it, label it. His language works like a brushstroke, realizing the artist's vision, always known on some level and only now expressed.

"Mama," Carter continues, "was Mr. Oscar's own sister. She was Mr. Dupree's daughter. And it was her mother, our grandmother Carrie, that Mr. Dupree killed." His words hang in the still air like shreds of smoke. "That he murdered."

Amy sits down in a chair and sobs soundlessly, her hands over her face. Hester stands behind Amy's chair, her hands protectively gripping Amy's shoulders. The only sound in the room is their collective breathing.

•   •   •

Carter and Dooly walk beneath the clear dome of afternoon sky. They have surveyed the damage done to Carter's house. "Good God," Dooly muttered over and over again as they made their way through the splintered and shredded house. They both turn their eyes quickly away from the dried blood still on the kitchen floor. Then they visited Rachel, who has simply moved into her kitchen, sleeping on a pallet in the corner. When they left her she was sitting calmly in a chair staring out the window.

"So Justina... It was Justina who told..." Dooly begins, struggling to keep up with Carter, as he walks quickly along the road to Justina's house. The air at Rose Hill is clear and dry, scented with honeysuckle and rain-washed alfalfa. As Dooly inhales he can smell the soil itself, its dense black richness.

"Yes," Carter responds. "When Mr. Dupree died, it was like Justina couldn't wait to tell us. To get it off her chest. Something she'd been livin with all those years. And I know what she wants now. Now that Gilbert is dead she wants to tell me where my grandmother's buried."

The police and fire authorities, combing through the charred ruins of Rose Hill, found old Gilbert's body along with the gas cans. Justina called Hawthorne to let Miss Amy and the others know. She also asked Carter to come out to Rose Hill to see her. Dooly wanted to go along, too.

"It could be just an old story," Dooly says. "Something the people on the place have told, something...."

"No." Carter stops him. "Nobody knew about it. The killing part. Nobody but Justina and Gilbert and Mr. Dupree. Mr. Oscar knows that my mother was his sister. I know he knows that. And he didn't care. That's the worse. He didn't care."

Dooly shudders at the knowledge that his father knew everything. But he does not doubt it. Carter walks so fast that Dooly practically runs to keep up.

"What are you going to do, Carter?"

"I don't know. I don't know."

They pass alongside the old pear orchard and the overgrown baseball field, with its rotting and sagging backstop. The tall magnolia trees come into view, absent the big house now.

"Gilbert," Dooly ponders. "Why would he do that? Burn the house?" He remembers mornings when he and Carter had slept in one of the heavy, high old beds upstairs at Rose Hill. Gilbert had awakened them, clucking his tongue and pretending annoyance that they'd slept so late, the sun already high, the white sheer curtains ballooning in the morning breeze.

"Who knows?" Carter replies. "Maybe Justina knows. But I doubt it. I don't think she would tell us if she did."

As they come down the lane they can see Justina sitting on the narrow front porch of her peeling cabin. They pass what is left of the big house, charred timbers and piles of ashes, bedsprings, burned stoves and refrigerator. Six redbrick chimneys tower nakedly toward the sky. The stink of fire lingers everywhere.

As they get closer, Dooly focuses on Justina's face, wrinkled and ancient, faded and familiar, a face from his past. Her neatly ironed house-dress seems too big for her tiny body, as though she draped and folded it to make it smaller. Her bare feet tap on the rough planks of her porch. The perfume of purple wisteria blossoms scents the heated air.

"Mornin, Justina," Carter calls, and she jumps, startled. Snuff clings to her thin lips. She tilts her head and peers toward them like a bird.

"Carter?" she responds, squinting at Dooly as she shades her eyes from the sun.

"And Dooly," Dooly adds.

"Lord Jesus!" she cries. "Mistuh Dooly!" She cackles and flutters the handkerchief she grips in her thin fingers. Dooly mounts the porch and embraces her in the chair. Though her body is as thin and wispy as dry sticks, she's not frail. Carter told Dooly that she still does all her cooking and housecleaning, and she walks to Hanson's Store and back every day in good weather.

They sit on the edge of the porch near Justina's old wooden rocker, which creaks as she rocks. She leans over and spits into a wrinkled brown paper bag next to her chair.

"How you feelin this afternoon?" Carter asks.

"Fine. Bad bout old Gilbert, though."

"Yeah. They think he set the fire," Carter responds. "Say it's just some more of the troubles. They think he fell and couldn't get out."

"Gilbert ain't set no fire."

"How do you know? I thought...."

"No. Gilbert ain't set no fire."

"He was a black man, and these are the times," Carter points out. He glances at Dooly, his face set and grim.

She waves his observation away with her thin, clawlike hand. "I don't care what they say. I'm too old for all these troubles. I'm sorry bout all Mr. Oscar's troubles, too, Dooly. I nursed him when he was a child. It too much for me to take in." She rocks.

Dooly leans back against an upright supporting the slanting tin porch roof. From here he can look across the broad backyard at the ruins of the big house. Boxwood grows in profusion around the chipped brick walkways and the old sealed well. He can see the outbuildings and the new spring green of the pear orchard. It's quiet and peaceful here. He hears a mockingbird somewhere in the fields and a blue jay chattering in the privet next to Justina's house. A dark gray hound trots across the yard and flops down in the shade, its tongue lolling.

"Sorry," Justina says. Dooly knows she means the dog. He smiles. "Sorry old dog. He just took up," she says. "How come you brought Dooly out here?" Justina then asks, catching them by surprise. "I told you I had somethin to tell you."

Carter looks at Dooly, then at Justina. "It's all right, Justina. He knows the whole story. I told him."

"Uh-huh," she nods. "Uh-huh." She peers at Dooly. "I don't reckon it matter no more. Here I am so old I'm bout to die and Mr. Oscar gone off to be the governor. Uh-huh."

"What you want to tell me, Justina?" Carter asks.

"Gilbert. I tell you now about Gilbert cause he gone on to glory. Can't nothin hurt him no more. He helped him. Mr. Dupree. Gilbert helped him bury her under the smokehouse."

"What?" Carter sits up.

"The next morning. Carrie Winfield. Christmas Eve mornin. Mr. Dupree tried to bury her that night, before he came back in and stood there for me to see the dirt all over him and know what he was doin without havin to be told. But the ground was hard and packed in that smokehouse, and it was freezin weather, so the next mornin early he went and got Gilbert, fore daylight even, and Gilbert helped him dig up the floor of the smokehouse and bury her there. That's where she's buried. Under the smokehouse."

Carter looks across the lane to the outbuildings, vacant, leaning, whitewashed haphazardly. He notices the old smokehouse standing apart, its door sagging on rusty hinges. "Are you sure, Justina?" he whispers.

"Course I'm sure," she answers. She fans herself with her knotted and wrinkled handkerchief, nodding, pursing her lips. "Whyn't y'all go there and dig? Look for that snake ring. Then you'll know."

"Maybe I will," Carter says.

"Maybe we will," Dooly adds.

"That's why she walks," Justina explains.

"What?"

"That's why she walks. All this time since she died. She always in the yard, round bout midnight. Eyes starin like she ain't seein nothin. When I was a girl I called out to her, but she ain't heard me. Her eyes look like they lookin at somethin else, somethin way far off somewhere where can't nobody but her see. She sings songs don't nobody know. She can't rest, I don't reckon, knowin her peoples don't know what happened to her nor where she is."

Dooly feels a chill and shivers like a child. He looks up at Justina. The old woman smiles at him. He watches her pull a Garrett's Snuff can out of her apron pocket, take a pinch, and put it between her lower lip and her toothless gum. She smacks her lips and leans back in the rocker, fanning herself as though chasing insects away.

"It sho hot already, ain't even summer yet," she says. She cackles. "Old Mose, he say that on the final day, if your name come up on the wrong side of the ledger, then all you got to do is tell the Lord that you done lived all your life in Noshobe County and He'll wave you right on through, cause you done already served your time in the fires of almighty Hell!"

• • •

The oldest building at Rose Hill, the smokehouse is a two-room log cabin with a packed dirt floor. Its logs and joints are chinked with mud. Its old brick chimney is made of the same pale red bricks that form the fireplaces and chimneys of the big house. To make the structure more airtight, board siding of four-by-sixes was added to the outside walls and over the windows. At some point a tin roof replaced the original shingles, now rusty and pocked with holes.

The thick door, also made of unfinished four-by-sixes, hangs on rusty hinges, cobwebs sealing the cracks around it where the mud has long since crumbled into dust.

"We'll need a light," Dooly notes as they approach the smokehouse equipped with a pick and shovel borrowed from Justina. Carter shrugs. He seems suddenly distant, passive, his actions hesitant, slowed. "Look around the back porch, see if there's not a lantern or something that wasn't burned up," Dooly suggests. He watches Carter cross the overgrown yard to what's left of the porch. Dooly turns back to the smokehouse. The story belongs to him now, as well as to Carter and Rachel. Moody and silent, Carter wants to deny Dooly his place in this tragedy. But he can't. It was his grandfather, too. The hinges squeal as Dooly pulls open the door. The interior is musty and dark, lit only by shafts of sunlight peeking through the holes in the tin roof. The cobwebs drift like limp banners in the air.

Carter returns with an old coal-oil lamp, its glass chimney smudged and smoked. He takes a box of Diamond matches from his shirt pocket and lights the lamp. He leads the way inside.

Rows of rusty baling wire with iron hooks for the meat hang from the ceiling. Ashes and chunks of charred hickory from the fires litter the floor. (Dooly can't remember when the smokehouse had actually been functional. But he recalls his grandfather talking about it, about hog-killing time, the first real cold spell of the winter. They'd sometimes kill up to fifteen hogs and butcher them, hang the hams and butts and shoulders and sides for bacon in the smokehouse. For years the smokehouse fires had been supervised by his grandfather's uncle, old Thomas Mereweather Waverly. A widower, Mr. Thomas moved to Rose Hill after his wife, Mr. Dupree's mother's sister, died. He had lived to be over a hundred, carrying out his job to oversee the fires under the meat and to parch and grind the coffee beans purchased in bulk in town.)

"Where do we start?" Dooly asks.

"Maybe you...maybe you better wait outside." Carter looks at him.

"No." Dooly lifts the pick.

"All right," Carter says. "Wait a minute."

"What?"

Carter peers at him in the lamplight. "What do you have to say about all this, Dooly?"

"I don't know," Dooly answers. "I don't know what I think, even. I can't take it all in."

Carter shakes his head, looks away, then back at Dooly. He points to the floor. "He would have buried her in this front room," Carter speculates. "He would have stopped right here because he was freezing." He sighs. "And maybe his heart was broken." Standing there looking at the ground, Carter seems distant and lost again, then he shrugs and shakes himself. "And she would have been heavy by now, by the time he got this far."

"Yes," Dooly agrees, swinging the pick high over his head and down onto the black dirt foor packed as hard as cement. The dirt breaks up in clots almost like stones. He swings again, twisting the handle back, freeing the blade again and the dirt loosens. Carter begins to shovel. The old lantern casts an orange glow on the ancient log walls, smoke- and soot-stained.

No air circulates in the smokehouse at all. The captured air smells of mildew and decay. Sweat runs down both their faces and into their eyes, and they have to pause from time to time to wipe their faces. Gloveless, their hands blister, but neither cares. They exchange tools to vary it and keep working. The black loamy dirt, looser now, breaks up in clumps.

Side by side, they work together like two other young men must have worked sixty years before, black and white, too. Unlike the other men, who toiled in the predawn chill, Carter and Dooly sweat in the late-spring heat, sweat through their clothes before they've dug ten inches into the earth.

They labor for a long time, then rest. Dooly leans on the shovel. Carter squats, balancing himself with the pick.

"Maybe we're in the wrong room," Dooly wonders aloud. "Maybe there's nothing here."

"Shit, dig."

"But...."

"If she's not here," Carter says, "we'll dig the other room, too. Maybe it was another one of the outbuildings, and we'll dig those, too. Maybe Justina got it wrong, or Gilbert remembered it wrong. Dig."

Their shoulders and hands ache. Wringing wet, they find it difficult to breathe in the close, dank, old smokehouse. They widen and deepen the hole they dig, but still there is nothing. They swap tools again, Dooly wielding the pick and Carter shoveling behind him.

Suddenly Carter's shovel hits something, something hard and rigid and unyielding in the soft earth.

He kneels quickly, scooping the dirt with his hands. "Bring the lantern closer," he orders. Dooly holds the lantern high, and it floods the gaping opening with light. They now sees bones, yellowed and stained dark from the soil. Carter leans close to look at what he thinks is the top of a skull. But a glint, almost a sparkle captures his eyes, freezes him completely. Grasping what he thinks are the bones of a hand, he brushes at them with his own fingers gently and reverently. Then he sees it: the silver, coiled ring gleams in the lamplight, the snake head where a stone might be is raised as though to strike.

Dooly sees it at the same time. "May light perpetual shine upon her," he prays. He makes the sign of the cross over the grave, staring steadily at the snake-head ring. His eyes lock on it. He sees nothing else. The ring seems to throb and glow in the dimness, to gleam with a light of its own much brighter than the lank yellow spilling of the old lantern. He watches as Carter gently brushes black soil from the face of the smallish skull, no bigger than that of a large child. The chilling empty eye sockets stare blindly up at them. Two rows of perfect white teeth lock in an eternal and time-wasted grin.

"Yes," Carter whispers. "She would be right where Justina said she'd be, of course." Though his tone sounds oddly objective, Dooly hears his grief, the immensity of his sorrow. Carter sits back on the edge of the grave, holding the skull. His fingers continue to caress it, to lightly brush away all the loose soil as though he's trying to feel the smooth skin, long since passed back into the earth, it warmth absorbed and transformed into the oily loam itself. "Justina said…" He pauses, wipes his eyes with the back of his knuckles. "Justina said her eyes were 'feisty.'"

"I'll bet," Dooly says. He wants to pray but he doesn't. He realizes that this moment, this discovery, is prayer enough.

Carter opens his fist, revealing the ring in his red, blistered palm. Both men look at the ring, thin and delicate, so tiny it would barely fit their little fingers. The snake head curves up gracefully, its eyes minuscule rubies the size of pinheads. "She had not even got her full growth," Carter whispers, his voice thin, barely audible.

Carter turns the ring in his palm. Its shiny, polished circle shimmers in the muted sunlight and the glow of the old lamp. For a long time they crouch in the old smokehouse, close together, their bodies rank, their clothing soiled, kneeling in the imprisoned air of Carrie's grave, air full of the smells of the deep, rich soil and the lingering scent of the hickory-wood fires, the mold and the decay.

# Dooly

THE WARM HUMID AIR SPREADS NORTH FROM THE GULF
of Mexico, pumped by a high-pressure area over North Carolina. Hurricane
Donald hovers in the Gulf before heading toward Florida's southwestern
coast. High clouds form early each afternoon turning the Alabama sky purple and bruised, and loud claps of thunder accompany spears of lightning.
Then thick and heavy rain sweeps across the landscape in sheets.

The marchers keep to the pavement as much as possible, avoiding the
dark, muddy quagmires of the highway shoulders and ditches. After the
rain passes, the people camp at night in soaked fields.

Because most everyone is on the march, the countryside around Rose
Hill seems deserted of human souls. No one sees the effect of the heavy
rains on the earthen dam of the lake inside the fence. Where Mose's path
crossed the fissure in the middle of the dam, the ground has crumbled, and
creamy, heavy sludge now spills over the top. The thick liquid oozes down
the steep hill above Crockers Crossroads and the valley near the little
church, which houses Rachel's school and the graveyard out back. The spill
goes unobserved by even Marcus Hanson. So accustomed to blight, to the
dead trees and undergrowth, Hanson and other residents can't differentiate
the toxic sludge from the landscape's day-to-day lifelessness.

•   •   •

The early-morning fog hangs in gray shreds like the Spanish moss that
drapes the trees along the highway. By midday, the sun bakes the asphalt,
and Dooly can feel the heat through the soles of his shoes. Then,

predictably, the rains start. They are closer to Montgomery than to Hammond now, and the marchers are tired. Medics come out and doctor blistered feet. The marchers are accompanied by a fleet of Alabama state troopers' cars and several National Guard personnel carriers, their guardsmen armed with M-1 rifles. Guard encampments have been set up along the route. Soldiers and spectators, who travel from the farms and little towns, watch the marchers go by. A National Guard tank truck carrying water follows them. It's operated by two young white men, curious and friendly, dressed in fatigues.

"Where y'all from?" they ask everyone. They both come from Uniontown and work at Marathon Paper Company down along the Alabama River.

"From Hammond," Dooly tells them. They look at his collar. They look at Kitty. They're shy. They know who she is, have seen her on television and heard her records on the radio.

They look back at Dooly. "Hammond? No shit?" They say incredulously. He knows they don't believe him. They hand out paper cups of water. "It takes all kinds, I reckon," one comments. His name, stitched on a white canvas patch over his shirt pocket, is Joe Rattiwig. The other man's name is Earnest Briney.

Kitty is distant and moody. She thinks about her mother over in Meridian, only fifty miles west of Hammond. As they march east, she turns and looks behind them. The sun sets brilliantly among the lavender clouds, shafts of gold exploding across the sky.

"Maybe we are going the wrong way," she says to Dooly. "Maybe we should be following the sun."

"No," he responds, "we're going the right way." Their faces drip with perspiration. They can smell each other. Dooly and Kitty make love at night in a little pup tent, revel in each other's funkiness. It excites them, drives them deeper into one another, unable to distinguish the odors of their bodies from the dark rot of the soil on which they lie.

Rachel watches them march. Dooly limps. She knows his feet are killing him. Kitty walks like a woman out for a Sunday stroll. Beneath Kitty's beauty Rachel sees a woman who knows evil, knows the depths. Kitty's restless. Her nervous energy signals that she's lost direction. Her age is hard to determine, as though she's been dropped into the midst of living. She's not a woman Rachel would have thought that Dooly would choose. From Christmases and Thanksgivings at Hawthorne, Rachel knew his wife, comfortable and serenely attractive. Dooly left her and their children, left it all for this woman. As Rachel observes them, she can see the end.

Kitty hugs her, stays near her. Whenever Rachel looks her way, Kitty is always looking back at her. Kitty's intense black eyes lock on her own, beg for approval, try to peer all the way through her.

"Sister," Kitty says to her softly.

And Rachel sees it in her eyes: the end of something.

•  •  •

Everyone knows by now that Dooly is the governor's son. The marchers go out of their way to speak to him, to stare at him curiously. They spread out along the highway. Only two more days. They should reach Montgomery the day after tomorrow. Gray and black state trooper cars precede them, crawl along with lights flashing. Some marchers slush along the mushy ground, avoiding the hard paved road, unforgiving to sore feet. More photographers accompany them now and take pictures of the marchers' shoes in the mud.

Carter, with Eshu, always walks near the front of the line. He walks briskly, next to King and Mose. King has been on the march from the start, along with Fred Shuttlesworth and Eldon Long and Andrew Young. Carter's stride is confident, fresh; he gives everyone else renewed energy. Wearing a backpack with Eshu's bottles and diapers, he sometimes holds the baby above his head like a talisman. They sing "We Are Marching to Jerusalem" and cheer lustily.

•  •  •

Martin King's eyes are a soft warm brown, like a blanket. Sitting cross-legged on the ground, across the small campfire from Dooly, he seems younger than Dooly would have imagined, younger than he looks on television. He wears a light blue work shirt; wrinkled khaki pants; and black clodhoppers, thick-soled shoes that look as though they've been carved with a hatchet from chunks of coal. The night feels cool after the sun of the afternoon.

"You can heal," King says, "I've heard it said." His voice is muscular and hale, with an undertone of melancholy.

"Yes," Dooly replies. "But not now. I'm not worthy."

"Nonsense."

"He thinks he healed me," Kitty tells King, "I'd be dead now. Maybe I am dead now. I don't know."

King's eyes shift to her. He looks at her as though he's seeing her for the first time, as though he'd forgotten she's even there. He nods, looks back at Dooly, and nods again. Camp noises surround them. Crickets chirp back in the brush.

"If I believe I can, I can heal," Dooly explains. "But if the faith flickers, even a little...."

"Yes," King nods, "all right. I understand. And there is no 'logic' to it, is there? God has no 'logic.'"

"That's right," Dooly agrees. "Sometimes I just can't do it, and I know it."

"And there is no pattern."

"No."

King nods again and settles back. Groups around some fires sing, others ripple with laughter. Dooly doesn't know where Rachel, Carter, and Eshu are. Most nights he and Kitty sleep near them. Dooly smells the sweet-acrid scent of marijuana mingling with cooking smells and wood smoke. Guitars strum among the singing tree frogs.

"Your father," King asks after a long moment, "how long is it since you've seen him?"

"Several weeks. At a funeral. At two funerals, actually. My...."

"Your grandfather and Carter Taylor's mother," King interrupts. "I know. Eldon Long told me."

"My father is not someone I know any more. If I ever did."

"Which of us has known his own father, huh?" King smiles. "Our name is Legion, and we are many." He chuckles, a smooth and rich laugh. His wide and steady eyes and his skin gleam in the firelight. "Your father," King continues, "he came to my church, Dexter Avenue, once. Back during the bus boycott. He was lieutenant governor then and he came and sat through the service, listened to my sermon, sat there like just anybody. His was the only white face in the church. He looked angry. One of my people described him as 'swole up like an old bullfrog.' When he left the church he shook my hand hard, squeezed it really, and he leaned toward me and said, 'We'll meet again.'" King looks around, looks over his shoulder in the direction of the capitol, waiting for them. Dooly's father waiting behind the walls, like a king in his castle, behind the moat. Dooly sees the glow of the city's lights against the night sky. "I guess this is what he meant," King says.

The marchers don't know what to expect. They plan to march into downtown and up the avenue to the capitol where they will deliver the voting rights petitions on the capitol steps. Governor Legrand has said he will not meet with them.

Newspaper and television reporters from the local stations and the networks blanket the place. The people who return to Hammond at night bring back word that everyone is watching them, the whole free world is tuned in. But it's hard to comprehend that out here, so far away from everything. They have one more full day of marching and will camp at a school right outside Montgomery. Then they'll make the final walk to the capitol early the next morning. Though it has only been days, it seems years since they started, took those first tentative steps across Rooster Bridge and headed east into the morning sun.

"You and I are even then," Dooly says to King. "He's only attended one of my services, too."

"Just one?" King asks. "You're serious, aren't you?"

"Yes," Dooly responds, "and this is what he meant, too. This is the 'again' he meant. He would have been able to know that even back then."

*   *   *

The governor's office is on the first floor of the capitol building. Outside the tall windows stands a marble statue commemorating the old Confederacy. At each corner of the statue flies one of the flags of that lost nation. The inscription on the statue reads: "Fame's temple boasts no higher name, No king is grander on his throne; No glory shines with brighter gleam, The name of Patriot stands alone." The neatly manicured lawn slopes down from the capitol in all directions, and aimless traffic circles it in the bright afternoon. The capitol building itself is so blindingly white that a person can hardly look directly at it in the day's bright sun.

Police put barricades along Dexter Avenue, where the march will come. Even though only a couple hundred people march along Highway 80, more are waiting south of the city to join the group. And in Montgomery, thousands are expected to join in, creating a mass of humanity moving up the avenue like a flood, moving toward the white and gleaming steps. Those are the very steps where Jefferson Davis stood a little more than a century ago to take his oath of office, a sacred spot marked by a large bronze star embedded in the marble. Generations of schoolboys have stood on the star and raised their hands in a mock oath. From here one can look down the broad street at the sluggish traffic, the heat waves already rising up and wavering in the air to mark the beginning of another long Alabama summer.

The yellow sawhorse barriers stenciled POLICE LINE DO NOT CROSS stretch all the way through town to the campus of St. Andrew's Catholic School, the marchers' final camping place. There, thousands of people will listen to speeches and entertainment: Peter Paul & Mary, Dick Gregory, Joan Baez, and Kitty Wiggins. People pour in from all over the country, rowdy boys from eastern schools and horny coeds from the Midwest. Montgomery braces itself.

Oscar Legrand stands on the second floor of the capitol building, alone. His bodyguards play cards in an outer office on the first floor. He paces the long hallway outside the old House chambers. The oil portraits of all the Alabama governors who have preceded him stare down from the walls. He pauses to look out the windows, down Dexter Avenue. He stands for a long time, gazing, waiting.

• • •

In the middle of the night a hand reaches into the tent and grips Dooly's arm, shocks him out of a strange, multicolored dream. Kitty's arms and legs are tangled with his. Her body warms his; he doesn't want to pull away. His bones are stiff and aching. His mouth, dry and pasty, still tastes like the beans he ate for supper.

"What is it, what...?" Kitty murmurs when he pulls away. He pats her shoulder reassuringly, rolls out, and sits up. Carter stands there in the moonlight, with Rachel behind him holding Eshu. The night is bright; everything around them, the undergrowth and the leaves of the trees, is touched with silver. Rachel wears a long black skirt and work shirt like the one King wore. A blue bandanna wraps her head. Her huge hoop earrings dangle and sparkle in the light from the waning moon.

"What time is it?" Dooly asks.

"Midnight," Carter answers. "King wants you. He needs you."

"What is it?"

"Somebody's sick."

Dooly's arms go slack, and his legs weaken. Rachel and Carter stare at him. "Hurry," Carter urges, his eyes anxious and focused. Rachel gazes at Dooly over the bundle of the baby. He sees in her eyes that she knows what he's going to say.

"I can't," Dooly replies.

"What you mean? Come on," Carter insists.

"Wait," Rachel says.

"I can't do it anymore," Dooly explains.

"Martin says you can," Carter says. "It's a boy, Philip Music. He's havin a seizure. You got to help him."

"The medics, call them out here. I couldn't help him. It's gone from me, all gone."

"Wait," Rachel urges again. "Both of you wait a minute."

"We ain't got a minute. The boy is dyin," Carter responds.

"All right," Dooly murmurs. He's willing to try, but even as he says it, he feels empty, hopeless. "All right."

"Don't," Kitty says from the tent. "Don't do it, Dooly. You don't have to." She scrambles outside, stands looking at them, hair matted and tangled. "I'm afraid."

"You're afraid?" Rachel asks.

"Yes," she answers. "Please, Dooly."

"I have to try," Dooly responds, his voice tired, without energy.

"Just stay with me," Kitty says. "Stay with me. Come on. We're safe."

Rachel watches them, watches Dooly waiver. She knows Dooly has no idea what a huge and momentous decision he's about to make. It's just as well that he doesn't.

"Wait, hold him." Rachel hands Eshu to Carter. She motions to them to stand there while she moves into the bushes, into the shadows. They hear her rummaging around among the leaves and sticks on the ground. After a minute she comes back toward them, holding her hands cupped in front of her. In her hands sits a live frog. She holds it out and they all stare. "Give me your pocket knife," she says to Carter. He impatiently hands it to her, and they watch her kneel and neatly slice off the frog's left rear leg, then toss the wriggling frog back into the underbrush. She fumbles in the large pockets of her skirt and comes out with a red flannel cloth bag with strings. She puts the frog's leg into the bag and ties it around Dooly's neck. "Go now," she tells him.

"No," Kitty argues. "He doesn't want to."

A sickness comes over Dooly, a bitter, stinging bile fills his belly. He feels helpless, useless. He also feels the frog's leg move against his chest, a still-living thing, squirming inside the bag. It feels cold, like a lump of ice. He knows it will do no good. No good at all.

"Dooly, I don't believe any more," Kitty says. "I never did."

Dooly feels the severed frog leg thump against his chest like an extension of his own heart. Nausea fills him, burns his insides. Carter leads the way. The others trail behind. Their little caravan passes through the sleeping camp and gently smoldering cookfires. A small group awaits them ahead. Dooly sees King there.

A boy lies stretched out on a blanket on the ground. Several people kneel beside him. Dooly recognizes the boy's close friend, David Miles, crying, his head thrown back. Dooly has met them, talked with them, even counseled them. They're young, a long way from home. They're foolish, will experiment with any drug they can get their hands on.

"David says Philip is asthmatic," King informs him, "that he has all kinds of allergies. His medicines are a hodgepodge, over-the-counter stuff."

"And no telling what all else," Dooly adds, moving toward the boy on the ground.

"Yes," King says. "I envy you your gift." Dooly pauses and looks at him. King's eyes glow in the darkness.

"It was bestowed on me by a madman," Dooly tells him.

"Many good gifts are," King responds. "The Nazarene was a madman."

Philip Music's head jerks back rigid on his neck, his eyes rolling back in his head. His mouth foams flecks of discolored spit, and his body trembles violently in spasms. His hands claw at those who hold him down. King kneels next to Dooly. He whispers, "The answer of Jesus is not an argument but a life."

"Yes," Dooly says.

"Blessed are your eyes, for they see: and your ears, for they hear."

"Amen."

He places his hands in the middle of Philip Music's chest. He feels the boy's chest muscles as tight as steel bands. Dooly's breathing becomes rapid and desperate. For a moment he feels his own brain will be deprived of oxygen, that he will suffocate in the damp air. He senses Kitty somewhere behind him. He knows that Carter and Rachel and Carter's son are there, too. The ring of sympathizers and onlookers becomes oppressive. "Get back," Dooly orders. "Give us room, give us air." King motions and they loosen and move raggedly farther away.

Dooly feels the boy's body jerk in an irregular pattern as though jolted by random electrical shocks. He hears the friend sob, knowing the boy is close to death and miles from anywhere. He has no idea what causes the boy's seizure. It doesn't matter. Froth at his lips has turned bloody. His eyes seem completely white. Dooly smells that the boy shat his pants. The odor overpowers.

"If thou canst believe, all things are possible to him that believe," King prays, and Dooly knows exactly where the words sit in the Gospel of Mark, sees them in his mind as though they're etched in flame and his eyes move rapidly down the page. Printed in red are the words: Thou dumb and deaf spirit, I charge thee, come out of him and enter no more into him. Dooly feels his fingers begin to burn and his arms tingle all the way to his shoulders. He hears Kitty's breathless sobbing right behind him and he hears Rachel chant "Holy Mary, Mother of God" in a steady, low monotone, "Holy Mary, Mother of God."

Then Dooly and the boy are alone on a vast sea, surrounded by silence, unmoved by the tossing of the waves, suspended there. Dooly's body spasms as though he draws the rigors out of the boy and into himself. He smells the boy's shit and the dark moldy earth and the cold sour ashes of the dead fires. Both of their bodies jerk in an insane dance. Dooly feels as though someone's hitting him across the back with a two-by-four. His body hurts with the intensity of a boil. Dooly thinks he's going to pass out—his heart races out of control, and he sees only the boy's head moving back and forth and then slowing, slowing. There's an audible gasp behind Dooly as the boy suddenly opens his eyes and looks at him, looks at them all with the eyes of a frightened animal. After a moment of complete stillness, Philip Music tries to sit up, his eyes darting about. He asks "What? What?" Behind him Dooly hears Rachel say, "Praise Jesus."

Finally, Dooly struggles wearily to his feet. Every muscle in his body aches. The sudden movement around him smears his vision as the others comfort Philip Music. He sees Rachel, her dark eyes fixed upon him, a smile on her lips. And he sees Kitty, standing apart, her cheeks streaked with tears, looking at him as though he's a stranger.

● ● ●

The Rose Hill fire completely singed off Billy Singleton's eyebrows and eyelashes. The absence of brows gives his face the pale, doughy look of a plucked chicken. It's the only mark the fire left on him. He hasn't a single burn or blister. After he finishes showering, scrubbing away the remains of his earlier bath in Rattlesnake Branch, he can't believe his good fortune as he peruses himself in the long, plastic-framed mirror he tacked for Jessie Merle on the back of the bathroom door.

He still can't bear to think of the old man. Every time he closes his eyes he hears the dull thunk of the hammer hitting the old man's skull. Thank the good Lord he hadn't really seen him, that he didn't have the old man's eyes, his face, to contend with in his imaginings. He dreams all night of dancing flames surrounding him and wakes up hot and sweating, thrashing around under the limp, damp sheets, cursing.

And the cold pain has returned to lodge itself in his bowels. It's there all the time, along with a constant pain like pinpricks—almost like a catfish's fins, he imagines—but he can live with it if he has to. It's a part of him now, like a rotten tooth in his jaw, and maybe it isn't the worst burden he has had to carry around in his life. Maybe a man can learn to live with anything once he grows used to it. Jessie Merle brings home every purgative she can find in the drugstores. But he's given that up. She has his prescription from Dr. Hughes filled, the ulcer pills, but he doesn't take them. He throws them down the well. He knows better. He knows very well what's inside him.

Billy wants to tell his buddies about setting the fire but he dares not. They talk about the fire, even speculate on who might have set it besides old Gilbert Washington.

"That old nigger didn't have sense enough to set that fire," Lucious Willie comments.

"Somebody else done it," Wayne Scroggins says. A car salesman for Derry's Chevrolet, Wayne is tall and thin and likes to wear vests, unbuttoned and loose.

Billy planned to tell them, planned to brag about it, to be their hero, and then the old man screwed it up. Now he's scared to admit anything. As long as the police believe that the old man did it, then they keep on believing that Gilbert fell down and accidentally managed to get himself burned up in it at the same time. Or at least Billy hopes they keep believing that. But they probably won't, since even his friends seem skeptical.

"Maybe it was them northern niggers, them outside agitators, that done it," Lucious says. "That house was a symbol of the Old South, like the Stars and Bars."

Billy hasn't thought of that. He can't believe it escaped him, since it's so obvious now that Lucious points it out.

"Maybe that old man was even tryin to stop em, you can't know," Lucious speculates.

"Maybe you done it, Lucious," Wayne says, "I mean with your name and all."

"Why don't you go fuck yourself," Lucious sneers.

"I might just do that," Wayne responds. "At least I would know it's clean!"

Jessie Merle has painted eyebrows on Billy with an eyebrow pencil. To make them appear dark and thick, she used a mascara brush, too. "You better have sense enough to come in out of the rain," she told him. "Wear your baseball hat and pull the bill down low."

She still hasn't asked him where his eyebrows went or why he showed up at the house in the middle of the night naked as the day he was born. Billy knows that she knows without having to be told. Every now and then Billy sees someone staring at his painted-on eyebrows or glancing at them with a questioning look. But so far nobody has mentioned them. None of his buddies seems to notice at all. But Billy suspects that they notice and are just waiting for the right moment to pounce on him.

Johnny Lee Bobo, the Grand Imperial Wizard of the White Knights of the Ku Klux Klan of East Mississippi, speaks at a rally out at French Creek, east of town. They burn three twenty-foot crosses and shoot off some firecrackers. The women—not Jessie Merle; she prefers to lie around the house in her slip reading movie magazines and yelling at the kids to shut up and leave her alone—serve Brunswick stew with light bread, potato salad, Moon Pies, and Coca-Colas.

Johnny Lee Bobo tells them the world is going to hell in a handbasket. That Martin Luther Coon is a communist followed around by degenerates of all stripes and colors, and if they don't believe it, all they have to do is go and look for themselves. He says the Jews and the niggers are trying to take over the world and put all the white people into concentration camps. He says the buck niggers are after the white women, that that is what they really mean by "integration." He reminds them of the sons of Ham in the Bible and shouts that the Lord wields a mighty sword of vengeance! "We are that sword! We are the vigilante, an idea as American as apple pie!"

A minister in the Church of the Everlasting Jesus, Johnny Lee Bobo vows that he personally is willing to die protecting the southern way of life and the sacredness of southern womanhood. He asks everyone else to pledge the same. They shout back in agreement. He whips them into a frenzy. A little short man with a balding head and a protruding upper lip, he yells prayers at them with his eyes closed and makes them get down on their knees in the Johnson grass and damp dirt. He urges them to hold hands, but Billy and his friends won't go that far.

After the ceremony, a small group from the Hammond Klavern stand around smoking cigarettes and talking. Rooster Wembley, the one-legged barber, is there. The former Grand Dragon of the Klavern, Rooster retired recently, and Luscious has taken over. All the boys who work over at the landfill are there, except for Goodlowe Lewis and Bobby Musgrove, who've disappeared in Goodlowe's truck. (Billy heard them talking about going down to Pensacola to fish. He and Goodlowe's wife figure they just got drunk and took off.) They're joined by Frank Fite, Clarence Mack, and Mesta Follett, the woman from Birmingham dressed in men's clothing with her hair up under a red baseball cap.

Mesta infiltrated some of the march to Montgomery. "I think they was suspicious of me," she tells the men. She loves all the attention. Bobo comes over especially to talk with her. "I knew I was in danger the whole time," she reports. "They got voodoo folks with em."

"What?" Billy asks, his ears pricking up. "Who?"

"Some woman. She could look right straight through me." Billy knows she means Rachel Taylor. "All they could talk about was having the governor's son on the march. He wears one of them collars, claims to be a Catholic priest."

"Naw," Billy corrects her, "he's a piscopal."

"Same damn difference," Mesta says. "You never saw such a bunch of depraved humanity in your life as the crew they got on that march."

Billy remembers Dooly Legrand from when he was a boy, coming out to Rose Hill to fish and play with Carter Taylor. They'd never have anything to do with Billy, called him white trash, wouldn't even play ball with him. They made up silly songs about him, called him Billy Simpleton. And what would Carter Taylor have said if he'd known that all along Billy was fucking his sister? Billy always figured Dooly Legrand was after some of that, too, but it was him who was gettin it!

He knew all about Dooly Legrand, big college man, making a fancy preacher. Legrand probably didn't possess a bit more sense than Brother Kenneth Grable, probably less. A rich man being a preacher. Billy couldn't figure that at all.

Bobo wants Mesta to tell him all about Dooly Legrand, Father Legrand he calls him with a sneer. "The son turns against the father," Bobo comments, "the oldest story in the book." He still wears his red robes and tall pointed hat. "How can a man live with hisself havin no more loyalty to his state and his region than that?"

"He lives in Tennessee," Wayne Scroggins says, and Johnny Lee Bobo just stares at him, his dull eyes tinged with green, like olives. The shortest man in the group, shorter even than Mesta Follett, except for his hat, he gazes at Wayne as though from a great height and then abruptly turns his eyes back to Mesta.

"What is this man up to?" he asks. At first everybody thinks he's talking about Wayne Scroggins, and then they realize he means Dooly Legrand.

"He's a married man with children at home, travellin with another woman. Kitty Wiggins. The singer."

"Ahhhhhh," Johnny Lee Bobo nods. "The degenerates of Hollywood." He looks around. His flat gaze settles on Billy Singleton. Bobo stares at him. It makes Billy uneasy, the way the shiny red silk cloth frames his face and makes him appear to be peeping out at the world. Billy hopes he doesn't look that silly in his own plain white robes. He sees Bobo's eyes flick up to his eyebrows and linger there for a moment. Here it comes, thinks Billy. "And what is your name?" the Imperial Wizard asks.

"Billy Singleton, sir," Billy replies, snapping to attention, nervous and excited. I've got a catfish in me, Billy wants to say, put there by a nigger.

"You have the look of destiny about you, son," Bobo observes, which thrills Billy. He suspects Bobo is bullshitting him like Brother Kenneth Grable did, but he doesn't care. He's proud to be singled out. When Bobo looks at him he forgets about the fire and Gilbert Washington, forgets about the catfish and the pain.

"Do you have a shotgun, son?" the Imperial Wizard asks, and it's as though they're the only two people in the world right then.

"Yes sir, I've got a 20-gauge pump, best damn bird gun I ever...."

"All right," he interrupts, and Billy just stands there flat-footed, looking at the older man.

"Why? What you want me to do with it?" Billy asks. The other men and Mesta look at him, the focus now of the entire group. He could have said, Anything! Anything! Just tell me, and I'll do it!

"You gonna have to pray about that, son," Bobo tells him. "Ask Jesus to set down with you and have a talk."

"Jesus ain't studyin me," Billy says.

"Jesus cares about everybody, son," Bobo responds. "And he's got a message for you. He's got a plan for you. All you got to do is tune in to it."

•　•　•

Billy drives home and comes into the bedroom where Jessie Merle sits reading a magazine called *True Crime Detective*. He reaches for his shotgun on top of the chifferobe.

"Where you going with that thing?" Jessie Merle asks, propped up in bed on both pillows. She motions toward the shotgun with the magazine. A large, round, pale green ashtray full of cork-colored cigarette butts sits next to her. The close air in the room is dense with gray smoke.

"Quail huntin," Billy replies.

"You lyin like a dead pig in the sunshine. It ain't even quail season."

"I don't know where I'm goin with it. It's my gun. What do you care?"

"You gonna get yourself in trouble, Billy. Worse'n you already are."

"What the hell you talkin about, woman?"

She just stares at him for a minute. She colored her hair again recently, unnaturally light this time like finely spun gold. Her hair spreads out thin against her pink skull. She wears a wrinkled blue blouse and khaki Bermuda shorts. "That fire," she says. "Sheriff Tate come by here this mornin. Lookin for you. He wanted to know if I knew where you'd been that night, and I told him right here in the bed with me."

"You did?" he asks. "Well, I was."

"Yeah. After you come in butt naked with your pecker hanging out and your eyebrows burned clean off!"

"Now listen, woman...."

"I told him you was here all night. I told him we went to bed early. Even acted silly about it to make out like we had went to bed to do it and I'd remember it because of that."

"Good," Billy responds.

"So I guess you done made me a accessory. So put the gun back. I don't like all this shit, Billy."

"No," Billy says, "Bobo told me to pray about it."

"Bobo who?" Billy doesn't answer, doesn't even look at her. "You actin peculiar, Billy."

"These is peculiar times, Jessie Merle," Billy tells her. "I don't want you worryin none. You just stay here in the house with the young-uns."

She sits up and the magazine falls flat on the bedspread. "Now you just...." she begins.

"No, woman," he yells, "just shut up. You hear me?" The look in his eyes, fierce and heated, makes her sit back against the pillows. His clothes hang on him, the waistband of his pants gathered and bunched, his black leather belt, much too long for him now, dangling down his front. His eyes are hollow, darkened. The painted eyebrows remind her of some ceramic plaques she once had, masks, one laughing and the other frowning. She hung them on the wall over the sofa. Soon as Henry could climb, he pulled them off the wall and broke them, dropped them on the floor and shattered them into a million pieces. Billy looks like the frowning mask now, driven and haunted. Jessie Merle shivers inside. She feels cold. She sees Billy's face breaking, cracking. She knows that when Billy leaves the house this time he'll never come back.

• • •

It's dusk when Billy stops the truck, as far back in the swamp as he can go, following the old rutted logging road that runs loosely parallel to Maconoco Creek. The road ends near an overgrown clearing where a crumbling, deserted old church, a sagging, unpainted one-room structure sits up on brick pylons. There's no glass in the windows, nothing inside the church but ancient, faded Sunday school papers. He and Rachel once found an old Bible there, when they brought their quilt for one of their parties. They smoked reefers and did it on the quilt thrown over the rotting floorboards. An old Negro church, it was deserted years ago, given back to the swamp, which overtakes it and reclaims it. Kudzu curls up over the roof and around the front door, and honeysuckle vines in full bloom drape the outside walls.

The ground under Billy's feet is soft like flesh. The afternoon storms have left everything damp. Kudzu and honeysuckle grow on the trees and the undergrowth around the clearing, too, making otherworldly shapes in the fading daylight. The old church sags there, motionless and still, as though momentarily arrested midway in its journey back into the earth. There's little sound, little movement in this suspended moment before twilight.

Billy prepares to stay all night if necessary. He has several quart jars of shine under a sack in the cab. And he has drunk half of one jar already. It's a good batch, only slightly oily, without any of that faint turpentine taste of his last batch. If it were aged, he thinks, even a Legrand would like this. He unloads some stove wood he brought in his pickup and finds kindling littering the ground. Tall hickory and sweetgum trees rise up toward the sky, and pines, too, narrow and straight. Brown pine needles cover whatever part of the church roof is not yet consumed by the kudzu. He knows he's three miles from the river. He can smell it, damp and fertile. And even though he's miles upwind from it, he can smell the familiar smell of the landfill, like ammonia or nitrate.

Maconoco Creek narrows in the woods behind the church. Billy hears the soft gurgle of the water cascading down the creek's limestone falls. When he hears the water he feels the fish move within him, a slow twisting as though the fish hears it, too, and Billy walks out into the clearing and gazes at the sky. It's violet with a few stars already out, forming gold pinpoints. A clear night, the sky will soon radiate with a waning moon. He hears a bullfrog start up back along the creek.

As he walks in the clearing, his boots cause lightning bugs and little yellow butterflies to rise up and float about in the air, the fireflies darting at eye level and twinkling. Billy thinks the yellow butterflies are the same ones that fluttered between branches the night when Billy, Goodlowe, and the others tried to run down Carter Taylor. They drift up and away from him, swarm toward the trees. Thousands of them. Billy wonders if they're some new plague of centipede, some new form of boll weevil or something. He's never seen butterflies quite like them before—pretty and harmless enough but with something ominous, something mysterious about where they have come from. As silent in the air as snowflakes, they make Billy think of the unusual late snow back in April. "These is peculiar times, Jessie Merle," he repeats aloud, as though she's right there with him in the darkening clearing.

Billy builds a fire. He lets the tailgate down on his pickup and sits on it, avoiding the damp ground. The shotgun, loaded, rests behind him. The fire crackles and snaps, the thin smoke rising straight up to the now-black sky. Billy tries to pray. He closes his eyes, squinting them shut. He realizes he is almost drunk, and he is glad.

"Now Jesus," he says aloud, his tongue thick, "Bobo said you had somethin to tell me. So come on out here and tell me. I'm ready."

He sits for a long time that way, until he begins to see tiny stars dancing behind his heavy eyelids. His mind draws a blank. He knows he was wrong about the first sign, the burning of Rose Hill. He thinks Bobo is pointing him toward what must surely be the real sign.

"Jesus," he continues, "I've done prayed mightily to you to take away this here pain in my gut, to remove this evil fish that's been cast into me by the devil's handmaiden, but you ain't seen fit to do it. Maybe, like Brother Grable says, you got your own reason for lettin me hurt. But I be dog if I can figure it out."

The only sound in the clearing is the popping of the fire.

"Maybe I ain't supposed to figure it out. Maybe I ain't supposed to know no more'n my own name, but look like you could tell me, one way or the other. Tell me what you and Bobo want me to do."

He hears a rustling in the underbrush, like an animal. Then he hears it again. He opens his eyes. And Jesus stands there, right before his eyes. It's like he's got his own light. His face glows from within, creamy and smooth. He wears a crown of thorns. His long, soft, brown hair looks just like the pictures Billy has seen. But he doesn't wear the flowing robes. Instead he wears what looks like a long black overcoat. He just stands there, looking at Billy, his eyes as large and brown and downy as a doe.

"Jesus?" Billy's heart thumps in his chest. He can barely get his breath. He'd been confident that Jesus would appear but hadn't actually expected him to. "You come to give me a message?"

"Yes," Jesus replies, his voice so faint that for a moment Billy isn't sure he said anything. He sits up straighter.

Billy's whole body tingles. "What? What is it?"

Jesus stands motionless. The butterflies seem to hover just over his head. Fireflies dart about and twinkle, and Billy thinks he can see them right through Jesus. He doesn't answer for a long time. Billy's so tense he feels as though he'll jump from the truck any second. Jesus smiles. He holds out his hand, his right hand, toward him.

"Tell me, Jesus," Billy stammers breathlessly, "I've done handled the snakes and everything!"

Jesus begins to speak. His mouth moves, and Billy leans forward to hear, then jerks his head back when Jesus's voice suddenly booms as though someone turned up the volume: "BLESSED AND HOLY IS HE THAT HATH PART IN THE FIRST RESURRECTION. ON SUCH THE SECOND DEATH HATH NO POWER, BUT THEY SHALL BE PRIESTS OF GOD AND OF ME, AND WILL REIGN WITH ME A THOUSAND YEARS!"

Confused by the words, Billy cannot grasp what Jesus says. It goes right by him. He shakes his head, tries to concentrate.

"AND WHEN THE THOUSAND YEARS ARE EXPIRED, SATAN SHALL BE LOOSED OUT OF HIS PRISON!"

"Yes, yes." Billy knows what that means anyway. He thinks he knows what Jesus is telling him, what Bobo meant for him to hear, if he can just put it together. It's about Satan, the snake, the snake that he himself tried to wrestle down. He knows enough about the Bible to know Jesus won't explain it, that he puts the truth way down inside stories that sometimes don't seem to make a lot of sense. "All right," Billy says. "What else?"

"AND SATAN SHALL GO OUT TO DECEIVE THE NATIONS WHICH ARE IN THE FOUR QUARTERS OF THE EARTH, TO

GATHER THEM TOGETHER TO BATTLE, AND THEY SHALL COME DOWN LIKE A MIGHTY FLOOD AND THEIR NUMBER SHALL BE AS THE SAND OF THE SEA!"

"Yes, yes." Billy's eyes are open now. He knows what Jesus is saying, as clear as spring water. He's talking about the marchers.

"AND THE DEVIL THAT DECEIVES THEM SHALL BE CAST INTO THE LAKE OF FIRE AND BRIMSTONE!"

Billy, his mouth hanging open, stares at the figure before him. It seems to grow larger, to fill up the entire clearing. The eyes implore Billy, plead with him. Billy can feel his heat, like a raging fire. Sensing that Jesus is beginning to fade away, Billy asks, "Wait a minute, now, what do you want me to do, Jesus? What? Just tell me."

The voice, already dimmer, still resonates: "BLESSED IS HE THAT KEEPETH THE SAYINGS OF MY PROPHECY." Jesus's words throb inside Billy's brain until he thinks his head might explode. He smells a sulfur smell, like spent matches, and watches as the figure begins to spin and wrap inward upon itself. Billy hears the steady beating of drums and the distant howling of laughter. Fumbling in the dark, Billy finds the mason jar of shine. He needs the hot, bitter liquid to cleanse his mind like a kind of Communion. He gulps it, holds it on his tongue, feels its soothing bite.

The clearing is empty now. The tiny, fading flames lick at the charred and smoldering stove wood. He blinks, looks around. Sipping the whiskey, sniffing its fumes, he feels its heat coursing through his body. Billy sits there in his truck, reflecting that Jesus came to him exactly the way Johnny Lee Bobo had predicted. That fool Brother Grable waited all his feeble life for such as that. It had come to Billy in an instant, because he really believed it would. And his pain is gone, in its place a coolness as though he's been eating his fill of ice cream.

He remembers the last time he was pain free, following the snake bite. But the pain came back. He's confident now that it won't this time. All he has to do is fulfill Jesus's prophecy. He drinks the rest of the jar of moonshine, opens another, then stretches out in the bed of his truck and sleeps a dreamless, restful sleep.

Billy awakens in the wet, cool dawn. A fine layer of dew covers him. Curtains of fog hang like spiderwebs about the clearing. He sits up, rubbing his eyes. His mouth dry, he takes a long drink of the shine, chilled now by the departed night. Taking an old towel, he rubs the moisture off his shotgun, polishes the stock. A squirrel chatters in the trees somewhere. Billy looks at the clearing. He looks at the sacred spot where Jesus stood. He knows who Satan is, all right, knows it as clearly as if Jesus had spelled it out for him. Billy hefts the shotgun, its perfect balance. Billy knows the truth and he knows the truth will finally set him free.

# Rachel

AS CARTER WALKS ALONG IN THE BRIGHT MORNING SUN, carrying Eshu, his shoulders ache the way they ached when he picked cotton as a small boy, side by side with Dooly. Dragging heavy adult-size bags, they competed to see who could pick the most before sundown. It was a game. They picked until the tips of their fingers were raw and bloody and the older folks in the field poked fun at them. The older folks, shining with sweat, worked with a steady precision that was no game. Some of the very people who labored in that field all those years ago walk beside him now, limping, stooped, their feet blistered.

"We're gonna make it," Eldon says, grinning at him.

"Yes," Carter agrees, "yes, we are." They're getting close to Montgomery now. In this flat, marshy country, close to the wide Alabama River, lonely, tall trees rise beside the roadway with curly Spanish moss streaming down from their branches. Wedged between broad fields of alfalfa, soybeans, and cotton are more houses, more filling stations and stores. Bigger crowds gather and watch them go by. White children observe them silently and curiously out of their lean faces and big hungry eyes.

The sky is cloudless blue now, the sun unforgiving. Folks break out their straw hats as though they're returning to the fields. Rachel wears a yellow straw hat over her bandanna. She grins at Carter, too. Weary, they move now on excitement and adrenaline. But with the excitement comes anxiety and fear.

Laughter and nervous chatter ripple through the lines of marchers. They sing "On Jordan's Stormy Banks" and "Swing Low Sweet Chariot."

Kitty sings, her voice sweet and separate from the rest. Her voice soars. Dooly watches her. She's already gone. From the moment he healed Philip Music she drifted away like wildflower pollen on the wind. It's as though Dooly's healing confirmed that he was not wholly hers, had never been completely hers. She hasn't said a word, but he senses it clearly.

He looks around and sees Philip Music walking beside David Miles. They giggle, flirt with a young girl as though last night never happened. He focuses again on Kitty, her head thrown back, revealing the long, thin line of her neck. "Comin for to carry me home," she sings, her eyes closed, the words moving in the mysterious darkness behind her eyes.

• • •

Johnny Lee Bobo addresses a huge rally of Klansmen from across the South. Assembled in a field near the town of Hoke's Bluff, they all wear their robes. Lucious Willie's heart thumps nervously in his chest. He's excited, senses that something is happening at last. Lucious looks around, surveys most of the Hammond Klavern. But there's still no sign of Lewis and Musgrove. And now it looks like Billy Singleton has flown the coop as well. Lucious sneers, pats the .38 revolver under his robe. He left a thirty-ought-six rifle in his car.

"They just wouldn't listen to reason," Johnny Lee Bobo yells, standing on a flatbed hay wagon. "When what happened at the Rooster Bridge happened, the niggers should have known that they can't just take over the roads and the highways and anything else they just up and decide to. But they just keep on. And then the federal government comes in and tells the state folks that you got to let em march! Not just let em, but escort em, with the state police and the National Guard and God knows what all else!"

The crowd grumbles and stirs. Their heavy boots, caked with black mud, grind down the shoots of spring flowers. The high sun blindingly reflects off the sea of pristine white robes. There must be at least five hundred of them, Lucious thinks, five hundred brothers united!

"Well then we'll stop em!" Bobo shouts, waving his fist in the air. "It falls to us, brothers, and we'll do it. We'll form a human barrier outside

Montgomery. We'll make a stand! At Ticen's Station, we'll take our stand and block the highway, and they'll have to come through us to get to the capital of this hallowed state!" Cheers rise up. "When they get that far we'll be there to meet em, and say to em 'Niggers, this here is the END OF THE LINE!'" More cheers, shrieks, long rebel yells rend the air. "Let this be just one more battle in a war that ain't over yet, the Battle of Ticen's Station!" Bobo waves both fists over his head now. Lucious again feels the pistol tucked into his belt and smiles.

●   ●   ●

Billy has to drive way down through Camden and Lowndes County and make a loop back up to US 80 to get ahead of the marchers. At noon, he pulls into the gravel parking lot of a country general store and barbecue cafe in the little crossroads hamlet of Ticen's Station. He travels with his loaded shotgun leaning against the seat beside him. High in the sky, the sun casts a wicked light that waters his eyes, makes him squint.

Billy's pickup rocks and scratches in the gravel lot. Several men, women, and children, waiting to watch the march, look at him.

"They sposed to pass through here in a half hour," a women says to him. She has traveled all the way from Thomasville down in Clarke County to see it. All dressed up for the occasion, she wears big white ear bobs, large plastic pearls, and white high-heel shoes. She stares at Billy.

"Yeah, well, what makes you think I care?" Billy responds. "I ain't studyin em."

"It's history," she says. "I told Helen Grace, no matter what you think about it, it's history."

"Everthang's history, woman," Billy sneers, slamming his truck door and turning toward the little cafe. The children stare at him with their mouths open. One of them, a little blonde girl licking a green all-day sucker, asks, "What's wrong with that man's...."

"Hush up, Helen Grace!" the woman interrupts.

Inside, the cafe is dim after the harsh sunlight. Billy stands a moment to let his eyes adjust. The smell of barbecue makes his stomach knot. He hasn't eaten since lunchtime yesterday. Suddenly he feels weak, light-headed, dizzy. He wonders then about the milking, whether Jessie Merle got the kids up out of bed to do it. He'd lay odds she didn't.

Billy walks up to the counter, and the waitress looks directly at his eyebrows. Then he realizes what the little girl was asking about, remembers the early-morning dew.

"What ails your...." the waitress begins.

"Where's your men's room? I'm in a hurry."

"Back there," she tosses her head. Wearing a black frilly dress with a little white apron, she inspects him curiously. Her name tag reads ANGEL. "You look a sight," she says, "you...."

"Shut up," he growls, hurrying toward the hand-lettered sign reading "Restrooms for Cafe Customers Only."

"Hey!" She protests.

The cramped little restroom stinks. A big turd floats in the toilet, and the urinal is half full of green water. The sink, stained and chipped, offers no hot water. Billy examines his face in the blistered mirror. His eyebrows, now streaked down the sides of his face, make him look like somebody done up for Halloween. Billy lets the cold water run. There are no paper towels, only a dingy circular cloth hanging from a jammed dispenser on the wall. The same filthy section of towel has been used over and over. The bottom of the loop of cloth lies bunched on the damp floor. No telling who's been using it. But Billy has no choice. He washes his face carefully, trying to leave some eyebrows.

Drying his face on the gray towel, he inspects his distorted image in the warped mirror. He's done a pretty good job. The eyes stare back at him as though they belong to somebody else. He wonders what Jessie Merle is doing right now. He wonders what she thought last night when he didn't come home, what she told the children. He thinks about the cows standing out by the barn bellowing, their udders swollen and painful, and Jessie Merle in the kitchen painting her nails, watching "As The World Turns." He knows his family will see him on the television news tonight. They'll hear his name broadcast all over the country.

He remembers Mesta Follett's words: "There ain't no real security for the march. It's just a show. Them cops up front. And some high school boys dressed up in National Guard fatigues. The marchers stop along the way to eat, like at lunchtime, at a store or somethin. They'll buy cheese and cinnamon rolls and sardines and cold drinks and sit outside. Nobody'll let em use the bathroom, so they go in the woods out back, or if there's a privy. When I was with em and we got to Marion Junction at old Haskins Clayborne's store, he told us the white folks could use the toilet but not the niggers, and the whites wouldn't use it neither. The men just walked off into the bushes. The women made a circle out back to squat in. It was downright comical."

Billy notices everybody in the crowded cafe looking at him as he comes back from the men's room. He doesn't care. He goes back to the counter. "Gimme a barbecue sandwich with all inside meat," he orders. "To go." The waitress named Angel smirks at him, rolls her eyes.

"All right," she says. "But you got no cause to tell me to shut up, buster."

"I didn't go to," Billy explains. "I was in a hurry." Billy looks around the room, filled with animated talk and laughter. It's like a big party, all these people gathered to see the agitators. Maybe the fact that there are so many people will make it easier. On the other hand, the crowds may make the agitators more wary. Mesta told them that King always marches right at the front, along with a fellow named Andrew Young. And Dooly Legrand and Kitty Wiggins. And the voodoo woman. Billy knows that has to be Rachel and figures Carter will be nearby, too. And both of them will recognize him instantly. He does not know what will happen if they see him.

The main challenge will be getting close enough to King with the shotgun, which will be difficult to hide or disguise. But Billy is confident he can do it.

Angel hands Billy a grease-stained brown paper sack. "You want somethin to drink?"

"Gimme a Pabst."

She rings his purchase up. "Ninety-nine cent total," she tells him.

Outside, more people stand along the highway, jostling and laughing and joking as though waiting for a Mardi Gras parade. Billy leans against his truck and eats his sandwich, swallows the ice cold beer. When he finishes, he climbs into the cab of his truck, which feels as hot as an oven. Billy immediately starts to sweat, pulls his jar of liquor from beneath the seat and sips it, even though it's lukewarm. Sitting up high he sees flashing red and blue lights of the state trooper cars in the distance as the march rounds a curve and moves toward him.

He turns his head lazily back to the right and gasps at the sight of more Klan than he's ever seen before in one place. They fill the highway and its broad, flat shoulders; they spill into the fields along the road. Their white robes glare in the sunlight. They wave American and Confederate flags.

"Jesus Christ Almighty," Billy murmurs, holding the jar midway to his mouth.

•   •   •

The marchers notice people gathering ahead, more and more onlookers. The atmosphere shifts from somber one moment to carnival-like the next. Crowds jeer at them, laugh at them, watch them with drawn and funereal expressions, standing in a sober, almost respectful, silence. They point at King and whisper, hoist little children on their shoulders to get a better look.

Then the escorts stop in the road, their lights continuing to swirl. The marchers smell the barbecue from the Ticen's Station Café. It's gut-wrenching. The heated, humid air of the cafe's parking lot is full of the mixed scents of the pork's slow cooking, motor oil, and dust. They've smelled exhaust from the troopers' cars now for days, for almost fifty miles. The high-noon sun beams down. The strip of gray asphalt ahead runs straight as a plumb line through thickets of willows and through low swampy places marked by stunted water oaks. It traverses three short bridges and six more miles to the Montgomery city limits.

Then they see the highway fill with white robes, hear the stirring and shouting, the laughter, the astonished pointing from the crowd in the parking lot.

"My God," Kitty says.

The bleached robes and the red and blue Stars and Bars flags create an oddly beautiful contrast against the cloudless sky and the road's green frame of undergrowth and fields. Dooly's breath quickens when he sees them. Murmurs ripple through the lines of marchers.

"Don't worry," King reassures them. "It's just a show."

Rachel peers across the fifty-odd yards separating them from the Klansmen, who stand defiant and terrible. She focuses on the eye holes, trying to find Billy. She'll know him, even behind a mask. He's not there. But she senses him, feels him on her skin.

Rachel knows that something is bad wrong, even beyond the sudden appearance of the Klan. She knows Billy Singleton is near. Like suddenly remembering a dream, she can smell the chalky, bleached odor of his body as he forces her to the ground and falls on top of her, can hear his raspy breathing. A stinging pain surges between her legs, as though a hot poison inside her is pressuring to be released.

She looks around, at the highway with its heat waves rising and wavering, at the white-robed men, the people in the parking lot. She notices King and Dooly talking to a state trooper who leads the two men into the parking lot. They walk along gesturing with their hands, looking from the trooper to the Klansmen. The trooper shakes his head and stalks off. Rachel focuses on King and knows it will be him. But it is Dooly who is surrounded by a kind of glimmering aura, edged in a pulsing light. Rachel realizes it will be Dooly first. She sees an image of King on the ground, bleeding, dying, other black men kneeling beside him. Dooly's face spins through her vision, Dooly as a child. Now she pictures Dooly hurtling backward, his arms outstretched, covered with blood.

●   ●   ●

Braced by the shine, Billy no longer feels hungry. He feels as strong as a mule, fortified by the presence of the hundreds of Klansmen. He recognizes Bobo by his stature and red robes even though his face is covered. It's all part of Jesus's plan that the little man would be here. Billy understands exactly how Jesus and Bobo worked together: the Imperial Wizard anointed him, knighted him. Then Jesus pointed him toward his destiny.

Suddenly it seems like the other people scattered about the parking lot disappear, giving Billy an unobstructed view of Martin Luther King. He talks to a fellow in a priest's collar. Then Billy recognizes him: Dooly

Legrand. Dooly looks like the father of the kid who once taunted Billy, made fun of him when they were boys. The kid who used to drive like a maniac all around the countryside in that fancy car with fancy girls grabbing all over him. Rich boy.

Billy grips his shotgun. Before he knows it, he is out of the truck, his feet hitting the loose gravel. An almost blinding pain slashes through his belly then, like a red-hot ice pick. And he sees Rachel over there with that bandanna on her head and big gold earrings glinting in the sunlight. He knows she's turning up the pain, escalating it until he thinks his gut is going to burst. He stumbles and runs toward the two men who see him now amidst the screams and shouts and people running away. The two men freeze, stand flat-footed, as though awaiting him. Neither one looks frightened. They look as though they've been expecting him all along.

He raises the shotgun to his shoulder. He quickly gets King in his sights, aiming at his chest. And just as he starts to pull the trigger, Dooly Legrand jumps in front of King, shielding him. As Billy squeezes off the round and the gun bucks back against his shoulder, he sees that he hit Dooly square in the chest, sees his astonished expression, sees his body jerk violently backward, his arms flung out, sees blood spatter in all directions as Dooly's body soars through the air and comes to rest on his back. There's a moment of complete stunned silence. Billy smells the spent shells and the barbecue, watches wisps of smoke rising from Dooly Legrand's shattered chest, watches his eyes slowly filming as they gaze blankly upward at the sky.

Something stings him on the shoulder like a huge wasp, and another. And he hears the crack of pistol shots quicker and finer than the deep boom of his shotgun, which still echoes. He thinks he hears gunfire all around him, like a war. He hears screams and crying. He sees the two state troopers aim at him, hears their pistols pop like firecrackers. All right, he thinks, all right. But at least I got that goddam Dooly Legrand. They'll be proud of that, at least. The bullets spin him back, and his arms flail the air as he tries to run and then crumbles in a heap to the ground.

• • •

When Rachel sees Billy, she screams. The images of Billy in her mind and Billy in the parking lot with the gun merge, and she screams at King and Dooly, she watches Dooly jump in front of King just as Billy's shotgun fires.

• • •

When he hears the shotgun blast and the quick pops of pistols, Joe Rattiwig aims his M-1 out the window of the tank truck and fires off four quick rounds at the Ku Klux Klan across the highway. Reacting quickly and precisely, he's proud of his decisive response.

"Jesus!" Earnest Briney yells from behind the wheel. "What are you doin, man?!"

Three Klansmen go down, fall into piles of white sheets on the ground. Joe hears enraged shouts from the Klan lines.

"What the hell are you doin?!" Briney screams again.

• • •

Lucious is standing right next to Johnny Lee Bobo when the shots ring out, first the unmistakable boom of a shotgun, then pistol and rifle shots. Everything begins to swirl around him. He's bumped from the side. "Goddammit!" he hears. "Git down! Git down!" Someone pushes him. Only then does he realize they're under attack. Dropping to one knee, he pulls from beneath his robes his thirty-ought-six, which he grabbed from his car just as the agitators grew close. Frantic and scared, he fires up the road, pumping the lever action and spraying randomly. Through the blur of sweat stinging his eyes, he sees people scatter. Brown-clad soldiers group along the road, aiming rifles at him. American soldiers! Firing at them. Lucious can't believe it. He hears the crack of the rifle fire and bullets whiz around him.

He hears a blubbering noise next to him and turns to see Johnny Lee Bobo jerk his headdress off to reveal blood gushing from his face and mouth. Bobo stands there for a moment with a curious, expectant look on his face. Suddenly, half of his head disappears as he's hit again. Lucious cries out and whimpers, covers his head, and crouches close to the rough, hot asphalt. He hears shots all around him as his remaining buddies return the fire.

● ● ●

Caught between the two warring armies, the marchers have no place to hide. Philip Music stands with David Miles and Michelle Ranelli, a young girl from Detroit, when a steel-jacketed bullet rips through his chest, shattering his ribs and heart, and exits grazing the side of Michelle's head. Philip is dead before he hits the ground. David catches Michelle as she falls, her face ashen and pale, her eyes wide open in shock. Crying, David hunkers over the girl, shaking and trembling. Frightened people stumble over him as they run in circles seeking cover.

● ● ●

The young Guardsmen don't know what to do. Some fire at the marchers, some at the Klansmen. Some run for cover in a grove of cotton-wood trees across the highway from the cafe. Rifle and pistol shots spray everywhere. The onlookers in the parking lot duck behind cars. People rush into the cafe, trampling several small children. Crouching behind a parked van, Carter holds Eshu tightly against his chest. Rachel stands in the middle of the parking lot, staring at the bodies of Dooly and Billy Singleton. She sees a little girl with a green all-day sucker get hit by a bullet, her head splitting open like a melon. The plate glass windows of the cafe explode, creating thick mists of shards that glitter like rhinestones in the sunlight. People scream and moan. Children cry.

•  •  •

Several pellets from Billy's shotgun nicked King's arm. After King fell
to the ground, Dooly's body hurtled on top of him, as if thrown by a giant
hand. Dooly's blood has splattered everywhere, on King, on Rachel, even
on Carter standing off to the side, blood and tiny pieces of flesh clinging to
Eshu's blanket. Kitty Wiggins begins to scream and shriek hysterically.
Carter pulls her to the ground next to him, behind the van, as the gunfire
rings out all around them.

•  •  •

And then it stops, as suddenly as it had started. A heavy, deep silence
sweeps across the landscape, broken only by whimpers and the sound of
distant sirens. People mill around in shock, spectators mingling with
marchers. The Klansmen retreat, gather in the open field, pull their dead
and wounded after them. Angel steps outside the cafe. She sees the bodies,
sees Billy's pale, distorted face turned toward her, his lifeless eyes open,
faint traces of eyebrows painted on his forehead like a store window man-
nequin. A few feet from him lies a little girl, her head a bloody mass, her
legs splayed clumsily out, one of her shiny patent leather Sunday sandals
missing from her white-socked foot, a green sucker covered with gravel and
dirt still in her fingers. Angel vomits on the ground.

Sirens riff through the air. Parents hustle their children back to cars,
trying to quiet their crying and fear. People gather around the injured and
the dead. "Ambulances are coming," someone shouts from the door of the
cafe. "And more police from Montgomery!" Kitty Wiggins kneels next to
Dooly's body. King bends over his chest, listening in vain for a heartbeat.
Kitty's face turns to the sky, her eyes tightly closed, and tears stream down
her face. King stands and shakes his head, his legs unsteady. Someone takes
his arm.

Rachel also kneels next to Dooly. Flecks of his blood already dot her
shirt and bandanna. She takes him in her arms, lifts his upper body, holding his head lolling limply back. His blood is still hot against her; but even

as she holds him, she feels his body growing stiff and cool. She holds him for a long time, until the ambulance comes.

No one approaches Billy Singleton's body, heaped on the gravel like a pile of greasy old rags.

●   ●   ●

The marchers and a contingent of National Guardsmen and federal troops camp that night at St. Andrew's School on the outskirts of Montgomery. All the planned festivities are canceled. But the march to the capitol will go on. In spite of everything, the march will continue tomorrow to its destination. Thousands gather. As the news of the day's events spreads around the country on news bulletins and evening broadcasts, thousands more begin their journey to the capitol.

Many National Guardsmen and armed Klansmen have been detained and even arrested. But not Joe Rattiwig and Earnest Briney. No one knows that Joe was the first to fire on the Klansmen. Or even that he fired at all. Joe and Earnest pitch their pup tent, build a fire. Then they take the tank truck to a nearby McDonald's drive-through and return to their campsite to eat Big Macs for supper.

"Jesus," Earnest Briney keeps muttering, "Jesus!"

"Stop sayin that," Joe says.

They camp apart from everyone else, near a patch of woods behind the football field, wanting to hide, afraid.

"But you...but you...."

"Shut up! Shut up!"

It's late. They both know they won't sleep. The lights over the football field have been doused. Sleeping people cover the campus. The talk is that every hotel and motel in town is full. Joe and Earnest sit beside their small fire, staring at the flames.

And then they see him, see him walk by, the priest—the one who said he was from Hammond, the one rumored to be Governor Legrand's son, the one shot and killed dead in the parking lot.

"Hey, that's...." Joe says.

"Shush," Earnest interrupts, shaking all over. They see him clear as daylight, walking slowly, see the open wound in his chest and the blood-splattered, shredded clothes. Despite their bright campfire, he doesn't look their way. He walks slowly but purposefully, his eyes focused straight ahead. They hear his footsteps in the grass, he's that close.

And then he's gone, disappears into the darkness, leaving them breathless and halted, unable to move or speak, only to listen to the gentle popping of the fire, the crackling of flames.

•  •  •

At that same time, fifty miles west, Amy Legrand sits in a maroon velvet armchair in her darkened parlor. She spent the afternoon weeping for the loss of her only son. Holding a glass of bourbon and water, she hears Hester in the kitchen washing dishes. Hester had prepared her a pork chop and a salad for dinner. Sitting alone at the long table in the dining room, Amy tried to eat but chafed under the blissfully benign stares of the ornately framed Legrand ancestors lining the walls. They remained stubbornly unaware of her grief or of any sorrow they themselves had imposed and inflicted on all the family to come after them. Amy wanted to rip them from their frames and choke them, every damn Legrand of them.

She picks up her red leather prayer book and thinks she hears her mother say, I don't like to say I told you so, Amy, but there you have it. She cannot imagine anything worse than burying her own son. His death was violent and bloody in a confrontation that was all too truly about his own father. At the hands of a Singleton! She'd known those Singletons for years, and everyone knew them for the worthless white trash they were. And now this. This senseless thing.

Hester steps quietly into the room. "You need anything, Miss Amy?"

"No thank you, Hester. As long as there's plenty of liquor. And ice."

"You don't need to be drinkin all that stuff, Miss Amy, you got to...."

"That will be all, Hester."

"Yes mam." Hester doesn't leave, just stands there silently. Amy stares at the strip of night peaking through the almost-closed drapes. Finally,

Hester says, "I be in the kitchen for a while. I'm gonna do the crossword and then go to bed."

"All right," Amy says. Since her husband died four years ago, Hester has slept in one of the guest rooms upstairs. Amy and Hester occupy the house like two spinster sisters, with Hester doing all the shopping, cooking, and cleaning, and Amy keeping the books and paying the bills. Amy hasn't seen Oscar in weeks, since his father's funeral.

Amy opens her prayer book. With only one lamp lit, she squints to read the words. Looking through the sacrament of "The Burial of the Dead," she reviews the list of suggested Old Testament and New Testament readings. She will choose the readings for Dooly's funeral. ("You do it!" Paula sobbed on the phone. "I am devastated. The children are devastated! Why, Amy? Why in God's name?") Amy puts the prayer book down and picks up her Bible, resting next to her whiskey on the small marble-top side table. She opens it to the selection from Revelations.

"And I saw a new heaven and a new earth," she reads, "for the first heaven and the first earth were passed away; and there was no sea." She blinks. She nods, knows without even thinking that this is what Dooly would want. She reads on: "And God shall wipe away all tears from their eyes; and there shall be no more death, neither sorrow, nor crying, neither shall there be any more pain: for the former things are passed away."

She crosses herself.

"No," Dooly says. She looks up and he's seated in the other chair, next to hers, his white collar smudged with dirt and blood, his denim jacket ripped to shreds. She remembers recently commenting to him, "Dooly, you don't have to dress like a field hand!" The sight of his blood pains her, causes her to die a little herself, but she's grateful that he's here, that she can see him again. She sits holding the Bible, and he smiles at her, impishly, mischievously, like when he was a child.

"What do you mean, 'no'?" she asks.

"Just no," he says. "Isn't that plain enough?"

She stands up to refill her empty glass. "Do you want a drink?" she asks.

"Yes. A Scotch," he nods. She turns her back to the room and puts ice in two glasses, her hands shaking. She thinks about the day at Rose Hill when she saw Dooly's grandfather, become young again. His ghost was as cocky as the old man had ever been in life. Amy fully expects Dooly to vanish before she turns around again. But he's there, sitting, one leg thrown over the other at the knee, foot jiggling. He takes the drink from her, gulps it, and says, "I needed a drink."

"Yes," she says, "I suppose you did." She wants to embrace him, to touch and soothe his wounds, but she fears he'll leave if she tries to. She sits back down.

"You know better than that," he says, pointing to the Bible. "You know there will always be sorrow. And the problem with the 'former things' is that they're not former. They're now."

"Yes," she says. "Of course you're right, Dooly." He smiles the same wan and resigned smile she's seen him smile for as long as she can remember. She gestures toward the portrait hanging over the mantel of Nicholas Desnouette Legrand with that self-same smile. "Yes," she says again, "look at that smug old bastard."

"Uh huh," he says. "I've always been afraid of him, ever since I was little. I didn't even like to come in here where he was."

Dooly sighs and settles back in the chair. She hears it creak with his weight. Throwing his head back on the chair, he gazes at the frescoed ceiling, the bright painted figures swimming in shadows.

"Well, Mother," he says, "I have to know. Did you know?"

"About what?" she asks, but she knows what he means.

"Did you know about Grandfather? And Carrie Winfield? And the fact that he murdered her? And about who Rosa actually was?" She doesn't speak. "My heritage," he says, "what has been passed down to me...."

"Stop, Dooly," she interrupts, "don't."

"Because," he goes on, "I was there with Carter, my brother, when we brought Carrie up from that lost grave. I held part of her, you see, in my hands. I was in her presence. It was...it was complete. She and I, you see, we have a great deal in common. You might even say things have come full circle, that...."

"No," she insists. "It's not the same."

He looks at her with his dark and hollow eyes. "I must know," he says after a moment, "I will know. You're the only family I have, and you're not a Legrand and never have been. So it's important to me to know if you...."

"Yes," she says, "all right. Yes. I knew. Not that he killed her, no. But I knew about Rosa. Yes."

"And Father, he...."

"Of course. Yes."

"Of course." He sits up.

They both sense Hester in the doorway and look over at her. She stands there looking at them, her eyes wide with astonishment. "Mist' Dooly?" she asks, standing very still. "Sweet Jesus above," she murmurs.

Dooly stands up then. A sharp, sweet odor like burning hickory surrounds him. Then he is gone. He doesn't fade, just vanishes as quickly as he had appeared.

Amy crosses herself again. The parlor is quiet, no sounds but their breathing. "Yes," Amy repeats, to the room now empty of her son. "I'm sorry."

● ● ●

Brother Kenneth Grable sits with Jessie Merle in the living room, on a sagging sofa covered with a green chenille bedspread. The children are put to bed, and Brother Grable holds Jessie Merle's hand. They've prayed for hours. "It's the Lord's will," Brother Grable repeats. "It's the Lord's will."

Even though the night sky is clear and is peppered with millions of stars, a sudden wind rattles the windowpanes. It soughs in the pine trees at the edge of the woods and snarls in the eaves of the little dingy house.

They hear the wind moaning, almost like a mournful song.

● ● ●

A few miles away from the Singleton house, as the wind shakes the naked limbs of the dead trees around the old lake, the dam gives way. The sludge, swollen by the spring rains, rolls through the crumbling dam, making a long, sustained rumble like the earth clearing its throat. Sudden cracking noises disturb the night's stillness as dead trees on the side of the hill snap like matchsticks under the weight of the oozing avalanche. The wall of brackish sludge rolls relentlessly and implacably down the slope toward the village.

The village sits deserted—even Marcus Hanson is gone. Everyone is in Montgomery. Hardy Siddons and his parents, their neighbor old Ruby, everyone has been transported by car and pickup truck and old school bus to the capital city to join the marchers. Though empty of people, the village is filled with life—dogs and cats, chickens and hogs, and even a milk cow or two, all caught in the briny, chemical mess oozing in and around the houses, filling ditches and wells with its poison. It pushes at the sides of the houses, toppling the less sturdy ones as easily as children's stick houses. The oily flood covers the kitchen gardens, flattening new green pole beans and tomato plants. It obliterates the streets and paths, carries away fences and outdoor furniture and children's toys left outside. Hovering over it all is the choking odor of solvents, of creosote, and of a kind of burning formaldehyde smell. The sludge rolls like lava beyond the village and into the rest of the valley, seeps into the rivers and toward the unsuspecting town of Hammond, sitting peacefully on its bluff across the way.

The metallic and poisonous residue covers the entire valley, settles into the topsoil and forms thick puddles several feet deep in every low place. In future years everyone in Alabama will refer to the village once called Crockers Crossroads as "Devil's Town." The only visible reminders of its former life will be the skeletal remains of the houses, the sagging Oak Grove Calvary Church, and the decaying caved-in Hanson's Store with its rusted metal soft drink and snuff and Martha White Flour signs.

It will be many years before anyone will attempt to restore the dark, loamy land between the rivers, to return the area of Rose Hill Plantation to its original fecund state, to prepare it for those who will next exploit it, who will try once again to wrench their living from its soil.

•   •   •

Rachel walks through the sleeping campsite, leading a strange and silent parade. From time to time someone rouses and stands up and falls in behind her: old people, bent and stooped, young girls, young men who carry drums, old Joe Bynymo, his overcoat brushing the ground. Carter follows, too, carrying Eshu.

Rachel turns down a side street, a road really, a dirt road already dusty from the long day's sun. After weeks of rain, the night is clear and pure, cool, the stars a glittering canopy. Rachel still wears the clothes stained with Dooly's blood. She plans to wear them all the way to the capitol tomorrow.

Lights shine from the houses along the road, small houses, sagging and in need of paint, like those in Frogbottom in Hammond. A few people come out of the houses to join her small midnight procession. Soon they reach a concrete block church, whitewashed, its windows dark. Out back is a graveyard. Rachel and her followers cut across the dirt churchyard and pass through a rusty metal gate into the cemetery. The people fan out into the cemetery, past rows of stone slabs and graves covered with splashes of colored, plastic flowers, reds and oranges and blues, bright hued but dulled by the darkness of night. Bynymo sits on a tombstone.

The group grows still and quiet. Rachel walks to the center of the cemetery and kneels next to a grave covered with a fine and powdery dust. She doesn't know whose grave it is. It doesn't matter. She scoops up some of the dust and examines it. Then she sits on the ground, holding the dust out before her. Leaning her head back, she looks up at the sky through the nubby branches of black cedar trees, letting the thin, dry dust filter through her fingers onto the ground.

"Benga, manman moin," she chants, "Benga, my mother." Her eyes are closed. The group watches her, her face like an icon, delicately carved from the finest mahogany. Her skin glows. "Basket covers basket," she continues, "Ibo gods. Billy goes to rest. Take Billy to rest. Basket covers basket."

"Basket covers basket," the people repeat.

Bowing her head, she begins to dig a small hole in the earth. "That hole, that hole, is called the Salengro hole," she chants. "My talisman is there. Test it! O! My talisman is there, test it, lock it up!"

She dusts off her hands and takes from her skirt pocket an empty matchbox, a small jar, and a little pincushion. She opens the box and puts in some of the graveyard dust. Then she unscrews the lid from the jar and scoops out chimney soot, black and oily, which she mixes with the dust. She closes the box and sticks nine pins from the pincushion into the box. She puts the box in the hole she has dug and buries it there. "Billy Singleton," she says, "rest in peace."

"Amen," says Bynymo.

"Amen," Carter repeats, along with all the others.

She sees it all happen again, stretched out before her: Dooly flying through the air, his body jerked backward by the force of the shotgun pellets, the sound of the blast flooding the sun-splashed parking lot and splitting all their ears. She'd seen Billy for only that one terrifying moment before the shell exploded. Rachel then sees the quiet, tree-lined streets of Hammond, the great straight stretch of highway leading away and back toward Hammond, empty now and waiting, a monument.

And she thinks of her son, of Cap, remembers him as a baby, the way he smelled, the way he felt when she held him close. She imagines him as he must be now, growing, becoming a young man.

She packs the dirt over the hole and takes out a small cloth bag of white gris-gris powder and makes geometric patterns, lines, and concentric circles over Billy's tiny grave. She sits back on the dirt. It's long after midnight now, and she and the others begin their vigil.

•   •   •

Not a cloud dots the open sky as thousands march through the shanty towns of Montgomery toward the center of the city. They cheer and sing, hold hands, march in step, and then skip along raggedly to keep up. Old people watch from cramped porches holding tiny children; older children run beside the stream of marchers. Dogs, sensing the excitement, bark, dash back and forth between yards and the crowds.

King leads the march, with everyone following behind him, forming one long serpentine creature. Rachel and Carter march near the front. Carter carries his child. The inner city is farther than they thought. A great cry goes up when they turn the corner onto Dexter Avenue and see the gleaming white capitol up ahead. The broad avenue stretches out open and inviting until the marchers see the crowds of jeering white people who gather on the sidewalks, behind sawhorse barriers.

Police helicopters hover overhead; photographers and television cameramen walk backward in front of them. From almost a mile away, they can see the Confederate Stars and Bars atop the capitol. They sing "When I Leave for Heaven Don't You Weep After Me." They sing "Just a Closer Walk With Thee." The capitol building looks deserted, but Oscar Legrand is there. Standing in a window on the second floor in the old House chambers, his hands gripped behind his back, his jaw tightly clenched, Oscar Legrand watches the sea of people move inexorably toward him.

●   ●   ●

As he walks, Carter enters a waking dream. Inside the wide, echoing halls of the capitol building, Mr. Oscar stands before him. Alone, they look into each other's eyes.

Carter takes the razor from around his neck, holds it, tests the sharpness of the blade against his thumb. Mr. Oscar doesn't move. His face is slack and passive, his eyes swim in the most intense terror Carter has ever seen. His lips tremble as he looks at the razor in Carter's hand. He's an old man. He doesn't know his own soul. Carter moves closer, holding the razor in his hand.

The old man is defenseless, totally at Carter's mercy. Carter remembers how vigorous he once was, how his hair was the color of slate, not white like cotton. His face was ruddy and burned by the wind and the sun; his eyes were sparked and fiery. He smelled of whiskey and horses and tobacco, of the rich black soil and the honeysuckle and wisteria of Rose Hill—a smell masculine and sweet.

"In God's name. In God's name," the old man pleads, his contorted breath wheezing out around his words. "I'm not worth it."

They stand there like that for a long time, an eternity, locked into a mock tableau of father and son.

"Yes, that's right," Carter finally says. He folds the razor and loops it back over his neck, letting it drop harmlessly beneath his shirt.

•   •   •

Rachel falls into her own waking dream. In it, she can see the mass of people stretching all the way back up the avenue, away from the capitol building. King mounts the marble steps. No one's there to accept the petitions. So King places them at the top of the steps, near Jefferson Davis's star, as loud cheers ring out and echo in the spring blue sky. The flags hang almost limp, occasionally stirred by a slight breeze. The white columns of the old capitol rise like something ancient to the clock face with its black Roman numerals, its hands joined at noon under the high, searing sun.

Standing on the steps, Rachel unwraps the blanket covering Eshu. The baby's dark eyes gaze curiously out at the world. In her heart's vision, untamed now and free, Rachel dreams Eshu's deformities into wings and horns. She releases him like a falconer would her bird. Eshu rises, unbound now and redeemed, flying over the gleaming white rotunda. Oceans of upturned faces watch Eshu soar higher and higher into the cloudless blue, until they can see only a tiny speck against the domed and royal sky.